Roman II – The Rise of Caratacus

Kevin Ashman lives in South Wales with his wife and dog and has been writing for eight years.

Mainly concentrating on Historical Fiction books, especially in the Roman and Medieval eras, he found significant success with the India Summers Mysteries, a series of books about a Librarian and her Special Forces Partner who delve deep into history to solve modern-day problems.

Also by K. M. Ashman

The India Summers Mysteries

The Vestal Conspiracy
The Treasures of Suleiman
The Mummies of the Reich
The Tomb Builders

The Roman Chronicles

Roman – The Fall of Britannia
Roman II – The Rise of Caratacus
Roman III – The Wrath of Boudicca

The Medieval Sagas

Medieval – Blood of the Cross
Medieval II – In Shadows of Kings
Medieval III – Sword of Liberty
Medieval IV – Ring of Steel

ROMAN II
THE RISE
OF
CARATACUS

K.M. ASHMAN

1C CANELO

First published in the United Kingdom in 2012 by FeedaRead

This edition published in the United Kingdom in 2021 by

Canelo
31 Helen Road
Oxford OX2 0DF
United Kingdom

A CIP catalogue record for this book is available from the British Library.

Print ISBN 978 1 80032 370 4
Ebook ISBN 978 1 78863 930 9

Look for more great books at www.canelo.co

Printed and bound in Great Britain by Clays Ltd, Elcograf S.p.A.

1

Chapter 1

The Land of the Khymru
44 AD

Cassus crawled through the bracken and peered down into the valley. For an age he could see nothing, but eventually movement caught his eye and a group of riders crossed the river below him. Even at this distance he recognised his pursuers and he cursed silently, as he realised his false trails had failed to fool the native tribesmen, who had been following him for the last two days. He knew he could not evade them much longer, and when they caught him they would kill him without a second thought.

The riders were dressed in coarse plaid leggings and soft leather boots up to their knees. Each man had a cloak around his shoulders secured by a single brooch and Cassus knew from painful memory that when it came to battle, the cloak would be discarded instantly so he could fight unencumbered, naked from the waist up. Their arms were muscular and tattooed with strange imagery, unfamiliar to Cassus's eyes and even their faces were marked with swirling Celtic images. Their jet-black hair hung halfway down their backs, intertwined with lengths of red fabric, and they wore Torcs of Celtic gold around their necks.

The horses were strong but relatively small, much smaller than those used by the Roman cavalry and Cassus guessed correctly that they would be far better suited to the hilly terrain found in this part of the world. Their saddles were simple and rose into a horn at the front, against which the riders could lean to achieve a stable platform as they loosed their arrows from their short but powerful bows. Hanging from the left side of the saddle was a simple scabbard containing the sword that every warrior carried, but though most Britannic Celts Cassus had encountered so far had wielded the larger broadswords, these were smaller and much more versatile. The sword's blade narrowed in the centre before widening again toward the point and the hand guard had two lethal points curving outwards from the main blade. Even the heavy metal weight on the top of the hand grip was designed not just as a counterbalance for the blade, but as an additional option as a cudgel during a backhand swipe. Overall, it was a compact lethal weapon, designed for ease of use in a quick attack on any foot soldier unlucky enough to meet them in combat.

The men below paused to let their horses drink from the river and Cassus hesitated as one of the warriors turned his gaze toward his hiding place. Even though Cassus knew there was no way he could be seen, it was still unnerving and he froze until the warrior looked away again. Finally Cassus crawled back through the bracken toward the glade where he had left his horse.

He knew the mount wouldn't last much longer, as he had ridden it hard for two days away from the Khymru where the Silures had just slaughtered an entire cohort of Nasica's ninth Legion. The Catuvellaunian king, Caratacus, had been within the grasp of the cohort sent by Nasica and if it wasn't for the intervention of the Silures, the Roman unit would now be returning in glory to the

Legion, with the king of the Britons as prisoner. As it was, Cassus was the sole Roman survivor of the battle, fleeing for his life with a head start, granted to him by his childhood friend, Prydain.

Cassus patted the horse's neck and whispered encouragingly into his ear before swinging up into the saddle and turning eastward once more.

'Come on boy,' he said, 'one more effort,' and with a kick of his heels, spurred the horse forward once again, desperate to place as much distance as possible between him and the pursuing Silures.

—

The following morning, Cassus stripped the saddle from the exhausted horse and threw it into a nearby thicket of brambles. There was no way the horse could go on, so he let it go free out onto the plains. Without further ado he continued his journey eastward. Even though he was used to twenty-mile route marches with the Legion, he was weak from hunger and there was no way he could outrun the horsemen. The one good thing was that he could pick terrain that was difficult for the pursuing horses to negotiate.

A few hours later, an enticing smell caused him to detour into a wood and he watched from a thicket as a huntsman roasted a squirrel over a fire. Cassus considered the options. Though he was weak, he was still a trained Legionary at the peak of fitness and the huntsman seemed overweight and elderly. Just as Cassus was considering rushing the man, fate intervened and the man got up and walked to relieve himself against a nearby tree. The Roman seized the opportunity and ran into the clearing to grab the meat off the spit.

'Shit,' he shouted as the hot meat burned his hands and the man turned around in fear.

Cassus spotted the man's knife stuck in a log and grabbed it quickly, before facing him again with a look of menace on his face.

'Stay back,' he said in Latin, 'I just need some food.' He pointed at the cooked squirrel now lying in the dirt.

The old man glanced to one side and following his gaze, Cassus saw a broadsword lying against a tree. He considered taking the weapon but knew it would slow him down and it would be useless against the Silures arrows.

'Don't try anything stupid,' said Cassus, and bent slowly to pick up the meat.

The man answered in his own language and though Cassus didn't understand him, the tone of voice suggested there would be no resistance.

They stared at each other in silence, one tearing chunks of half-cooked squirrel from the carcass with his teeth while the other looked on, hoping this strange man would hurry up and leave. Finally, Cassus threw the remains into the fire and wiped his mouth on the sleeve of his dirty tunic.

'Water?' he said, imitating the actions of drinking. 'Have you got any water?'

The man pointed at a nearby water skin and Cassus drank his fill.

'Thank you,' he said grudgingly at last and lowered his knife.

'Romans,' he said, pointing at himself, 'have you seen any Romans?'

'Romans?' mimicked the huntsman.

'Romans,' repeated Cassus, and pointed at his own eyes. 'Have you seen any Romans?'

The man nodded in understanding and looked toward some hills on the horizon.

'Romans,' he said in his strange accent, and pointed at the arc the sun would have made in the sky, from dawn till dusk. He did this twice and lifted two fingers.

'Two days,' guessed Cassus, 'Romans two days in that direction, yes?'

The man just stared back in silence.

'I guess I'll just have to trust you,' he said and picking up the water skin, walked backwards out of the copse, careful to ensure the man didn't follow.

Within minutes he was running across open moor land again toward the distant hills, desperate to reach the safety of their crags before night fell. By the time he wedged himself into a damp crack of a cliff it was pitch dark, and he looked back over the plain he had crossed that day. Soon he saw the flickering light of a campfire and realised how close the tribesmen actually were. There was no doubt about it; unless he could find safety, they would catch him the following morning. He closed his eyes, desperate for a few minutes sleep, but knowing full well he had to be long gone by morning.

–

The last twelve months had been a whirlwind of action and emotion for Cassus. Since leaving his father's home in Picenum on the eastern coast of Italy, he had travelled up the west coast of Europe to Gaul, taken part in the brutal recruit training demanded by the Ninth Hispana Legion and ultimately taken part in the invasion of Britannia. During all this he had been accompanied by his childhood friend, the freedman Prydain Maecilius, sharing every ache and every success as they were turned from boys into men by their instructors. They had even fought alongside each other against the Germanic warrior Hanzer at a conflict near their training fort in Gaul, and despite Cassus being a true blood Roman and Prydain a freed slave from his father's estate, they had been the closest of friends.

The day Prydain had defected to the enemy in the Khymru all that changed, and they had finally met as foes on the battlefield where Cassus's had come up against Caratacus and the remnants of his army. The entire cohort had been wiped out by the Silures that day and only the intervention of his old friend had stopped him being executed along with the rest of his comrades, gaining him a day's head start before the Silures warriors started their pursuit. Prydain had saved his life and Cassus hated him for it.

Cassus pushed the branches before him as he came to the end of the thicket. He had been running since morning and knew the Silures warriors were not far behind. He had chosen the most difficult routes to slow the riders down, but they always seemed to catch up as soon as the going got easier. He was on his last legs and knew unless he did something drastic, he would soon be caught.

Before him lay another swathe of open land that had been cleared for farming by some local tribe. Cassus groaned as he realised he would be exposed once again until he reached the far tree covered mountains, but also knew he couldn't stay where he was. Though it would be a gamble, tomorrow would mean the pursuers would be that much closer and he would have no chance of reaching the relative safety of the high ground. One last effort and he could be safe amongst the mountains and perhaps buy himself a few more days. With a deep breath, Cassus broke from the cover and ran down to the open pastures.

He had been running for just over an hour and was more than halfway to the mountains when a blood curdling cry rang out behind him. He spun around and was horrified to see four riders break free of the forest edge and gallop down the slope in pursuit. Cassus discarded his cloak, armour and water skin to lighten the load and turned away to sprint as fast as he could, toward the safety of the hills. Within minutes his strength gave out and he staggered to a halt, knowing he could go on no more. He turned in defiance and drew the only weapon he had been allowed to take with him, his Pugio, the knife that every Legionary carried on his belt. It may be useless against arrows but if they fancied their chances with their swords, Cassus was confident at least one of them would accompany him to the afterlife.

Decision made, he was surprised at the calmness that descended upon him and he looked up at the sky, saying his last prayer to Mars, the Roman God of war.

'Prepare thy table for visitors, Mars,' he shouted, 'for tonight I dine at your side.'

He dropped his gaze and stared at the red painted riders galloping toward him, with their swords raised.

'*Come on barbarian filth,*' he screamed, 'let us meet our gods together.' With that he started running toward the oncoming riders, fully aware that attack was the best form of defence.

Suddenly the riders pulled up short in a cloud of dust, staring at the sight before them.

'What's the matter?' he shouted. 'What are you waiting for? Come on, you heathens, and let me show you how a real soldier dies.'

The riders milled about in hesitation before turning around and galloping away as fast as they could.

Cassus stared after them in confusion, not understanding why they were ignoring this opportunity to kill him in cold blood. A few seconds later all became clear as twenty uniformed riders thundered past him in pursuit, each holding a lance parallel to the ground.

Cassus spun around and stared in amazement as a full cohort of auxiliary cavalry trotted up toward him. Behind them, up on the hill, another cohort of Batavian infantry stood in ranks watching events unfold before them. Cassus had never been so happy to see anyone in his life. The Praefectus in charge trotted up and spoke down to him from his horse.

'Who are you, soldier?' he said.

'I am Cassus Maecilius,' he responded, 'a Decurion of the Ninth Hispana. I have been on a special mission led by Tribune Mateus and centurion Remus of the first cohort.'

The Praefectus looked past Cassus and surveyed the surrounding landscape.

'I am aware of the mission,' he said, 'where are your comrades?'

'All dead,' said Cassus, 'slaughtered by kinsmen of the men you have chased off.'

'All of them?' asked the centurion by his side. 'An entire cohort, dead?'

'Yes, sir,' said Cassus, 'there were no survivors.'

'Except for you,' the Praefectus sneered.

'I can explain,' said Cassus.

'Save your explanations, soldier,' said the Praefectus, 'I am not interested.' He turned away and addressed the officer by his side. 'Centurion, take your unit and support the squad in front. The rest of you,' he called to the other assembled centurions, 'take your men back to the hills and prepare a camp. We will stay here tonight and return to the Legion at first light. Post double guards for we seem to have an enemy worth fighting at last.'

The men rode back to their units to make the arrangements, while one complete century galloped after the squad in pursuit of the Silures. The centurion in charge pulled up his horse as he passed.

'Any orders, Sir?' he asked.

'Catch them up and be back by dusk,' he said.

'Yes, Sir,' shouted the centurion and galloped off in pursuit of his men.

'What about me?' asked Cassus.

'You?' the Praefectus sneered. 'Until I can make sense of all this, you, soldier, are under arrest.'

'Under arrest? For what?'

'Desertion,' said the officer. 'Optio, take him into custody.'

'Desertion?' gasped Cassus. 'But Sir...'

Before he could say anything else, two soldiers grabbed him and tied his hands behind his back.

'But nothing,' said the Praefectus. 'If your story is true, you have nothing to worry about. If desertion is proved then you will be crucified in front of the Legion. Nasica will decide but until then, you will remain under arrest. Optio, take him away.'

The burly soldier threw a noose around Cassus's neck and tied the other end to the pommel of his saddle.

'Come on, soldier,' he said, 'let's go.'

9

Cassus jerked forward as the tether tightened and trotted behind the Optio's horse, spitting the dust from his mouth as he went.

Chapter 2

Gwydion swung the axe with all his might, the cast iron blade cutting deep into the flesh of the oaken trunk. He was stripped to the waist and the sweat ran in rivulets down his torso. His long black hair was tied back into a ponytail and his ever-present sword was leaning against a neighbouring tree. He paused for a moment and took a long drink from the skin he had filled at the nearby spring.

The day was warm, but he knew that it would not last as winter was on the horizon. It would be the second winter he and Gwenno had spent in the forest and though the woods had protected them from the worst of the snows, he had lost no time that first spring making a simple wooden hut. It was especially needed since the birth of his son, Taliesin.

As a boy Gwydion had seen the men of the Blaidd making the large round huts that were typical of their people, but it had always been a job for a group rather than an individual. Nevertheless, he had used the same principles but formed an oblong shape rather than a circle, simply because it would be easier to form a lean-to roof. He had sunk the poles into the ground to form the walls while Gwenno had woven the more flexible ash saplings between them, to form a latticework base. Finally, they had mixed river clay, grass and horse dung together and packed any gaps to make it weatherproof.

The final result was simple but effective. The roof was similarly constructed, though sealed with chords of bracken sandwiched between sheets of stripped bark.

The hut had been finished for months and Gwenno had made it as comfortable as possible for their new family. Gwydion was an expert with his bow and they seldom hungered for meat, so when there was a surplus they traded with nearby clans for salt, cloth and anything else they needed. A half a dozen chickens roamed around the hut and their latest acquisition was a milking cow.

This was the reason Gwydion was cutting trees. They needed to make a shelter for the cow before the snows came. At the moment it was brought in during the night to protect it from the wolves that roamed the area, but it was far from ideal, and when Gwenno had given him an ultimatum that either he or the cow had to move out, he knew that he could put it off no longer.

Gwydion smiled at the recollection. It wasn't that he was a lazy man, but the last few months had been idyllic for him and his childhood sweetheart. Gwenno had fully recovered from the trauma of almost being sacrificed by the druids and though the pain of knowing her father had been murdered with the full complicity of her mother had eased, the hatred of the man responsible still burned like an ember at the heart of a fire. Her mother had drugged her father's ale enabling Robbus to kill him in an uneven contest, and when the usurper had grabbed control of the clan, Gwenno's mother had joined him as joint leader – a pact made between Robbus's bed furs weeks earlier.

Despite this, the two intervening years had numbed the pain and Gwenno was happy living with Gwydion in the forest. When their child was born, they had decided to stay in the glade where they had first pitched their tent after the battle between the Romans and Caratacus had ended in the Briton's favour a few miles away. The outcome would have been so different if it hadn't been for the timely intervention of Prydain and the Silures. Gwydion found himself frowning at the memory and picked up the axe to resume his task.

'Pointless worrying about something that never happened,' he thought. But nevertheless, he knew how close they had come to death that day.

'Gwydion,' called Gwenno a few minutes later.

'Over here,' he answered, resting his axe once more.

Gwenno appeared through the trees and Gwydion caught his breath at her beauty as he always did. Her long hair hung below her shoulders like a golden cloak while the white linen dress hugged her slim figure like a second skin. Taliesin was wrapped in a shawl in one arm while the other carried a woven basket.

'What are you doing here?' he asked.

'I've brought you some lunch,' she said.

'Gwenno,' he said, 'what have I told you about wandering the forest alone? You could get easily lost.'

'Oh, stop moaning,' she said as she sat down on a clear piece of grass, 'I know these woods as well as you. Here, sit down and have something to eat. Anyway, Taliesin was missing you.'

She pulled some mutton and flat bread from the basket along with a small skin of milk, and they sat together enjoying the afternoon sun. After feeding their son,

Gwenno placed the baby in the basket and once he was asleep, turned to Gwydion with a twinkle in her eye.

Despite there being work to do, the rest of the afternoon was spent talking, laughing and making love as they spent the time enjoying the peace and safety of their lonely existence, so different from the way of life they had known back in the clan.

Finally the baby stirred and Gwenno knew they would soon have to return to the hut. 'Looks like you'll have to come back tomorrow,' she said standing up, 'it's getting dark.'

'Don't worry,' he said, 'I'll have it done this week.' He gazed into her clear blue eyes and leaned forward to kiss the woman he loved, but at the last moment her gaze altered to focus on something behind him. He hesitated for half a second but before he could say anything she called out in fear.

'*Gwydion,*' she screamed, 'look out!' She pushed him to one side. Gwydion tripped over the basket and fell sprawling to the floor. As he fell, he spun around in a defensive manoeuvre and watched in horror as a spinning hand axe embedded itself deep into Gwenno's chest.

For a second, nothing seemed to happen apart from Gwenno staggering back a few steps. She stared at the weapon hanging down from her body and looked over to Gwydion in shock. Slowly she raised her hand toward him and just before she fell forward, Gwydion saw a single tear roll down her face.

'*Gwenno!*' screamed Gwydion in horror, and jumped up from the ground. Across the clearing a warrior turned to run back down the hill, and though every cell in Gwydion's body demanded he catch and kill the unknown man, his first thought was for his wife and he ran across to lift her up and cradle her in his arms.

'No, no, no,' he murmured as he brushed her hair from her eyes, 'not you, not now.'

The girl half opened her eyes and forced a weak smile.

'Worry not, Gwydion,' she said weakly, 'there's no pain.'

Gwydion looked at the axe, still embedded in her chest, and knew she would be dead within minutes.

'Gwenno, my beautiful wife,' said Gwydion through his tears, 'we had it all, a new home, a new life, a future…'

'Gwydion,' whispered Gwenno, 'I know I am dying, so I want you to listen carefully.'

'What is it, sweetheart?' asked Gwydion, the tears running freely down his face.

'That man, I know him.'

'Who is he?' asked Gwydion. 'For I swear I will tear his still beating heart from his chest with my bare hands.'

'I know not his name,' she whispered, 'but I have seen him in the village.'

'Lanbard?'

'Yes, a few weeks ago, he was staring at us but turned away when I met his gaze…' Gwenno started to cough violently and blood spurted from her mouth.

'But why attack you?' cried Gwydion. 'It makes no sense.'

'I don't think the axe was meant for me, Gwydion,' said Gwenno, 'he was trying to kill you.'

Tears flowed freely down Gwydion's face, as he stroked her hair.

'Oh my beautiful, beautiful wife,' he said, 'what pain have I caused that the gods punish me so?'

'Don't berate yourself, Gwydion,' whispered Gwenno, her voice faltering, 'just cherish the time we had and do something for me.'

'Anything,' said Gwydion.

'Look after Taliesin,' she said. 'Keep him safe and one day, take him to the Blaidd and help him claim what is rightfully his.'

'I swear by all that is holy I will,' sobbed Gwydion.

'One more thing,' whispered Gwenno as her breathing got weaker, 'bury me in the clearing where we first made love.'

Gwydion nodded and wiped away the tears once more.

'I will, Gwenno,' he said quietly, 'I promise.'

'Then I die happy, Gwydion,' she said, 'and will await you in the next life.'

Gwydion turned and picked up his son, now wide awake and oblivious to the drama unfolding around him. He lowered the baby gently into Gwenno's arm, carefully avoiding the handle of the axe still sticking out of his wife's chest. Gwenno turned her head and met her son's gaze.

'Goodbye, my beautiful child,' she said weakly. 'Be good for your father and one day you will be a great chief.' Despite the pain of movement she stretched her head forward and kissed her baby for the last time, and as her eyes closed and her life slipped away, Gwydion tilted his head back and let out a primeval scream that echoed all around the valley.

–

Gwydion stumbled through the forest, carrying the limp corpse of his childhood sweetheart in his arms. He had removed the axe, and the basket containing his son was cradled in her blood-soaked lap. He entered the clearing where they had started their new life together, passing the hut they had worked on for so long, the hours of aching limbs outnumbered by those of laughter, as they shared the labour of love. He continued on past, blind to the animals looking hopefully in his direction, and made his way to the grassy clearing next to the spring before placing the basket and Gwenno on the ground.

It had been their special place, the place where they had first shared their love together and where they sat most evenings to watch the sun go down over the distant mountains. Leaving Taliesin alongside his mother's dead body, he returned to the hut to bring the digging tools. For the next few hours he dug her grave, taking out his frustration on the reluctant soil as he swung the pick furiously at the soft ground. Uncovered rocks were cast down the hill in fury, followed by curses and tears as he screamed at every God he knew, demanding they return her and take him instead.

Occasionally he stopped and held his son, crying uncontrollably as he absorbed the tragedy and the enormity of the task before him, but when Taliesin's cries became constant, the fog cleared momentarily and Cassus brought a jug of cow's milk from the hut and fed the baby from a hole in a leather water-skin.

When his son slept once more he wrapped Gwenno in their best blanket, recalling the way she'd squealed in delight when she'd first seen the vibrant colours and felt the softness of the lamb's wool lining. It had cost them all the coins they had managed to save from the sale of the meat they traded in the nearby village, but it had been worth every one just to see her smile at the first bit of luxury they had seen for two years. The thought suddenly hit him that the day she selected the cover for the marital bed, she could never have guessed that she was also selecting her shroud.

He wrapped her body tight in the blanket, leaving her face uncovered so she could see the sunset one more time beside him. He lit a small fire and brought two tankards with a skin of honey wine from the hut, laying them out as they always did on any night where the weather allowed.

Everything was perfect, exactly as Gwenno would have wanted, and Gwydion talked to her as if she was still there, forcing himself to stay awake all night, reliving every last minute he could recall with the girl he had known all his life. The childhood games and silly pranks they'd played on the adults when they were children, the stolen walks in the forest and swimming in the river as teenagers, and finally the shy glances as their feelings had changed along with their bodies. Even the dangerous time where she had been almost sacrificed by the druids was looked back on with fondness, the terror and hardship of that time subdued by the subsequent happy times that had enveloped their relationship. Gwydion allowed himself to wallow in grief and memories the night through, but as the sun rose, he was a different man. He fed the baby and, ignoring his cries, turned to the task that he knew would break his heart.

He gave Gwenno's now-cold face a final kiss before sealing her shroud one last time and lowered the body into the grave, back-filling it with the loose earth. His mind was numbed from the sound of soil falling on the body of the woman he loved. Finally, he planted an oak sapling he had dug up from the forest edge and patted down the soil firmly around its base, knowing full well that Gwenno would have loved that last gesture.

'One day, my love,' he said quietly, 'I will return to sit beneath the boughs of this oak, and we will watch the sunset together once more.'

Without another word, he picked up the basket containing his son and returned to the hut.

-

Less than an hour later, he left the clearing for the last time. In his saddle bags he had food and water for several days along with any smaller essentials he might need as he travelled. Across his saddle he had Angau, the Parthenian recurved bow given to him by his father years ago and on top of that, his son looked up at him from the basket that had become his makeshift crib.

Behind him, the hut he and Gwenno had built as a labour of love blazed fiercely in the morning air, his last gesture of mourning. He headed across the valley to the hut of a woodsman and his wife who had become their friends and as he approached, the man looked up from chopping firewood.

'Gwydion,' said the woodsman, 'you are welcome. To what do we owe this visit?'

'It is not a happy visit, Derwen,' said Gwydion. 'I have tragic news and a great favour to ask.'

A portly woman ducked out of the timber hut followed by two small girls.

'Gwydion, what's the matter?' she asked, seeing the stress on his face. 'Where's Gwenno?'

'She is dead, Lynwen,' said Gwydion coldly, 'murdered by an assassin's axe meant for me.'

'Oh, Gwydion,' gasped the woman and ran forward to his horse. 'What about Taliesin?'

'He is here,' said Gwydion, 'and he is fine though he cries for his mother.'

'Give him here,' she said tenderly and took the basket carefully from the horse's back. 'Derwen, help the man down, he looks exhausted.'

'No,' snapped Gwydion, 'I am fine. But I have a favour to ask. I promised Gwenno I would look after our son but I have thought the night through to seek the way. I know nothing of raising children and fear my son would suffer at my hands due to my ignorance. I will give my life for him, yet I cannot look after him. I have no right to ask but would request you take him from me and raise him as your own. I have no coin to pay you though my animals are across the valley and are yours to keep.' He paused. 'I know I ask a lot, Lynwen, but I know not which way to turn.'

The woodsman's wife glanced at her husband before replying.

'Gwydion, we don't have much and life is often hard. Sometimes we go hungry and as you know, brigands abound. Not a day goes by where we do not worry what the morrow will bring and only the gods know the future. However, and I know I speak for my husband in this matter, if this is what you must do then your son is welcome in our home and will be treated as our own. When times are good, he will share our meat yet when times are hard, he will hunger alongside us. If you are happy to do this, then we will bring him up as our son. We can offer no more.'

'And it is all I can expect,' said Gwydion. 'Bring him up as a man of the woods and one day, if the gods are willing, I will return to take him back to our people.'

'What about you, Gwydion?' asked Derwen.

'I don't know, yet,' said Gwydion, 'but at the very least I need to find the man who took Gwenno from me.'

'I understand,' said Derwen, 'but why don't you stay for a while and get some rest?'

'I appreciate your concern, Derwen,' said Gwydion, 'but there are things to do.' He glanced down at the baby in the woman's arms.

'Goodbye, Taliesin,' he said. 'With the gods' will, one day we will ride alongside each other as father and son,' and with a simple nod toward his two friends, he turned his horse and galloped away.

–

Gwydion's face reflected the determination he felt. The time for weeping was done and from now on he would return to what he knew best. It had been two years since he had wielded any weapon in anger, but that brief interlude had ended. It was time to pick up on the ways he had known for most of his adult life, the way of the warrior. He had a debt to pay and an anger in his heart that burned like a roaring fire.

Without a backward glance he headed down from the hill and made his way toward the nearby village. Gwydion of the Blaidd, son of Hammer, warrior of the Deceangli, had returned. And he was on a mission.

Chapter 3

The River Tamesas
46 AD

Plautius stood in the watchtower overlooking the river Tamesas, contemplating the events of the last two years. After ceremoniously accepting the surrender of Camulodunum, Emperor Claudius had returned to Rome within weeks and left Plautius in charge of the country. Claudius had given the general the title 'Governor' and tasked him with achieving the domination of Britannia within three years. He had been left with four Legions to aid him in the task, as well as twenty thousand auxiliaries including Batavians and Thracians, a total of over forty thousand military men in all. Allowing for all the usual traders and camp followers the total invasion force counted over sixty thousand individuals.

A main route was cleared from their initial landing site at Rutupiae and a never-ending stream of stores was unloaded by hundreds of slaves and transported along the route supplying the string of fortresses they had built between the bridgehead and the country's capital, Camulodunum.

The task was enormous. Along with the invasion force, he had to deal with the constant stream of refugees that warfare always produced, along with the obligatory slaves that Rome demanded. Only the young and fit would last the long and arduous journey and were sent to Rome, while the older ones were set to work building the straight roads that Rome's engineers were famous for. Quite apart from the enormous bureaucracy, the post demanded he still had the task of organising the military campaigns needed to dominate those tribes further afield, which had so far refused to bend the knee to Rome. With this in mind, he had deliberately avoided setting his base within the city and instead had ordered a fort built overlooking the narrows of the river Tamesas where he had outwitted Caratacus two years ago. As soon as it had been erected the camp followers quickly established a settlement around the fort and within weeks had named it Londinium. It was a small town, split down the centre by the river Tamesas, though both sides were linked by an impressive wooden bridge built by the Roman engineers. Within months the shores of the Tamesas had been secured from Londinium right back to the sea, allowing stores to be sailed almost right up to the settlement, supplementing those transported by road.

With the river secured and the fortresses dominant, Governor Plautius allowed himself to once more think about the military campaign that had faltered for far too long. He had summoned the four Legion commanders to the fort and whilst three were already relaxing in their quarters, he still awaited Nasica from the Ninth Hispana who was stationed two days ride away to the west. Of all four Legions, the ninth had had the worst of it since the invasion two years previously and had already lost an entire cohort when they failed to come back from an ill-thought out expedition westwards two years previously.

He stared out over the river, lost in the memories of home. The sun-soaked vineyards and crystal-clear waters of the Mare Nostrum were a stark contrast to the constant rain and muddy waters of the lazy river before him. His reverie was short-lived as the guard commander approached along the ramparts.

'My lord, Nasica's column approaches,' said the Tribune quietly.

'Thank you,' said the governor. 'Let him freshen up and then bring the Legates to my quarters.'

'Yes my lord,' the Tribune responded before disappearing into the dark.

Plautius lingered a few moments longer, drinking in the fresh air of the night, before descending from the ramparts and making his way to the briefing room.

–

An hour later the four men were standing around the briefing table drinking warm wine. Before them lay a map of Britannia as far as they knew it. It was drawn onto the scraped inside of a softened cow hide and had been brought from Rome with the invasion force. The coastal outline was clear and had been mapped by a cartographer from on board a Bireme that had circumnavigated the islands years previously. Major population centres had been drawn in from information gleaned from the many traders who had plied their trades for many years in these lands, while any further information gathered since the invasion was added as it was discovered. The map was detailed, with most tribes marked within circles along with relative strengths and weaknesses. Tracks were marked with dotted lines while paved roads were added as solid lines as they were made. Along with the main rivers and mountain ranges, the map was a detailed and very important weapon in Plautius' armoury.

'Gentlemen,' said Plautius, interrupting the quiet conversation that had permeated the room for the last half hour, 'enough small talk, let's get down to business.'

All the officers in the room gathered round the table.

'As you know, we now have control over most of the tribes in the immediate vicinity. Trinovantes, Catuvellauni and Cantiaci have all bent the knee and we have received tribute from many of the other tribes accepting our governorship. However, we have allowed ourselves to become complacent. Over the last few months, to my shame, I have allowed myself to become detached from the situation on the ground. Our men grow fat from inactivity, and those tribes yet to kneel to our fist become more confident every day their blood remains unspilled.'

A murmur of excitement rippled around the room from senior and junior officers alike. This was what they had been waiting for. Their bridgeheads had been secured and they were impatient to carry out the task they had trained so hard for.

'Our supply lines are secure,' continued Plautius, 'our fortresses well manned and the granaries full. The winter is behind us and we have a full campaigning season before us. As you know, I have been collating the reports from our scouts and have drafted the plans for the second phase, our move inland. What we have achieved so far is impressive but, make no mistake, the more difficult part is to come. Our forces have overcome the local tribes due to our superior numbers and discipline. Add to this the proximity of the four Legions in a relatively small area and the locals know it would be suicide to undertake any sort of offence against us.

'However, that luxury has now come to an end. I have sent a message to Claudius requesting four more Legions. A few days ago I received his response; the request has been denied so it is down to us in this room and the men we currently command.'

More whispers filled the room as the size of the task before them sank in.

'It is a big ask,' continued Plautius, 'as the further we campaign, the more we will be stretched and the further away from support we will be. However, the die is cast and we will make it work.'

He placed three scrolls on the table.

'I have thought long and hard about your deployment, taking on board your relative strengths and allocating tasks accordingly.' He picked up the first scroll and handed it to the Legatus nearest him.

'Nasica, you will take the Ninth Hispana North-West toward Caledonia. You will have to cross the lands of the Coritani but should have no problem; they are reported to be relatively weak. However, beyond the Coritani lies the Brigantes and they are a different proposition altogether. Your task is to find a main route deep into the Brigantes territory and establish a foothold from which you will spread our control. Once they have been subdued, further campaigns can be launched north into Caledonia at a later date. I have no doubt your task will be difficult so prepare well.'

Nasica took the scroll and saluted the general.

Plautius turned to the second Legatus.

'Geta, the Valeria Victrix will go westward to the heartlands of this country. There are still clans of Catuvellauni at large and we have yet to cross swords with Cornovii. Your task is to wipe out any remaining resistance from Caratacus's people and try to reach agreement with the Cornovii. If that is not possible, use all necessary force to make them see the error of their ways. Campaign no further than Cambria but establish a fortified town close to the river that borders their lands. I also want a road built from Londinium to your final location. I have managed to obtain an extra unit of engineers as this will be a key task. Take prisoners as you go and put them to work on the road. Work them twenty-four hours a day if necessary, for if we are to invade Cambria, we will need quick and reliable supply routes.'

'We are going into Cambria?' asked Geta.

'Eventually, yes, but one step at a time. Build the road and subdue the locals first. Cambria is a different proposition altogether and we need to be sure that our rear is secure.'

'Understood,' said Geta and took his scroll from Plautius.

The general turned to the last Legatus, Vespasian. The man's features seemed younger than his thirty-six years and though he came from ordinary stock, his sharp mind and tactical mastery of his Legion meant that he was talked about in high circles as one to watch. His father had been a minor official, gathering taxes for the government in Rome, but his grandfather had been a feared centurion and fought under Pompey at Pharsalus. Vespasian had his sights set on other things and after serving in the military for three years in Thrace as a Tribune, he had also served his required time as a minor magistrate in Rome, a necessary requirement for anyone not of the senatorial class who aspired to higher office.

'Vespasian,' said Plautius, 'to the Augusta falls the biggest task of all. First of all I want you to campaign south and secure the tin mines on the south coast. You should not encounter too much trouble on the way as many of the tribes are relatively friendly. However, your mission is twofold. When the south is secured you will turn west and start probing the lands of the Khymru. This is the most dangerous part of our expedition so far. In the south of the Khymru there is a tribe called the Silures that we know little about. Your task will be to gather as much information as possible with a view to nullifying their threat.'

'These Silures,' said Vespasian, 'are they not the same ones who slaughtered one of Nasica's cohorts?'

'They are,' said Plautius, 'and I suggest that you spend time with Nasica to glean whatever information you can, though I fear that is precious little.'

Vespasian took the third scroll and as the other officers in the room read their own documents, his remained unopened as he tapped it repeatedly into the palm of his hand.

'You look troubled, Vespasian,' said Plautius.

'Not troubled, my lord, but intrigued.'

'Explain.'

'Can I speak freely?'

'Indeed.'

'My lord, I understand the need for each task but to me they seem to be fragmented. Neither is linked to each other and when you consider the overall mission, surely there needs to be a more cohesive approach.'

'You are a very astute man, Vespasian,' said Plautius, 'and yes, you are right. There is an overall link here – the Druids.'

All the officers stopped talking and their heads turned toward the general. Plautius stepped forward and leaned over the map to indicate the land to the west.

'As you know, this is Cambria,' he said, 'otherwise known as the Khymru. Like Caledonia it is a place of high mountains but not on the same scale. There is one major mountain range that splits the land but it is easily travelled. On the northern shore of the Khymru lies the island of Mona, the heartland of the Druids. As you know, every act of every person on this island is guided by the hand of the Druids. They decide when to plant the crops, when to harvest and when to fast. There are Druids in every clan of every tribe throughout this land and they are responsible for gathering tribute and for ensuring the dead meet their gods. However, we also believe they are responsible for organising the resistance to our armies.'

'But I thought they were no more than simple priests,' said Geta.

'This was indeed the understanding,' said Plautius, 'but the more we interact with these people, the more we realise they hold far more influence. Apparently, they have their own warrior clans and have made their island a fortress. Every tribe in Britannia looks to the Druids for guidance and I believe it is essential to minimise their influence.'

'And how do we do that?' asked Nasica.

'To kill a snake, you must take its head,' said Plautius. 'I believe that if we take the island of Mona, the remaining tribes will lie down like a sick puppy.'

'Then why don't we just march in there and squash these priests under our heel?' asked Vespasian.

'It's not as simple as that,' said Plautius. 'Between us and them lie three tribes, the Cornovii, the Deceangli and the Ordovices. All are threats in their own right though they are all relatively quiet at the moment. If we want to reach the Druids, we need to overcome them.'

'Can they be bought?'

'I doubt it; they have more gold than they need and are fiercely loyal to the Druids.'

'Give me three Legions and I will bring back the head of the chief Druid himself,' said Vespasian.

'Your confidence is admirable,' said Plautius, 'but don't forget, two years ago we lost an entire cohort to these barbarians. No, first of all we need to isolate them from the rest of the country, hence the individual tasks. With the south, north and central areas secured, the Khymru will be isolated and we can move in without fear that our rear will be compromised.'

'But that could take years,' said Geta.

'There is no rush,' said Plautius, 'we are here to stay and if it takes years, then so be it. It would seem that the Khymru is very rich in gold and minerals so this has to be done right. First of all we will isolate them. During this time, we will also gather intelligence and when the time is ready, we will strike like a blacksmith's hammer. With the loss of the Druids the tribes of Caledonia will also lose the stomach for a fight and if there is one thing we Romans have in abundance it is patience. Now then, let's talk detail.' The four men gathered around the cow hide map and spent the rest of the night talking tactics, breaking only for food. When the servants served bowls of broth,

Vespasian sat next to Nasica on a couch, engaging him in conversation.

'I hope you don't mind I've got the west,' he said, between mouthfuls of gravy-soaked bread.

'Why would I mind?' asked Nasica.

'Well, with all this business about losing a cohort back then, I thought you would be keen to take revenge. It must hurt after all.'

Nasica ignored the thinly veiled jibe.

'Oh it hurts,' said Nasica, 'but ultimately Tribune Mateus overstepped the mark. He went further than his authority and got isolated.'

'Why would he do that?' asked Vespasian.

'A bitter mix of inexperience and greed,' said Nasica. 'He thought he had the chance to take Caratacus and ploughed further into the country than was safe. When the locals turned nasty, they were far too committed to escape or expect reinforcements.'

'Didn't he have any experienced officers with him to guide his arm?'

'Actually he had one of my most experienced men with him,' said Nasica. 'A centurion called Remus who has seen more battles than most men, yet even his vision was clouded and between them they led their men to slaughter.'

'Caratacus would have been a great trophy,' said Vespasian.

'Admittedly, and perhaps we would all have been tempted so.'

'Sometimes these things come off, sometimes they don't. Pull it off and you're a hero, fail and you are a pariah.'

'Such is the burden of command,' agreed Nasica. 'Tell me, how is it you know so much of the battle? I thought your men were wiped out.'

'All except one,' said Nasica. 'A Decurion named Cassus Maecilius. He was released by a freed slave who joined the enemy. Apparently, they knew each other in their youth.'

Vespasian's eyes narrowed as he absorbed the information.

'Wait a minute – you have a man who has not only been into the Khymru, but also engaged them in battle? You kept that quiet.'

'The loss of a cohort, a Tribune and a respected centurion is not something you shout about,' said Nasica. 'Plautius was given a full briefing but the tale is of disgrace and treachery. The story was told of a valiant battle where our men fought overwhelming numbers but were eventually cut down in the service of Rome. The detail of individual stupidity, greed, treachery and desertion were kept from the troops.'

'And what about this Cassus? What happened to him?'

'He was taken under the wing of Plautius and I know not his fate. A shame, really, as he is a formidable Legionary, one of the best. He had a good future in front of him and I would have him back in a heartbeat.'

'Why did Plautius take him?'

'Probably to make sure he kept quiet. The last thing we needed so early in the invasion was a severe blow to morale. For all I know he could be dead.'

'Nasica, Vespasian,' called Plautius, 'enough chatter. Let's get back to work.'

The two men returned to the planning table and the rest of the night was spent discussing detail. Finally, Geta and Nasica said their goodbyes and left for their own lines as the sun rose. Plautius was talking to a junior officer in the corner and turned to see Vespasian still waiting at the door.

'Vespasian, you are still here,' he said as he held out his cup for a servant to refill.

'Yes, my lord,' said Vespasian, 'I have a question to ask you.'

'And you had to wait until the others had gone before voicing it?'

'Yes, my lord, as it may be one you do not want to answer and I do not wish to put you in a compromising position.'

'Intriguing,' said Plautius, 'ask your question, Vespasian.'

'My lord, the Legionary called Cassus. Does he still live?'

Plautius sipped on his watered wine thoughtfully, all the while staring at Vespasian. Finally he broke Vespasian's gaze and looked over his shoulder toward the servants.

'Leave us,' he said and they scuttled out of the room without a backward glance. 'You too,' he said to his personal bodyguards at the door and after a perfectly synchronised salute, they also retired, leaving the two Legati alone in the room. Finally he turned back to Vespasian.

'That is a very strange question Vespasian,' he said, 'why do you ask?'

'My lord, if he is dead then my request is irrelevant, but if he still lives, I would request that he is posted to my Legion for the coming campaign.'

'Why would you want him?' asked Plautius. 'He has been branded a coward and a deserter.'

33

'Mere words,' said Vespasian. 'I care not what he has done in the past; I am only interested in what he knows. From what I can gather we have no knowledge of these Silures you speak of in the Khymru, yet there is one amongst us that has been there, fought them and lived to tell the tale. The task you have bestowed on me places my men in the vanguard of our assault on these islands. A task I hasten to add that we will embrace gladly, but embracing a task is not enough; success is also paramount. If the testimony of this man saves one life of my Legionaries, then it is worth a fortune. However, I believe it is worth far more. He has seen them fight, seen their weapons, and been on the receiving end of their tactics, all invaluable intelligence that will benefit my men.'

'Your comments have merit,' said Plautius, 'and yes, the man is indeed alive, but I cannot grant your request.'

'Why not, my lord? Is he not but one man?'

'He is, but he has been tasked to other duties.'

Vespasian was quiet for a while but decided to push the point.

'My lord, forgive me but I am at a loss to see how the duties of one man are more important than the security of a Legion.'

Plautius slammed his cup onto the table causing the wine to shoot out of the top.

'Do not question my decisions, Vespasian. This man was the sole survivor of a humiliating massacre inflicted on us by a tribe of backward heathen. Yes, he was a good soldier and for that reason only I spared his life, but I cannot and will not risk that information contaminating our Legionaries' minds. We routed Caratacus at Medway and our men are confident this country will fall like wheat before the scythe as we march inland.'

'But it is common knowledge that we lost a cohort in the Khymru, my lord. The stories of their demise are shared around every campfire from here to Camulodunum.'

'They are,' said Plautius, 'but the tale is one of bravery and a last stand of unbelievable courage against an overwhelming force many times their size. There is no mention of treachery, cowardice or desertion, nor will there be. As far as the men are concerned, Mateus's cohort was defeated in a battle covered with glory and now stands alongside Mars in the heavens. If I release this man, there is a possibility that a tale less honourable will raise its head and we cannot allow that to happen.'

'Then why do you not just take his head?'

'I don't know, Vespasian. There is something about him. A look in his eyes that reveals a hunger that burns to the heart of him. Perhaps an opportunity will come where I may harness that fire and turn it upon my enemies.'

'Then let this be it, my lord,' said Vespasian. 'Allow me to use his knowledge to our advantage. If it is of use, then your leniency in allowing him to keep his life will be justified. If not, then at least his sword arm will be suitably deployed in the service of the Emperor. Let that anger loose on Rome's enemies and if he is indeed proved a coward, then I promise it will be my own blade that pierces his heart.'

Plautius thought for a while before nodding slowly.

'Your words make sense, Vespasian,' he said. 'Rome's investment in this man demands payment. Take him off my hands and use him as you will.'

'Tell me where he is,' said Vespasian, 'and I will send my best riders for him.'

'He is here, in this very fort,' said Plautius. 'Return at dusk tomorrow and he will be handed over.'

'Until tomorrow, my lord,' said Vespasian and after saluting his superior, left to attend his own quarters.

Chapter 4

Britannia
46 AD

Vespasian rode through the gates of the fort for the second time in thirty-six hours. He was accompanied by a century of auxiliary cavalry as a bodyguard, as although they may have subdued the local tribes, there were always those who resented the intruders and fancied themselves as heroes. He dismounted outside the general's quarters and gave the reins of his horse, along with his heavy cloak, to a waiting slave.

Before he could walk up the steps, the general walked out of the door and down toward him.

'Vespasian,' he said, 'perfect timing. Retrieve your cloak and come with me.' He strode away from the officers' quarters closely followed by Vespasian and the ever-present bodyguards. Vespasian caught up with the general.

'Your stride seems purposeful, my lord,' he said. 'Where are we going?'

'I want to show you something,' said Plautius, 'something that will astonish you.'

'Is it in regard to the campaign?'

'You could say that,' said Plautius. 'How goes your preparations?'

'My camp echoes with the sound of Gladii being sharpened,' laughed Vespasian. 'Even my toughest centurions are surprised by the enthusiasm shown by the men.'

'Yes, it is good to have a focus again,' said Plautius. 'Politics have a way of blunting a Gladius quicker than any training post.'

'I still can't see why Claudius doesn't just flood this island with Legions and crush every tribe like beetles,' said Vespasian. 'All this pandering to barbarians who see themselves as kings makes me sick to my stomach.'

'Oh for the old days,' laughed Plautius, 'it was so much simpler back then.'

They walked through the rows of barracks toward the outer palisade. Finally Plautius stopped before a building that had no shutters in its solid walls.

'Here we are,' he said.

'Slave quarters?' suggested Vespasian.

'Similar,' said Plautius, 'but these are used for incarcerating those we take captive.'

'Plautius running a prison,' laughed Vespasian, 'wonders will never cease. Any taken by my men are sent to the road gangs, Rome, or sold on as soon as possible. Prisoners take up too many resources for my liking.'

'I agree,' said Plautius, 'but sometimes the intelligence gained is useful before they are despatched.'

They walked into the candle-lit building, past the fully armed guards and waited as the inner door was unbarred.

'After you,' said Plautius and followed Vespasian into the inner cells. Before them was a room with a barred front containing three prisoners, all sat on the floor with their backs against the wall. They were all dressed in plaid leggings and naked from the waist up. Their hair was dark, matching their full beards, and the scowls on their faces told Vespasian they had not had an easy time of it at the hands of Plautius's guards.

'Catuvellauni?' suggested Vespasian.

'Yes,' answered Plautius. 'A few misguided individuals who thought they could be a thorn in our side.'

Vespasian walked toward the bars of the cell and smirked at the three men.

'Pathetic,' he said.

One of the captives suddenly sprang forward and smashed into the bars, swearing in his own strange language. Vespasian stepped back in alarm.

'Still got some spirit though,' said Plautius.

'So what is all this about?' asked Vespasian.

'You are about to find out,' said Plautius. 'Guards, bring one of those men outside, the one with attitude.'

Four Legionaries entered the cell and subdued the captives at the point of their Gladii, before dragging the volatile one out by his heels and throwing him in the dirt before the doors. Another group of guards surrounded him, forming a circle of spear points. Plautius walked to the guard commander and whispered in his ear. The guard commander ran to another nearby block and disappeared inside. A few moments later he returned to the circle closely followed by a young man dressed in full Lorica Segmentata, the flexible armour of the front-line Legionary. In his right hand he carried a Gladius already unsheathed. He walked into the makeshift circle.

Vespasian looked at the young man with interest. He was young, obviously strong and had an air of arrogance about him which was evident in the way he strutted around the stationary captive.

'Vespasian, meet Cassus Maecilius,' said Plautius, 'the most ruthless killer I have ever met.'

'Quite a statement,' said Vespasian, 'I could name a hundred of my own men who could stake a claim to the same title. What makes this man so special?'

'You are about to find out,' said Plautius and turned to face the circle. 'Cassus Maecilius,' he shouted, 'kill this filth.'

—

Vespasian and Plautius both turned their attention to the scene before them. The well armoured Legionary adopted the classic stance, holding his oval shield before him with his left hand while the Gladius was held in his right with an overhand grip, levelled just below his shoulder and pointed forward at the dirty Celtic warrior to his front. His legs were shoulder width apart with the left slightly forward of the right, providing a stable base from which to launch any attack.

'This is stupid,' said Vespasian, 'and provides no sport. Why not arm the heathen?'

'It provides sport enough for my purpose,' said Plautius, 'patience, Vespasian.'

The Legionary sneered at the dishevelled warrior in front of him and took three measured paces forward. The warrior bent into a semi crouch and met the stare with a steely gaze of his own. As the soldier approached, the warrior skipped lightly sideways, forcing his adversary to follow him around the makeshift circle. For several moments, he followed the lighter warrior, unable to corner him to administer the killing blow. Finally he anticipated the next move and managed to corner the bedraggled figure at the juncture between the perimeter of soldiers and the wall of the prison.

'Got you, you pathetic excuse of a man,' the Legionary sneered and stepped in to slam the warrior against the wall. As he did, the Celt dropped into a crouch and slammed his foot into the enemy's knee below the shield. Though it failed to smash the joint, it forced the soldier to stagger backwards in pain, causing him to lose composure for a few seconds. This was the opening the warrior had wanted and he followed the blow by launching himself onto the shield of his adversary, forcing him back even further across the dirt. So aggressive was the assault that the soldier struggled to get enough balance and though he swung his Gladius frantically, the blows were easily avoided by the prisoner as he pressed home the surprise.

'The animal has spirit,' said Vespasian, 'this is much more interesting.'

The Legionary regained his composure and smashed the warrior backwards with his shield, following it up with a carefully aimed swipe of his Gladius, but where he anticipated flesh, there was only air.

The warrior caught his arm in full swing and before the Legionary could do anything, the unarmed man sank his teeth into his inner forearm, tearing flesh and tendon free from bone and causing the soldier to scream in agony as the Gladius fell to the floor. The Legionary stepped back, but despite the pain, his training kicked in and he renewed the assault, using the shield to force the warrior back once more. To his surprise, the warrior dropped down once again but alert to the danger, the Legionary lowered the shield to protect his knees and legs.

This was exactly what the warrior was waiting for and grabbed the bottom of the shield, to pull it outwards. As the soldier naturally pulled back to get it out of the smaller man's grip, the shield tilted backwards and the Legionary's eyes widened in horror at his basic mistake. A split second later the warrior slammed the shield upwards and the top edge caught the soldier under the chin, sending him flying backwards into the dirt. Before he could recover his senses, the warrior pounced onto his opponent's body and pinned him to the floor, his iron grip clamped around the soldier's throat. The other hand sought out the soldier's own Pugio and pulled it from the sheath before placing it between the lapped scales of the armour, and against the soldier's under vest just below the heart.

'No,' gasped the soldier, 'don't do it, please.'

'Guards, stop him,' shouted Vespasian.

'Hold still,' shouted Plautius and the soldiers re-sheathed their swords in confusion.

'Plautius,' answered Vespasian, 'he is about to kill one of your men, you can't allow this to happen.'

'Be quiet,' ordered Plautius, 'this will be seen to its natural end.'

Silence fell again until the beaten Legionary's pleading voice floated once again across the makeshift arena.

'Don't do it,' he pleaded again, 'I will speak for you, get you released to your people. I can do that; I am a Decurion.'

The warrior leaned forward and whispered into his ear, and as the soldier's eyes widened in confusion, the warrior eased the knife upwards and into the man's heart.

-

Vespasian drew his own Gladius and stepped forward.

'Vespasian, hold still,' ordered Plautius. 'What's done is done.'

'You cannot be serious,' hissed Vespasian, 'that filth has just killed Cassus Maecilius, the one man who could shine any light on the ways of the Silures. Since when does the great Plautius allow any Celtic filth to kill one of his own men without retribution? We have wiped out entire villages for less.'

'Grab him,' shouted Plautius to the surrounding guards, 'and bring him to me unharmed.'

The ring of Legionaries closed in on the now-standing warrior and dragged him unceremoniously to stand before the general.

'Release him,' ordered Plautius, 'and return to your posts.'

'What are you doing?' hissed Vespasian, holding his Gladius at the ready, 'he could attack you.'

'He won't attack me,' said Plautius. 'But enough theatre for one day. Vespasian, meet Cassus Maecilius, soldier of Rome.'

'What?' gasped Vespasian, staring at the bedraggled warrior before him. 'This is Cassus?'

'It is.'

'But I thought…'

'Well you thought wrong, Vespasian. At no time did I say that Legionary was our man. You drew that conclusion on your own. Cassus has worked himself into the locals' trust over the last year and is a passable imitation of the real thing, don't you think?'

'It is amazing,' said Vespasian, and took a step closer, 'he even stinks like a local.'

'All part of the cover,' said Plautius.

'Wait a minute,' said Vespasian and looked over to where two men were dragging the corpse of the dead soldier away. 'I don't understand. Why allow the death of a soldier to prove a point?'

'Oh, him?' answered Plautius. 'He was nothing. I would have had to deal with him anyway. He was caught raping one of the locals last night.'

'Spoils of war, surely,' suggested Vespasian.

'Women, yes,' said Plautius, 'children, no.'

'Oh, I see,' said Vespasian and turned to Cassus who was waiting patiently in front of the two officers. 'So, soldier, I am intrigued. What did you say to him before you pierced his heart?'

'He told me he was a Decurion,' said Cassus in perfect Latin, 'and I replied, so am I.'

Vespasian nodded an acknowledgment and turned to Plautius.

'So, my lord, can I take him?'

'You can,' said Plautius.

'Get yourself cleaned up,' said Vespasian to Cassus, 'and report to my quarters at first light.'

'What about those men in there?' said Cassus, nodding toward the jail. 'They will suspect something.'

'You are right,' said Plautius and turned to the nearby guard commander. 'Soldier, execute the prisoners.'

'Do you want them crucified, my lord?' asked the soldier.

'No, make it quick and burn their bodies when you are done.'

'Yes, my lord,' said the soldier and saluted his commanding officer before spinning around and making his way back to the jail.

'Anything you need, soldier?' asked Plautius to Cassus.

'No, my lord,' said Cassus.

'Then get some rest. I will see you tomorrow.'

The two officers strode away leaving Cassus alone in the dust circle. A nearby soldier wandered over and approached him.

'Did I hear right?' he asked. 'You are a Decurion?'

'I was,' said Cassus.

'What unit?' asked the soldier.

'I don't have one,' said Cassus, 'now, where can a man get a meal around here?'

'Follow me,' said the soldier and the two men headed off into the barracks.

—

The following morning saw Cassus waiting patiently before the doors of the officer's quarters. He was dressed in a plain white tunic, secured around the waist with a leather belt, and a black cloak kept out the morning chill.

'What do you want?' barked the guard.

'I have an appointment with Legatus Vespasian,' said Cassus.

'Name?'

'Cassus Maecilius.'

The soldier consulted his comrade who nodded his agreement.

'You are expected,' said the soldier, 'surrender your arms.'

Cassus withdrew a Pugio from his belt and handed the small dagger over to the nearest soldier.

'What sort of knife is this?' asked the soldier.

'A local one,' answered Cassus. 'Better made than our own Pugios and balanced to my own hand.'

'Looks too light to me,' said the soldier. 'Anyway, where's your Gladius?'

'I have no sword,' answered Cassus.

'Then you are improperly dressed for duty in this fort,' said the soldier. 'Centurion Rufus will wear your arse-skin for slippers if he finds out.'

'Then don't tell him,' said Cassus.

'Don't be funny, boy,' said the older man, 'or I'll kick your arse from here to the guardhouse for insubordination. Now, wait there and I will see if the Legatus is ready for you.'

Despite his urge to wipe the sneer off the man's face, Cassus held his tongue, knowing it was important to draw as little attention to himself as possible.

'Yes, Sir,' he said and waited as the man disappeared inside. A few minutes later he emerged and summoned Cassus in, patting him down for hidden weapons before allowing him past the door.

'Nothing personal,' grunted the soldier, 'I just haven't seen you around here before and we can't take any chances, can we?'

'No problem,' said Cassus and followed the man inside. They walked down a corridor decorated with paintings of Roman architecture and past marble busts of various gods.

At the end of the corridor another guard opened a door to allow Cassus through into the room beyond. The room was very large with walls of solid stone plastered to a smooth finish and decorated with drapes of hanging silk. A fire raged in a giant hearth, carefully tended by an industrious slave. Vespasian stood in the centre of the room facing away from Cassus, a further two slaves securing his armour.

'Cassus, come in,' said Vespasian without turning around, 'take a seat. I will be with you as soon as these two imbeciles finish this simplest of tasks. Perhaps a whipping will make them concentrate more, what do you think?'

'Perhaps so, my lord,' said Cassus, knowing the words were for the benefit of the two slaves and not him. The two slaves finished their task and stood back as Vespasian checked the finished effect in a full-length bronze mirror.

'It will do,' he said eventually, 'now get out of here.'

The relief on the two slaves' faces was immense and they retreated out of the quarters as quickly as they possibly could without falling over. Cassus rose from his seat as the Legatus approached the table.

'At ease,' said Vespasian. 'Have you eaten?'

'Yes, my lord, I have been well looked after.'

'Glad to hear it,' said Vespasian and took a seat opposite Cassus at the table. For what seemed an age neither man spoke as Vespasian took in the features and demeanour of the young man before him. Finally he broke the silence.

'So, Cassus Maecilius, I expect you are wondering why you are here?'

'Yes, my lord.'

'Well, before I enlighten you, why don't you tell me about your background and in particular, what has become of you since Mateus's disastrous foray into the Khymru?'

–

'Well, my lord,' said Cassus, 'after I escaped the clutches of the Silures, I was brought back to the fort to face my accusers.'

'Ah yes, I understand you were accused of cowardice.'

'I was,' said Cassus, 'and to be fair, I understand why. I was the only survivor from a complete cohort to escape with my life. Even then it was not by my own efforts but as a result of so-called kindness by one I once called friend.'

'Prydain Maecilius?'

'Yes, my lord. He released me out of some sort of false allegiance. As I rode away, the hills echoed with the death screams of my comrades as the Silures slaughtered everyone in cold blood.'

'Yet still you fled.'

'Yes, my lord. I know it sounds like cowardice, but it was the only way I could ensure that one day the traitor would pay for his treachery.'

'And did your accusers believe you?'

'No, my lord, though Plautius stayed my execution. My record was good and he saw a glimpse of truth in my words.'

'He released you?'

'No, my lord, he gave me an impossible task to prove my allegiance and bravery.'

'Which was?'

'To execute a troublesome king in the territory of the Atrebates.'

'And I assume you were successful?'

'I brought him the king's head within a month.'

'Impressive,' said Vespasian. 'Did you lose many men in the execution of this task?'

'No, my lord. I had no men.'

'You went alone?'

'Yes, my lord.'

'I am impressed,' said Vespasian. 'And how did you accomplish such a feat?'

'Subterfuge, my lord. I took on the identity of an escaped Gallic slave and was taken into their village. That night, I killed the guards and cut through the walls of the king's hut.'

'He was alone?'

'Apart from his family, yes. His arrogance brought his demise. He thought the location of his village was safety enough. He was wrong.'

'And his family?'

'I killed them all,' said Cassus without any hint of compassion. 'His line will not bother us anymore.'

'So,' said Vespasian, 'you brought back his head. What happened then?'

'When I returned, it was difficult to place me in a unit. The accusation of cowardice had preceded me and it seemed nobody wanted me. For a while I was assigned kitchen duties, but Plautius knew my skills lay elsewhere. Soon he sent me back out to infiltrate the local tribes. At first I used the cover of being an escaped slave, but soon picked up their tongue. After that it was easier. I allowed myself to become as them and now I can mix with most, albeit as a Gaul to explain my strange accent.'

'Hence your appearance,' said Vespasian.

Cassus lifted his hand to the large beard now hanging from his face. His hair hung about his shoulders and he looked every bit the native.

'All part of the subterfuge,' said Cassus.

'Tell me, Cassus,' said Vespasian, 'how do you feel about another posting into enemy territory?'

Cassus shrugged his shoulders.

'It makes no difference to me, my lord. I have a debt to fulfil to Plautius. When he feels I have proved my innocence in the slaughter of Mateus's cohort, only then can I return to the Legion's lines. One day I will do so and continue to serve Rome as she sees fit. One day, I hope to once more face Prydain Maecilius and plunge my Gladius deep into his heart.'

'Hmm,' said Vespasian. 'What if I was to say that I can make that day come much sooner than you think?'

For the first time, Vespasian saw the glint of interest in Cassus's eyes. He knew he had touched a nerve.

'If that were the case, my lord, I would carry out your orders without question, or die in the process.'

'I thought you would say that,' said Vespasian, and turned to nod at the guard at the door. The soldier left the room but returned a few moments later followed by a simply dressed local. The strange man was clean shaven and dressed in a tunic and leggings. He strode toward the two waiting men and after a brief nod of the head toward Vespasian in recognition, stopped to stare at Cassus.

Cassus was surprised, not only at the lack of humility but at the fact that the man held a knife and was casually cutting slices from the apple in his hand. Cassus could see that the man was well built and probably from farming or warrior stock.

'Is this him?' asked the stranger in perfect Latin.

Again, Cassus was surprised to realise that he was Roman. What sort of man could act with such impunity in front of a Legatus?

'It is,' said Vespasian.

The man turned toward Cassus and spoke in fluent Briton.

'Stand up,' he said.

After a moment's pause, Cassus did as he was told and faced the stranger.

The man placed the half-eaten apple on a side table and returned to face Cassus.

'Defend yourself,' he said and lunged forward to stab Cassus.

Cassus was unprepared but despite his shock, managed to throw himself to one side avoiding the thrust. He jumped up and spun to meet his attacker.

'What trickery is this, my lord?' he shouted. 'Was I brought here to be murdered?'

Vespasian kept quiet and stepped back to watch the events unfold.

'Shut up and fight,' said the stranger.

Cassus knew he had no choice and adopted the defensive stance he knew so well, legs slightly apart with the left slightly in front of the other. His left hand extended out to deflect any attack and his right was held loosely at chest level, ready to take advantage of any opportunity.

Again the man attacked, but this time Cassus was ready for him. He took a pace back, but as he did he grabbed a beaker of wine from the table and threw it into his attacker's face.

The wine caused the man to adjust his position slightly and Cassus pushed home his advantage. He picked up a stool and aimed it at the man's head to crush his skull, but as he did, the man regained control and ducked out of the way. The chair smashed harmlessly against the wall, and though Cassus spun around as quickly as he could, it was too late. The stranger was immediately behind him and as he turned, smashed him in the jaw with his fist. Cassus crumpled against the wall and his attacker followed up with his knife. Within seconds, Cassus was still, feeling the cold steel of the attacker's blade against his throat. Though he didn't understand the reasons, he knew that his time had come. This was where he died.

The assailant's face was less than a hand's width from Cassus's own and for an age, he stared into Cassus's eyes, as if seeking something within. Finally, he removed the knife from Cassus's throat and pushed himself away.

'Well?' asked Vespasian.

'He'll do,' said the stranger, 'those eyes have seen many men die.'

'Good,' said Vespasian, 'when do you want him?'

'Have him outside the fort gates at dawn,' said the man and without another word, retrieved his apple from the table before leaving the room.

One of the slaves ran around picking up the broken furniture and Vespasian held out his hand to help Cassus up from the floor.

'Who was that man?' asked Cassus.

'That, Cassus, was Tribune Ocelus, an officer in the Exploratores.'

'Exploratores?' asked Cassus.

'Yes, are you aware of them?'

'I came across one in the Khymru,' said Cassus.

'And what did he have to say for himself?'

'Not much, really. He told us where to find Caratacus but that was about it.'

'I'm not surprised, they keep their own counsel. A wise trait in their game, I feel.'

'So there are more here?'

'Yes there are more. They are currently deployed throughout Britannia and have been since long before the invasion even set sail from Gaul.'

'I thought the scouts paved the way,' said Cassus.

'Indeed they did,' said Vespasian. 'The scouts did an excellent job clearing the signal fires from the cliffs and letting us know the strengths and weaknesses of those armies directly opposing us as our ships landed. But the Exploratores were on a different kind of mission. Claudius knew that the invasion of Britannia was unavoidable. If he wanted to keep the mantle of Emperor, the people demanded a big victory. Gaul was already ours; Germania was too dangerous and the Eastern countries were old news. What he needed was something new to raise him to the ranks of his predecessors, somewhere new and previously unconquered. Bearing in mind that the great Caesar himself had been repelled from these shores on two occasions, Britannia was the perfect target. A full year before the invasion, a unit of Exploratores were sent into Britannia to mingle with their people. They came as traders and were welcomed accordingly.'

'Didn't the language pose a barrier?' asked Cassus.

'All had received basic instruction back in Gaul,' said Vespasian, 'but don't forget, this was a peaceful time and there were many such Roman traders on the roads of Britannia. During this time they were tasked with learning the language and integrating into the tribes, nothing more.'

'To what end?' asked Cassus.

'Despite his apparent buffoonery, Claudius is a clever man,' said Vespasian, pouring himself a mug of watered wine. 'He knew that the invasion was but the first step of many. Our spies had already told him that there were many tribes in these lands and many battles lay before Rome, before she could claim these islands as hers. So he took a longer view and infiltrated the enemy. Tell me, what do you know about the Exploratores?'

'Not much,' said Cassus, 'just that they are an elite fighting unit that are hand-picked from the best the Legions have to offer.'

'Hmm,' said Vespasian. 'Not quite right but near enough. Let me explain. As you know the scouts often hand pick their men from the best Legionaries throughout Rome's armies. These men often have dubious backgrounds and would probably see out their lives in the salt mines had they not possessed some skill deemed desirable by the officers of the scouts. Some are fantastic riders or have particular weapons skills whilst others have been selected due to their ability to live off the land, or simply their willingness to kill at a moment's notice. The Exploratores take these skills one step further. You cannot ask to be transferred to the Exploratores as they do not officially exist. They are hand-picked individuals who spend their lives in a solitary existence, living behind enemy lines and reporting back on the enemy's strengths or weaknesses. Sometimes that means infiltrating their armies, fighting amongst them and killing fellow Romans to prove their allegiance. Others live in the wild, eating off the land and living wherever they can find shelter from the weather.'

'For how long?' asked Cassus.

'However long it takes,' said Vespasian. 'Sometimes it could be a few months, other missions could take years. In Germania, I am aware of one who still reports back to the Senate after ten years in the enemy's camps.'

'Ten years?' gasped Cassus.

'He has become a member of this particularly troublesome tribe's elder council and his word is trusted. He has even married one of their women and has children.'

'But why so long?' asked Cassus. 'Surely he knows all there is about them.'

'Perhaps so, but his position now influences the decisions of that tribe and many of our countrymen have been able to be deployed to more troublesome lands as their threat has diminished.'

'And this is something you would have me do?'

'Well, perhaps not to that extent but there is a task that would benefit from your particular skills and experiences.'

'And this is?'

'Let's not get ahead of ourselves, Cassus,' said Vespasian. 'First of all we need to see if you are as good as you make out. The little test given by Tribune Ocelus a few minutes ago was no more than an introduction. Luckily, he liked what he saw and if you are willing, he will take you under his wing and bring you up to the standards required. Now more than that, I am unable to share. So if you are willing to take this step into the unknown, then the opportunity is there.'

'Do I have an option?' asked Cassus.

'Of course you do. The Exploratores want nobody in their ranks who wouldn't die to be there. They are very secretive and look down on every other unit in the army. Often, they will be attached to home units just to keep their sword arm strong but usually they move between missions decided by none less than a Legate. When you are not deployed, you cannot share what you do with any outside of your unit. No one except your comrades will know what you do, and then only those you work closest with. Be successful and the rewards are great.'

'And if I am unsuccessful?'

'There is no such thing as unsuccessful Exploratore,' said Vespasian, 'you are either successful or dead. Take some time and report back to me with your thoughts.'

'I need no time,' said Cassus. 'I accept your offer.'

'Are you sure?' asked Vespasian. 'You are probably signing your own death warrant.'

'I understand what the risks are,' said Cassus, 'and I accept them wholeheartedly.'

Vespasian nodded quietly.

'So be it,' said Vespasian. 'I will make the arrangements. Be outside the camp gates at first light. Someone will contact you directly. Now, if you don't mind, I have a cohort to inspect.'

Cassus saluted and left the officer's quarters to return to the barracks. This opportunity was exactly the sort of thing he relished and the chance to be part of an elite group of men who shared his values, put meaning back into his existence. As he went, Vespasian followed him out and stood in the shade of the portico. A smaller man joined him from the side of the building.

'Well, Ocelus,' he said, 'do you think he'll make the grade?'

'He has fire in his stomach,' said Ocelus. 'I don't think he realises what he is getting into but he has the raw materials. Give me a month and I will bring you either a corpse or an Exploratore.'

'You do that, Ocelus,' said Vespasian. 'I have a very important mission in mind for that young man.'

Ocelus nodded and walked away without saluting. For a second Vespasian was annoyed at the seemingly blatant disregard for his authority, but he stopped himself reacting and sighed inwardly. Ocelus never showed allegiance to anybody. It was annoying, but that's the way it was. After all, he was an Exploratore.

Chapter 5

The Lands of the Ordovices
46 AD

The village of Lanbard was situated on the side of a winding river and was the central village in the area where many local clans came to trade. As usual the gates were wide open, though flanked by a brace of guards primed to close them should any threat be detected.

The predominant tribe of the surrounding area were the Ordovices, and the main thrust of the tribe's success was farming. The rich soil and regular rainfall ensured that crops grew in abundance and the surplus was traded with the surrounding tribes. Wheat fields were rotated religiously and after a few years production, they were left to lie fallow. In turn, herds of cattle were allowed to roam free on the natural grass, fertilising the soil with their droppings before the fields were once more planted and the cattle moved elsewhere.

The local hills had long been cleared of trees by their ancestors and shepherds watched over huge flocks of sheep, nurtured for their meat and wool. Though renowned for their farming capabilities, the Ordovices also had their own warrior caste which looked after the farmers, herdsmen and shepherds. Throughout the land the hills were dotted with smaller palisades, used in emergencies to corral the herds, should any unfriendly interlopers pass by. Though the warriors were indeed adequate to see off smaller groups of brigands, they were no match for the warrior clans of Deceangli or Silures that often rode unchallenged through their territory.

Gwydion walked up to the gates of the palisade surrounding the village. One of the guards stood up from the log he was sitting on and stepped onto the path to block his way, peering over the young man's shoulder to check he was alone. Gwydion sighed quietly to himself as he approached the boy, as he was obviously no more than sixteen years old. It was always a nervous time when approaching a village, especially a fortified one, but when the access points were guarded by youngsters it was always a lot more stressful. These were the ones who were out to make names for themselves and though they did not trouble Gwydion, it was not in his interest to engage in argument.

'You seem lost, stranger,' said the guard.

'I am fine,' said Gwydion, coming to a halt.

The boy's hand played about his sword hilt; an action not lost on Gwydion.

'You dress in the way of the Deceangli,' said the boy, walking around him, playing up to his comrades who were watching the unfolding scene in amusement.

'You are blessed with good eyesight,' said Gwydion, 'as I am indeed proud to call that tribe my people.'

'Then I was correct,' said the boy, 'and you are indeed lost. This is the land of Ordovices and we don't like Deceangli around here.'

Ordinarily Gwydion would enjoy the banter, but with the death of Gwenno, he had no inclination to join in the boy's games. He turned away and faced the three remaining men still sat on the log. Whilst two were enjoying the baiting, the third, the mature one of the group, was more composed and watched quietly. Gwydion addressed himself to him.

'Friend,' he said, 'I recognise the importance of your role here, indeed all your roles, and on another day would gladly clash wits with you, but not on this day.'

'Hey,' interrupted the young boy from behind Gwydion, 'don't turn your back on me, I haven't finished with you.'

Gwydion continued addressing his words to the older man.

'I am Deceangli in the lands of the Ordovices,' continued Gwydion, 'and I am at the mercy of your hospitality. I see you are a man of experience, so would ask you as an equal, please call off your pup before both he and I both suffer the consequences.'

The laughter stopped immediately and the younger men stood up, their hands firmly on the hilts of their sword. Behind him, Gwydion heard the boy's sword being drawn.

'Hold,' ordered the older man and stood slowly before approaching and standing directly before Gwydion.

'Strong words, stranger,' he said, 'and perhaps uttered without thought of consequence.'

'There was thought in my words,' said Gwydion, 'and I stand by them.'

'And what consequences do you envisage?' asked the older man.

'Both he and I will die,' said Gwydion, 'he by my sword and I by the hands of you and your fellows.'

'You insult me.' The boy's voice came from behind and Gwydion heard the step as the boy walked forward with sword drawn.

'Stand firm, Drew,' shouted the older man, 'and hold your tongue.'

Throughout, neither man's eyes left the other. Eventually the older warrior spoke again.

'I think your appraisal is accurate,' he said, 'and though my blade has tasted Deceangli blood before, it craves none today. However, I am intrigued. Why would a man whose eyes hold the memories of so much conflict risk death for the words of a boy who knows no better?'

'It is a fair question,' said Gwydion, 'and deserves the truth. At this moment in time life and death holds the same attraction to me. Life so I can find the man who killed my wife and death so I can hold her once more in my arms. Either is welcome.'

'How did this man kill your wife?'

'With a throwing axe meant for me,' said Gwydion. 'She stepped into its path to save my life.'

'And do you know why?'

'No, but one day he will tell me, just before I rip out his heart.'

The warrior nodded his head in agreement.

'I will not deny you that day, stranger,' he said eventually, 'and besides, in my experience, a man who holds no distinction between life and death is the most dangerous man alive. What is your name?'

'My name is Gwydion of the Blaidd,' he answered, 'a clan of the Deceangli.'

'And I am Gerald of Lanbard, son of Bryn,' said the warrior. 'I have heard of the Blaidd; they were once a respected clan who traded hard but fair. Occasionally we had need to clash swords but honour was always kept. Recently they are better known as people of false promises and are seen as a stain on the good name of the Deceangli.'

Gwydion didn't answer.

'Do my words offend you, Gwydion?' asked Gerald.

'Without knowing the facts behind such claims I cannot answer either way,' said Gwydion.

'Then let me enlighten you,' said Gerald. 'Just before last winter, the Blaidd sent a trading party south to barter for cattle. Though the request to meet halfway was strange, we trusted their word and met as requested. The cattle were handed over and we received a sack of gold jewellery in tally. However, on our return journey, our men were ambushed by a party of Blaidd far superior in number. They killed all our men and stole back the tally.'

'If all were killed, how do you know they were Blaidd?' asked Gwydion.

'One boy survived,' said Gerald. 'Not for long, but long enough to tell about the Wolf Torcs they wore about their necks.'

'If what you say is true,' said Gwydion, 'then I am shamed, but I have not been part of my clan since the death of Erwyn. I can only assume that the new leader, Robbus, has taken them down a path that is new to my people.'

'I suspect you are right,' said Gerald, 'but there was more than one sword doing the killing.'

'Then I have no explanation,' said Gwydion. 'It is the first I have heard of this news.'

'It matters not,' said Gerald eventually, 'if every man was killed for the actions of his comrades the land would be full of beasts only. We do not hold you responsible and despite the bitter memories, we are a peaceful clan and welcome your trade. You may pass.'

'No,' shouted the boy, 'I have been insulted and demand redress.'

'Be quiet,' said the man, 'you may live longer.'

'The pup has a loud bark,' said Gwydion.

'But a weak bite,' said Gerald, 'take no heed.' He held out his hand and grabbed Gwydion's forearm. 'I hope you find the man who killed your wife, Gwydion,' he said, 'no man should carry such a burden.'

'I will,' replied Gwydion, 'but now I must go.'

Gwydion turned to enter the village but had not gone a few steps before the boy's voice called out one more time.

'Wait,' he shouted, and Gwydion turned to face the angry young warrior.

'I have not finished,' said the boy. 'You have insulted me and I demand redress.'

'Shut up, Drew,' said Gerald, 'let the man pass.'

'I will not,' shouted Drew. 'This Deceangli pig has dishonoured my name and I am owed payback.'

'How have I dishonoured you?' asked Gwydion calmly.

'You called me a pup,' said Drew, 'and that offends me. Draw your sword, Deceangli.'

'Don't do this, Drew,' said Gerald quietly, 'he will kill you.'

'It is my right,' shouted Drew, 'now stand clear – this is a matter of honour.'

Gerald sighed and stepped back. Age, experience or even rank always came second to matters of honour and though he knew there could only be one victor, Drew was correct. Where honour was concerned, it was his right as a warrior to demand conflict.

'I do not want to fight you,' said Gwydion, 'but you should know, if you pursue this course, then I will offer no quarter.'

'It is you who will beg for quarter,' snarled Drew and launched forward into the attack. Gwydion drew his sword and swatted the blade of his opponent to one side. Drew rained blow after blow at Gwydion's head, forcing the Deceangli backwards across the path. Those people passing nearby stopped in their tracks to watch the conflict with interest, most knowing that the heavy, double-handed sword of the local boy would smash through the smaller Romanesque blade favoured by the stranger.

In less experienced hands this would indeed have been the case, but Gwydion had spent most of his youth practising with the smaller sword and had perfected a technique unique to him. If he tried to block any of the blows directly with his blade, he knew it would shatter within minutes, so instead he used the smaller blade to absorb and deflect the blows to either side. Any side strokes aimed at his torso were similarly deflected downwards toward the ground with surprising ease and little effort. Within minutes, the attacker was tiring while Gwydion was still relatively fresh. The strength of the blows weakened and the frequency slowed as the young boy struggled to keep up the intensity and finally his sword slumped as he gasped for breath.

'Why do you not fight me?' he gasped. 'Are you a coward?'

'A fight is not defined by the more aggressive,' said Gwydion, 'but by the victor. One last chance boy, stop now while we both have honour, or my blade will taste blood.'

'Brave words,' said the boy, 'yet I have seen nothing to worry me.' With that he raised his sword and rushed forward to renew the attack. Gwydion deflected the blow one last time and stepped forward to inside the reach of his opponent, grabbing the back of the boy's neck with his left hand.

'I warned you, boy,' he snarled into his ear, and thrust his stabbing sword through the flesh of the teenager.

Drew's body stiffened in shock and he dropped his own sword to the ground. Gwydion withdrew his blade and pushed the boy away from him. Drew looked down at the blood starting to run from the wound before falling to his knees.

Gwydion span around to defend himself from any attack that may come from the others, but there was no need – all three stood firm in a silence broken only by the gasps of pain from the wounded boy.

'Do we have a problem?' asked Gwydion.

'There is no problem,' said Gerald, 'the fight was fair.'

'And I am free to continue?'

'You are.'

Gwydion nodded toward the boy still kneeling in the dust.

'If you stem the blood, he may live yet. I placed my blade outside of the organs.'

'I noticed the thrust was pulled,' said Gerald, 'and you have my gratitude.'

'Why gratitude?' asked Gwydion. 'As a warrior he knows death is always a bedfellow.'

'Because he is my son,' said Gerald. 'Now be gone before I change my mind.'

After a moment's pause, Gwydion sheathed his sword and nodded acknowledgement.

'Then I hope he lives, Gerald, for his father's sake.' Without another word he turned and walked into the village to continue his business.

–

An hour later Gwydion sat at a wooden table in the village square, drinking ale from a wooden goblet he had purchased from the nearby vendor. He sat patiently, waiting for the contact he knew would come. Finally a man with familiar features limped toward him, relying heavily on a walking stick and Gwydion signalled to the nearby vendor to bring more ale.

Marius was a Catuvellaunian warrior who had served with Caratacus and been severely wounded at the famous battle of the Silures two years previously. Caratacus's army had been at the point of annihilation at the hands of Mateus and his cohort but had been delivered by the timely intervention of a war band of the Silures. When Caratacus and the remaining survivors of the Catuvellauni travelled south to join with the Silures, those wounded who couldn't travel were dropped off at the village where the elders were well paid to ensure they were cared for until they were well again. Many did indeed follow on but some, like Marius, stayed and sought work in the busy trading village.

'Gwydion, good to see you again,' said Marius, extending his hand. They grabbed each other's forearms in greeting before Marius looked around the square. There was an awkward silence before Marius spoke again.

'I heard about what happened to your wife,' he said.

'How? It only happened yesterday.'

'News travels fast, Gwydion, though I don't know the details. What happened?'

'I will tell you over ale,' said Gwydion. 'Take a seat.' The two men sat back down and sipped on the tankards as Gwydion retold the story of how Gwenno lost her life. Finally he sat back, the tale told. 'And that is why I am here,' he said eventually, 'I seek the man who took her life and have reason to believe he is in this village.'

'But even if he is,' said Marius, 'what makes you think they will let you kill him, especially if he is one of their own?'

'I will challenge him to trial of arms,' said Gwydion, 'they will grant me that right.'

'Not necessarily,' said Marius, 'especially after that business with the cattle last year.'

'I heard about that,' said Gwydion, 'and it leaves a bitter taste in the mouth, but a challenge must be recognised across all peoples. It is our way.'

'Unless he was sent by the elders,' said Marius. 'It is common knowledge that you and Gwenno live in the hills. Perhaps when our cattle were stolen you were seen as the easy option for retribution. After all, the people were screaming for Deceangli blood and you fitted the bill nicely.'

Gwydion stared at Marius, not sure how to take this news.

'Are you telling me that the Ordovices are behind the death of my wife?' he asked eventually.

'Look, Gwydion,' said Marius, 'I am not party to the meetings of this tribe but do hear things said in passing. Whether the elders were involved or not, I can't say, but what I do know is that there were no tears shed when the news reached the village.'

'I don't understand,' said Gwydion. 'We traded here every month, made friends and became involved in the village. I thought we had been accepted.'

'But your blood is Deceangli,' said Marius, 'as was the blood of those who killed their kin.'

'Then I will speak to the elders,' said Gwydion.

'There is no point,' said Marius, 'they would not turn him over. All you will do is alert them that you seek retribution. You may even be executed yourself. No, you must leave this place and move on.'

Gwydion considered Marius's words carefully.

'I can't, Marius,' he said, 'my life would be spent in shame for not addressing the imbalance. This man killed my wife and I will take his or die trying.' He stood up to leave. 'Where will I find the council?'

'No, wait,' said Marius, 'if I can't turn you from this path, at least let me arm you.'

'I have my own weapons,' said Gwydion.

'Not with steel, but with knowledge,' said Marius. 'I work in the stables of the council and have taken up with a lady who serves their tables. Let me speak to her first and see if I can glean any knowledge. At least you won't be entering the lion's den as a blind man, though I fear the outcome will be the same.'

'This woman would share such things with you?' asked Gwydion.

'She will,' said Marius. 'We have a child together and share everything.'

'Ha, you old devil,' said Gwydion, 'you wasted no time planting your roots.'

'This injury was the best thing that ever happened to me,' said Marius. 'It has made me think twice about the way of the warrior. Oh, I miss the camaraderie and even the rush of blood during battle, but my eyes have cleared enough to see there are other things in life.'

'I know what you mean,' said Gwydion. 'For the last two years I too have realised that there are other things outside of war, but since…' He drew a deep breath, leaving the sentence unfinished.

'I understand,' said Marius. 'Look, you stay here and I will be back in an hour. If I don't find anything out, at least you have only wasted time.'

'Thank you,' said Gwydion, and sat back down as Marius limped away.

-

For over an hour he waited, adding a platter of chicken and a chunk of bread to his bill with the tavern. Finally he saw Marius limping out of the gloom and stood to meet him.

'Marius,' he said, 'you have news?'

'I do,' said Marius, 'though not good I'm afraid. The man you are looking for is known as Badger, named for the white streak in his hair. He is a brigand without a clan and known for deeds of murder. On this occasion, it would appear he was indeed in the pay of the council, though I doubt they would admit to it.'

'I don't believe it,' said Gwydion. 'Why would they do this to me? I have done nothing to raise their ire.'

'You were just an easy target, Gwydion,' said Marius. 'The people demanded action and you were available.'

'It matters not,' said Gwydion eventually, 'I still have the right to a trial of arms.'

'Perhaps so,' said Marius, 'but he is not here.'

'Where is he?'

'When his blade found Gwenno's flesh, he knew you would seek him out so left for someplace where he thought he would be safe.'

'Where has he gone?'

'North, to the lands of the Deceangli.'

'Why does he think he would be safe there?'

'Are you not a wanted man within your own people?'

'That may be so,' said Gwydion, 'but if he thought he would be safe there, then he thought wrongly. Wanted or not, my blade will spill his blood or I will die in the process. When did he leave?'

'Immediately,' said Marius, 'he probably has a day's start on you.'

'Then I have wasted enough time,' said Gwydion, 'I should leave now.'

'I thought you would say that,' said Marius, 'so have prepared this.' He handed over a bag of food. 'Right, you had better be gone – darkness falls, and you have a long way to go.'

'Enjoy what peace you can, Marius,' said Gwydion, mounting his horse. 'I doubt our paths will cross again.'

'Good luck, Gwydion.'

Gwydion turned his horse and trotted back toward the main gates of the village. Within minutes he approached the gates and was dismayed to find them closed for the night. A guard looked down from the wooden platform, while another approached from the shadows.

'The gates are closed, rider,' he said, 'come back in the morning.'

'I need to leave tonight,' said Gwydion, 'I will take my chances.'

'You're not listening, stranger,' said the guard, 'I open the gates for no man except my peers.'

'Then open them for me,' called a voice from the shadows. Gwydion turned in his saddle and saw the older warrior whose son he had injured earlier that afternoon.

'Gerald,' said Gwydion, 'how is your son?'

'He will live,' said Gerald, 'though it is more than I can say for you should you stay here this night.'

'I am in danger?'

'My son's comrades are still aggrieved that someone who has wounded one of their own walks freely in their own village. They are drinking heavily and despite my counsel, I fear they will seek retribution before the night is out.'

'And what about you, Gerald? Do you seek revenge?'

'I see the honour in what happened, the young bloods only see the wound. Be gone quickly, Gwydion. With this deed we are even and should we meet again as foes, there will be no debt on either side to stay our blades.' He nodded to the guards to unbar the gates.

Gwydion walked his horse forward and stopped on the other side of the wall.

'One more question, Gerald,' he said, 'what news of the Romans?'

'They have become bogged down by Catuvellauni women and wine around Camulodunum,' sneered Gerald. 'Fear not, Gwydion, they won't venture this far west for they know Khymric steel is sharper and wielded more expertly than that of the Catuvellauni, a lesson learned not two days ride from here.'

'I am aware of the battle you refer to, Gerald, for I witnessed it myself.'

'You were there when the Roman cohort fell at the points of our blades?' asked Gerald.

'I was, though my recollection is that it was Silurian steel that slew the enemy, not Ordovician.'

'The source of the weapons is irrelevant in this instance,' said Gerald, 'for it is common Khymric pride that bore them. Silures or Ordovices, the result would have been the same.'

'Perhaps so,' said Gwydion, 'but it is Silures steel I seek now.'

'You are going south?'

'I am,' said Gwydion.

'Then you are a fool,' said Gerald. 'The Silures welcome very few strangers into their territory.'

'I will take my chances,' said Gwydion, 'for there is one amongst them who owes me a favour.'

'Who is this man?' asked Gerald.

'His name is Prydain,' said Gwydion, 'and I call him friend.' With that, he turned his horse and headed into the darkness toward the land of the Silures.

Chapter 6

The Lands of the Ordovices
46 AD

Gwydion kept riding south, occasionally coming across farmsteads where the advice was always the same. *Travel no further, or you will die.* Despite this he continued on his journey, having little other option. Soon he left signs of civilisation behind and entered the forests of the south, still thick and un-felled, unlike the farmlands to the north. Every moment he imagined hidden eyes watching each step he made, but still he advanced. Two nights were spent this way, until finally he woke on the third day and knew instantly he was in trouble.

His horse was still tethered to the nearby tree but its ears were pricked up and its nostrils wide as it detected danger. Gwydion stood slowly, and deliberately held his sword at arm's length, dangling uselessly from his fingers.

'I am Gwydion of the Deceangli,' he said loudly, 'son of Hammer and I come in peace.'

When there was no answer, he took a risk and threw the sword away from him. A movement in the bushes caught his eye and he turned to face the hidden warrior.

'I offer no threat,' he said, 'and seek only to talk with the one called Prydain.' Again there was no response, so he reached inside his tunic to withdraw the Wolf's head Torc, the insignia of the Deceangli tribe.

'I carry the true sign of Erwyn, chieftain of the Blaidd,' he said, holding up the Torc, 'and claim protection as is the way of all tribes of the Khymru.'

To his front, more bushes moved and slowly a warrior stepped out to face him, aiming a bow directly at his chest. Gwydion held his breath. Should the warrior release his arrow, Gwydion would be dead within seconds.

The warrior remained silent and they stared at each other across the clearing. Gwydion was about to speak again when he realised he had been tricked, as a spear point pressed against the back of his neck.

'Get down on your knees, stranger,' said a voice, and Gwydion did as he was told immediately.

'Why do you trespass in our lands?' asked the voice.

'I only seek to talk to your leaders,' said Gwydion, 'I offer no threat.'

'We agree there is no threat,' the voice sneered, 'just a solitary man who trespasses without invite.'

'I agree I have no invite,' said Gwydion, 'but I have something greater, a debt that needs repayment.'

'The Silures owe debt to nobody,' said the voice, 'tell me why I shouldn't kill you right now.'

'For I once saved the life of one of your leaders and would seek his aid in return.'

'Name this man.'

'He is known as Prydain and he is the son of a chieftain.'

'I know of this man,' said the voice, 'and I hear he is a man of weak character and poor skills.'

'Then it is not the man I seek,' said Gwydion. 'The man I know is strong of arm and rich with honour.'

'Stand up,' said the voice. 'If you are who you say you are; you would know what his first meal was when he was released from confinement in the lands of the Catuvellauni.'

Gwydion's eyes narrowed in confusion and though he knew the answer, it was a strange question to be asked.

'I gave him a wood pigeon,' said Gwydion.

'You did,' said the voice, 'and it was well received.'

Understanding dawned and Gwydion spun around to face his questioner in disbelief.

'Prydain,' he shouted, recognising the grinning man before him and walked forward to grasp his friend's forearm in recognition. 'You jest with me.'

'I couldn't resist,' laughed Prydain, 'and I offer apologies. Gwydion, you are well met yet you took a great risk coming here. Not many get as far without feeling Silures steel.'

'Then I am lucky I ran into you,' said Gwydion.

'There was no luck,' said Prydain. 'Our scouts have followed you for days and sent word to me about your arrival.'

'How did they know it was me?' said Gwydion.

'Our spies are everywhere,' said Prydain, 'and I knew of your quest the same day you left Lanbard. It was simply a case of finding you.'

'Well you found me,' said Gwydion, 'and I am grateful for it.' He stepped back and looked Prydain up and down. The ex-legionary had changed a lot in the two years since last they met. His black hair now fell below his shoulders and he wore plaid leggings as well as the wolf skin cloak that typified his people. A Celtic tattoo sat on his right temple and a Silures Torc lay about his neck. A short sword hung from his belt and he held a wooden spear with a barbed metal blade in his hand.

'You look well,' said Gwydion, 'like a true native of the Khymru.'

'It feels right,' said Prydain before adding, 'I am sorry to hear about Gwenno. I share your pain.'

'It is indeed a terrible thing,' said Gwydion, 'and part of me died with her that day. Yet I swear to make that man pay for her life. That is why I am here, to seek your help.'

'I will do what I can,' said Prydain, 'but first let me offer you our hospitality. There is a place nearby where you can rest and get fodder for your horse. Come, we will ride together.'

As they rode away, they were joined by Prydain's comrades, as warrior after warrior emerged from the shadows to form a column of over thirty men.

'Are these your men?' asked Gwydion.

'Some of them,' said Prydain, 'though the main force isn't mobilised unless there is a threat. These belong to the border patrol that has been following you these past few days.'

'So,' said Gwydion, 'tell me about your life these past two years.'

'Not much to tell,' said Prydain. 'These people have a very different way of life to any that I expected. In this part of their lands they allow the forests to run riot as a barrier to any large force, but further south, the hills are free from trees and we farm herds of sheep and cattle. Villages are many, but all are overlooked by hill forts populated by the young warriors of the tribe. At times of danger, the villages seek protection within the stockades.'

'Similar to the Deceangli,' said Gwydion.

'There are similarities,' said Prydain, 'though our main strength lies in the forests and the hills.'

'And what of you, Prydain?' asked Gwydion. 'Have you taken your place as chieftain?'

'I am not the chieftain of these people, nor ever will be,' said Prydain. 'The identity of my father precludes that honour. To be honest I'm not sure they know what to make of me. They placed me in a village to learn the language and then sent me to the border patrols, learning their ways in conflict.'

'But your grandfather is the chieftain,' said Gwydion.

'And that is acknowledged,' said Prydain, 'but holds little sway until I prove myself alongside my fellow warriors.'

For the next hour they rode together, catching up on each other's lives over the preceding two years. Finally the smell of wood smoke filtered through the trees and they broke into a clearing containing a long wooden cabin. A shackled man stood near a fire, roasting a forest pig on a spit.

'This is it,' said Prydain, reining his horse to a halt.

More slaves appeared from the building and took their horses to the nearby stable while Gwydion followed Prydain inside. Inside consisted of one long room containing a large table, a giant hearth and rows of sleeping alcoves along both walls, these formed from bundles of dried straw and bracken. Several men were fast asleep in the bays, while one sat at the table sharpening his blade with a whetstone.

'A warrior hut?' suggested Gwydion.

'Something similar,' said Prydain. 'There are many of these situated across our lands and are for the use of the men that constantly patrol our borders. They are open to any of our people as a place to rest during those patrols, as they can often last months. Slaves maintain them, overseen by two keepers, ensuring they are well stocked with food, water and bedding.'

'An interesting concept,' said Gwydion, 'and the straw bales must prove a welcome comfort for those tired of weeks on horseback.'

'They are,' said Prydain, 'yet that is their secondary purpose. The straw is nothing more than fuel for the flames that would engulf this place within moments should any enemy approach.'

'You would burn it?'

'In a heartbeat. Our strength lies in forests, not in buildings and we would deny our enemy any comfort it offers.' Their conversation was interrupted by one of the slaves, entering the hut with head bowed.

'Lord, the beast is done,' he said.

'Good, then bring it in,' said Prydain.

Ten minutes later the hut filled with warriors coming in from the rain, but despite the plates of steaming meat and pile of rough bread from the stone oven, all stood back while the slaves filled a leather bag with the choicest cuts.

'For the guards,' said Prydain, answering the unspoken question on Gwydion's face.

Finally, when the slaves had run off to take the food to those still on duty, the remaining warriors took it in turns to slice slabs of meat from the carcass, before breaking chunks of bread and sitting in any space they could find against the wooden wall.

'So,' said Prydain between bites, 'what is it you want from me, Gwydion?'

'To be honest, I'm not sure,' said Gwydion. 'When I set out from Lanbard I had it all worked out. I was going to come down here and ask you to ride north with me. A task similar to the one we carried out when we took Gwenno from the druids, though this time our mission would be one of death, not life.'

'You seek the one who killed Gwenno?'

'I do,' said Gwydion, 'and thought we could ride together. However, now I am here I see I have made a mistake and underestimated your role here. I had no right, Prydain, I see that now. It is good to see you again but our lives have taken different paths. So allow my horse to regain its strength and I will ride north alone.'

'Do you know where this man is?'

'All I know is he seeks protection in the lands of the Deceangli.'

'Why would he go there?'

'Because he knows they would kill me on sight should I pursue him. The gods play with my life, Prydain. I seek to kill a man who killed my woman, yet I am denied by my own people.'

Prydain was quiet for a few moments before answering.

'Not necessarily, Gwydion,' he said, 'this meeting could be advantageous for all. There are things afoot that may aide your quest.'

'What things?'

'As you know, after his defeat at the hands of the Romans, Caratacus sought refuge with my people. During this time he has garnered favour with the elders and sought joint effort against those who drove him out. His request fell on willing ears and ever since he has been building his forces in the south. Survivors from Medway and Tamesas sought him out, as well as warriors from other tribes who share his hatred. Within two harvests he has built a formidable army with fire in their bellies, all willing to drive the Romans back to the sea or die trying.'

'How does this help me?' asked Gwydion.

'You could join with them,' said Prydain. 'He knows you and would surely give you command of a unit, for your hatred of the Romans is as strong as any warrior who stands beneath his banner.'

'Make no mistake, Prydain,' said Gwydion, 'I too would love to see the rivers of Britannia run red with the blood of retreating Romans, but my desire to revenge Gwenno's death burns stronger. To join Caratacus would cause distraction.'

'Perhaps not,' said Prydain, 'there is talk of taking his army north into the lands of the Deceangli to engage their support. Caratacus learned a lot from his defeat and seeks an alliance of all tribes. If you are with him, you can ride with head held high. Nobody would dare strike against you while you are at the side of the king and while you are there, you could seek this man and pour your revenge upon him.'

Gwydion stared at Prydain, deep in thought.

'There is merit in your words,' he said eventually. 'Though my heart burns enough to fight many men, I am outcast from my own people and sought by the druids but through my pain even I can see I would not get within a day's ride of the Blaidd.'

'Then take this opportunity,' said Prydain. 'Join with Caratacus and carve out your future. I am not saying forget Gwenno, for that would not befit you or your gods, but pause for thought. Instead of stealing that man's life like a thief in the night, build the pathway to your revenge with sword in hand and honour in your manner.'

'And if opportunity does not present itself?' asked Gwydion.

'Then your quest becomes mine also and we will ride shoulder to shoulder into Hades itself. This I swear by my own gods.'

Gwydion smiled at his friend's intensity.

'And I believe you will, Prydain,' he said. 'I accept this challenge and though it hurts to bend the knee to a Catuvellaunian king, I see it is for the greater good. Where can I find him?'

'That part is easy,' said Prydain, 'I travel there myself. Tomorrow we will ride south, into the heart of my people's homeland.'

–

Over the next few days, Prydain and Gwydion rode south, leaving the rest of the Silures warriors behind to continue the defence of their border with the Ordovices. The forests thinned out and meadows appeared, vast tracts of cleared ground containing herds of livestock under the watchful eyes of slave herdsmen and the obligatory mounted Silures warrior. Hills loomed before them and flocks of sheep covered them like a snowstorm. Occasionally Gwydion spied lone warriors shadowing their movements from afar, but Prydain reassured him it was the way of his people and nothing to worry about.

'Tell me,' said Gwydion, 'why do the other tribes of this island hold the Silures in such awe?'

'I am still learning,' said Prydain, 'but I don't think we are that much different to anyone else. The clan leaders lead the people fairly and allow them to live their own lives in the hills and the forests. Seldom do the people take arms unless we are threatened by outsiders; when they do there is no quarter considered. Every man is called to arms and while they do field big armies if necessary, their strength lies in the tactics of the huntsman.'

'What do you mean?'

'Many warriors take to the hills in small groups or even alone. Their task is simple and does not need coordination; it is to kill the enemy and then disappear like the mist to hit them again in a different location. Confrontation is avoided wherever possible and arrows are preferred over swords.'

'Some would say it is a dishonourable way to wage war,' said Gwydion.

'Honour is in living to protect your people, not rotting on a battlefield floor,' said Prydain. 'Unlike other tribes, the Silures don't collect the heads of their enemies as trophies to hang in our huts. Our homes are places of family and respect, not blood and warfare.'

'It sounds like a peaceful existence,' said Gwydion.

'It is,' said Prydain, 'though it is hard earned. Our borders are permanently patrolled by our warriors and strangers are rarely allowed in. Kill one of ours, and we will kill a hundred of yours. Steal from our herds, and we will wipe out your village, every man killed without quarter and every woman sold into slavery, irrespective of age.'

'But surely you must trade with other tribes,' said Gwydion.

'We do,' said Prydain, 'though always on our terms and on neutral ground.'

'What about the Romans?' asked Gwydion.

'They are a concern,' said Prydain, 'and despite their isolation, even the Silures see the threat. Allow the

Romans to spread and it will only be a matter of time before their cloaks blow in the Khymric breeze. That is why my people have embraced Caratacus. In him they see a kindred spirit, a man who will fight to the death to protect Britannic lands. The fact that he is also a respected king adds to his value and they offer a sympathetic ear to his plans.'

'And what plans are these?'

'He wants to combine all the Khymric tribes under one banner and drive the Romans back to the coast.'

'Will the Silures join him?'

'That remains to be seen,' said Prydain and reined in his horse. 'There it is; the seat of the Silures chieftains, Llanmelin.'

Gwydion followed Prydain's gaze. Before him a series of rolling hills had been cleared of all vegetation and in the distance, on the highest of them all, he could see a huge hill fort, dominating everything before it.

For a few moments, Gwydion stared in awe. Even though it was still an hour's ride away, its size was evident and though there were no roundhouses in the shadow of the fort, Gwydion could see a tented village less than an hour's ride to one side.

'Is that the camp of Caratacus?' he asked.

'It is,' said Prydain, 'and his numbers grow by the day.'

'Why are there no roundhouses?' asked Gwydion.

'Like I said, we are different to other tribes. The land around Llanmelin is kept clear of dwellings to not only provide clear line of sight for any defenders, but also to deny any attacker shelter or ammunition.'

'Another strange concept,' said Gwydion.

As they approached, he eyed the fort with interest. The hill rose steeply before him and he could see several deep ditches running around the entire circumference, each being defended on the far bank with palisades of sharpened stakes and alert guards. Each ditch was crossed via a simple easily removed bridge and any visitor had to climb a formed path following the contours of the slope, before reaching the next bridge around the opposite side of the hill.

Gwydion could see that any attackers hoping to breach these defences would either have to climb the almost vertical slopes, or use the paths to reach the access points, while running the gauntlet of any defenders manning the palisades above. It was simple but very effective.

Throughout their ascent they were constantly challenged by guards, but eventually stood before the main entrance and waited while a messenger was sent in to seek permission for them to enter.

Again Gwydion was impressed. High above, the almost vertical final rise of the hill was enhanced with a stone wall the height of two men and on top of that, one final timber palisade formed the last line of defence. Out of all the hill forts Gwydion had seen, this was surely the most impregnable and the magnificent entrance only added to that impression. A narrow roadway had been carved through the rock just wide enough for a single cart or two riders to ride alongside each other, a deliberate ploy to limit the size of any force lucky enough to have reached this far. On either side, the natural rock provided sheer walls, from the top of which defenders could unleash a hail of deadly rocks and arrows at any attackers assaulting the enormous oak doors that now blocked their way.

'For a people who claim to be peaceful, this fort seems ready for war,' said Gwydion.

'In peacetime we are peaceful,' said Prydain, 'in times of war we are warlike. The time in between is often but a heartbeat and we will always be ready. Don't forget, although the Romans are only focussed on the eastern coast, it takes but a moment to cast their eye this way and their Legions are only ten day's march from here. We will not be caught unawares.'

For the next hour they were kept waiting outside the giant gate, until eventually it creaked inward and a warrior stepped out to face them.

'Prydain, you are not expected,' he said, 'and you bring a stranger.'

'I do, and I would present him to my grandfather.'

'You know our ways, what reason is there to push them aside?'

'For this man is no normal man – he saved my life when we fought alongside Caratacus. I believe my grandfather would share bread with him.'

The warrior paused before nodding in agreement.

'It is acceptable,' he said and turned to lead the way.

Prydain and Gwydion walked behind him, leading their horses by the reins. Within moments Gwydion realised that the giant oaken door was one of three, each equally as thick as the others. Finally the hill levelled out and Gwydion paused to stare around at the hill fort of Llanmelin, capital of the Silures.

Chapter 7

The Lands of the Durotriges

47 AD

Vespasian sat in his tent warmed by the fire prepared by his servants. In his hand he held a mug of warm watered wine and he leant back in the sheepskin armchair, allowing himself the luxury of resting his eyes after hours of boring administration that came with the role of Legatus. It had been a year since he had led the Augusta south through Britannia and though they had encountered some resistance, overall it had been a fairly painless campaign. However, the movement of so many men at arms across unknown territory was a drawn out and complicated process. The Legion was currently encamped in a temporary fort, forced to take shelter from the autumn storms that ravaged the country. Usually the marching camps were only used for a few days at a time but they had become bogged down for almost a month, while they took stock of their situation. He knew he would have to find somewhere more permanent before the winter snows came and needed to ensure they had adequate stores to last them through the winter, until the campaigning season started again.

Vespasian's command consisted of almost five thousand Legionaries, two cohorts of Batavian infantry, two more of Thracian Sagittaria, the expert bowmen from the western coast of the Black sea, another of Cretan slingers and four centuries of Gallic cavalry. Added to this, there were almost half as many camp followers and though he wasn't directly responsible for their welfare, it was in his interests for them to flourish. Overall that meant a total force of almost ten thousand men and a civilian following of five thousand more that needed feeding and shelter.

Despite his annoyance with the followers, their presence was accepted as a part of modern warfare. Their numbers included bakers, blacksmiths, leather workers and butchers. Prostitutes were never short of customers from the ranks and temporary ale houses were always full of those soldiers lucky enough to get leave. Much of the Legion's needs were met by the camp followers as though there were permanent supply lines reaching back as far as Londinium and the coastal ports; the followers traded and hunted locally to acquire fresh meat and vegetables. In turn these were often sold to the Legion's camps and along with any stores taken forcibly by the Roman patrols from the smaller villages en-route, supplies were usually adequate.

In addition, due to the time it took for ox drawn carts to travel from Rutupiae, the main port formed during the initial invasion three years previously, the Legion were often shadowed offshore by the Roman fleet, always on the lookout for native fishing villages suitable for the landing of store direct from the mainland. Those villages that resisted were dealt with mercilessly and it was always in their interests to comply rather than being wiped out and their ports used anyway.

Vespasian had junior officers and civilian clerks to deal with most administrative tasks, yet Roman efficiency demanded he still had to be involved at a higher level, when authorisation was required to spend huge amounts of money from the imperial coffers. These were the tasks that tired him the most and though he relished the weeks when he had to strategize any potential conflict with the local tribes, recently he had even handed this control over to his second in command, as the limited imagination of his enemies failed to tax his military mind.

'Oh for a foe worth fighting,' he sighed to himself, and though he didn't know it, his desire was about to be met.

—

On the outskirts of the camp, a guard peered through the rain toward the commotion on the road to his front. Though the Legion always had patrols out for miles around, there was no real expectation of trouble, so when a group of ten horse mounted scouts galloped out of the darkness and shouted up to open the gates immediately, he and the other guards reacted cautiously.

'Watchword?' demanded the guard.

'I have no idea,' snapped the voice from below. 'I am Lucius, centurion of Vespian's second scout unit. We have been on patrol for the last ten days and have wounded who need tending. Open the gates. That is an order.'

'My lord, I cannot until I have someone verify your identity,' said the guard, 'you know that.'

'Soldier,' shouted the centurion, 'if you don't open this gate right now and any of my men die for your actions, I will hold you personally responsible and trust me, you don't want that.'

'But my lord...' started the guard.

'Let him in,' said a voice behind him.

The Decurion turned to look at the Tessarius in charge of the guard.

'It is indeed Lucius,' said the Tessarius, 'I served with him in Gaul. I will vouch for him.'

'Guards to arms,' shouted the Decurion, relieved that the decision had been taken out of his hands, 'open the gates.'

Within moments the scout unit came through the gates, obviously the worse for wear after days on patrol in awful weather. Two of the riders were slouched over their saddles nursing wounds of some description.

'Get them to the Medicus,' ordered the centurion as soon as they were within the boundary and as the rest of the patrol cantered into the centre of the camp, he turned to face the guard commander who had descended from the temporary defences to greet him.

'Hail, Lucius,' said the Tessarius, 'what events cause your unexpected arrival?'

'I have little time to explain,' said Lucius. 'Suffice to say the fort may be in imminent danger. Stand-to the garrison and prepare for battle, I have to speak to Vespasian.' Without another word, he continued deeper into the fort, leaving the guard commander behind him.

'Your orders, my lord?' asked the Decurion.

'I don't know what's going on,' said the Tessarius, 'but it doesn't look good. Sound the alarm.'

-

Vespasian was already halfway into his armour when his personal guard entered his tent to announce the arrival of Lucius.

'My lord, centurion Lucius begs audience.'

'Granted,' said Vespasian.

Lucius ducked into the tent and saluted the Legatus.

'Hail Vespasian,' he said.

'Lucius,' said Vespasian, 'I trust you are behind the call to arms?'

'I am, my lord, and have made haste to give meaning.'

'Then make it good, Lucius, for this unit has not been called to defensive stations since we left Medway.'

'My lord, as you know, ten days ago my unit patrolled south to select suitable camp sites for the Legion's advance. The route was clear and we found many such locations, but as we went, we found most villages deserted. This did not worry us unduly as many flee at the sound of the Legion's feet. On the sixth day, we spied a well-armed party from the Durotriges making their way eastward with purpose. Their numbers were ten times ours so we watched from a distance. At first their threat was minimal but within hours their number was swollen by many more such patrols joining them and within a day, their number were several thousand.'

'Did they see you?'

'No my lord, at least not at first. We followed from a distance and their purpose soon became clear. Less than six day's ride from here there is a Durotriges hill fort and it seems that a vast force is assembling at this place. At first, we kept hidden but were spied by one of their patrols. We fled to raise the alarm but they were relentless in their pursuit and we were forced to turn and fight. Many felt the steel of our arrows though their aim was just as keen.'

'You suffered casualties?'

'We did, my lord. Four dead and two wounded. It was all we could do to get away with our lives and we have ridden two days without rest.'

'And your pursuers?'

'I know not, my lord, they could be on our heels, that's why I raised the alarm.'

'You did right,' said Vespasian. 'Can you put meaning to their actions?'

'I saw nothing that suggests they will bend their knee,' said Lucius, 'they are forming their forces as we speak. They seem well armed and are certainly warlike. I believe they intend to face us in battle and try to achieve what the Catuvellauni failed to do.'

'You think they want a fight?'

'I do.'

'Then a fight they shall have,' said Vespasian. 'How many units of scouts are still within the camp?'

'Another six, my lord.'

'Then instruct them to deploy around the fort at a distance of one day's march. If as much as a leaf falls out of place, I want to know about it.' He turned to the young man standing to one side. 'Send word to the Camp Prefect, the Primus Pilus and the Tribunes. There will be a war council in my tent at first light. In the meantime, place the men on alert and double the guard.'

'Yes, my lord,' said the young man and disappeared out of the tent.

'An eager man,' said Vespasian after he left, 'but so much to learn.'

Lucius nodded. The position of Tribunus Laticlavius was a strange one within the Legions. On paper they were second in command of the whole unit but in practise they were fresh faced and inexperienced. Their family influences back in Rome often bought their position, as active duty stood them in good stead for a future life in politics. Shadowing a Legatus gave them a unique insight into the workings of the Roman military. In reality, they acted as clerks to the Legatus and though they enjoyed the trappings of military privilege, in times of battle they retreated to the shadows to watch and learn.

'Lucius,' said Vespasian, 'you have done well. I will organise the defences, you see to your men and get some sleep.'

'But my lord…'

'But nothing,' said Vespasian, 'you need the rest. If what you say is accurate, the pursuers are no more than a few hundred strong and provide no serious threat to a Legion. Report back here in the morning and join the war council. I will expect accurate report as to the enemy locations so ensure you are well rested. You have done well, centurion, now go and see to your command.'

'Yes my lord,' said Lucius and left the tent before making his way over to the barrack lines where he knew his men would be located.

–

The rain had long stopped as the new day dawned and hundreds of men peered over the ramparts into the cold mist beyond. Despite their numbers, the silence was absolute as every man strained to hear any noise from the surrounding forests, for it was well known the Celts favoured the dawn attack.

Down on the floor of the camp, units of archers with extra quivers of arrows waited to be deployed to any area of the fortifications should an attack come and behind them, row after row of Legionaries stood in reserve.

In the centre of the camp, all the remaining cohorts were on parade, again waiting for deployment should the need arise. Every man was wet through from the dawn mist, but the nearness of potential battle meant every heart beat faster, pumping the hot blood through their veins in expectation. In the headquarters tent, a group of men stood around the planning table, waiting for the arrival of their commanding officer to lead the war council.

The flap opened and every man turned to salute the Legatus.

'As you were,' he said and looked around the room as he removed his cloak. 'Report readiness.'

The camp prefect stepped forward.

'My lord, the fort is battle ready. All scout units are in the field and report no threat.'

'Cavalry?' asked Vespasian.

'Already patrolling the hills, my lord, with more at the followers' camp along with a cohort of Batavians as you requested.'

'Good,' said Vespasian, 'the last thing we need are those civilians panicking and clouding our judgement. Right, Lucius, show us what you found on patrol.'

For the next hour, Lucius leaned over the animal skin map of the land of the Durotriges, drawn from the accounts of prisoners and informers. Calmly and clearly, he described the country he had followed over the previous ten days, pointing out safe routes, places of potential danger and any obstacles they had encountered. Where something was mentioned that was not already represented on the map, a junior officer sketched it in with chalk, knowing the cartographer would draw the detail later with inks.

Questions came thick and fast as each officer probed the centurion for details that affected their own forces and Lucius answered each the best he could. His role as a scout centurion meant he was used to taking in detail and his concise answers meant everyone soon had the information they needed. Eventually Vespasian was happy; he had gleaned as much information as he could and he called for quiet around the tent.

'Lucius,' he said, 'as usual your information is excellent and you have our gratitude.' He turned to face the rest of his officers. 'Overnight I have sent men into the follower's camp and dug out a couple of local traders. At first, they were reluctant to talk but were soon convinced otherwise. The fort to our front is the base for a clan leader called Eadric, a minor chief but one with big ambition. He is known as being arrogant but a good war leader and has designs on the leadership of the entire Durotriges. I fear he may see the encroachment of an invading army as opportunity to show his worth in battle. Defeat us, and the other clans will come running to join him. It is an irritating itch but one that needs scratching.

'There is no way we can continue south leaving an aggressive tribe in our wake,' he continued, 'so we will send a message into the heart of these people demanding their surrender. Lucius, you will lead the cavalry back to the area of the hill fort. Take the prisoners with you and make sure they are well versed in our demands. When you are a day's ride away, send them in with my message. Tell them we are willing to accept their surrender on favourable terms, but we will ask only once. Failure to accept or even respond will result in their annihilation.'

One of the Tribunes stepped forward.

'My lord,' he said, 'I applaud your decision but would ask if we shouldn't wait until we know their strength?'

'You are right,' said Vespasian, 'the decision has wings but we cannot afford to wait. The Catuvellauni were the strongest tribe by far yet were no match for our fist. The Durotriges are not well known to us but their numbers will be smaller, at least at the moment. If we give them time, who knows who else will rally to this man's call. No, we will mobilise the Legion and take advantage of the moment. Tribune Natta, you will take three cohorts in the main column as well as the slingers and a cohort of archers.' He pointed at a series of valleys on the map weaving their way toward the enemy fort. 'Your route lies here, heading as an arrow straight to the heart of them. Your role is to form a defensive line here on the plain between these hills. Tribune Lanatus will lead another three cohorts and the rest of the Batavians, shadowing your movements two miles west. Maintain close contact and be prepared to offer support if required. I will take the remainder south before wheeling east and approach their hill fort from behind. Unless you are challenged on the approach, we will time our arrival for seven days from now. Send word to the engineers to prepare all siege engines, I have a feeling we will need them before the next full moon. You are all good men and I know I need not outline your tactics should you come under attack.' He paused and looked at the faces of every man around the table. 'Gentlemen, this is our first time to confront the enemy without the back up of Plautius so let's get this right. Are there any questions?'

Silence fell in the tent.

'Good,' said Vespasian, 'then strike camp and prepare to march.'

–

Four days later, centurion Lucius stood high on a hill awaiting the return of the prisoners with the answer to his demands of surrender. Beside him was his trusted second in command, Optio Vetus, a veteran of many a campaign in several countries. The sun was setting and in the far distance they could make out the campfire smoke of the Durotriges hill fort.

'What do you think?' asked Lucius. 'Will they return?'

'I fear not,' said the Optio, 'they faced the wrath of a Roman Legatus and were released with their lives. Would you return?'

'Probably not,' said Lucius, 'but we will give them until daybreak tomorrow.' He looked around the landscape before settling his gaze on a nearby hill covered with a tangled willow forest on the opposite side of the valley.

'Are the men fed?' he asked.

'They are,' said Vetus. 'I will instruct them to smother their cooking fires before dark.'

'No,' said Lucius, 'let the flames burn themselves out.'

'But their glow will attract unwelcome eyes.'

'If the prisoners reach the fort, they will tell them of our position anyway. I want our fires to add credibility to their words. Build up the fires but as soon as it is dark, retrace our steps and circle to that hill beyond the river. It has good all-round vision but enough undergrowth to conceal our mounts. If they send word of response, we will see them coming yet if they sneak upon us like assassins in the night, they will find nothing but embers and horseshit.'

'It will be done,' said the Optio and vaulted onto his horse before galloping back down the hill to where the rest of the century were hidden deep in the forest.

Lucius mounted his own horse before pausing one more time to stare toward the hill fort.

'What's it to be, Eadric?' he said to himself. 'Peace or war?'

—

The following morning the scout patrol waited in the treeline alongside the river while Optio Vetus and four men drew their Gladii and crept through the undergrowth to the original camp from the night before. The prisoners had been instructed to return with Eadric's answer by dawn and should be there. However the presence of hundreds of hoof prints in the mud paid witness to far more visitors than Vetus had expected. Finally they came across the remains of their own fires and at first could not see any sign of the messengers, but a slight movement in the undergrowth caused Vetus to spin around and stare at the sight before him in disgust.

The prisoners had indeed returned and though they were incapable of speech, the message was clear. Both men had been gagged, stripped naked and tied between two trees with their arms and legs stretched out wide. Their bodies had been cut just deep enough to allow them to bleed without dying and the scent of human blood must have been irresistible to the animals of the night. The lower halves of their bodies had been ripped apart and entrails strewn across the forest floor told the story of the carnage the predators had wreaked before being interrupted by the approach of Vetus and his men.

'They were of the same tribe,' said one of the scouts, 'why throw them to the wolves?'

'To send us a clear message,' said Vetus, 'let's get out of here.'

Chapter 8

The Fort at Tamesas
46 AD

The morning after his meeting with Ocelus, Cassus waited outside the gates of the fort as instructed. Though there was no sign of the Tribune, there was a man leaning against a tree wrapped in a waxed cloak against the morning drizzle. Cassus approached to address him.

'Are you waiting for someone?' he asked.

'Perhaps,' said the man. 'What is your name?'

'Cassus Maecilius.'

The man nodded.

'Then you are the man I seek,' he said. 'I have a message for you. You are expected at the village of the Ysbryd. Be there by sunset in three days.'

'The village of the Ysbryd,' repeated Cassus. 'I do not recognise the name. Where will I find this place?'

'I know not,' said the man, 'I am just a messenger.'

'But it could be anywhere.'

The man shrugged his shoulders and turned to walk away.

'Wait,' said Cassus, 'what about rations, weapons, a horse. Surely Ocelus has left me these things.'

'I am just a messenger,' he repeated and without another word, strode away leaving Cassus staring after him in confusion.

Cassus wandered back into the fort, not quite sure what to do next, but eventually he realised this was some sort of entrance test and turned his mind to the problem. Ysbryd was not a Roman word so therefore had to be the name of a local clan and though he spoke the language, it was not one he was familiar with. Looking around he saw a group of slaves unloading firewood from a cart and made his way over to talk with them.

'Hold,' he said, using the local language and all four stopped immediately, their eyes lowered to the floor. 'Who of you are from these parts?'

'I am, Lord,' said one.

'Good, I am seeking a clan,' he said. 'They go by the name of Ysbryd and their village lies less than three days ride from here.'

'I do not know of this clan, Lord,' said the man.

Cassus cursed but continued his line of questioning. Having lived amongst these people for the past year, he knew they would never voluntarily give up any information that may help the Romans.

'What about the rest of you, surely you know this place?'

When no answer came, Cassus picked up a thin branch from the back of the cart. He stripped the twigs and flexed it between both hands.

'Look at me,' he said and all four lifted their eyes in fear. One of them was younger than the rest and little more than a boy.

'You,' he said, 'remove your tunic.' The boy whimpered but did as he was told. 'Lean against the cart,' ordered Cassus and as the boy did, Cassus turned to face the three men who now glared at him with hatred.

'Right, I will ask again,' he said, 'but this time, you will give me the information I seek. If not, this boy will pay the price of your silence. Let's try again. Where is the village of Ysbryd?'

Nobody answered and without pause, Cassus swung his makeshift whip across the boy's naked back. The boy screamed and fell to his knees as the blood started to flow from the stripe cut deep into his flesh.

'No!' shouted one of the men. 'Lord, he is but a boy.'

'Then answer my question,' said Cassus. 'Where are the people they call the Ysbryd?'

Again there was hesitation but as Cassus raised his arm again, the man called out again.

'Lord, stop. I will tell you what you wish to know.'

'Good,' said Cassus, 'tell me about them and where I can find their village.'

The man looked around nervously before answering quietly.

'There is no clan called Ysbryd,' he said quietly.

Cassus raised his hand again but the man grabbed his arm and stared into his eyes.

'Stop,' he shouted, 'I tell the truth, there is no clan called Ysbryd for the word means something else.'

Cassus punched the slave with his free hand and watched in disgust as he scrabbled in the mud of the fort floor.

'Touch me again, slave,' spat Cassus, 'and you will feel the point of my blade. Now explain your meaning.'

The man looked up with blood running from his mouth.

'Lord, the word you are saying means spirits or ghosts. There is no clan by this name but there is a place. Three days ride upstream lies a village that is said to house the spirits of our ancestors. I think this is the place you seek.'

'Then why didn't you tell me?' asked Cassus.

'Because it is a sacred place,' said the slave, 'and no man goes there; to do so would invite curses from the gods.'

Cassus smirked. It made complete sense. If these Exploratores were so secretive, surely, they would use such a place as a base.

'You could have saved the boy much pain,' said Cassus and threw the branch to one side. 'Now, see to the boy and get back to work.'

Over the next hour, Cassus managed to swindle a food pouch from the fort quartermaster as well as rations, a Gladius and a waterproof cloak. He walked out of the fort unchallenged and followed the road into the forest, seeking a suitable victim. Within minutes he saw a lone trader riding toward the fort, followed by a group of manacled slaves.

'Hail stranger,' said Cassus, blocking his path, 'what business do you have on the road?'

The man eyed him suspiciously before answering.

'I seek to sell these men,' he answered. 'I am expected at the fort.'

'Then I need to check you for hidden weapons,' said Cassus and approached the horse.

The man was no fool and immediately drew his longs-word, aiming it at Cassus's head.

'I have ridden this path many times, stranger,' he said, 'and have never suffered this indignity. Who are you to demand this of me?'

'My apologies,' said Cassus, 'I did not mean to offend. It is just that...' Without finishing the sentence, Cassus lunged forward beneath the man's sword arm and punched him in the ribs, hearing the satisfying crack of a rib under his fist. The man cried out in pain and with a helping push from Cassus, fell off the opposite side of the horse.

Cassus vaulted up onto the back of the horse before addressing the slaves looking impassively up at him.

'You men,' he said in Briton, 'carry this man to the fort. Tell him that one day I will pay him fair price for his horse. Run if you dare but you will be hunted down and crucified, the choice is yours.' Without another word he turned the horse and rode toward the river. He knew this village of spirits was three days away and he had already wasted enough time. Ocelus wouldn't wait.

–

Three days later, Cassus sat upon his mount watching the evening mist rolling into the village at the bottom of the valley before him. He had ridden hard, following the river Tamesas as it got narrower toward its source, carefully avoiding the random groups of brigands who still made the forests their home since the defeat of Caratacus and the surrender of Camulodunum.

The village of spirits, he said to himself. This had to be it. Night fell and though he watched for several hours, he saw no sign of movement. Finally he decided it was safe to descend, and slowly made his way down the slope.

Apart from the sound of the river, the silence was profound and he knew that if there ever was life in this place, it had left long ago. As he swung around the outside of the hut, the horse pulled up abruptly, its nose flaring in fear. Before them lay a rotting corpse, held upright by a stake driven down through its chest and into the ground. The fleshless skull screamed in silent agony and beyond the corpse, Cassus could see a ring of small fires alight in the centre of the village. Though his heart raced, Cassus urged the horse slowly forward.

As he went, Cassus started to make out the shapes of human corpses in the darkness, carefully arranged into poses of everyday life. The remains of a woman leaned over a long cold cooking pot, while another sat against her hut, alongside a dead dog. Rotting warriors leaned on their spears, every one with their heads stripped of flesh and the gleam of their skulls adding to the horror of the scene.

Slowly he continued and when he reached the ring of fires, he dismounted from the horse before walking into the centre. The silence was absolute and the combination of the flickering fire light and the swirling mist cast an air of otherworldliness across the whole scene. Beyond the fires he could see glimpses of seated corpses, as if gathered to see a contest but before he could investigate further, the sound of a sword being unsheathed reached him through the gloom. Cassus quickly drew his own Gladius and seconds later a man appeared menacingly out of the rapidly receding mist bearing a sword of his own.

Cassus adopted the defensive stance; feet shoulder width apart with the left foot slightly ahead of the right. He held his sword at shoulder height pointing forward while his left hand reached out as if judging the distance.

The man kept walking silently toward him. He was dressed in leather scaled armour and a full faced Gladiator's helmet. In his hands he carried a broadsword almost twice the length of a Gladius but Cassus knew it was also twice the weight and very unwieldy.

'Who are you?' asked Cassus as he got nearer but the man didn't answer. Within seconds he was upon Cassus and launched an overwhelming attack, swinging the heavy sword skilfully as if it weighed nothing. Cassus hardly had time to defend himself and was forced back under the ferocity of the attack. Frantically he used his sword to deflect the blows but without warning the warrior punched him across the jaw and Cassus fell to the ground. He knew he was in serious trouble but as he spun in the dirt to face up toward his opponent, he was confused to see the man walking quietly away into the mist, leaving the clearing silent once more.

Cassus got to his feet and stared around in confusion.

'What is this?' he called. 'Some sort of sick test?'

When there was no answer, he bent down and picked up his Gladius.

'Come on then,' he shouted, wiping the blood from his mouth and raising both arms high, 'here I am. What are you waiting for?'

A whooshing sound whistled through the air and before he could react, his Gladius was knocked from his hand by an arrow from an unseen archer, causing sparks to fly as metal struck metal. The force of the strike jarred his arm and Cassus spun around as the sound of laughter whispered from the gloom.

His mind raced. Surely this place was of the dead and the slave was right, no living man belonged here.

'By the gods, show yourselves,' shouted Cassus. 'Face me on equal terms, or are you all cowards?'

Another man emerged from the mist, though this time was dressed in a simple tunic and carried nothing but a wooden staff.

'So you are the champion,' Cassus sneered, bending down to pick up his Gladius again. 'Well here I am, stranger, no more children's games for I am insulted at your mockery, do your worst.'

Cassus took the initiative and attacked the man only to find himself face down in the dirt, having been smashed across the head by the man's staff. The man stepped away and Cassus picked himself up to renew his attack, embarrassed at how easily he had been bettered. Again, the man avoided his lunge and this time knocked Cassus's feet away from under him so he sprawled in the dirt once more. Cassus picked himself up again and launched himself forward in a frenzy of aggression. At first the other man retreated, using his staff to deflect Cassus's frantic assault, but within moments struck a crushing blow against Cassus's ribs before knocking him sprawling again with a blow to the head. Like the man before him, the staff bearer walked across the clearing in silence and disappeared into the gloom, leaving Cassus alone once more.

Cassus got to his feet and wiped the blood from his face as the sound of laughter once more rippled quietly around the arena. He looked around at the long dead audience, realising that this whole thing had been staged for effect and nothing more than some sort of initiation.

'Enough,' called Cassus, turning slowly on the spot, 'you have made your point. I have been bettered. Show yourselves and stop this farce.'

A murmur seemed to ripple around the long dead audience and Cassus's heart missed a beat as he saw some of them start to move. Frantically he invoked the names of his gods and stared in horror as the dead got to their feet.

'*What witchcraft is this?*' he screamed and threw his Gladius toward the nearest approaching body, his heart racing in terror. As the shape stepped into the firelight, Cassus breathed a sigh of relief to see what he thought had been a corpse was actually a mere man dressed in the same manner of the staged bodies around the camp. The man walked silently forward passing close to Cassus before ducking into a nearby hut. Behind him, five more followed his steps and each stared at him as they passed without uttering a word.

'Very clever,' Cassus sneered as they passed, 'a game for children, played by men.'

'Yet a lesson learned,' said a voice and Cassus saw Ocelus emerge from a hut, once more slicing pieces from another apple.

'And what lesson is this?' asked Cassus.

'To beware of that which is hidden before your very eyes,' said Ocelus, 'to understand that no matter how good you are, there is always someone better; to beware the hidden assassin; to understand that the unknown can be a powerful weapon. Do you want me to go on?'

Cassus considered what had just happened and realised there had indeed been lessons learned, though the delivery had been strange.

'Your point is taken, Ocelus,' he said, 'but your methods are new to me.'

'You will find many things different here,' said Ocelus, 'but come inside. It is time to eat and I will answer what questions I can.'

–

Cassus entered the hut and saw that three of the men were sitting around an enormous tree stump that served as a table. Each placed a bag on the table and were withdrawing whatever food they had stored within. Cassus sat to one side and waited as each man ate his meal in silence. Ocelus paused with a piece of bread halfway to his mouth.

'Did you not bring food?' he asked.

'Enough for travel only,' said Cassus. 'I thought there would be food available here.'

One of the men looked up at Cassus in derision.

'We fend for ourselves here,' he sneered, 'you'll want us to wipe your arse, next.'

'I expect nothing,' snapped Cassus in reply. 'Now I know what is expected, I will fend for myself.'

One of the other men grunted and reached into his food pack. A moment later a piece of cooked pork slid across the table, closely followed by half a loaf from somebody else.

'I don't need your charity,' said Cassus.

'They are not gifts,' said Ocelus, placing a skin of wine before him. 'Tomorrow night you will provide the meal. Consider it a loan.'

Cassus hesitated before reaching forward and breaking the bread in half.

'So,' he said eventually, 'who's going to explain how it all works around here?'

'Not much to explain,' said Ocelus. 'First thing, we need a name. It doesn't have to be your real name; we are not interested in your past.'

'My name is Cassus,' he replied.

'So be it,' said Ocelus. 'These are the men who will train with you over the next few weeks. This man here is Syrian born and the best bowman I have ever encountered. He spent five years in the Sagittaria until I rescued him from his life of boredom. He is known simply as Archer.'

The dark-skinned man didn't speak but nodded a brief acknowledgement toward Cassus.

'The next is Terrimus,' said Ocelus, 'he is a native of this country and his role is to teach you how to live off the land.'

'He is a Briton,' said Cassus in surprise.

'He is,' said Ocelus, 'is that a problem?'

'I don't know,' said Cassus, 'can he be trusted?'

'More than any man I have ever met,' said Ocelus.

'I trust no man who betrays his own people,' growled Cassus.

'Your point is well made,' said Ocelus, 'but this is different. Many years ago Caratacus wiped out his clan for a crime he did not commit. His wife and children were burned alive in front of his eyes, before he was set upon by Caratacus's men and his body thrown from a cliff. Somehow, he survived and swore to avenge their death. Heed his teaching carefully and you will never go hungry. By the time he has finished, you will move like a ghost and know the country better than one who was born here.'

'He doesn't say much,' said Cassus.

'He can't, they tore out his tongue,' said Ocelus.

Before Cassus could say anything more, Ocelus continued.

'Finally, that man there is Titus.'

'And what is his role?' asked Cassus.

'To kick your arse,' interrupted Titus without looking up.

'Titus is an ex-Gladiator who won the Rudis,' said Ocelus, referring to the wooden sword of freedom awarded to those who had excelled in the arena. 'Unfortunately he couldn't handle freedom and killed three fully armed men in a fight in Rome before he was sentenced to death by the magistrate. I saw him fight and bought his freedom.'

'So he is your slave,' said Cassus, staring defiantly at Titus.

'There are no slaves here,' said Ocelus, 'all are free to leave whenever they require, including you.'

'I can just walk away?'

'You can. We want nobody here who doesn't wish to be here.'

'What about those other men I saw outside?' asked Cassus.

'They are recruits like you,' said Ocelus, 'though further into their training. Many are called, few are successful.'

'And what does this training consist of?' asked Cassus.

'We will teach you how to live like a Briton,' said Ocelus, 'and though there will be weapons training, the main aim is to make you fit in as a native and keep you hidden from those who would challenge you.'

'Then why the weapon training?' asked Cassus. 'I can use a Gladius better than any man.'

'The natives of these lands don't use the Gladius,' said Ocelus, 'their weapons of choice are broadsword, axe and club. By the time we are finished you will be able in all three, but only enough to pass as a local. Should you have to rely on those skills to defend yourself against an attack, then you will have failed for the whole thrust of this place is to avoid conflict. Here you will learn to fit in and to be accepted by the natives as one of their own. The whole point is to become one of them and to hide before their very eyes. Knowledge is power, Cassus and the Legions need to know what their enemy intends to do almost before the enemy knows themselves. I understand you have some knowledge of living with the Britons.'

'I do,' said Cassus, 'and spent a year amongst them. I also know their tongue.'

'Which tribe?'

'Catuvellauni.'

'Then that is the identity you shall take,' said Ocelus. 'We will nurture that image and turn you into a Catuvellaunian warrior. Now eat and then I suggest you get some rest. The next few months will be the hardest you have ever known.'

'What about guards?' asked Cassus.

'We need no guards here,' said Ocelus, 'the natives won't come within ten miles of this place. A trait we encourage with our, shall we say, decorations.'

'The corpses,' said Cassus.

Ocelus nodded and continued with his meal. Finally he stood up and gathered his things.

'You can use any of the huts you see fit,' he said, 'make of it as you will for we provide nothing but instruction.'

'What about fodder for my horse?' asked Cassus.

'Your problem, not mine,' said Ocelus, 'from here on in, you will look after yourself. Every seven days you will be allowed to hunt and to rest. Make sure you do plenty of both. Now, we are done here. At dawn present yourself outside to start your training.'

Without another word he left the hut followed by the rest of the men. The last to leave was the ex-Gladiator Titus, who paused alongside Cassus before he left.

'I give you ten days maximum,' he whispered and followed the rest outside.

The following weeks were a whirlwind of training for Cassus. He spent hour after hour honing his weapon skills with Titus, not with Gladius or Pugio but with longsword and double headed axe. Though his instincts and basic skills were sharp, the weapons were strange to him and every session he seemed to end up in the dust; more than he was on his feet. Titus took great delight in taunting his lack of skill, which riled Cassus even more, causing him to lash out in anger, only to be swatted to the floor almost effortlessly by Titus.

For the first few weeks he spent every morning being beaten, admonished and insulted by the Gladiator while every afternoon was spent with Archer, sending hundreds upon hundreds of arrows into far off targets until his string fingers bled.

Evenings were spent with the silent Terrimus and though the warrior couldn't speak, his calm manner and easily learned sign language quickly conveyed the magic of the forest to Cassus's ever hungry mind. The enforced silence of the huntsman seemed to affect Cassus and without the distraction of speech, his mind focussed on the task in hand.

Soon he tuned in to the methods of his teacher and he found himself looking forward to the evenings and nights spent with the strange local. A simple nod or shake of the head when confronted with a choice would convey whether something was safe to eat or not. These berries would cause a bad stomach; those leaves when chewed were good for a wound while this mushroom will kill you. Tracks in the forest floor were soon identified by his strange and often funny interpretations of the animals they belonged to but better than that, whenever they found a new set and if it was possible, Terrimus tracked the animal down to show Cassus where it lived. Wolf packs were observed from a distance and their kills often stolen for the meat. Beaver were trapped with snares and even roosting birds were snatched from branches while asleep in the dark. Within two months Cassus walked lightly through the forests, hardly making a sound as he went. So quiet was his approach, often he was upon animals before they knew he was there and combined with his growing accuracy with his bow, hunting soon became second nature.

Within weeks Cassus found himself getting leaner and harder, relying on less food to sustain him yet feeling the strength in his muscles grow. All conversation was in Briton and he soon found out that most recruits selected never even made it to the village, as the initial lack of information and supplies was all part of the selection process and meant to test their resourcefulness. Of the two recruits who had already been there when Cassus had started, one had left to re-join his Legion, ready to be deployed on whatever mission his Legatus had in mind, while the other often trained alongside him and though it was discouraged, Dento had become a good friend.

On one of the rare evenings off from training, Cassus and Dento sat around a small campfire, talking quietly and sharing what food they had managed to catch in their snares.

'So, where are you from?' asked Cassus, leaning over to rotate the hare roasting on the makeshift spit above the fire.

'Southern Gaul,' said Dento, 'on the coast of the Mare Nostrum.'

'You are Gallic?' asked Cassus in surprise.

'I am, though my town has always been in Roman hands and I grew up desperate to join the Legions.'

'So why are you out here?' asked Cassus.

'Let's just say the Legionary life wasn't quite what I expected and I got into a lot of trouble. Somebody told Ocelus about me and he offered me the chance to change my fortune.'

'Did you have to fight him at your first meeting?' asked Cassus.

'I did,' laughed Dento, 'and he had me spitting blood within seconds. He's a tough little bastard.'

'He is,' agreed Cassus with a smile. 'So, do you think you made the right decision joining this lot?'

'I'm not sure,' said Dento. 'I love the training and I am certainly a better soldier for it. I just hope I can carry it off when deployed into the villages.'

'You'll be fine,' said Cassus. 'You already speak the language like a local and so many villages have been decimated by our army's hand recently, there are hundreds of lone refugees wandering the countryside. One more won't raise any eyebrow.'

Dento took the hare from the spit.

'It's done,' he said and laying it on a nearby stone, used his knife to split the animal down the centre before throwing half over to Cassus. The men used large leaves to protect their fingers from the hot flesh and ate their meal quietly, alone with their thoughts.

Since training with Terrimus, Cassus found that he enjoyed silence much more and his thoughts were often clearer for it. Now he considered the consequences of every action, whereas before he would stamp wildly into any situation, relying on his aggression to overcome any obstacle. Even in the training ring with Titus the contests were becoming closer; though the Gladiator invariably was the victor, Cassus often landed blows on the giant man.

'How much longer have you got left?' asked Cassus.

'I don't know,' said Dento. 'There isn't a time frame for this training; you are ready when they say you are. That could be weeks or months. I have known several men just disappear overnight and I can only assume they have been summoned by their Legions. One day soon, I assume that will happen to us.'

'And that's when we will be deployed into the wilds of Britannia?' asked Cassus.

'Not necessarily,' said Dento, 'you may be attached to a century back in your Legion until such time your skills are required.'

'That makes a mockery of all this,' said Cassus in disgust. 'What's the point if we are to rot in a fort?'

'It may not be that bad,' said Dento. 'They know we have skills they need so even if we are not needed yet, they will usually put us with a scout unit. At least that way we will be spared the boredom of camp life and guard duties.'

'Will there be other Exploratores there?' asked Cassus.

'There may well be,' said Dento, 'but don't announce yourself as such. Nobody else needs know except you, your Legatus and fellow Exploratores.'

'But how will I know them?'

'Don't worry,' said Dento, 'they will find you.'

Chapter 9

The Exploratore Camp
47 AD

Cassus lay on the straw mattress in his hut, listening to the pre-dawn chorus of bird song out in the forest. His eyes were still closed but he was awake, not sure what had interrupted his sleep. The past few months had been hard with constant training and learning weapon skills from the three instructors. His skill with a bow had become exceptional, his sword skills almost matched those of Titus and his survival skills were like second nature. Dento had gone, having left while Cassus was out on yet another learning expedition with Terrimus and though nobody would confirm it, Cassus assumed he had been deployed on a mission on behalf of his Legion. Occasionally new recruits appeared, but most left again just as quickly having fallen short of Ocelus's standards. Only a few were left to undergo the same rigorous training that Cassus had endured.

As he contemplated his time in the camp, something weighed on his mind. Something was wrong and he wasn't sure what it was. Suddenly he knew and rolled to one side to grab his sword; someone else was in the hut. He jumped to his feet and faced the man silhouetted against the faint light of the impending dawn.

'Declare yourself,' growled Cassus.

'Hold that reaction,' said the man, 'for it just may save your life in the next few hours.'

'Ocelus,' said Cassus, 'what brings you here?'

'It is time,' said Ocelus.

'Time for what?' asked Cassus.

'Destiny,' said Ocelus and ducked out of the hut.

Cassus followed him out and was surprised to see Archer, Terrimus and Titus standing in the clearing, each armed with their weapons of choice. Archer had his bow, Terrimus his staff and Titus his longsword.

'Your time here is done, Cassus,' said Ocelus. 'There are things afoot that need your involvement. But before you leave there is one more challenge, a trial of arms. You may choose one adversary but choose well for defeat will mean you leave without our endorsement.'

Cassus looked carefully at all three. He now considered himself the equal of both Archer and Terrimus and knew that he could expect a fair contest. Titus was a different matter. Cassus had never bettered him and he knew that should he choose the Gladiator, the chances of victory were slight.

'Consider carefully, Cassus,' said Ocelus, 'many have chosen the Gladiator but none have prevailed. Perhaps you should seek their advice?'

'They are here?' asked Cassus.

'Indeed they are; they have watched your every battle with Titus since the first night you arrived.'

Cassus looked around as the realisation sunk in. The corpses who provided their audience on a daily basis were not native dead but those Romans who had fallen to the sword of Titus at the last hurdle. The thought disgusted him. Despite this, his mind was set.

'I choose Titus,' he said.

'Then make ready,' said Ocelus, 'you fight at dawn.'

All four men left Cassus alone and he retreated to his hut. He prepared his horse and packed what food he had before sitting down and sharpening the edge of his broadsword. This is what it had all been about. Get it right today and his life would take a different direction. Get it wrong and his body would become nothing more than one more addition to the dead population of this cursed village.

Finally the time came and he made his way out to the arena where he had been humiliated on the night he had arrived. This time there were no theatricals, just Titus waiting with both hands resting on the hilt of the broadsword.

'Where are the others?' asked Cassus as he walked toward the Gladiator.

'Elsewhere,' said Titus. 'There are others that need their tuition now.'

'And what about us?' asked Cassus.

'We fight,' said Titus.

'With no witnesses?'

'Those already dead bear witness,' said Titus, nodding toward the cadavers situated around the arena in poses of normality.

'But I could say I triumphed, even if it was not true.'

'If you survive.'

'You would not report the outcome?'

'No.'

'Then what is the point of this trial?' asked Cassus. 'If the victor can never be proven, nobody will ever know.'

'You will know,' said Titus, 'as will your gods.'

'And would this be a burden?'

'Only to an honourable man.'

Cassus nodded and realised that the last few months had been about building not only his skills, but his character.

'Then let the trial commence,' said Cassus and walked over to take up position before the Gladiator. He withdrew his longsword from the sheath across his back and stuck the blade in the ground before him, matching the stance of his opponent. Months earlier he had launched wildly into the attack but that was a different day, a different man. He had changed beyond all recognition and now possessed a character that combined patience alongside skills in equal measure. Gradually he controlled his breathing, knowing that his heart rate was slowing as he concentrated on the man before him. The image seemed to get clearer and Cassus could see every mark on the leather of the man's armour. Minutes passed with each man motionless as they waited for their opponent to move, looking for any sign of weakness. Cassus's senses seemed to sharpen the longer they waited. The songs of the birds were louder, the smells of the forest were sharper and the light breeze on his face was like the strongest gale. Across the clearing, Titus was just as resolute, knowing that most men broke under the weight of tension and usually rushed into the attack out of frustration. He was happy to wait all day, but then something happened that sent a message to Cassus clearer than the loudest parade square order – a bead of sweat ran down Titus's face.

At that moment Cassus knew he had him and he withdrew the sword from the soil to replace it in his sheath before turning to leave.

'Hold,' shouted Titus, 'the contest remains un-fought.'

'There is no contest,' said Cassus, 'you are already defeated. Your fear echoes around the hills like a dying beast.'

'I fear no one,' snarled Titus. 'Turn and face me, coward.'

'For whose benefit, Titus?' asked Cassus. 'These dead men who have witnessed your vanity on so many occasions, or to satisfy your own doubt in your own skills? I know I will emerge the victor, Titus, and it is now for you to prove otherwise. Is that not a victory in itself?'

'A victory of words not steel,' snarled Titus swinging his sword before him, 'and mere words have not bloodied me yet.' With a deafening roar he charged across the clearing, not realising that was exactly what Cassus wanted.

Cassus drew his own sword with lightning speed and spun to one side, causing Titus to miss him completely and swing wildly into thin air. Cassus seized the opportunity and launched his own attack on the Gladiator. Though at a disadvantage, Titus's huge experience in the field of battle meant he reacted quickly and deflected the blows with his own sword but just as he was ready to go on the offensive, Cassus broke off the attack and walked away from him, exposing his back to the Gladiator.

Titus was confused. He could easily strike down this man but there was no honour in attacking a man from behind.

'Turn and face me,' he shouted.

'Momentarily,' said Cassus and paused at the far end of the arena before turning to face him.

'I am ready,' he said and adopted the defensive stance, holding the sword above his shoulder.

Titus stormed across the arena again and swung his sword toward his opponent's torso, but Cassus swung his sword downward with all his strength to knock Titus's weapon from his hands and sent it spinning away into the bushes. Again, Cassus walked away nonchalantly, knowing his demeanour was feeding the Gladiator's rage. Titus retrieved his sword and re-entered the arena.

'Enough games, *Cassus*,' he said. 'This trial will not end until blood is spilled. Stand and face me as an equal.'

'So be it,' said Cassus and walked forward to within a few paces of the Gladiator.

Moments later, steel crashed upon steel as both men threw everything they had into the contest. Every blow was met by an equally skilful riposte and the constant exertion took its toll on both muscle and breath. Both men raced around the arena and rivers of sweat ran down their faces as they sought non-existent openings in each other's defence. Clouds of dust flew from their feet and deflected blows from the swords were followed up by clenched fists from free hands as every avenue was desperately explored.

Realising he was tiring rapidly, Cassus took a calculated gamble and deliberately swung a weak strike toward his opponent's head, allowing his sword to be deflected easily by Titus's blade, but as his body was forced to twist to follow the sword's progress, he used every ounce of his strength to smash his elbow back into Titus's head, forcing the man to stumble backward. Cassus repeated the back-hand blow, though this time with the pommel of his sword and though the Gladiator's head was protected by his helmet, Titus staggered backward in a daze. Cassus saw his opening and quickly followed up his advantage with a kick to the Gladiators midriff, sending him crashing to the floor.

Cassus threw away his word and drew the dagger from his belt before dropping onto the prone man's chest. He lifted up the Gladiator's visor and both men stared at each other, one the victor and the other the vanquished. Both men were exhausted and for a few moments neither said a thing as they caught their breath.

'You have drawn your blade,' said Titus eventually.

'You said there had to be blood,' said Cassus.

'The agreement was made,' said Titus, 'and must be fulfilled.'

'So be it,' said Cassus and drew the blade across his own palm, before standing up and holding out his arm to help the Gladiator up.

Titus paused before accepting the arm and got to his feet.

'You could have taken my life,' said Titus, 'it was your right.'

'To what end?' asked Cassus. 'There are other men who need your tuition as once did I.'

'Perhaps my journey is ended,' said Titus, 'for you are the first man to better me.'

'That may be true,' said Cassus, 'but I have learned from the best.'

Titus drew his own dagger and cut his own palm before offering it to Cassus.

'Your time has come, Cassus. Go with head held high.'

Cassus gripped his hand and their blood flowed together.

'You have my gratitude, Titus,' he said and released his grip to walk out of the arena.

Archer appeared from behind the huts leading Cassus's horse. Behind him came Terrimus carrying his usual staff. The Syrian Sagittarius held out his arm and Cassus grasped his forearm to say goodbye. When they were done, Terrimus stepped forward and held up his staff as a gift. It was a very special gesture and Cassus hesitated, not quite sure what to do.

'Take it,' said a voice and Cassus turned to see Ocelus stood in a doorway, peeling his obligatory apple.

'I cannot take his staff,' said Cassus, 'it is the very soul of him.'

'There will be other staffs,' said Ocelus, 'honour him by accepting the gift.'

Cassus turned to face Terrimus. Of all the instructors, he had become closest and Cassus considered him a friend.

'Your ways have shone new light on my life, Terrimus and I will always be in your debt.'

Terrimus just smiled and stepped back as Ocelus approached.

'You are one of us now, Cassus,' said Ocelus, 'and the natives have no equal. Yet you are still flesh and bone. Use the skills learned here to avoid conflict. Your role is to disappear in plain sight and become the eyes of the Legion within the heart of the enemy. Return to Plautius for there are things afoot that need your skills but before you do, there is one last lesson. Learn it well.'

He bent forward and using his knife, scratched a design in the dirt. It was very simple yet Cassus recognised it immediately; it was the classic shape of a Pugio, the roman knife that every soldier carried.

'Remember this sign, Cassus,' said Ocelus, 'for it is the way we recognise our brotherhood. Keep the meaning hidden but if your path should cross with a fellow, hold back nothing in your support. Now be gone for your purpose awaits.'

Cassus nodded and after a final look around, rode his horse out of the village to follow the river East toward Londinium. He had ridden here as an opinionated soldier but was riding back an Exploratore.

Chapter 10

The Camp of Caratacus
48 AD

Caratacus strode through the camp followed by his personal guard. His army had grown to an enormous size and was now housed in hundreds of roundhouses, each housing several warriors, some complete with families and children. Since joining with the Silures, he had grown in political stature and was now counted as an equal amongst the tribal elders. Word had reached him that Caedmon, the chief of the Silures, was dying and it was in his interests to be present at the death bed.

'Gwydion of the Blaidd,' he roared as he passed through the village, 'attend me.'

Gwydion ducked out of the hut that had formed his home since arriving two years earlier. He had done as Prydain had suggested and joined the army of Caratacus, rising rapidly through the ranks to become one of his trusted warriors. Due to the rapid growth of his army, Caratacus's camp had been moved northwards across the nearby mountain ranges, to share out the burden of supporting so many men in such a small area. As the army grew, they started to raid the villages of the Dobunii tribe across the Eastern River, building a reputation for brutality against those who failed to rally to their cause and it was common knowledge that they would soon be ready to take on the Romans once more.

Caratacus himself was a large man and bore the scars of battle that proved his courage. As always, he wore his chainmail vest over a leather jerkin and carried his longs-word strapped to his side. His bodyguards wore a mixture of clothing, varying from chainmail armour to woollen jerkins, as though their fighting skills were excellent, they saw no merit in uniformity. Each man wore his own helmet of choice ranging from simple round helmets with leather straps keeping them secure to ornately decorated symbols of their tribe, crested with leaping wolves or soaring eagles.

Gwydion ran over to walk alongside the bearded king, matching him stride for stride. He had been expecting the call and knew that their destiny would be decided in the next few hours. When they reached the horse compound, they mounted the small but sturdy horses that were native to these lands and rode out to travel to Llanmelin, several hours ride away to the south.

'What news, my lord?' asked Gwydion as they rode.

'My spies tell me Caedmon will not see this sunset,' said Caratacus, 'and his legacy balances on the edge of a sword. The next chief will be chosen from his word and both of his sons claim power. One is considerate in his manner while the other is reckless and would attack Rome itself single handedly. We travel to lend support to the former.'

For the next few hours they rode hard and fast, desperate to reach Llanmelin before the chieftain died. Finally they were riding between the impressive oaken gates that Gwydion had first seen two years previously.

'What news of Caedmon?' asked Caratacus as he dismounted.

'He lives yet,' said the servant, 'though his men build a pyre in his name.'

Caratacus nodded. The preparations meant that though he was in time, the chief was not expected to live much longer.

'Take me to him,' said Caratacus, 'I would pay tribute.'

The servant led the way followed by Caratacus and Gwydion. On the way they passed a beautiful black stallion being harnessed with reins of gold and a blanket of fine silver links. The horse was being groomed until its coat gleamed in the afternoon sun and Gwydion couldn't help but feel it was a shame that such a magnificent beast was doomed to join the chief on his journey to the afterlife.

A few minutes later they reached a clearing in the centre of the fort and a crowd of warriors, thousands strong, sat silently in a giant circle around the solitary roundhouse at its centre. Caratacus paused at the outer edge of the crowd knowing that this magnificent display of warriors was but a fraction of those available to the Silures. If everything went to plan, these and many more could soon come under his command.

They made their way through the warriors and paused before the hut, waiting as word was sent inside to announce their arrival. A few moments later, Prydain emerged and spoke to Caratacus.

'We are honoured by your presence, Lord,' he said, 'please enter and pay tribute.'

Caratacus entered the hut leaving Gwydion outside. Prydain turned to Gwydion and the men grasped each other's sword arm in the recognised gesture of friendship.

'Good to see you, friend,' said Prydain, 'it has been a long time.'

'Too long,' agreed Gwydion, 'and I am shamed that it takes the death of a king to bring me here.'

'Worry not,' said Prydain, 'some things are beyond our control. Come; join me in tribute at the feet of a great man.' He turned and led the way into the roundhouse.

Burning rush torches lit the interior and the acrid fumes burned Gwydion's eyes. More warriors filled the interior, each sitting cross legged and focussed on the raised dais at the centre of the hut. Gwydion knew that every man there was a chief in his own right albeit of the smaller clans that made up the Silures tribe. In the centre, Caedmon lay dressed in the finery of a tribal chieftain.

The Shamen of the tribe stood around the dying king, chanting incantations to their gods to ensure a speedy passage. Behind the Dias, Gwydion could see two young men staring into the distance, seemingly oblivious that their king was dying before them. Ironbark and Hawk-wing were brothers and they knew that with the death of their father, one would inherit his empire and lead this tribe in an uncertain future. In the gloom, the old man held up his arm and the room fell silent. Despite the weakness in his voice, his words reached the back of the room.

'Silures,' he said, 'hear me. I have asked the gods to lead me in my thoughts and it is they who guide my words. Our lands are under threat from the Roman heel and our men tire from sharpening blades. I have been tortured by doubt these last days and the decision weighs heavy upon me. Our people need to be united and that means the strongest must lead.'

Caedmon started coughing and the room waited in silence, every man anticipating who he would name as successor. Slowly he caught his breath and the Shaman called for silence again.

'You wait for a name,' said Caedmon eventually, 'yet I cannot choose between my sons for both are worthy leaders. So, as is the way of our ancestors, I gift the choice unto the hands of the gods.'

The roundhouse erupted into argument and as the implications sunk in, many left the hut to pass on the news to those outside. Gwydion looked to Prydain in confusion.

'What does he mean?' he asked.

'It means a trial of arms,' said Prydain, 'between the two brothers. Whoever is victorious will lead the Silures without fear of question.'

'And what if the other survives?' asked Gwydion.

Prydain turned to face him.

'There can be no survivor, Gwydion,' he said. 'Caedmon has just sentenced one of his own sons to death.'

–

It took two more days for Caedmon to die and when he did his body was placed atop of the biggest funeral pyre Gwydion had ever seen. The bonfire had been built around a timber cage containing the magnificent stallion and a hundred slaves were tied amongst the branches to serve the king in the afterlife. As soon as it got dark, the two sons lit the pyre and the whole tribe gathered around the fort to gaze up at the light from the flames as Caedmon's spirit rose to the stars, accompanied by the screams of the burning slaves and the terrified horse. Gwydion thought it was a fitting end to the life of a king.

The following morning the ashes of the funeral pyre were spread out to form a large circular arena and the clan chiefs gathered as Caedmon's sons faced each other across the still smoking ashes of their father. Both were stripped to the waist and armed with a broadsword and a knife. Gwydion stood alongside Caratacus and across the clearing he could see Prydain standing amongst the descendants of Caedmon.

A Shaman walked to the centre and waited until silence fell.

'Let it be known,' he called, 'that by the dying words of our king and the ancient ways of our ancestors, today we choose a new leader. On pain of death, let no man intervene in the choice of gods.' As he retreated from the arena, the two young warriors closed in to speak one last time before the challenge began.

'It is a great path the gods have laid before us, brother,' said Hawkwing, 'and it falls on us to honour their will.'

'Then show no mercy, brother,' said Ironbark, 'for I will not hold my sword from taking your head.'

'I will meet your challenge, brother,' said Hawkwing, 'for we were born for this day, but let us pledge this: that whosoever stands at the end of the day, he takes arms against the Romans in the name of the other.'

'So be it,' said Ironbark and drew his longsword from the scabbard across his back. Hawkwing did the same and each man held his weapon high, crossing that of his opponent. In the distance, the sound of a thousand drums broke the silence of the morning air and each man took several steps back without breaking the gaze of the other.

'In the name of our father,' shouted Ironbark over the drums.

'In Caedmon's memory,' answered his brother and both charged forward to join battle.

–

Both men were strong and, as the sons of a chieftain, had spent their entire lives learning the skills of the longsword. Metal crashed on metal and both men applied every ounce of their strength to force each other back as each sword sought out unprotected flesh. High strokes followed body swings as each warrior reached into their very being, seeking the unexpected lunge that would catch their opponent unawares. Crash after crash echoed around the battlefield and each man enjoyed brief advantage, only to be forced onto the back foot as his opponent regained control. For an age the combat continued and Gwydion thought they would fight themselves to a standstill until suddenly, a rare mistake by Ironbark resulted in him misjudging a swing and completely losing his balance, albeit momentarily.

A communal gasp echoed from the experienced swordsmen around the arena; though it was a minor mistake, they knew it could be decisive.

Hawkwing also saw the mistake and without calculation, completed the now redundant swing of his axe in a complete circle to smash his blade into the body of his brother.

Though Ironbark's sword took the brunt of the blow, enough blade met flesh to cut deep into his side and he staggered backward in shock and in pain. Both men stopped and stared at each other, both gasping for breath after the exhausting fight. Ironbark looked down and knew he wouldn't be able to go on. The wound was deep and pouring with blood, and even if he had immediate attention from the Shamen it was unlikely he would survive. He looked back up at his brother.

'I am done, brother,' he said, 'you will lead the tribe as it should be.'

Hawkwing's aggression drained out of him as he realised he had struck a fatal blow. He had been close to his brother all his life and despite the warlike words before the fight, now the reckoning had come, the implications fell upon him like lead.

'Ironbark,' he said and started to step forward.

'Hold,' snapped Ironbark. 'You have taken my life; brother, do not take my honour.'

'Let me take you to the Shamen,' said Hawkwing, 'they may be able to stem the blood.'

'This is not about us,' said Ironbark, 'it is about our people. They need to see a strong victor; one they can look up to in battle. You are that man, brother; lead them as our father would wish.'

'Let me help you,' said Hawkwing.

'No,' snapped Ironbark, 'I am done here. All that remains is to finish what we have started.'

'I will not kill you, brother,' said Hawkwing quietly.

'You already have,' said Ironbark, 'and I do not hold grudge. Just bear me one favour, brother, allow me to die as a warrior before our people.'

'Ironbark, I...'

'Hawkwing, you have to do this, for both of us,' said Ironbark.

Hawkwing looked around at the thousands of men surrounding the arena and on the slopes of the fort. He knew his brother was right. Every man there was watching with bated breath, waiting to see the outcome and thus the direction of their people. Finally he realised his brother was right. This was something that had to be done. He turned once more to face Ironbark.

'You are right, brother,' he said, 'the Gods' will must be done. Take up your sword and strike low, I will make it quick.'

Ironbark stood up straight and gripped the handle of his sword in both hands.

'Strike strong and true, brother,' he said.

Hawkwing nodded slowly.

'Until the next life, brother,' he answered and refreshed his grip on his own sword.

With the last of his strength, Ironbark lifted his sword parallel to the ground and staggered through the ashes toward his brother with blood pouring from his wound. Without breaking eye contact, Hawkwing stepped forward and swung his own sword against his brother's neck, sending his head bouncing across the floor.

–

Hawkwing stood in the ashes of the arena, looking down at the body of his dead brother. The drums had stopped and the crowd had fallen silent. Even the rustling leaves seemed to pause for breath as the earth took in the momentous occasion. He took a step forward but staggered in pain and looked down at his own blood-stained body. Though he was covered in the blood of his brother, he hadn't realised that he had his own wound and now that the battle lust was falling, the pain came in waves. He staggered forward and bent to pick up his brother's body and everyone could see his strength was failing him yet despite this, they knew it was something he had to do.

Cradling the body of Ironbark in his arms, he walked over to where the ash stained head now lay and stood still, knowing full well he didn't have the strength to go much further.

Without warning he heard a voice behind him and he turned slowly to see Caratacus had walked from the crowd to join him.

'Lay him on this, Hawkwing,' said Caratacus and rolled out a blanket in the ash. Hawkwing nodded and knelt down to lay out the corpse of his brother. Caratacus gently picked up the dead man's head and placed it next to the body, before wrapping the blanket tightly around both. He picked up the bundle and knowing it was important that the new chieftain carried his brother from the field of conflict, placed him in Hawkwing's arms. The young man paused for a moment before slowly walking to the edge of the arena. Every step was laboured and he staggered often, knowing it was essential the victor walked from the field unaided. He was almost there when suddenly his legs gave way and he sprawled headlong into the ashes. This time, men ran out to help their chief and he was carried away to seek the help of the Shamen.

Back in the arena, the crowd looked on, unsure of the implications. The battle had been fought as was the will of the gods but there had been no outright winner. One brother was dead and the other lay at death's door. Caedmon's line had been chieftain for many generations and as there were no other brothers in line, it left a gaping hole in the tribe for a leader.

Caratacus saw the opportunity and walked back into the ring. He drew his sword and turned slowly, looking at the gathering of clan chieftains.

'Men of the Silures,' he called, 'hear my words. Two brave men fought for the right to call themselves chief today. A great battle was fought yet this great tribe now lies without leadership. Hawkwing's wounds are dire and the gods argue whether to claim him for the afterlife. I see your minds are troubled and for a warrior tribe as great as the Silures, this is an abomination.

'Despite the new fight that lies before Hawkwing, there is an even bigger battle to be won, the one against the Roman invader. As we speak, men are dying at their hand and women are raped for their amusement. Our children are sacrificed to their gods, and entire villages are wiped from our lands.

'You may not have seen this with your own eyes but I have, as have many of my men and make no mistake the Romans have set their eyes on the lands of the Silures. We cannot afford to wait until Hawkwing recovers to deal with this threat, we have to act now. Caedmon was with me on this and only his failing health stayed his arm. We could wait until Hawkwing recovers but by then it may be too late and if he dies, what then? Stand back and watch the great Silures rip itself apart?

'No, this is not worthy of you but there is a man who can lead this tribe to beat back the invader, not only a true leader of these lands but one who has faced them many times. That man is I, Caratacus, Chief of the Catuvellauni and true King of Britannia. Join with me and I will lead you against the Romans, pulling other tribes to our cause to eject this filth from our lands.

'Be the first to unify the tribes and fight alongside me and my men; Silures alongside Catuvellauni as brothers, sharing bread and killing Romans. Send out a signal to other tribes that we are as one and they should rally to our call. Forget tribal argument and become a nation for make no mistake, if we fight as one, then nobody can stand in our way.' He looked around the silent arena, waiting for someone to challenge him. Finally a man stepped forward.

'Caratacus,' he said, 'your name precedes you. You are a great war leader but we are Silures not Catuvellauni. When this is done, what is to stop you crowning yourself as chief of the Silures?'

'The answer to that is all around you,' said Caratacus. 'Not even I would face the Silures across the battlefield. I only offer leadership in a time of crisis. When this is done, I will return to Camulodunum and retake what is rightfully mine, the throne of Britannia. A Britannia free from the Roman heel and one that is a greater land made up of all tribes as brothers. Do this and never again will our children be thrown to the flames of our enemies.'

'Your skills in warfare are well known and men whisper your name in fear,' he continued. 'My spies tell me the Romans fear only one thing and that is if the tribes unite under common purpose. I can do that with or without you – I would prefer the former. Make no mistake, brothers, your lands, your very way of life is under threat. My army leaves within days to unite the rest of the Khymru so I will ask you one more time. Will the Silures march with Caratacus to drive our enemies from the lands of our ancestors?'

Caratacus feared the worse when the crowd stayed silent and was about to leave the arena when one man stepped forward.

'I will follow, Caratacus,' he shouted, 'as will my clan.'

'The Bear clan will follow,' shouted another man from the far side and Caratacus turned to acknowledge his support.

'The Eagle clan will follow,' shouted a third and gradually over half of those present stood forward to accept Caratacus's offer. When the calls stopped coming, Caratacus realised he had the oath of over half the Silures tribe, more than he could have dreamed. He held up his hand to silence the talk of the crowd.

'Silures, hear me,' he called. 'Today you have taken the first step to driving back the intruder. We do this in the name of Hawkwing and in the memory of Caedmon. Those who have decided to stay behind should strengthen their forts and ensure the safety of those families the rest leave behind. Those who have pledged their sword, be ready by dawn two days from now, for then we will march side by side as brothers and cleanse our country of Roman filth. This is my pledge.'

The whole gathering raised their weapons in salute and the surrounding hills echoed with their cheering.

Caratacus lifted his head and marched through the parting crowds. He knew this was a momentous day. Today, the fight back began.

Chapter 11

The Lands of the Durotriges

49 AD

Vespasian sat astride his horse looking toward the hill fort of the Durotriges. The Legion had made good time over the last few days and though there had been some skirmishes with patrols of Durotriges warriors, they had been but a minor inconvenience and quickly dealt with. This however was different. Below him, spreading across the open fields before the fort, hordes of warriors stood in deep defensive lines in challenge to the approaching Legion. At the moment they were relatively quiet for they couldn't see their approaching adversaries due to the forests, but they knew they were there and waited patiently for them to arrive.

Vespasian received report after report from his scouts and knew he had to make a decision quickly. The Legion was dispersed throughout the forest to his rear, waiting for his commands. Ordinarily he would have rained fire upon the enemy lines before committing any troops, but the carts containing the Onagers and the Ballistae had got bogged down in the mud from the constant rain and were still several days away. He would normally form a containment defence, keeping the enemy corralled within the battleground until the artillery arrived, but time was not a luxury he enjoyed.

Overnight, a messenger had arrived from Plautius telling him to halt his advance southward with immediate effect and await further orders. Further questioning of the messenger had revealed little else except the news that Plautius was being recalled to Rome and replaced with a new governor, Ostorius Scapula.

At first Vespasian had thought to turn immediately and retreat his Legion to the north east where the ground was easier to defend, but to halt an attack and retreat without inflicting a single wound on the Durotriges army would be seen as a humiliating defeat, not only to the enemy, but within the ranks of his own Legion and that was a situation he would not tolerate.

'Report,' he ordered as one of his Tribunes rode up alongside him.

'My lord, the men are ready and the cavalry in position.'

'Any sign of the carts?'

'No, my lord. They will take another three days to arrive.'

'Make it two,' ordered Vespasian, 'and gather my officers. There has been enough delay; I want to get this dealt with.'

'Yes, my lord,' said the Tribune and turned his horse to gallop away.

An hour later, eight mounted men formed a circle and faced inward for the impromptu orders from their Legatus. The group consisted of the Tribunus Laticlavius, the camp Prefect, the five Tribunes in charge of the battlefield tactics and the Primus Pilus, the senior centurion of the Legion.

'Today, we have had news of major political change in Britannia,' he said. 'Plautius has been recalled to Rome and a new governor warms his arse against the fires in the fort at Londinium. The new governor's name is Scapula and I know little of his military background. It may be that he is worthy of this post and I worry needlessly but we have received orders to hold firm and await further developments. This can mean only two things. Either he has a different plan for the Augusta and has his eyes on a different prize, or he will ask us to proceed with the colonisation of the southern tribes. Now, I may not know this man but I do know Claudius and he would not withdraw Plautius to replace him with a weaker man. Make no mistake about it, Claudius hungers for Britannia's complete subservience and I suspect Scapula's role is to hasten this outcome. As we have found, the southern tribes are quick to bend knee to our power and though the enemy to our front stamp their feet in defiance, they are the exception. We could do as ordered and retreat to the safety of the flatlands to our rear, but what message does this send to our men and more importantly, the enemy? They have set out a challenge and to see us retreating like frightened children would send an undesirable message throughout these lands and lend courage to those who would oppose us. In the longer term, that would cost Roman lives. So, what I intend to do is this. We will return to the lowlands as ordered but not before teaching those who stand against us a lesson. Our artillery is bogged down and we can't afford to wait but luckily, this Eadric seems so eager to impress, he ignores our strength and has chosen a battlefield favourable to us. If he thinks he can face a Legion on open ground and emerge victorious, then he is wrong. Eadric will have his battle and when that is done, we will burn his puny fort to the ground, sending a message to what remnants of this pathetic people still remain. Prepare your men. Deploy the Sagittaria on point along with the slingers to take the sting from their tail. First to fifth cohorts will form the spearhead, flanked by the Batavians.

'Tribune Lanatus,' he continued, 'order your cavalry to take that small hill to our front and defend it with the second auxiliary cohort. Take one Scorpio operator from every century and form them into a unit on the forward slope covering the approach from east. Without our artillery, they will provide some fire power. Once it is ours, withdraw the cavalry and hold them in readiness. The rest of us will form the reserve, standard operating procedure.

'Gentlemen, it is rare that we have the opportunity to use our training field skills in a manner that favours us as much as this. You are all here because you have vast military experience and have earned your rank. I do not foresee any problems here and expect an over-whelming victory but make no mistake, these people are no pushovers. We saw that at Medway and particularly Tamesas. Your men will have to be at their best if we are to keep our casualty numbers low.

'Centurion Barbatus, though I feel the first cohort has more than enough to prevail, I want you to blood the Ninth. They are untried in battle with many fresh from the training forts of Gaul. This will be a classic battle and an ideal opportunity to blood their Gladii.'

Barbatus acknowledged the command. As the senior centurion of the Legion, he was fully aware of the task before him. His position meant that he would lead the elite first cohort into battle and though his cohort had five centuries instead of the usual six, each was double strength and consisted of the best soldiers in the Legion. That meant he had an initial strike force of eight hundred crack troops. The Ninth cohort in comparison had four hundred and eighty men and though fully trained, few had battle experience. It was a good way to bring them on.

'Now,' said Vespasian, 'are there any questions?'

The group remained silent.

'Good. You have an hour to deploy, dismissed.'

–

Barbatus stood to the front of his cohort. Behind him and to either side, thousands of Legionaries had taken their positions out on the battlefield. They stood silently, waiting for the signal to advance. Each man wore their full Lorica Segmentata and held a Pilum in their right hand, the throwing spear designed to bend after impact to prevent re-use by the enemy. In their left hands they held the Scutum, the tall shields designed not just for defence against enemy weapons, but to punch into any attacker's faces, the bronze boss at their centres perfect for inflicting devastating blows.

Every man was well drilled and knew exactly what to expect. They would obey the orders of their centurion without question, acting immediately in response and at the height of battle, when all orders would be drowned by the sounds of fighting, they would carry out the drills they had learned during their training, confident that every man alongside them was doing the exact same thing. Over and above that, the trumpeters of the Legion would convey any strategic commands over the battlefield, with each man knowing what the other meant and what to do should each signal come.

In front of them on the far side of the battlefield, row after row of Durotriges warriors stood facing them at the base of their fort. Though there was no formality in their ranks, Barbatus could see they had strength in depth and stretched far on either side. Despite this, he knew there could be only one victor. If this would-be king had possessed any sense, he would have taken his people and run to the hills. Instead, he seemed intent on pursuing the one course of action that centuries of history had proved any enemy of Rome should never do – meet them on an open battlefield.

Across the field the sound of drums emerged from the ranks of the Durotriges and Barbatus knew the moment was nigh. Up on the hill, Vespasian recognised the overtures of battle and knew that they would work themselves into a frenzy before charging across the field.

'My lord, what is that noise?' asked one of the newer Tribunes.

'It is a trait of these people to build up their courage,' said Vespasian. 'They invoke their gods and the spirits of their ancestors before committing to the battle.'

'How long does it go on?' asked the Tribune.

'Until they are ready,' said Vespasian, 'but I see no need to fight this battle on their terms. Give the signal.'

The Tribune turned to the man beside him and gave an order. Immediately a lone trumpeter raised his instrument and blew a long solitary note that echoed around the hills. Below, every man in the ranks straightened up and flexed his sword arm. This was it; battle was about to commence.

–

At the sound of the Cornicine, Barbatus drew his Gladius and raised it high above his head before bringing it down sharply to point at the floor.

'Sagittarii ready,' he shouted and as one, every Legionary in the front two cohorts dropped to one knee, revealing row after row of archers lifting their bows to aim high above their heads. Barbatus raised his Gladius once more.

'Legion Secunda Augusta,' he roared, 'this is your time. For your country, your Emperor and your Legion; let them feel the pain of our steel.'

His hand dropped and the air was filled with hundreds of arrows flying through the air toward the enemy lines. Before the first flight landed the second was already in the air, raining a hail of death upon the Durotriges lines. Over and over the sky was darkened with their number and across the field, the enemy warriors crouched low to the floor raising their round shields above their heads. Following their orders, the Sagittarii emptied three of their four quivers before stopping the onslaught. The Legion got back to their feet and resumed their stance. Across the field the enemy lines were motionless and for a moment, Barbatus thought that the enemy had been wiped out by the arrows. That thought was soon erased as he saw them start to rise to their feet and it was soon evident that though some had indeed died, the shields had been expertly wielded and the number of dead was relatively small.

On the far end of the battlefield, a century of cavalry burst from the treeline and rode at breakneck speed toward the solitary hill, followed by a cohort of infantry. The relatively small contingent of warrior archers encamped on its slopes were taken by surprise and quickly overrun.

The Batavian infantry formed defensive lines at the base of the hill while hundreds of Scorpio operators carried their crossbows to secure positions overlooking the valley to the East.

Barbatus raised his Gladius one more time before levelling it toward the enemy's lines.

'Augusta, advance,' he roared and as one, every Legionary stepped forward, each banging the hafts of their Pila against their shields in time with their pace.

Across the battlefield, the Durotriges warriors were screaming insults and started their own advance to meet the Legion head on, stepping over their dead as they went. Every man wielded their weapon of choice and the Romans could see broadswords and clubs, battle axes and spears. Their faces were painted in strange designs and their hair was spiked into random shapes with animal fats. Most were bare-chested and many had scarred their own flesh with strokes of a knife's blade as a commitment to their gods. The overall effect was designed to strike terror into the hearts of their enemies but Barbatus was not impressed. He has seen it all before.

'Front rank, ready Pila,' he shouted and the command was repeated down the lines. Every man in the front raised their throwing spears to shoulder height and as the enemy closed in, Barbatus gave the order to release, sending another hail of death into the screaming hordes. As soon as their spears had been released, every Legionary drew their Gladius and presented their shields forward in an unbroken barrier of laminated wood and bronze. The ranks behind rested their own Pila over the shoulders of the front rank, presenting a hedge of steel as a further line of defence.

Barbatus slotted into the centre of front line and braced himself alongside his men. Behind them, the second and third ranks added their weight to brace the men in the front as everyone knew the initial impact was all important.

Suddenly the front wave of warriors smashed into the forest of Pila and though every spear found a target, the combined power of the assault drove them forward onto the shields of the Romans. The initial clash drove the Romans back a few steps and each man ducked behind their Scutum, offering the enemy no target for their terrifying weapons.

Up above, Vespasian watched the opening moves of the battle with interest, discussing the tactics with the young Tribunus Laticlavius by his side.

'It never ceases to amaze me,' said Vespasian, 'no matter where we encounter these Celts, from Hispana to Germania and right across Gaul, they always seem to think the frontal assault will prevail.'

'But my lord,' said the young man, 'our men go backward and are not striking back.'

'Patience, Natta,' said Vespasian, 'and watch the tactics unveil. Despite the enemy numbers, only the front rank can wield any weapon and while we are in close contact, even they are rendered helpless. Our men, however, have their sword arms free. As soon as the pressure eases, as it will, you will see the benefit of closed shields.'

Down below both armies had ground to a standstill and though the occasional warrior weapon found its way over the wall of Roman shields, they only found more protection above the Roman's soldiers heads, provided by the shields of the second rank.

Up above, the Cornicines sounded again and as one, the Legion thrust forward taking the initiative against the confused warriors. At the same time, each Legionary thrust their Gladius through the gap between their own Scutum and that of the man to their right. Many found flesh but before the enemy could take advantage of any gap, the ranks closed again denying any blade access to the men behind the shields. Again the Cornicines sounded and again they took a step forward, ensuring any wounded at their feet had their faces caved in beneath their hobnailed Caligae. Over and over again they stepped forward, each time cutting the men before them down with thrusts of their protected Gladii. Slowly the pressure eased and the warrior's ranks thinned out as they tried to attack seemingly easier areas of the Roman lines. This was exactly what Barbatus was waiting for and the front rank spread out, allowing themselves to wield their weapons to greater effect.

'*Advance!*' screamed Barbatus and the whole line stepped forward once more, though this time using the tactics they had trained for, every day of their military life. Each step forward was delivered alongside a thrust with their shield, smashing into their opponent's face before the killing blow was administered, with a thrust from their stabbing swords. Men screamed in pain as blades cut through flesh and fountains of blood spurted across Roman and Durotriges alike.

Despite their discipline, the Romans did not have everything their own way and in places, the lines broke under the pressure of the assault. Barbatus led the Legion's assault like a madman and men fell before him like corn before the scythe. So engrossed was he with the killing, he didn't notice the problem on one of the flanks.

'My lord,' shouted his Optio, 'Drusus has fallen.'

Barbatus spun around and saw the centurion leading the inexperienced Ninth cohort had been killed by a spear through his chest, but it wasn't the death of a comrade that concerned him but the chaos that ensued. The lines that were so important to the Legion's strengths were in disarray and Durotriges warriors were amongst them, finding their inexperienced opponents much easier fodder for their blades. Barbatus could see they were close to breaking and that would allow a substantial part of their enemy to access the rear of the lines and should that happen, it painted a completely different picture. The rear lines would have to turn and their strength would be halved. Reinforcements would be needed from the reserves back in the woods and that would be a shame on his cohort.

'Optio, carry on here,' he shouted, 'first three Centuries follow me, left flank.'

Two hundred and forty men broke off to follow the Primus Pius while the rear ranks ran forward to plug the gap. Barbatus led the men toward the breach, fighting their way through to reinforce the beleaguered cohort. The grizzled veterans fell upon the Durotriges in a frenzy of violence, hacking their way through bone and flesh to relieve the pressure. Barbatus saw a familiar soldier crawling away in the mud, his leg dragging uselessly behind him and blood pouring from an open head wound from the attentions of an enemy axe. He ran over and spun him around onto his back.

'Optio Galleo,' he shouted, 'what the fuck happened here?'

'The line gave,' gasped the man.

'What do you mean gave?' shouted Barbatus. 'These soldiers may be green but they are trained Legionaries. Nobody gives ground in my Legion.'

'The front line fell,' said the Optio, 'and the rear line ran in fear.'

'Ran,' spat Barbatus, 'who ran? What units? Name them.'

'The whole rear rank, my lord,' gasped the Optio, 'Centuries five and six. Without their support, the middle ranks gave ground and before we knew it, we had been breached.'

Barbatus looked around. His veterans had made a difference and the battle was swinging back in their favour.

'They will pay for this,' he growled, before looking down again at the man before him. He reached out and dragged a discarded shield to place under the dying man's head. Barbatus located the Optio's water bottle and poured a trickle between the man's lips.

'Galleo,' he said, 'I have to go for my men need me. I will not lie to you; your wounds are dire and there is much to do before the Medicus and the orderlies can seek out the wounded. Make peace with your gods, my friend, for I fear your life is done. It has been an honour to serve alongside you.'

'The honour has been mine, my lord,' said the Optio.

Barbatus nodded and gripped the dying man's shoulder momentarily.

'Until the next world, my friend,' he said and stood up to re-join the battle, leaving the man to die in the mud.

–

The next ten minutes were the bloodiest of the day for Barbatus as he and his men wreaked havoc on the warriors who had broken through the lines. Despite his training he had always preferred battle when it inevitably opened up into individual confrontations and the open nature of the breach meant man faced man over a large area. Ferociously he waded into the melee, flanked on either side by two of his trusted men. Each were fearless and they worked together, covering each other's backs as they carved their way mercilessly through the enemies ranks, hacking flesh from bone and cleaving skulls apart with their swords. The sounds of battle were deafening and men of both sides screamed in agony as their bodies were torn apart by sharpened steel or were crushed into the mud by the stamping feet of their enemies.

Up above on the hill, Natta turned to Vespasian.

'My lord, shouldn't we send in reinforcements?'

'Not yet,' said Vespasian. 'I know Barbatus of old and he is the best there is. He would not thank me for inter-ference.'

'Surely one man's pride is secondary to the needs of the Legion,' said Natta.

'Ordinarily yes, but this is different. Look to the Phalanx, the day is all but won and the enemy retreat to the fort. The only place to give is the left flank and Barbatus has that under control. Though it may cost a few extra recruits' lives, it is essential that Barbatus is allowed to redeem the situation. His pride is worth a thousand recruits and I would gladly trade them for a satisfied Primus Pilus.'

'What about those who ran?' asked Natta.

'There will be time enough for them,' said Vespasian.

A shout from one of the lookouts echoed across the hill.

'My lord, enemy chariots.'

Vespasian spun to stare into the distance and sure enough a dust cloud signalled the approach of almost a hundred chariots racing to join the battle.

'Shit,' shouted Natta, 'we have no Ballistae. Shall I send the cavalry?'

'Hold,' ordered Vespasian. 'This brings no surprise. If Tribune Lanatus is worth his salt, these chariots will not even breach the shadow of the fort. Watch and learn the value of intelligence, Natta.'

Every man on the hill looked toward the charging chariots and all felt a nervousness as the cloud got closer. If they reached the battlefield proper, the day would take on a completely different complexion and, without artillery, Vespian's reserves would have to be deployed in full. Even then the outcome would be messy and many of his men would die before the chariots would be overcome.

'Come on, Lanatus,' he said under his breath, 'don't let me down.'

-

On the rocky hill Tribune Lanatus had seen the threat and his heart beat in anticipation of the responsibility of what lay before him. The thundering chariots were just under a minute away and he knew the consequences if any got through. He had just under a hundred Scorpio operators under his command and every one was an excellent shot but despite this, the distance between them and their intended targets and the fact that the chariots were galloping at full speed, meant there would be a high percentage of misses. On top of that, the chariots were spaced quite far apart which meant that the chances of success were limited.

He had planned carefully, anticipating exactly this scenario. Eighty men stood in two rows of forty on the forward slopes of the hill, and another twenty lay hidden in the bracken at the bottom. Success hinged upon every man carrying out his role exactly and making every barbed metal bolt count. For what seemed like the hundredth time, he looked over at the pole mounted crossbows and the men behind them, each awaiting his orders. They were experts with their weapons and he knew he could rely on them. Finally he called out across the ranks.

'Listen in,' he cried. 'On my command I want the front rank to aim at the first ten chariots, ignoring those at the rear. As soon as the results are clear, the second rank will focus on those who escaped the first volley. Any that escape the first onslaught will be taken by the men below. Aim true and reload quickly. The safety of the Legion lays with us for make no mistake, if even one reaches our lines, many of our comrades will die. Now, look to your weapons.'

Every man leaned into their pole mounted crossbows, aiming at the rapidly approaching chariots.

'*Ignore the warriors,*' screamed Lanatus, 'take out the horses. On my command, ready, *fire.*'

Fifty metal pointed bolts flew from the crossbows and moments later, horses screamed in agony as the shafts thudded deep into their flesh. Some fell instantly, dragging down their companions and the trailing chariots on top of them. Behind those that fell, the following chariots were forced to slow down to avoid the carnage and this was exactly the result Lanatus wanted. Despite this, many bolts missed their targets and several broke free to continue the charge.

'*Second rank, fire,*' screamed Lanatus and once again the arrows flew across the sky to continue the slaughter. Horses crashed to the floor again and once more the charge was slowed. At the base of the slope, those Scorpios hidden in the bracken started to pick off the few stragglers who had somehow managed to get through unscathed. Behind the casualties, the majority of the chariots wheeled about in confusion, desperate to find a way through to help their fellow warriors. Lanatus saw his chance and cried out once more.

'Scorpios, target the rear chariots,' he called, 'they have fallen into our web, let's keep them there.'

Both ranks changed their aims and bolt after bolt scythed through the air to find their targets. Again, panicking horses bucked and screamed in pain, throwing their carts over. Realising they were trapped, the two men on each of the chariots dismounted to seek what cover they could behind their animals.

Several more volleys of bolts followed but made no impression on the warriors behind their chariots. Lanatus held up his hand.

'Hold,' he roared. 'The gate is closed; our job is done. The rest is down to the Batavians.'

Down below, a Batavian officer looked up at Lanatus, expecting a signal. Suddenly a flaming arrow streaked across the sky and he knew their time had come. As one, almost five hundred Batavian infantry rose up from the bracken and raced across the blood-soaked ground to face the dismounted Durotriges charioteers.

The result was slaughter. The Batavians outnumbered the charioteers five to one and apart from a few prisoners, the elite of Eadric's army were wiped out. At the treeline, Vespasian breathed a sigh of relief as the outcome became evident.

'Your gamble seems to have paid off,' said Natta.

'What gamble was that?' asked Vespasian.

'Focussing your entire Scorpio strength on that one hill.'

'There was no gamble about it,' said Vespasian. 'It was highly probable that they had chariots to call on. The plain before the fort is free of growth and that could only mean chariots or cavalry practised their manoeuvres there.'

'But what if it had been horses?'

'These islands are not well known for cavalry,' said Vespasian, 'and besides, whichever it was, I knew they had to come in via that hill.'

'How?'

'Because the ground to the south is too boggy,' said Vespasian. 'Learn from this, Tribune Natta, accurate and relevant intelligence often has a value equal to that of a thousand men.'

The two men stopped talking and watched as the battle below drew to a close. Hundreds of enemy warriors had broken and retreated to the fort, closely pursued by the cavalry. The front-line troops had withdrawn to tend their wounds while their replacements wandered the battlefield despatching wounded warriors with a stab of their Gladii. Severely wounded men were carried to the tents erected at the rear of the field and the Medicus orderlies did what they could to make them comfortable. Vespasian could see centurion Barbatus strutting around the battlefield offering words of comfort to the wounded and praise to those who had fought well.

'So what now?' asked Natta.

'Take charge of the Legion,' said Vespasian, 'and form defensive lines around the fort. I want no one entering or leaving that place until the wagons arrive. Deal with our dead but do not burn the enemy fallen, at least not yet. I have other plans for them.'

'Where are you going?' asked Natta as the Legatus mounted his horse.

'There is something I must do,' said Vespasian and turned to face the centurion who had been alongside him throughout the battle.

'Lucius, are your scouts well rested?'

'They are, my lord,' said Lucius.

'Good, then order them to arms. We have deserters to find.'

Natta watched them go before returning to view the scene below him. This was the first time Vespasian had entrusted him with the Legion and he was determined not to let him down.

Chapter 12

The Lands of the Deceangli

49 AD

Cassus lay hidden beneath a carpet of wet leaves, deep in the forests of the Deceangli. He had lain still like this for almost three days, sustained only by dried meat and any insects that foolishly wandered too close to his mouth. Though they tasted horrible, Terrimus had taught him well and he knew every morsel helped. His water bottle had but a mouthful left so he eked it out by squeezing water from the moss attached to the adjacent log. His shoulder ached from the wound he had demanded his comrade inflict on him before he left the fort and though it had been dressed, he knew that it demanded attention before it got infected.

Plautius's orders had been simple. He was to infilt-rate the tribes of the Deceangli and establish himself as a displaced warrior from Caratacus's army. At first he had sneered at the simplicity, but when Plautius had told him the fate of a Legion may well lie in his hands, his viewpoint changed and he focussed totally on the task before him.

Below him in the valley was a small village consisting of three roundhouses and a stable. A flock of sheep was penned in a walled compound and Cassus knew it was probably a family farm linked to one of the local clans.

The three days he had watched told him that there were no warriors as such, though there were two young boys who spent much of their time fighting with wooden swords, obviously as keen as other boys of their age to become clan warriors. It was perfect for his needs and he knew it was now or never; he had to make his move. He waited until it got dark before making his way down to the track that led to the farm. He knew the path was well trodden and that the older men used it every night to bring their small flock back to stay in the paddock, safe from wolves and brigands. Cassus found the track easily enough in the dark and sat against a tree as he waited for the flock to arrive. Finally he heard them approach and he quickly arranged himself on the side of the path as if he had passed out and waited to be discovered.

Five minutes later he heard the flock pass by and knew it would be followed by the men. A dog sniffed around his head and moments later he heard a man's voice in the darkness.

'Rhun, come here,' he said, 'the dog's found something.'

'Probably a rat,' came the answer.

'No, I think it's a body. Come and see.'

Cassus heard another set of steps on the rocky path and the second voice spoke again.

'Who is it?' asked the voice. 'Do we know him?'

Somebody poked Cassus with a staff and he groaned quietly.

'By the gods, he's still alive,' said the man and he knelt down to turn Cassus over.

Cassus opened his eyes weakly and looked at the man before him. Though it was dark he could see it was the white-haired man whom he knew looked after the flock.

'Water,' gasped Cassus and the old man pulled a water skin from beneath his coat to grant his request. Cassus gulped greedily as if he hadn't drunk in an age. When he had finished, he sat up and looked at the men with fear on his face.

'Who are you?' he gasped. 'Are you of the Dobunii?'

'No we are Deceangli,' answered the man, 'you are way outside Dobunii territory.'

'Thank the gods,' said Cassus. 'At least the Deceangli are a proud people and not afraid to shed blood in defence of their lands.'

'We would ask the same thing of you, stranger,' said the old man, glancing at Cassus's broadsword across his back. 'Who are you and where are you from?'

'I am a warrior of Caratacus,' said Cassus, 'or at least I was. I fought at Medway but was wounded in the battle. I and some others sought refuge with the Dobunii when we lost the day. At first it was fine but as the Roman patrols got more frequent, they lost their nerve and their king bent his knee. I could not countenance such abomination and left with my fellows to find Caratacus. I hear he survived the battle and rebuilds his army.'

'And where are your comrades now?' asked the man, looking around.

'I fear we were betrayed by someone in the Dobunii,' said Cassus, 'and were ambushed by a Roman patrol. My fellows fell but I escaped with an arrow wound. I have been walking for days, avoiding all contact, afraid that anyone I came across would be either Dobunii or Roman.'

'Well you are safe now, my friend,' said the man. 'Perhaps I can help.'

'Do you know the whereabouts of Caratacus?' asked Cassus.

'That I don't,' said the man, 'but I can offer shelter and food while you recover.'

'Madoc, wait,' said the other man, 'how do we know he is not a brigand and this is no more than a ruse?'

'You may be right, Rhun,' said Madoc, 'but I am not going to leave a wounded man to die out in the woods. We will take him back and take it in turns to guard him tonight. Tomorrow we will decide if he is friend or foe. Now help me get him up.'

They lifted Cassus to his feet and helped him walk to the roundhouses a few hundred paces away. Cassus played along as if exhausted but deep inside he was exhilarated. This was going exactly as planned.

–

The following morning, Cassus woke before dawn as the men of the roundhouse got ready for the day's work. The fire at the centre of the hut burned steadily, casting its light around the gloomy interior. Six men and boys made this space their home while four family units including the children shared the other two huts between them. Across from him Cassus could see one of the young boys sat against a wall, cradling an old sword and staring at him with concerned eyes.

'Madoc,' called the boy, 'he's awake but he doesn't look right.'

The white-haired man from the previous night entered the hut and walked across to face Cassus.

Cassus tried to rise but found his strength was gone.

'Stay down,' said Madoc, 'you need the rest.'

Cassus was confused. This shouldn't be happening. His ruse of being weak was nothing more than an excuse to get into the village, but he was actually feeling awful and had no strength in his body.

'What's happening?' he asked, his voice shaking. 'Have you poisoned me?'

'We haven't,' said Madoc, 'though I fear your wound has. It is infected and needs the attention of a Shaman.'

Cassus moved his body slightly and gasped in agony as the pain rolled across his back. The false wound had been a risk but he had insisted on it to help his cover. Now it could turn out it could end his mission before it had started. He almost demanded a Medicus but stopped himself, before he gave the game away.

'He has the fever,' said Madoc. 'Boy, go and bring the Shaman. Be quick or we could lose him. I will get some water.'

A few minutes later Cassus lay back on the straw mattress, his whole body shaking uncontrollably as the infection took hold. The rest of the men left the hut to take the livestock to the pastures but Madoc stayed until the Shaman arrived. Cassus slipped into unconsciousness and through his fever he could feel the pain in his back increase to excruciating levels. Hours later someone forced a bitter liquid between his lips and the subsequent coughing fit dragged him from the dark depths of pain-filled hell.

'Steady,' said a voice, and he opened his eyes to see the tattooed face of a teenage girl before him. Her hands held a beaker containing the disgusting liquid.

'You have to drink this,' said the girl.

'Who are you?' he asked weakly.

'The one who is saving your life,' said the girl, 'now drink.'

Cassus did as he was told though the liquid was disgusting.

'Where is the Shaman?' asked Cassus.

'I am the Shaman,' said the girl, but before he could voice his disapproval, the darkness dragged him down once more.

-

The next time he regained consciousness, the hut was busy and smelled of cooking meat. Men and boys sat around the fire having done a day's work in the fields and were now anticipating the evening meal, having slaughtered a lamb that had broken its leg in a fall from a cliff.

The smell of the meat made him gag and though he knew he needed nourishment, there was no way he could eat. His back ached as if it had been ridden over by a hundred horses and his skin crawled as if infected by a thousand insects. Again darkness called and the noises disappeared along with the smells. As he lay helpless in the hut, two of the men walked over and looked at his body.

'Do you think he'll make it?' asked one.

'I don't think so,' said the second, 'the infection was too deep.'

They left Cassus in peace and returned to the fire, impatient to taste the lamb stew in the pot above it.

-

The next time Cassus opened his eyes, the room was quiet and he could see the same strange girl sat cross-legged at the fire, crushing leaves into a bowl. His headache had gone and though exhausted, he felt as if a weight had been lifted from his body. His wound still hurt but it was more localised around his shoulder rather than burning across his back. He realised he had a raging thirst and tried to speak.

'Water,' he gasped but the sound that emerged bore no resemblance to what he had tried to say.

'Water,' he said again with more success and the girl turned to face him. Without speaking she walked to the door and poured a beaker of water from a skin hanging on the wall. When she returned, she lifted his head with one hand and poured a trickle between his lips, gradually increasing the flow as he drank.

'Steady,' she said, 'you can't have too much yet.'

Cassus finished drinking and lay his head back down on the sheepskin beneath his head.

'Well,' said the girl, 'you must have really angered some gods in your time.'

'Why do you say that?' asked Cassus weakly.

'Because none of them want you in whatever realm they command and you've been sent back here to suffer this miserable existence with the rest of us.'

'I don't understand,' said Cassus.

'It's quite simple,' said the girl, 'I have never seen anyone travel so close to the afterlife and return as you have done. What was it like there, stranger? Did you peer into the realms of the dead?'

'I don't recall,' said Cassus. 'How long was I gone?'

'I have sat with you for seven days,' said the girl, 'cleaning your wounds and administering the potions of the forest as if I was your personal slave.'

'You have my gratitude,' said Cassus.

'I don't need your gratitude,' said the girl, 'here, let me help you up.' She eased him to a sitting position and packed another fleece behind his back, taking care to avoid his wound. She brought another beaker of water and this time he managed to hold the cup himself as he emptied it again. 'Your thirst is a good sign,' she said, 'it shows your insides are awakening. In a while I will get you some broth, but let's see if you keep the water down first.'

Cassus stared at her. Her hair was messy and completely black with a hint of blue like a blackbird's wing and from the centre of her forehead an intricate Celtic design followed the left side of her face and down her neck to disappear below her cloak. Her eyes were deep hazel and apart from the tattoo, her young face was unblemished by disease or marks. Her eyes lifted to meet his as she realised he was staring.

'What are you looking at?' she snapped.

'Your markings,' said Cassus, 'are they a tribal sign?'

'They are the marks of my people,' said the girl.

'Deceangli?'

'We are of no tribe yet all tribes,' said the girl.

'I don't understand,' said Cassus.

'All my kind are Shamen,' said the girl, 'and we tend the sick in return for the things we need.'

'Do you have a name?' asked Cassus.

'You will not be able to say my true name,' said the girl, 'but these people call me Heulwen.'

'Then that is what I will call you,' said Cassus. 'What of your people, are they known by a name also?'

'We are known as the Asbri,' said Heulwen, 'and populate the hidden places where the real people fear to go.'

'The real people?'

'Those who live in the farms and the villages,' said Heulwen.

'So what payment are you receiving for saving my life?' asked Cassus.

'Five sheep,' said Heulwen.

Cassus smiled weakly.

'Five sheep. Is that the total of my worth?'

'That and an oath made on your behalf,' said Heulwen.

'An oath?'

'Yes, given by Madoc and one which you will keep,' said Heulwen. 'We have loaned you your life and one day may request it back.'

'You will want my life?' asked Cassus.

'Perhaps not your life, but certainly a favour,' said Heulwen.

'What sort of favour?'

'That is yet to be decided,' said Heulwen, 'but it will not exceed the one given to you.'

'And if I refuse to pay?' asked Cassus.

Heulwen smiled.

'You won't refuse,' she said, simply.

'And when will you demand payment of this debt?' asked Cassus.

'At a time of our choosing,' said Heulwen and stood up. 'I don't think you should try solids yet but there is Cawl left in the pot. Do you feel strong enough to drink of the broth?'

'I'll try,' said Cassus and watched the girl as she ladled a bowl of the rich liquid from the pot on the fire. A few moments later she crouched again before him and fed him the clear broth from a spoon. When he was done, she stood up and tipped the remains of the soup back into the pot.

'I am done here,' she said. 'Get some more sleep and try to eat something tonight when the men have their meal.

I will return tomorrow to change your dressings and give you a different potion. You are over the worst and now need to build your strength.'

Cassus watched her go before lying back down on the mattress. Though he had only been conscious for a short while, he realised just how weak he was and welcomed the sleep that enveloped him once again.

Chapter 13

The Land of the Durotriges
49 AD

Vespasian rode his horse slowly along the front of his Legion. Apart from the scout patrols guarding the Legion's rear, every man was on parade on the plains before the Durotriges hill fort. Rank after rank of soldiers stood shivering in the morning mist waiting for the horror about to happen before them, but it wasn't battle that chilled their souls but something far more sinister. Decimation.

Up above on the wooden ramparts, the remaining warriors of the Durotriges looked down on the massed ranks, nervous but defiant that their fortress would prevail. They had suffered assaults before by warring native tribes but had always prevailed. Though the army below was impressive, they were only men and men could be killed.

Vespasian halted in front of his officers and turned to face the massed ranks. Though they stretched far on either side his voice rang clear as a bell and was heard by even the farthest man.

'Men of the Augusta,' he roared, 'three days ago you won a mighty battle on the field beneath your feet. Some of our brothers in arms died but they sold their lives dearly and we are honoured to have called them comrade.

'However, there are also those who shamed the name of our Legion and ran in the face of the enemy. This is the ultimate disgrace and I will not let it go unpunished. Look to your left and behold those who ran.'

As one the Legion looked toward the place where Tribune Lanatus had slaughtered the chariots of the Durotriges and to the sound of the Legion's drums, over a hundred men were marched onto the battlefield, flanked by the auxiliary cavalry. As they passed, the soldiers in the front ranks jeered and spat at them in disgust and all the men of the shamed centuries had a look of fear on their faces as they knew the fate that lay in wait. When they reached the centre of the field, the drums stopped and the men halted before turning to face their Legion. Vespasian turned and faced the condemned men.

'Citizens of Rome,' he called, 'I will not address you by your unit names, for you no longer have a unit. You stand accused of cowardice in the face of the enemy, a charge punishable by death. Many of you are young and this was your first taste of battle but I cannot allow this act to go unpunished. Therefore, my judgement is this. Those of you before me are known to have run so are subject to decimation.'

A murmur rippled through the ranks; though it wasn't entirely unexpected, it was never a good thing to happen to a unit, especially to so many men.

'Centurions,' called Vespasian, 'split them into their Contubernia.'

Three centurions waded amongst the accused administering vicious blows from their Vitis sticks until there were fourteen groups of eight men each. Fourteen junior officers holding small leather bags marched from the ranks of the Legion and halted before each group.

'Begin,' shouted Vespasian, and one by one each man in their group of eight took it in turns to withdraw a pebble from the bag. There were ten pebbles in each bag and while nine men in each group drew grey pebbles, one ended up with a black one.

'Those who have drawn black, step forward,' shouted Vespasian. Across the group thirteen men stepped reluctantly forward, knowing only too well the fate that awaited them. Vespasian looked toward the last group.

'Who has drawn black in that group?' he called.

When nobody stepped forward Vespasian nodded silently toward centurion Barbatus. Barbatus marched over and a few moments later, dragged a crying young man from the rear rank before throwing him to the ground alongside the others. For a second, Vespasian was surprised how young the boy looked but immediately wiped the thought from his mind. Any sign of weakness now could have catastrophic effects later on when absolute obedience was demanded.

'Men of the accused,' shouted Vespasian, 'by fair means you have chosen one man from your own ranks to face penalty on your behalf. These are the men you trained with, ate with, bled with, and shared stories around the campfires at night. Many of you grew up with them and some may even be related. Until three days ago they were your brothers but because of what you have done in the face of the enemy, they now face the ultimate shame on your behalf. In a few seconds, a drum will strike one hundred beats. When it ends, these men will lie dead before us, victims of your beating, but know this. You will have no weapons but will kill them as you would a diseased dog and they will die knowing they have been kicked to death by those who are no better than them.

Know this also, any man holding back will share their fate and should any victim remain alive when the drum stops, then the whole Contubernium responsible will share his fate.'

Vespasian turned to the fourteen men singled out. Most had their heads hanging low though a few stared forward in defiance. The boy still knelt in the dust, sobbing quietly.

'You who are about to die,' he shouted, 'I offer no word of comfort except these. You are no worse than your executioners. Show us now the courage that failed you in the heat of battle and gain some respect before you face your gods.'

Without warning one of those selected for death pulled a hidden Pugio from his tunic and raced across the ground toward Vespasian, but before he had gone twenty steps, an arrow flew through the air and lodged deep into his heart. The man staggered a few more paces but fell dead before he had crossed half the distance.

Vespasian was furious and called out again.

'*Centurion Barbatus*,' he screamed, 'take the rest of that man's Contubernium and crucify them before the enemy fort.'

Barbatus signalled a century of men to follow him and they dragged the dead man's nine comrades away to carry out the punishment.

'Is there anybody else amongst you who would share their fate?' shouted Vespasian.

Nobody moved a muscle.

'Then let the decimation begin.'

–

A sole drummer started the beat and for a few seconds nothing happened. Finally one of the men in the groups

167

realised what was happening and ran forward to punch his former comrade in the back of the head, causing him to fall forward in the dust. Immediately the rest of the men realised what was expected and fell on their unfortunate comrades, beating them to death with their bare hands in an animalistic fury borne of fear. The young boy's screams of fear rang out across the battlefield as his comrades approached and though he knew it was necessary, even Vespasian felt a pang of regret at the young man's terror.

Two minutes later the drumbeats stopped and the disgraced men stood silently around their dead comrades. Some were in tears at the brutality they had just administered on those they once called friend, but others were just relieved it wasn't them laying in the dust, bodies broken and soaked in their own blood.

'Fall back in,' roared a centurion and each survivor shuffled back into line, thinking their punishment was over but Vespasian had other ideas.

'Let this be a lesson to all,' he shouted. 'We will not tolerate cowardice in this Legion. These men who have suffered decimation paid the ultimate price but their death does not pardon your disgrace. You survivors should give thanks for their sacrifice, for their deaths will enable you to redeem yourselves in the eyes of your Legion. In two days' time we will take this fort that looms above us. We will go straight up the slopes and show these heathen their puny fortifications are but nothing to us. We will show them the might of the Roman army and henceforth these lands will tremble in fear at the sounds of our marching feet. There will be no retreat, there will be no mercy and we will take no prisoners.' Vespasian paused and looked back at the two disgraced centuries. 'You men,' he continued, 'you who brought shame on yourselves and caused the death of your comrades will have the chance to redeem yourselves. You will lead the assault on the walls and it is you who will secure the breach we need. This is your chance to regain your units. Most of you will die but secure the breach and those who still live will re-join their cohorts with honour restored.'

He turned to the trumpeter at his side.

'Give the signal,' he said and seconds later the blast from the signaller echoed across the plain. Up above on the hill, a hundred Cornicines joined in the fanfare. Ranks of drummers beat out a marching pace and columns of carts emerged from the forest edge and out onto the plain. Rows of oxen pulled giant wheeled Onagers through the blood-stained soil to take up position in front of the fortress. Huge Ballistae lined up alongside them and the gathered soldiers watched in awe as cart after cart unloaded their cargo of missiles to feed the ever-hungry siege engines.

The drums and fanfares continued while the positioning took place and Tribunes shouted their orders above the din, deploying their cohorts around the fort. Thousands of fully armoured soldiers marched in perfect unison to their positions and no man in the fort above could fail to be impressed by the military accuracy of the manoeuvres.

Finally, at a given signal every sound stopped and over six thousand armed men encircled the fort in total silence. The artillery weren't aiming at the gate for Vespasian knew it would have extra fortifications, instead they were focussed on the timber palisade wall to one side. Every man held his breath as they awaited the final command for the assault to begin.

Vespasian rode his horse slowly toward the largest Onager in the line and spoke to the Decurion in charge of the giant catapult.

'Have the arrangements been made?' he asked quietly.

'Yes, my lord,' said the Decurion and nodded his head toward the adjacent cart covered with a hessian sheet. Vespasian nodded but forced himself to avoid having any reaction to the smell emanating from the cart. 'Then make ready,' he said, 'and send these heathen a message they will never forget.'

—

Up in the fort, hundreds of warriors lined the palisades, each armed with a variety of weapons from swords to bows, and each waiting for the onslaught they knew would surely come. Heaps of small stones suitable for slings lay piled against the ramparts and though the Durotriges army had some archers, their strength lay in their courage and skill in hand to hand fighting. Behind them in the village, hundreds of women and children crouched in the dust, looking nervously up at their men, confident in their ability yet apprehensive about the battle they knew was coming.

The whole clan had believed the promises of their young chieftain Eadric. For the past two years he had led them against other clans of their tribe and they had emerged undefeated against every one, gaining strength and tribute from those they dominated with their ferocity. Village after village had followed his call and when he had heard the Romans had invaded their lands, he had promised to swipe them as he did a fly. The tribe had followed him blindly and fully expected him to deliver a crushing blow on the invaders, but when they had been humiliated on the battlefield days earlier, they knew that this was no ordinary enemy.

Eadric strutted along the ramparts, staring at the deployment of the Roman army. Never had he seen such organisation. Hundreds of men marched as one, each giant square flowing across the field like rivers of blood as their red cloaks blew in the wind. Each side of the fort was surrounded by troops as every avenue of escape was closed and Eadric knew this was going to be a battle to the last. Despite this, his arrogance knew no bounds and he saw no other outcome except a glorious and bloody victory, raising him up as the true chieftain of the Durotriges. He also knew that a triumph over the Romans here would add argument to the need of one chieftain to rule all the tribes and who better than the one who defeated them here.

'Look at them,' he sneered to one of the men at the palisade. 'Prancing around like women in their solstice robes. Let them have their moments of pathetic ceremony. Their posturing fills me with mirth, not fear and I grow impatient for their attack. Despite their number these walls have never been breached since the time of my grandfather's grandfather.'

The old man at his side stayed silent; he knew better than to offer conflicting viewpoint to Eadric – his ears were closed to any but his favoured advisors who shared the benefits of youthful leadership.

'Look at the machines they have brought,' continued Eadric. 'What honour is there in fighting from afar? Where is their courage to meet us man on man? I'll tell you where, they have left it in that far off place they call Rome. Well they can fire their arrows if they like for our walls are made of stout oak, not horse flesh. Let them stud the palisade with arrows and when they are done, we will raise our heads to show them our steel.'

'They are not crossbows,' said the man quietly, no longer able to hold his tongue.

'What?' snapped Eadric.

'My lord, I have seen their like once before as a boy in Gaul. Those machines are not the Scorpions who lay waste to our chariots but Onagers capable of throwing missiles over our walls.'

Eadric stared at the strange machines.

'Like catapults?' he asked.

'Yes,' said the man.

'Catapults cannot reach up here,' said Eadric but his voice betrayed his doubt.

'These are much stronger,' said the old man. 'The other machines are Ballistae, similar to the Scorpion crossbows but much bigger.'

'Why fire bigger arrows?' asked Eadric. 'One arrow can kill but one man no matter what the size. It is a folly.'

'Perhaps so,' said the man, 'but knowing the Romans, I think perhaps they have other uses in mind.'

'Time will tell, old man,' said Eadric, the arrogance returning to his voice. 'Let them send their worst for when it is over, our steel awaits.'

The old man nodded silently. He had tried to offer advice but Eadric had already made up his mind. He watched the leader walk away along the rampart before fingering the tiny idol of a bull in his pocket. Somehow, he knew he would not survive this day.

—

Vespasian looked around the battlefield. Hundreds of small fires had been set before the ranks and groups of archers stood waiting at each fire. The Onagers were similarly primed and the large leather slings were soaking in buckets of water, ready to be loaded with their terrifying projectiles. Carts of clay pots lay alongside each Onager as well as small mountains of rounded river rocks, hewn into shape by an army of slaves back in the forests. Every Ballista was primed and loaded with their strange ammunition designed not to kill or maim but instil fear and terror in the enemy.

Finally he knew they were ready and nodded to the Tribune in charge. Without any further ceremony, fifty sets of twisted ropes released their stored tension as the giant crossbows fired their strange missiles high above the walls of the fort to reach deep inside. There was no damage nor any casualties caused, though the Legatus knew the impact would be just as great. Over and over the Ballistae sent up their strange missiles until finally they fell quiet as the ammunition ran out.

—

Inside the fort, the men on the palisades instinctively crouched as the missiles sailed silently over their heads to land amongst the village and they all turned to see what damage would be caused but were confused when the projectiles just landed amongst the huts and rolled harmlessly along the floor.

'What trickery is this?' growled Eadric. 'But before he could say anything else, a woman screamed as a child picked up one of the missiles and held it up for all to see.

'By the gods,' gasped Eadric, and a collective cry arose from the gathered families as they realised they had been bombarded by the heads of the men who had been killed in the battle days earlier. Children started screaming and women crying as they realised what was happening and even Eadric swallowed hard as he realised the implications. Though the dead men had fallen in battle, without their heads, their spirits would be denied access to the afterlife.

He realised this could have a devastating effect on his men and turned to face the warriors on the ramparts.

'*Ignore the insult*,' he screamed. 'Our men died a glorious death and those who desecrate their memory will pay for this sacrilege. Face your fronts and show them their pathetic gestures are not recognised by Britannic warriors. Men of the Durotriges, let them hear your answer.'

As one, hundreds of warriors roared their defiance from the ramparts, waving their weapons aloft and screaming insults at the Romans. Down below, Vespasian smiled and turned to the Tribune at his side.

'That woke them up,' he said, 'are you ready?'

'Yes, my lord,' said the Tribune.

'Then prepare to let them feel the heat of my wrath,' said Vespasian and rode out to face his Legion.

'Men of Rome,' he shouted, 'before you is the lair of the devils responsible for the deaths of your comrades. These are the men who would have feasted on your hearts given the chance. They think their evil ways are better than the civilisation we offer. These are the people who see rape as a God given right and child sacrifice a way of life. They see our ways as weak and belittle our culture. Well, today we will show them who are the weak ones and send them a message this land will never forget. Place steel in hand and harden your gaze for today we make our mark.'

He drew his sword and held it high.

'*Onagers* ready,' he screamed.

Behind him men placed large pots of oil into the sodden leather slings and lit the woollen wicks sticking out of the necks. The Ballistae that had just sent human heads over the walls were loaded with rocks of a similar size and every man braced for the order.

'*People of the Durotriges*,' he screamed, 'prepare to die, for we are the Legion Secunda Augusta, and we are Roman.'

His sword arm dropped sharply and immediately hundreds of missiles flew through the air toward the fort above. Vespasian stared in satisfaction as volley after volley flew over his head, and though the adrenaline coursed through his veins, he knew he would have to be patient if he was to be successful. He could not afford to get this wrong.

-

For an hour the barrage continued and as each cart was emptied of rocks, another immediately took its place, maintaining a constant supply of ammunition for the machines. Occasionally an Onager or Ballista was withdrawn from the line to have its ropes changed or sling replaced but when it was, one of the many in reserve was hauled forward to take its place.

Inside the fort, hundreds of huts were ablaze, their dry roofs of willow and thatch feeding the hungry flames. People panicked and tried to avoid the searing heat of the inferno, but the rocks breaking down the walls of the huts meant the whole fort was in chaos and a maelstrom of fire and flying missiles. Hundreds of fire pots fell from the sky and as they smashed on the floor, the burning oil within threw its clinging death over building and human alike.

On the ramparts Eadric and his warriors watched in horror as the enemy artillery ignored the defences and concentrated their fire on their families and homes within the fort. The slaughter was devastating and when the hail of death finally eased off, the village within the fort was nothing more than a burning mountain of crumpled wood, thatch and human flesh.

Visibly shaken he turned again to look down at the enemy below. He could see more carts being brought up to the machines, each no doubt full of fresh missiles ready for the next attack to begin.

–

Vespasian watched the next phase unfold. He knew he had shattered the enemy's confidence; now it was time to shatter their defences. A specialist Architecti led a team of Immunes to manoeuvre a giant Onager to the front of the ranks and secured it down with piles of rocks and stakes driven into the ground. A cart reversed up to the machine and the Immunes rolled a large boulder off the end and into the double strength sling.

The Architecti watched as his men wound the winch to stretch the double ropes made from horse sinews and when the arm of the catapult had reached a pre-marked notch in the frame, one man drove a block through a preformed hole to hold the arm in place. Finally he looked up at the Legatus in anticipation.

'Ready, my lord,' he shouted.

'Then do your work, Darrius,' shouted Vespasian. 'Give me a gate in their walls.'

The Architecti saluted and turned to his men.

'On my mark,' he shouted. 'Ready, fire!'

A soldier swung an enormous hammer and knocked the retaining block out of the frame, releasing the tension of the ropes, causing the giant arm to rotate on the fulcrum and send the rock flying toward the wall.

Every man in the Legion watched in anticipation but let out a collective groan as the rock fell short and bounced harmlessly against the wooden walls. Up above the warriors jeered but Vespasian was unmoved.

'I'll give you that one, Darrius,' he said. 'Make the next one count or you will be replaced.'

'Yes, my lord,' said the Architecti and turned to his men. 'Reload,' he shouted. 'Three more notches on the winch.' The process was repeated though this time the arm was visibly lower in its frame.

'Ready,' shouted Darrius. 'Fire!'

Once more a boulder flew through the air and this time the massed Roman infantry cheered wildly as the rock not only found its target but smashed right through it, causing several defending warriors to fall to their deaths on the rocks below.

'That's more like it,' said Vespasian. 'Make sure all your shots are as accurate. I want a breach wide enough for fifty men marching line abreast by midday.'

'Yes, my lord,' said the Architecti and turned to focus on the task.

'You heard the Legatus,' he growled, 'let me down and you will form the point of the infantry assault, now bend your backs into it.'

Vespasian turned to the Tribune in charge.

'Stand down half the men,' he said, 'every other cohort to get fed and rested. Let me know when the breach is complete, I will be in the command tent.' As he rode away, he heard the crash of the second boulder as it smashed through another part of the wall. As well as the giant Onager, dozens of smaller ones added their power to the assault and slowly but surely, the wooden palisade that had stood for decades fell in smithereens to the rocks below.

Chapter 14

The Lands of the Deceangli
49 AD

Cassus spent the next ten days in the men's hut of the farmstead and every day Heulwen attended him to dress his wounds and apply different pastes from the leaves of the forest. Gradually his strength returned and he was able to help out around the farm, even spending some days out alongside Madoc with the flocks. Over time he became accepted by the family and spent many happy days alongside them yet, beneath it all, he always remembered the reason he was here in the first place. One evening he returned to the huts and as he was about to go in, a voice called from the treeline.

He wandered over thinking it was one of the other farmers but when he reached the edge of the forest, there was no one to be seen. Nervously he felt for his knife in his belt but paused in disbelief as he recognised a design, freshly carved into a tree. The sign of a Pugio.

'Who's there?' he asked nervously.

'My name is irrelevant,' said a voice. 'I have a message – listen carefully. You are to infiltrate the ranks of Idwal, King of the Deceangli. There are plans afoot to come this way and we would know his strengths.'

Cassus nodded.

'And how will I relay this information?' he asked.

'You will be contacted on the first night of the solstice celebrations,' said the voice. 'Ensure you are alone and bring what information you can.'

'How do I gain this trust?' asked Cassus, but there was no answer. The man had gone. Cassus returned to the hut and ate his meal alongside the other men in silence.

'Does your wound cause you pain?' asked Madoc.

'No,' said Cassus, 'I am almost as strong as I ever was. Why do you ask?'

'You are very quiet,' said Madoc, 'and your face betrays your concern.'

'You are a visionary man,' said Cassus, 'and indeed you are correct. I am very happy here but my heart demands I seek my fate elsewhere.'

'But why?' asked Madoc. 'Are you not warm at night and fed good mutton?'

'I am,' said Cassus, 'but a man needs more than meat and warmth.'

'If it is a woman you want,' said Madoc, 'there are slaves in the village available for a mere coin.'

'No it's not a woman my heart desires,' laughed Cassus, 'but retribution. My sword grows dull through lack of use and my knife should be washed with Roman blood, not that of mere lamb. Your hospitality has been better than any man could desire, but I have unfinished business. I need to find fellow warriors with whom I can ride in defence of our country. My kinsmen are long gone but surely there are others like me who strain at the leash to kill the Roman filth.'

'You seek Caratacus?' said Madoc.

'Eventually, yes,' said Cassus, 'but I hear tell he lies in the lands of the Silures, a perilous journey for any man.

Despite this, it is a journey I feel I must make. I can fight as well as any man but if I stay here any longer, I fear my skills will rust quicker than my blade.'

Madoc sighed.

'I knew this day would come,' he said, 'yet I hoped you would stay. My daughter has been caught looking your way once too often and though at first I had my doubts, I thought perhaps one day you would make a good son.'

Cassus smiled.

'I am flattered by your thoughts and indeed by the interest of your daughter. She is a pretty girl and will make a fine wife but I fear it will be for someone else. My fate lies alongside Caratacus or those who share his vision. Tomorrow I will set out to find him or die on the journey.'

'There is another option,' said Madoc. 'The Romans are a threat to all clans and the Deceangli are no different. We have a proud and honest king who also hates the invaders with every sinew of his body. He has an army as large as Caratacus and always welcomes men at arms. Why not seek a place in his army and fight alongside us?'

'Who is this king?' asked Cassus.

'Idwal, King of the Deceangli.'

'I have heard of him,' said Cassus, 'and good things were said, but would he welcome a Catuvellauni stranger to his cause?'

'I think you would be welcomed with open arms,' said Madoc, 'especially if you can wield that sword half as good as I think you can. Besides, I had dealings with his father as a young man and he knows my name. I will give you reference. Is this a path that will suit your needs?'

Cassus could hardly believe his luck. After only a few weeks he was on the verge of getting a place deep in the ranks of the enemy forces. It was almost too good to be true.

'Until I meet with Caratacus once more, it will suffice,' he said. 'You have my gratitude.'

'Then finish your meal,' said Madoc, 'and if this is to be your last night amongst us, we will share a skin of wine.'

–

Two days later Cassus stood in a field with hundreds of local men, many talking in groups amongst themselves. All had weapons of some description though most were aged due to lack of use. Some even wielded farming implements in place of military weapons as they waited for Idwal to arrive. Cassus stood alongside Madoc, talking quietly. Finally a commotion to one side grabbed everyone's attention and a column of Deceangli warriors galloped into the field and dismounted before those gathered in the morning light. One man still on his horse stood up in his stirrups and addressed the would-be recruits.

'Men of the Deceangli,' he called, 'your presence does you honour. Today you will join thousands of others making a stand against the coming Roman wave. There is a place for all but we need to see your strength. These men will come amongst you and select according to strength and prowess.'

'Is that Idwal?' asked Cassus.

'No, Idwal is the quiet one next to him,' said Madoc.

Cassus stared at the king. His leggings were of leather, as was his tunic. A chain mail jerkin covered his upper body and a longsword was strapped across his back, as was the way of most Celtic warriors.

'He is young for a king,' observed Cassus.

'He is,' said Madoc, 'but his head holds wisdom beyond his years. He and his men have attacked the supply lines of the Romans for the past two years but now the main threat comes closer, he seeks to build his army.'

'Some army,' said Cassus, looking around. 'These are but old men and boys. What use would they be against the enemy?'

'The strong men have already joined Idwal's ranks,' said Madoc. 'They lie in and around the Cerrig to the north. These men will be used to strengthen his numbers should we face the Romans on the field of battle. Every man is here of his own free will.'

Cassus looked around and knew that should they advance against a Roman line, they would all be dead within a minute at the hands of the Sagittaria.

'What's the Cerrig?' asked Cassus.

'The stronghold of Idwal,' said Madoc. 'It is a hill fort like no other, built from the very rock upon which it stands. No man has ever breached its walls.'

'No fort is impregnable,' said Cassus.

'This one is different,' said Madoc. 'It has its own water source and at night, herds of cattle are corralled within its walls. If necessary, they could live for a year under siege without going hungry.'

'It sounds magnificent,' said Cassus.

'It is,' said Madoc, 'and is the ancestral home of the Deceangli Kings.'

Both men fell silent as the king's men worked their way toward them, separating the volunteers into two groups. Soon the split became evident, as the very old and the very young were at one side while those who looked as if they could handle themselves in a fight stood to the other.

Finally they reached Cassus and one warrior looked him up and down in interest.

'And who are you, stranger?' he asked.

'I am Cassus of the Catuvellauni,' said Cassus.

'Catuvellauni?' the soldier sneered. 'I hear they all died at Medway.'

'Not all,' said the other warrior, 'some fled for their lives like frightened puppies. I guess you must be one of the second group.'

Cassus didn't rise to the bait but waited quietly.

'So did you run, stranger?' taunted the second man. 'Or did you fight?'

'I fought alongside Caratacus at both Medway and Tamesas but we were bettered by a stronger foe. There is no shame in that.'

'There is every shame in that,' spat the man, 'Idwal would never have run like Caratacus. The Deceangli would have faced them down and driven them back to the sea.'

'Have you ever fought them?' asked Cassus.

'We have,' said the man. 'Our horses tire from pulling the Roman carts stolen from their supply lines. We have not lost one warrior in these attacks.'

'Then you have not fought Romans,' said Cassus, 'but their civilian supply chain. I would wager any man on this field would enjoy similar success.'

'You insult us, Catuvellauni,' snarled the man, 'guard your words carefully.'

'I mean no insult,' said Cassus, 'but I have seen these men fight at close hand and they are a worthy foe.'

Both men stepped aside as a horse approached and Cassus saw Idwal looking down at him.

'You wear your sword like a warrior, stranger,' said Idwal, 'do you have the right?'

'I do, my lord,' said Cassus, 'though lack a cause to support its blade.'

'We have a common cause,' said Idwal, 'and there is a place here for all men, but some skills are needed more than others. Are you a wolf or a sheep?'

Cassus looked at the larger group gathered at the far end. It was obvious they were the weaker group and were there to make up the numbers, nothing more.

'I am neither,' said Cassus.

Idwal dismounted and walked over to face him.

'You are a strange one,' he said, 'but any man can strap a blade to his back and call himself warrior.' Idwal stepped back and drew his sword. 'Put meaning behind your words, stranger,' he said and the surrounding men formed a circle to witness the contest.

Cassus drew his own sword and held it above his shoulder. He stared into the king's eyes and a moment later, swung his sword downward to deflect the lightning quick blow that came at him. Without a pause, Idwal rained blow after blow toward Cassus and the surrounding men gasped in awe at the prowess of the king. Cassus defended himself frantically but even though his hands were working quickly, his mind worked even faster. He had no doubt he could better this man but that would serve no purpose in the greater scheme of things. Yet if he allowed Idwal to defeat him too easily he could easily end up little more than target practise in the front ranks of the farmers.

Idwal was a formidable foe but as soon as he over swung by the slightest margin, Cassus launched his own attack and the king retreated, deflecting Cassus's sword with expert swipes of his own. Both men were well matched and the crowd widened to watch the excellent display of sword play. For several minutes the advantage swung back and fore and finally Cassus felt the smallest of changes in the king's blows, a sign that he was tiring. Without making it obvious, Cassus started to lighten the strength of his own blows and allowed Idwal to seemingly better him. Idwal grasped the opportunity and forced Cassus back across the clearing until his back was against a tree. Finally, Cassus lowered his sword and yielded to Idwal, gasping as if exhausted. It was a gamble but one he knew he had to take.

Idwal placed his sword against Cassus's throat and panted heavily as he stared into Cassus's eyes. The whole crowd fell silent and waited for the deadly thrust, but the king lowered his sword and held out his arm.

'You are a formidable foe, stranger,' he said, 'and for a moment I thought I would be bettered.'

Cassus grabbed the king's forearm in mutual respect.

'I also thought I had the day, my lord,' he said, 'but now see why you are king.'

'What is your wish, stranger?' asked Idwal. 'Why are you here amongst these sheep?'

'I want to fight, my lord,' said Cassus, 'and revenge the slaughter of my people.'

'Then fight you shall,' said Idwal, 'though not amongst the weak but as part of my warrior fist. Do you have a horse?'

'I can supply a horse, my lord,' said Madoc.

Idwal turned to look at the old man.

'Madoc,' he said, 'friend of my father, it is good to see you again.'

'And you, my lord,' said Madoc.

'You can vouch for this man?' asked Idwal.

'I can, my lord, and will furnish him with a steed.'

'And what about you, Madoc,' asked Idwal, 'do you see yourself facing the Roman steel?'

'I'm afraid I am too old to wield a weapon in anger, my lord, but would support you in other ways perhaps.'

'Like what?'

'I can hunt, sharpen weapons, and groom horses. Perhaps my skills could allow your men more time to kill the enemy.'

'Then so be it,' said Idwal and turned to Cassus. 'Welcome to the Deceangli, stranger,' he said, 'gather your things and be at the Cerrig in two days' time.'

Chapter 15

The Lands of the Durotriges

49 AD

The Legion reformed before the Durotriges fort. Though missiles continued to fly over their heads, the sounds of crashing timber had long ago ceased as there were no more walls to demolish and the rocks sailed into the interior of the fort to create havoc amongst any survivors. Huge clouds of smoke swirled high into the sky and the hillside was a tangled mess of timber and bodies, signs of how effective the catapults had been.

At the base of the hill five hundred engineers crouched behind a wall of shields provided by their Legionary comrades. The engineers were split into fifty groups of ten with each group holding a giant ladder designed to make the assault of the Legion's infantry up the hill much easier. Behind them, another three rows of shields hid the archers that would cover the assault and even further behind them were the Batavian infantry that had been selected to take the ramparts. But in amongst all these specialists was one frightened group of young men. The hundred or so who ran at the initial battle and were to be the van of the assault. They would be the first men to climb the ladders and though it was a military honour, it was also a sentence of almost certain death. Many made peace with their gods while others stayed silent, accepting their fate as inevitable, accepting their time had come.

Vespasian gave the order and fifty gaps appeared in the shield wall. Immediately the engineers grabbed their ladders, five on each side, and ran toward the slopes. At first, they managed to get quite far and some were astonished to find they managed to deploy their ladders on the lower slopes without as much as a shout from above. The second wave ran forward and used the first ladders to aid their ascent but as they climbed, a frightened voice from above raised the alarm and arrows started to rain down upon them.

Vespasian spotted the threat and immediately ordered his own archers to provide cover. Within moments, volley after volley of arrows filled the air and fell among the defenders on the remains of the wall.

'Onagers fire,' roared Vespasian, and the catapults leapt into action again, this time firing piles of smaller jagged rocks at the wall breach. The giant hole in the defences became indefensible due to the number of missiles and the engineers took the opportunity to lay ladder after ladder on the steep slope, providing easy passage for those who would follow in a few minutes.

Barbatus stood before the disgraced Centuries and knew their time was almost upon them. He turned to face them and saw the fear in their faces.

'You men listen in,' he said, 'yours is the disgrace and the penance is yours but now is the time for you to regain your honour. Those who are about to die, do so in the knowledge that your debt is cleared but for those who prevail and provide a secure route for our infantry, return with pride restored and in the knowledge there will be a place for you in the first cohort.'

The men murmured amongst themselves. The first cohort was the elite of the Legion and led by the Primus Pilus himself. If they survived this assault, they had a chance of a future after all. Buoyed by his words, their will became hardened to the task and hands grasped the hilts of Gladii a little firmer. Their larger oblong shields had been discarded and they carried the smaller round shields favoured by the Batavians.

'Upon my signal,' shouted Barbatus, 'you will run straight for the assault ladders. The whole hill is covered and the engineers have laid them right up to the breach. The archers will provide cover as you approach but climb as fast as you can and if the man before you is struck, tip him clear; you cannot afford to stop or every man behind you will die. Today you have a second chance. Do this and your debt is paid. Now, are you ready?'

The young men roared their commitment and Barbatus nodded in approval. It was the best he could hope for.

The archers had replaced their steel tipped arrow for those wrapped with wads of wool and soaked in oil. Similarly the Ballista changed their missiles for fire pots and lowered their aim to the slopes. Combined with the thousands of arrows now burning on the forward slope, the hill was covered with black smoke, providing perfect cover for the assault troops. At a signal, archers, Ballistae and Onagers lifted their aim to bombard the defences again and Barbatus screamed the order everyone had been waiting for.

'Assault troops, for your names and for your honour,' roared Barbatus, '*advance!*'

The disgraced men stood up and ran toward the hill. Behind them, four cohorts of Batavian infantry waited to follow them up the ladders, over two thousand men specialising in open hand to hand fighting.

The men hit the ladders running and swarmed up the slopes, driven by adrenaline and fear. At first their approach was covered by the smoke but as it started to thin out, individual defenders stood up from the rubble and roared their defiant challenge to those below.

'Scorpios, target those men for as long as you can,' shouted a Tribune, and the accurate crossbows unleashed their hail of death for the second time in days. Up above, men fell with crossbow bolts lodged in bodies or heads but despite the devastation, there always seemed to be others to take their place. The rocks ran red with blood but within a minute, the first Legionaries reached the shattered defences. Behind them the hill swarmed with the main body of the assault and thousands of soldiers covered the slopes like ants. The first wave of inexperienced Legionaries crested the ridge only to be met with Celtic steel and man after man fell backward onto their comrades, with their skulls cleaved open.

The defending warriors fought like madmen, desperate to repel the assault and defend their homes. For what seemed like an age the attack seemed to falter as the bottleneck ground everything to a halt, but suddenly one soldier broke through to stand on the shattered defences, fighting off three defenders with his sword and shield. A roar of approval echoed up the slope and though the man fell under the enemy blades, the fresh impetus pushed upward and this time several men broke through to take on the fight. Having made the breach, albeit small, it gave the assaulting troops the opportunity to pour more men onto the defences and the trickle became a flood. As the defenders were caught up in hand to hand fighting, more ladders were thrown against what few walls remained and the Batavian troops swarmed over the defences like a surging tide.

The defences were breached and down below Vespasian breathed a sigh of relief, knowing full well that it was now just a formality. One cohort of the Batavians had been tasked to take the gates from the inside and when they did, the third and fifth cohort would march straight into the hill fort via the main entrance, every one equipped with full shields, armour and Pila. Their punch would be unstoppable and the hill fort would fall within hours.

'Will you be going in to take the fort, my lord?' asked Natta.

'No,' said Vespasian, 'I've seen it all before. There is nothing up there that interests me. When the message comes that the day is won, bring me the head of Eadric.'

'Yes, my lord,' said Natta and looked up at the fort. Troops were swarming over the walls unopposed and he knew that on the other side of the hill, any defenders trying to escape would be mopped up by the waiting cavalry. From here on in, it would be slaughter.

-

By the time night fell, the battle was over. The air was thick with the smell of smoke and Durotriges lay dead throughout the fort and on the surrounding hill like autumn leaves on a forest floor. A group of a hundred or so prisoners crouched miserably on the floor of the battlefield, each with their hands tied behind their backs. One man in particular was kept separate and guarded by a circle of Legionaries who took great pleasure in taunting him.

Vespasian rode down from his command tent with his usual unit of mounted bodyguards.

'Tribune Natta,' he said as he approached the prisoners, 'report.'

'These are the only survivors,' said Natta. 'Most are wounded so could not offer resistance at the end. Their lives were spared.'

'Why?'

'The battle was over, my lord. We saw no further need for killing.'

'That is my decision, not yours,' said Vespasian. 'Did you find the body of their leader?'

'We did better than that, my lord, we found him alive hiding like a child within the rubble of a hut.'

'Where is he?' asked Vespasian.

'Over there,' said Natta and pointed to the miserable figure separated from the rest.

Vespasian dismounted and walked over to the leader and stared down at him in disgust.

'Get me a translator,' he shouted and Natta called over a nearby slave.

'Repeat my words,' said Vespasian and the slave nodded in fright, careful not to meet the eyes of the Legatus.

'Tell him to look at me,' said Vespasian. 'Tell him to gaze into the eyes of the man who has wiped his clan from the face of the earth.'

The defeated chief lifted his face to look at the general.

'So, you are the man who had the audacity to challenge the might of Rome,' he said, 'the sole reason I have lost over a hundred of my men. How does that feel, Eadric, how does it feel to be the man who single handedly caused the annihilation of his entire clan?'

'It was the will of the gods,' said Eadric. 'They frowned on me today but there are a thousand others waiting to take my place. Do your worst, Roman, for my blood will nourish the soil that sustains my people. Eventually we will prevail. This year, next year or a thousand years from now, your ships will take you crawling back to Rome. I am just one of many, Roman; the first to have the bravery to face you down.'

'That wasn't bravery,' sneered Vespasian, 'that was stupidity. Your ego cost the lives of your people, and whatever heathen God it is that you worship will surely hold you to account in the afterlife.'

'I will stand in honour before my gods,' said Eadric, 'so take my head, Roman. I do not fear death.'

'No, I'm sure you don't,' said Vespasian, 'and I understand that every warrior craves death in battle. But what warrior hides while his men die?'

'The gods told me to save myself for further battles,' said Eadric. 'My men were expendable but I am meant for greater things. You are looking at a future King of Britannia, Roman. Send message to the chief of the Durotriges and they will pay good ransom for my return.'

'No, I don't think so,' said Vespasian, 'the time for negotiation is done. My men build a pyre for our fallen and you are responsible. For that you will pay.' He turned and called to his second in command. 'Natta!'

'Yes, my lord.'

'Execute the prisoners.'

'Yes, my lord. Crucifixion?'

'No, they fought well. Give them the death they crave. Take their heads.'

'And this one?' asked Natta.

'Guard him well,' said Vespasian, 'I have other plans for him.' Vespasian turned to face the chief for the last time. 'I gift you twelve more hours of life, Eadric. I suggest you plead for mercy from your gods.' He walked away from the defeated chief for the last time and summoned his second in command to join him.

'Natta, attend me,' he called and the Tribunus Laticlavius trotted over to join him as he walked across the battlefield. All around, scores of fires lit the looming darkness, and those who had fought sat around the fires tending their wounds or sharpening their weapons. Vespasian ordered his bodyguards to withdraw while he and Natta walked amongst their men offering encouragement and support. Anyone trying to stand to show respect was ordered back at ease and both officers crouched occasionally to chat quietly with the combatants.

Any with serious injuries had been taken by the orderlies to the Medicus tents back in the woods whilst those with minor wounds were tended by their comrades within their own Contubernium. Extra rations were being distributed by the Legion's slaves as well as skins of watered wine. Vespasian knew it was important to let the men unwind and enjoy the victory yet they couldn't totally relax until they were within the walls of a Legionary fortress. They were still in enemy territory and could face attack at any time, so those units who hadn't fought that day were deployed in a wider perimeter guard over a two-mile radius allowing the combatants to recover from the battle. As they walked, Vespasian could see all the other officers carrying out the same task as indeed did the centurions. It was an important gesture and one that engendered comradeship and respect between the men and their leaders. Vespasian took his time and tried to visit as many of the fires as he could, listening patently to the stories of their individual battles. Every man had a story to tell and every one was important to them.

Finally he came to a fire with only five men sitting around the flames. In the firelight he could see Barbatus sat amongst them, passing around the wine skin and sharing the stew now bubbling nicely in the communal pot on the fire. The men didn't notice his arrival until the last moment and Barbatus called them to attention.

'As you were,' said Vespasian and looked around the smaller group. Contubernia were made up of eight men and this was almost half the size.

'Barbatus, the Contubernium is light on numbers,' he said, 'where are the others?'

'All are dead,' said Barbatus, standing up, 'as indeed are the rest of their Centuries. Apart from one other with the Medicus, these are all that remain of the condemned men.'

Understanding dawned and Vespasian realised these were the sole survivors of the men who had led the assault up the ladders.

'You fought well,' acknowledged Vespasian. 'Your losses are heavy but were the price to be paid. I am aware that without your ferocity at the cusp, the breach may not have been made. Consider the debt paid and your honour restored. Centurion Barbatus will arrange redeployment when your wounds are healed but until then, consider yourself Immunes.'

The men looked around each other in surprise. As Immunes, they would be exempt the more menial tasks of the Legion and would not be selected to fight any forthcoming battles.

'Thank you, my lord,' they murmured.

'It has been earned,' said Vespasian before turning to Barbatus. 'Join us for a few moments,' he said, 'I have news.'

Barbatus joined the two officers a few steps away and they talked quietly amongst themselves.

'As you know, Governor Plautius has been replaced,' he said. 'During the battle I had a message from Londinium; Scapula wants us to move north as soon as possible.'

'North,' said Natta, 'but we haven't finished down here.'

'The intelligence is that the Durotriges chiefs intend to send representation to Scapula and will bend knee to Rome. We are to leave the rest of the task to politicians and traders.'

'What is so important in the North that demands the recall of an entire Legion?' asked Barbatus.

'The threat is many fold,' said Vespasian, 'but in particular, Caratacus has raised his head once more and raids our positions unchallenged.'

'Which tribe?' asked Barbatus.

'Our Exploratores say he now leads the Silures,' said Vespasian, 'and our role is to strike deep into their territory and seek him out.'

'The killing of a king is indeed a task worthy of a Legion,' said Barbatus.

'It is,' said Vespasian, 'but that is for the morrow. Give our men this night to let off steam but pass word we move out at midday. I want to be crossing the Sabrina River within ten days. Dismissed.'

Barbatus returned to the campfire to retrieve his helmet before disappearing into the dark to spread the word. Natta returned to the officers' tents to make the arrangements for the move. The logistics of moving a

Legion were huge, especially when on campaign and he knew he would be awake all night making the arrangements for the enormous range of support needed by the Legion, ranging from medical support to spare equipment and food. Luckily, they already had established supply lines but he would still need to send a stream of messengers to ensure any supplies en-route met them at agreed places along the way. It was going to be a long night.

–

The following afternoon the entire Legion was formed up on the battlefield for the last time. Before them, their dead comrades were stacked neatly on the top of a huge bonfire, each wrapped in the blood red cloaks of their Legion. A cohort of men formed a guard of honour and encircled the funeral pyre with heads bowed. The silence was profound and eventually an officer approached and gave Vespasian a burning torch. Reverently he walked over to the pyre and without a word, lit the kindling at its base. The flames licked upward and soon the fire became an inferno. The honour guard could feel the heat at their back and the Legion looked on with heavy hearts as they bid farewell to their fallen comrades.

When it was fully ablaze Vespasian gave a signal, and within moments, the assembled Legion heard a commotion to the far end of the field. One by one, every soldier present turned to see the source of the disturbance and were surprised to see a mounted centurion leading a tethered man toward the centre. It soon became clear that the prisoner was none other than Eadric himself, struggling with all his might to escape his bonds as well as cursing his captors and invoking the wrath of his gods against his enemies.

The horse came to a halt and Eadric picked himself up from the dust where he had fallen. Vespasian ignored him and turned to face his Legion.

'Men of the Augusta,' he roared, 'we are Legionaries and are prepared to die in the service of Rome. We go in peace but those who oppose us feel the wrath of Rome. No man wants to die but sometimes the decision is not ours. Sometimes it is taken by great men, like Plautius or Claudius but sometimes that decision is taken by lesser men, men not worthy to carry your shields. Before you stands one such man. He is Eadric of the Durotriges, leader of this hill fort and pretender to the Kingship of Britannia. This man alone is responsible for the death of your comrades and has requested he be ransomed back to his tribe. If we do this there will be bounty for all, but that decision is not mine. His life is yours to grant or deny, so, men of the Augusta, what say you? Do you grant this man his life?'

The Legion's response was deafening and exploded in deafening shouts of 'nay, kill the scum,' or 'death to the Durotriges'. Vespasian turned slowly on the spot, looking at the angry faces of his men and finally held up his hand for silence. When he could be heard once more, he turned to speak to Eadric.

'The men of the Augusta have spoken, Eadric,' he said, 'you have been judged by your betters.'

'But I am a king,' said Eadric, his voice breaking. 'I am worth a hundred of your men, a thousand even. Sell me to my people and you will be a rich man, you all will. There is gold enough for all.'

'We are not interested in your gold, Eadric,' said Vespasian, 'it will be ours soon enough. What we are interested in is making sure those who have fallen are served in the afterlife in the manner which they deserve.' His voice lowered and became little more than a growl. 'They will need a servant, Eadric; one to cook for them, to clean their armour and to see to their every whim until the end of time. They were great men who deserve the best and who better to serve them than a warrior king?'

Eadric's face fell and he looked over at the fire with terror on his face.

'No,' he groaned, 'not that. Take my head if you must but not the fire. Please, I implore you, not the fire.'

'Enough,' shouted Vespasian. 'Silence your cowardly tongue and face death like a man. Centurion, throw him to the flames.'

'No,' moaned Eadric, 'please no.'

Four Legionaries approached and untied his bonds before dragging him toward the fire.

'No,' wailed Eadric, 'please no.'

The four soldiers ran forward and threw the screaming prisoner into the flames before retiring quickly away from the heat. For a few second the massed ranks heard him scream in pain as he thrashed futilely in the flames, but slowly the screaming stopped and his body slumped into the base of the fire.

Vespasian turned and raised his Gladius.

'*Men of the Augusta*,' he roared, 'our men are avenged and our time here is done. We move onward to greater things. Legio Augusta, *advance!*'

The hills echoed to the sound of a hundred horns and thousands of men marched across the plain before the roaring funeral pyre. The enemy bodies had been left where they fell and many were already suffering the attentions of the crows and magpies. That night beasts of a different kind would soon arrive and wolf packs from miles around would have full stomachs for a long time.

As the columns passed the fire every man saluted in deference to their dead comrades. The guard of honour remained on station and would do so until the remains of their dead comrades had been entirely consumed by the flames. After that, they would bring up the rear of the Legion on their long march northward to confront the Silures. The phoney war was over – the real struggle was about to begin.

Chapter 16

The Lands of the Silures
50 AD

Caratacus led his men through the forests of the Khymru. He had waited years for this moment and his army numbered over ten thousand strong. Half of those were the survivors from the battle of Tamesas who had found their way south, but the rest were made up of the clans of the Silures, who had agreed to ride under his banner.

Since they had left Llanmelin a year earlier, his army had harassed the Romans all along the borders of the Khymru and deep into the lands of the Dobunii, proving a thorn in the side of the enemy Legion based there. The Valeria Victrix had been sent to oppose him and had established a permanent fortress on the far side of the great river separating the Khymru from the rest of the country and though Caratacus felt he was now strong enough to take on a Legion, he had learned from his defeat at Tamesas and held back from confronting them on the open battle field.

Instead he adopted the hit and run tactics of the Silures and wreaked havoc on the supply lines of the Romans. Cavalry were often sent out in response to Caratacus's attacks but by the time they arrived, the Silures were nowhere to be seen.

As well as the Roman supply lines, Caratacus preyed on the clans of the Dobunii and lost no sleep in killing his countrymen. They had bent the knee to the invaders and deserved everything they got but more than that, as a client clan of the Romans they were entitled to the invaders protection and soon there were so many clans begging for their aid, Geta's Legion were unable to patrol aggressively and had become static along the banks of the river.

The incoming governor had seen the threat and had redeployed Vespasian's Second Augusta to drive into the Silures heartland, endeavouring to kill the troublesome king. But the continued hit and run warfare meant that Vespasian's men hardly caught sight of their enemy, let alone engaged them in battle. For a year the Augusta chased shadows around the southern hills of the Silures so in response, Caratacus had led his army north into mountains of the Ordovices, avoiding the attentions of the Romans by staying constantly on the move. All the Khymric tribes were supportive and for two years Caratacus proved an astute and successful leader, inflicting loss after loss on the Romans. Finally Scapula had enough and called a briefing of all the Legates to meet him at the Legionary fortress in Londinium, the first time he had met the Legates of all Legions in one place. All four left their Legions in the hands of their junior officers and travelled for days cross country with their respective cohorts of bodyguards. Finally they reached Londinium, where they were summoned to the quarters of Scapula himself.

Vespasian was the last to arrive having had the furthest to travel and had only been in Londinium for a matter of hours. He entered the officers' quarters and looked around with interest. Since his last visit the timber buildings had been replaced by stone and the city outside the fortress sprawled for miles in each direction.

The other Legates were already there and turned to greet him as he entered.

'Hail Vespasian,' said Geta.

'Gentlemen, good to see you all again,' said Vespasian. 'I wish it could be in different circumstances.'

'Indeed,' said Geta, 'this Caratacus turns out to be an itch that refuses to be scratched.'

Nasica handed Vespasian a goblet of wine and for the next half hour they all discussed their relative campaigns of the last two years. Finally the door opened and Governor Scapula walked in. He threw his cloak to one side and demanded wine from a nearby servant.

'Gentleman, thank you for coming,' said Scapula. 'I know you yearn to return to your Legions but this matter will not wait.' He sat back in his chair and took the proffered wine from the slave. 'Leave us,' he said and the woman left the officers alone in the room. Scapula drank deeply before refilling his own goblet from the nearby amphorae. 'Please sit,' he said waving toward the chairs situated around the table. 'So,' he said eventually, 'let's get straight to the point. This so-called King of Britannia, somebody tell me why he still lives.'

The assembled generals looked around in surprise. The demand was curt and the governor was obviously annoyed.

'Well,' said Vespasian, breaking the awkward silence, 'the first thing to realise, my lord, is that this man does not fight like other kings. He uses the cover of darkness and only attacks small targets before retreating into the night. Sometimes he attacks many targets at the same time and our forces are stretched thinly over a wide area.'

'I understand that he targets our supply columns,' said Scapula. 'That says to me he needs the stores they carry.'

'He does, my lord,' said Geta. 'One of the reasons is that he maintains a large army and though he has the support of the other Khymric tribes, their resources are stretched and that means there are a fewer men tending the fields, thus food is at a premium.'

'Have you increased the guards on these columns?' asked Scapula.

'We have, my lord,' said Geta, 'but once one column is reinforced, he changes target to something not so well defended. Strengthen a column and he targets a granary. Put troops around the granaries and he steals our cattle. Protect the cattle and he'll target the wagons. It's as if he has spies in every camp.'

'Everyone in this entire country is a cursed spy,' growled Scapula. 'So,' he continued, 'what if we were do the same and burn his crops at source. Target his villages and destroy their families. Would this not have a positive effect and force him into the open?'

'Perhaps,' said Vespasian, 'but don't forget we are not dealing with just any tribe here. The Silures are not as the Durotriges or the Dobunii. These people are warriors to their core and every man, woman and child will stab you as soon as look at you. Their entire culture is one of warfare and they have left just as many warriors back in the hills as are on campaign, if not more. Strike at their heart and I fear they will mobilise an entire nation behind Caratacus. Even with four Legions I fear we will not have the strength to overcome such a threat.'

'I disagree,' said Scapula, 'but take your point. One way or another we have to bring this king to his knees. His name is now being spoken in the villages of the vanquished as a potential saviour and one who will drive us out. Now, I don't believe for a moment that this is the case but that's not important. If the people believe it could be the start of something greater, something we may not be able to control, the question I put collectively to all you men is this. How are we going to deal with this threat once and for all?'

For the next few hours they discussed the options for dealing with Caratacus but always came back to the same thing; they had to lure him out of the shadows to face them on the field of battle. Gradually they came up with a plan, and though it meant committing huge resources and would take time, they final agreed a strategy they hoped would finish the troublesome king for good. Food was brought by the servants, and finally Scapula summarised the plan.

'So,' he said, 'what we have is this. The Augusta will raise their campaign against the Silures homeland, forcing Caratacus northward through the Khymru. Increase your patrols; though keep the aggression to a minimum. We want Caratacus to be at ease moving northward and not see the Augusta as a major threat. At the same time, the Valeria Victrix will make it known they are to campaign against the Deceangli in the north. If my perception of this man is right, he will see this as an opportunity to catch an entire Legion between two tribes and inflict a devastating defeat on Rome.

'I think he will ride north as fast as he can to join with the Deceangli and that will be our opportunity to catch him in the open. If we time this right, there are open swathes of farmland they will need to cross before reaching the mountains of the north.' He pointed to a blank area on the map laid out across the table. 'Unfortunately, we cannot set a trap as it's unlikely an entire Legion can remain hidden in such sparse country, so what I propose is this. The fourteenth Gemina will remain in the fortress at Corinium and will continue to provide support to the client kings around that area. However, they will maintain a high proportion of the Legion at instant readiness in case relief is required.

'Geta, the Victrix will continue to campaign against the Deceangli in the north but the moment we know for certain that Caratacus has taken the bait, you will immediately turn south and confront him head on. With the Augusta behind him, he will be forced to go to ground in this open area to the south of the Wrekin hills.

'As soon as that happens, send signal to Corinium with the fastest riders and I will personally lead the Gemina in support. If this works, there are potentially three Legions available to call on should battle be joined.'

'My lord, the plan has merit,' said Geta, 'but relies on very tight timing and up to the minute intelligence.'

'Well, that's where Vespasian comes in,' said Scapula. 'I understand he has spies deep within the enemy camp and should be able to give us intelligence as to their movement. Is this not the case, Vespasian?'

'It is true I had a unit of Exploratores in the field,' said Vespasian, 'but recently their subterfuge was uncovered and many died at the hands of the tribesmen.'

'So there are none?' asked Scapula with concern.

'There is one,' said Vespasian, 'and he enjoys a high position, but he lives within the forces of Idwal, not Caratacus.'

'This is a concern,' said Scapula. 'Do the two tribes have regular communication?'

'Almost certainly,' said Vespasian. 'They are all tribes of the Khymru and see us as a common foe so I would imagine the communication is constant.'

'Then your man is tasked with finding out the information we need,' said Scapula, 'even at the cost of his own life.'

'Yes, my lord,' said Vespasian.

'Gentlemen,' said Scapula eventually, 'the plan is made and though there is no meat on the bones, I will leave the final details with you. I want this to happen before the winter sets in less than three months from now. Now I have to retire for I have an ague, but know I can leave the rest in your capable hands. Goodnight.'

All the officers stood up to salute and watched the governor leave.

'He looks ill,' said Vespasian eventually.

'I noticed,' said Nasica. 'The weight of command lies heavily on his shoulders, I fear.'

They returned to the table and spent the rest of the night thrashing out the detail of the plan and by morning, all were much happier about their chances of success. However, as they dispersed, Vespasian knew that it all relied on one man, a man who had to risk his life to find out the mind of a secretive and astute king. That man was Cassus Maecilius.

–

Just over two hundred miles away, Cassus Maecilius sat in the giant hall of the Deceangli Cerrig, the stone-built fortress that overlooked the sacred island of Mona and the northern coastline of the Khymru. He had been fully accepted by Idwal and due to his prowess in battle had been rapidly elevated to the king's close circle of confidantes.

Cassus had been with the Deceangli for almost two years and his loyalty was no longer in question. On many occasions he had killed men in the name of Idwal, but luckily they had always been from local clans and so far, he had not been pitted against fellow Romans. Cassus was thankful for that, but knew there could be a time approaching when he might be confronted with an ex-comrade and may have to slay him to prove his allegiance. When that time came there would be a decision to be made which could signal the end of his cover if not his life. Little did he realise, that time would come quicker than he thought.

Around the hall, men talked quietly in groups, discussing the politics of the area or the next trial of arms often held between the local clans. Idwal was sat on a giant wooden throne near the roaring fire, listening to a messenger from Caratacus imploring the Deceangli to support his cause with food and military supplies. It was the latest of many such requests and Idwal had already sent five hundred men south to aid the Silures army in their constant struggle against the Romans, along with herds of cattle and carts of grain. While their granaries were full, Idwal was happy to support their cause and besides, there may come a time when he needed the help of Caratacus.

The need to join together was accepted by Idwal but as the Silures were their ancestral enemies, the situation was not straightforward and his warriors still failed to see the benefit of such an alliance. The timing was also awkward as rumours abounded that the Romans intended to march against the Deceangli in the near future, and if that happened and the Cerrig was put under siege, the

Deceangli would need every morsel of food available to feed the people within its walls and indeed, the army he would have to field.

'I will send ten more carts of grain and a hundred head of cattle,' said Idwal. 'I will also send a fist of one hundred men to aid his cause. This is the best I can do until we know the threat from the north has eased.'

'Anything is gratefully received,' said the messenger and stood to leave. 'I will ride to tell him of your generous support and in his name, I pledge our swords when the time comes to defend your lands.'

'Hopefully that time is still far off,' said Idwal, 'but the pledge is comfort enough. The wagons will be sent at dawn and will be at the usual place in seven days from now. I need not remind you to ensure no Silures are present at the handover in case matters get out of hand. The last thing we need now is a pitched battle between Khymric tribes.'

'I agree,' said the man, 'and assure you there will only be Catuvellauni present.'

'Good,' said Idwal standing up. 'Give my regards to the king and assure him that one day we will ride side by side.'

'Your words will be welcomed,' said the man and walked out of the hut with the rest of his men.

Cassus got to his feet and turned to the king.

'My lord, I have business in the village,' he said, 'and would beg leave to attend.'

'Does this business have the bluest eyes and hair down to her waist?' asked Idwal.

Cassus smiled as Idwal described Madoc's daughter, the girl who had taken a shine to him two years earlier. Though not interested at the time, the girl had grown into a fine young woman and they had since grown a close friendship, meeting regularly in the village of Treforum below the walls of the Cerrig.

'She does,' answered Cassus with a sigh, and the rest of the men in the hall jeered in mock derision.

'Why fixate on one farmer's girl when there are dozens of professionals just a moment's walk away?' asked Idwal. 'You can take your pick and there will be no charge.'

'I appreciate your offer,' laughed Cassus, 'but I don't think Sioned would see the saving as a good enough excuse.'

Idwal roared in laughter.

'Probably not,' he said, 'but trust me, the experience would be well worth the grief.'

'Perhaps next time,' said Cassus.

'Leave is granted,' said Idwal. 'You go and play house with this girl while we real men take our pleasure with real women. Be back at dawn tomorrow.'

The warriors started laughing again and Cassus turned to leave the hall. In truth he had no problem at all in taking to the beds of whores or slaves, but his relationship with Sioned meant he had an excuse to leave the Cerrig regularly, a task that was essential for the continuation of his mission.

He rode out of the Cerrig and down the hill toward the village where he knew Sioned would be waiting. They would spend the rest of the day together in the village, exploring the market and watching the boats unloading their catch from the sea before making their way to Madoc's farm several miles away. There he would spend the night with Sioned but not before carrying out the main reason for his request, making contact with his Legion. It was a monthly arrangement and each time the date and location of the next meeting would be agreed based on the state of the moon. This month the date had been moon plus three which meant the last day of the full moon plus three days and the location had been given as a stream junction near to the farm.

He knew the next few months would be a challenge as the respective powers of Britannia jostled for position. Whatever happened he knew his people wouldn't allow the tribes to get the better of them and whether it took months or years, Rome would prevail.

A voice called out, interrupting his thoughts, and he saw Sioned waving from the village edge. Cassus smiled and pushed the thoughts of war to one side as he rode up to greet the young woman.

'Sioned,' he said, 'it is great to see you again.'

'And you,' said Sioned. 'I have been waiting for ages and thought you would never come.'

'We had a delegation from Caratacus,' said Cassus, 'and I couldn't leave until they left the Cerrig.'

'Well you are here now,' said Sioned. 'Come, we'll stable your horse and walk to the sea. The fishermen cook some of their catch straight from the nets sometimes; perhaps we still have time to join them.'

Cassus rode over to the nearby paddock and paid the boy a coin to look after his horse before re-joining Sioned on the road. Sioned took his arm and they walked through the village together. Sioned chatted endlessly and Cassus made the effort to look interested in her girlish banter, but all the while his eyes took in everything around him. Warriors were abundant in the village, and many sat outside huts drinking ale or getting stuck into bowls of Cawl, the local meaty soup that was the staple diet of the Khymric tribes. The mood was quiet and there was definitely a feeling of apprehension in the air. Men talked quietly amongst themselves knowing that the day was near when their skills would be put to serious use for the first time in many years.

As Cassus passed, many nodded toward him in recognition. Over the past two years he had participated in many trials of arms and had garnered a reputation as a fearsome warrior. His face was well known and he had the respect of all who knew him. His cover was well established and he walked freely amongst the Deceangli as one of their own.

The rest of the day was taken up with walking, drinking, eating and laughing. He enjoyed Sioned's company and knew that perhaps in another life, she would be the sort of woman he could settle down with. But that was not an option he could consider for any length of time.

Whatever the near future held, there was no way he could settle down. He enjoyed his new life but it was one he knew could not last. Despite his comfort, deep down inside he was still a Roman at heart and he knew that when the time came, if forced to choose sides, it would be Rome every time. That's why he had refused to wed Sioned. They had discussed it on several occasions but he always fell back on the excuse that war was coming and it wouldn't be fair to tie her to one man in case he fell in battle.

It was a weak excuse but one he could maintain. Eventually Sioned accepted his reasons and resigned herself to waiting until these dangerous times were over. Madoc had turned a blind eye to their union as although there had been no ceremony, he could see they were committed to each other and Cassus seemed a good man.

Over the past few months, Cassus had built a small hut with the aid of Madoc and when Cassus spent time at the village, he and Sioned shared the privacy of the hut away from the rest of the families and the farmhands.

–

Toward late afternoon, they retrieved Cassus's horse and he lifted Sioned up to sit behind him as they road back to Madoc's farm. When they reached the farm, they shared the evening meal with Sioned's family before retreating to their hut, to enjoy their private time together.

Hours later, Cassus listened to the gentle sound of Sioned's rhythmic breathing and, confident she was fast asleep, gently disentangled himself from her arms and crawled out from beneath the bed furs. Though naked, he made his way outside, picking up his clothing as he went, wanting to make sure he didn't wake her up.

The night was cold and he pulled on his leggings and boots quickly, followed by his tunic and cloak. He had left his broadsword in the hut, but knew he had a knife in the side of his boot in case of any unexpected threat. One of the camp dogs stared at him in interest and Cassus held out his arm to entice him over.

'Shhh,' he whispered, smoothing the dog's head, 'no barking now.'

When ready he walked quietly down the path and headed into the forest. He found the stream and followed it up to where it was fed by another. For a while he waited in silence, listening for the sound of anyone breathing in the darkness but after several minutes, he sat back against a tree to await the messenger he knew would soon be there.

It wasn't a footstep that eventually warned Cassus he wasn't alone, but a quiet growl from the dog lying at his side. An hour had passed and the cold air was seeping through his cloak, so, despite the need to keep hidden, he was glad to stand up and get the blood circulating. Still he couldn't see anyone, but the dog's continued growling told him someone was there.

'Declare yourself,' said Cassus quietly.

For a moment there was no answer but finally a voice came from the darkness.

'Who's your friend?' it said.

'Don't worry about him,' said Cassus, 'he'll only attack if I tell him.'

A shadow moved and someone stepped out from the black tree line.

'Hello, Cassus,' said the man and Cassus was shocked to see Dento, the man he had shared his training with.

'Dento,' he said, grasping his friend's arm, 'it's good to see you.'

'And you,' said Dento, 'though for a few moments there I wasn't sure it was you.'

For a second Cassus was confused but then realised he was referring to his appearance. Cassus's hair was tied back from his head and fell below his shoulders and his moustache was full, arching down past the sides of his mouth.

'I suppose I do look a bit different,' said Cassus, 'it's the way of the Deceangli.'

'I can't say it suits you,' said Dento, who was clean shaven with freshly cropped hair.

'So where did you go after training?' asked Cassus.

'I was attached to the Victrix,' said Dento, 'and spent time amongst the Trinovantes, a strange tribe but not one that poses a serious threat.'

'So how are you here in the Khymru?' asked Cassus.

'I was sent to see you,' said Dento.

'But what happened to my usual contact?'

'He was killed by a Cornovii patrol on the way back to Londinium after the last time he came.'

'If he was killed, how did you know where and when to meet me?' asked Cassus. 'We only agree the details one meeting in advance.'

'The location was obviously one of three he always used,' said Dento, 'and as for the time, we knew it would be one of a few days either side of the full moon. Two others wait at the alternative meeting places while I covered this one as it was nearest to the farm. I have been here for five days.'

'There are three other Exploratores in the vicinity?' asked Cassus.

'There are,' said Dento, 'it seems you have suddenly become the most important Roman in Britannia.'

'I assume this has something to do with the oncoming assault from the Victrix,' said Cassus.

'You know about that?'

'Everyone knows about that,' said Cassus. 'We receive riders almost every day telling us of their progress, though it seems Geta takes his time getting here.'

'There is good reason,' said Dento, 'and that is why I am here. You have an important task to undertake and the whole campaign relies on the outcome.'

'State it,' said Cassus.

'Geta's advance on the Deceangli is but a lure to draw Caratacus from the south,' said Dento. 'Vespasian pressures him from behind and we know they are currently somewhere in the lands of the Cornovii. The thing is, Caratacus moves constantly and is hidden from our spies. Scapula has decreed that...'

'Scapula?'

'The new governor,' said Dento, 'Plautius was recalled to Rome to receive his glory. Anyway, Scapula has tasked three Legions against Caratacus and it is essential we get up to date intelligence. That's where you come in. We need you to somehow join Caratacus's army and stay with him until the time is right.'

'I don't understand,' said Cassus.

'If Caratacus comes north, as we think he will, there will be a short period of time when his army will be in open ground and a prime target for our Legions. At that time we need to alert the Gemina to support the Victrix or there will be a risk they will be overpowered. With early warning, it is hoped the Gemina can get within a day's march of the battle and with that amount of men, we can certainly hold them until the arrival of the Augusta. With three Legions in the field, there is no doubt Caratacus will be routed no matter how many men he has.'

'Really?' asked Cassus with a hint of sarcasm. 'So how do you explain Teutoberg?'

Dento paused, remembering how three Legions had been entirely wiped out in the Germanic forests forty-one years earlier.

'A point well made,' said Dento, 'but that was in the depths of a Germanic forest and is why it is so important we catch Caratacus on open ground.'

'So what do you expect of me?' asked Cassus.

'We want you to try and link up with Caratacus and let us know which route he chooses to travel. We think there are three possibilities, the west coast, the valley route and the lowlands to the west of the river. Hopefully he will choose the lowlands as it will be closer to our forces but whichever is selected, we will need to know.'

'And how am I to achieve this?' asked Cassus.

'Only you can answer that,' said Dento. 'You are the only man we have in the enemy ranks and there is no time to deploy others to any effect.'

'On whose authority?' asked Cassus.

'The highest,' said Dento. 'Scapula himself demands your deployment and expects compliance at all costs.'

'I suppose it had to happen eventually,' said Cassus. 'How much time do I have?'

'That is in the hands of Caratacus,' said Dento. 'The sooner he moves north the sooner we can close the trap. You should go immediately.'

Cassus nodded thoughtfully.

'As it happens, there are events afoot that lend themselves to this task,' he said. 'It may be achievable though carries some risk.'

'Explain?'

'Idwal sends a fist of a hundred cavalry to aid Caratacus. If I can get attached to them, I will be close to his command structure. The thing is my claim to be Catuvellauni may not hold water when confronted with others from that tribe. We run a risk that my cover will be unravelled.'

'Then that is a risk you must take,' said Dento. 'Join this fist but keep a low profile and avoid engaging the men of Caratacus in conversation. Perhaps the ruse will last long enough to achieve our aim.'

'I will take my chances,' said Cassus. 'The first leaves in a few days and I will endeavour to be amongst them. In the meantime, I will spend one more day with the family of Madoc.'

'I have watched them from afar these last few days,' said Dento, 'and in particular, a pretty girl with long hair.'

'That's Sioned,' said Cassus, 'and she shares my bed when I am here.'

'Lucky man,' said Dento. 'So, is there anything you need of me?'

'There is one thing,' said Cassus. 'If the fight comes this way, take Sioned and her family from the danger and hide them in the woods. They are good people and don't deserve to die in this conflict.'

'I will do what I can,' said Dento.

They spent the next few minutes covering the details but eventually Dento rose to leave.

'I have to be going,' he said, 'I can only travel by night as the patrols around here increase by the day. Be safe, Cassus, and perhaps one day we can get lost in an amphorae of wine, behind the safety of a fort's walls.'

'I'll look forward to it,' said Cassus and watched his friend disappear into the darkness.

He returned to the farm and crawled back under the furs to hold Sioned, knowing full well it may be the last time he had the opportunity to do so.

Chapter 17

The Camp of Caratacus
50 AD

Prydain sat at the campfire alongside Gwydion of the Blaidd. Since leaving the south, they had campaigned alongside Caratacus and found him to be an able leader and a very charismatic king. He had embraced the hit and run tactics of the Silures and used them to ravage the Roman supply lines, as well as the villages of the Dobunii on the far side of the great river. Morale was high but despite the army's successes, they knew the time was coming when they would have to confront the Legions, if they were to expel them from their land.

'Yeuch,' said Gwydion and spat out the food he had only just placed in his mouth, 'what in the name of Aerten is this?'

'They are olives,' laughed Prydain, 'and come from trees to the north of Rome.' He dipped his hand into the small barrel once again and withdrew another handful. 'I had forgotten how much I like them.'

'They are disgusting,' said Gwydion, 'and I think I broke a tooth on the stone within. What else was on that cart?'

'Wine, dried beef and Garum,' said Prydain. 'Obviously some officer has a simpler fare on his table tonight.'

'Wine and beef, I know,' said Gwydion, 'but what is this Garum you speak of?'

'If you don't like olives, I fear you won't like Garum,' said Prydain.

'Why not?'

'It is a sauce formed from heavily salted fish entrails and allowed to ferment until liquid.'

'Sounds disgusting,' said Gwydion with a grimace.

'It's actually very good,' said Prydain, 'and sounds worse than what it is. It spices up the blandest of meals.'

'Keep it,' said Gwydion. 'I thought you Romans, or should I say ex-Romans, were supposed to be civilised people, yet you cover your food with rotting fish guts.'

'You don't know what you're missing,' said Prydain and carried on dipping into the barrel of olives they had taken from an ambushed supply train.

'So,' said Gwydion, 'how do you see this campaign going?'

'I don't know,' said Prydain, 'Caratacus is a competent leader but I fear we are still too weak to face any Legion head on.'

'I'm not so sure,' said Gwydion, 'this is an impressive army and your people never cease to amaze me with their bravery.'

'Bravery is one thing,' said Prydain, 'but I know how they work. You haven't seen them at their best and if they are given time to use their formations, they are unstoppable. You saw them at Medway.'

'Yes, but there we were unprepared. Caratacus is a man who learns quickly and I have been around many fires as he discusses tactics. He knows full well what the Romans are capable of and I think the next time, he will prevail.'

'Perhaps,' sighed Prydain through a mouthful of olives as he stood up to leave.

'Where are you going?' asked Gwydion.

'To find some meat and Garum,' said Prydain, 'it's been far too long.'

'Yeuch,' said Gwydion again and turned his attention to the fire where his Cawl was bubbling nicely.

–

Prydain made his way over to the captured wagons to seek the food he hadn't tasted for over eight years. Most had been distributed to the clans who had taken part in the assault, but some remained for the bodyguards of Caratacus.

One of the guards stood to confront him as he emerged from the dark but then recognised the man he had fought alongside many times in the last two years.

'Prydain, I thought you would be drunk by now,' said the man.

'Not yet,' said Prydain, 'there will be time enough for that. I seek the wagon containing the rich foods intended for the Roman officers. Gwydion of the Blaidd yearns to taste the flavour of Garum.'

'There's nothing left,' said the warrior. 'All the carts have been shared equally.'

'What about our share?' asked Prydain. 'Has it all gone already?'

'It hadn't,' said the guard, 'but a fist of men arrived from the Deceangli a while ago and they were hungry from their ride.'

'So you gave them the rest of the food,' said Prydain.

'It was the least we could do,' answered the guard. 'They come to aid our cause so we won't see them hungry.'

'A fair point,' said Prydain. He paused before continuing. 'Any news on what the morrow brings?'

'Nothing yet,' said the warrior, 'though Caratacus seems distracted. I believe he seeks a big victory before we return to our clans for the winter.'

'I hope he knows what he is doing,' said Prydain, 'these are dangerous times.'

'He has to succeed,' said the warrior, 'there is no one else.'

'So,' said Prydain, 'what strength is this Deceangli fist?'

'They say a hundred mounted men,' said the warrior, 'they are camped by the waterfall.'

'I might take a walk over and bid them welcome,' said Prydain.

The warrior laughed.

'What's so funny?' asked Prydain.

'You,' said the warrior, 'you offer the hand of welcome but I suppose it is a coincidence they also have the last of the Garum.'

Prydain smiled.

'A side benefit to my gesture,' he said and walked into the dark.

–

Cassus lay wrapped in his oiled cloak against the base of the cliff. The ride had been hard and he yearned for sleep yet the sound of the waterfall prevented him from slipping over the edge of consciousness and into the sleep that he required. He watched his comrades sitting around the fires talking quietly amongst themselves. They had been sent by Idwal to aid Caratacus and after leaving the farm, Cassus had petitioned Idwal, requesting permission to join them on the task.

At first Idwal had resisted, but Cassus had persisted, using the excuse that he yearned to fight amongst his own tribe. Eventually Idwal had given in and allowed him to leave with the hundred other men. They were all good warriors and had the best horses available. It was important for Idwal to impress Caratacus with the quality of his men as when this was all over, there would be a repositioning of power and Idwal intended to be an equal partner in any division of land.

The conversation murmured gently, matching the sounds of the water. Suddenly the talk at one of the fires stopped, and all three men stood up to confront the man walking into their camp.

'Declare yourself, stranger,' said one of the warriors.

'I am a friend,' said Prydain, 'and have come to welcome you on behalf of your fellow warriors.'

'Are you Catuvellauni?' asked the nearest warrior.

'No, I ride alongside Caratacus but my name is Prydain and I am Silures.'

–

Cassus's eyes flew wide open as he recognised Prydain and he pushed himself further back into the shadows so he wouldn't be recognised. It had been seven years since the battle where Prydain had discovered his true Silures roots and had defected to the enemy, but though the chances of being recognised were slight, Cassus could take no chances. He wanted to kill Prydain with all his heart but he knew there were bigger things at stake here, possibly the future of the whole of Britannia and despite his hatred, it took precedence over his oath to slay his childhood friend.

For an age he sat back against the rock, hidden by the blanketing shadows watching the man he had sworn to kill, talking less than twenty paces away. Even in the flickering light from the fire, Cassus knew he could place an arrow between Prydain's eyes or sink a throwing axe into his chest with no problem. But Cassus knew that wasn't an option, for apart from the fact his mission took precedence, there was no way he would kill Prydain from a distance. He wanted to do it up close and personal, preferably with Gladius or Pugio, so he could watch the life drain slowly from his eyes.

Prydain stayed for several minutes, laughing and joking with the Deceangli warriors but eventually left to return to his own lines, complete with a small amphorae of Garum.

Cassus watched him go and stared after him for a long time. The gods seemed to be playing games with him. He was deep inside enemy territory, assuming the identity of a tribesman at a time of war. As well as that, the one man he had sworn to kill had just been offered to him on a plate, yet killing him could jeopardise Rome's entire invasion, a jest indeed by the gods.

Despite his exhaustion, the events of the night meant Cassus struggled to sleep and spent most of the night planning how he could stay out of Prydain's way, at least until the coming battle was done. Then he would hunt him down like a rabid dog.

-

The next few days saw Cassus and his men settle in to Caratacus's army. They were tasked with patrolling the hills to each side of the main force, protecting the flanks from any intrusion. This suited Cassus perfectly as it meant they were kept separate from the main force and his cover remained intact. Despite this, he was occasionally called to the tent of Caratacus to receive his orders and though he had never spoken to the king directly, he had close contact with his warlords.

It was on just such an occasion ten days later when the dominance of Caratacus's army came to a sudden and unexpected halt. Cassus was approaching the command tent to receive fresh orders when a rider burst from the forest and galloped across the clearing toward the king's tent before jumping from the saddle without stopping his horse. Two guards grabbed the man and a fight ensued before Caratacus came out of the tent to see what the commotion was all about. 'Leave him,' ordered Caratacus and the guards let him go. The rider dropped to his knee, waiting for the king's acknowledgement.

'Arise,' said Caratacus and he looked at the messenger in anticipation. The Silures warrior was covered in sweat-streaked dust and had obviously been in the saddle for a long time. 'You have news?'

'My lord, I have come from the north,' said the rider, 'and have ridden two days without rest. My other horse lies dead in my wake.'

'What news causes this haste?' asked Caratacus.

'The movement of an army,' said the rider. 'The northern Legion marches on the Deceangli as we speak.'

'You are sure of this?'

'I saw it with my own eyes,' said the rider. 'A column of armed men march four abreast reaching back further than the eye can see. Cavalry flank their sides and hundreds of carts follow in their dust with strange constructions of wood and ropes.'

'Artillery,' said Caratacus quietly.

'They have many different styles of clothing,' continued the rider, 'and march to the sound of drums. To the rear, thousands of people carry their homes on their backs or in carts. It is as if an entire nation is moving.'

'Come inside and show me on the map,' said Caratacus. 'You men join me; you too, Cassus.'

The assembled warlords followed Caratacus into the tent and crowded around the deer skin map, as the Silures scout pointed out the location of the Legion on the map.

'They march along this valley,' said the scout, 'and offshore, a fleet of ships shadow their route.'

'Why bring ships?' asked one of the clan leaders.

'I don't know,' said Caratacus, 'perhaps they plan an assault on Mona.'

'They wouldn't dare attack the holy isle,' said a warrior, 'they would have an entire nation rise against them.'

Caratacus sneered.

'Then perhaps we should hope that is their intention,' he said, 'for it will bring the cohesion this country needs.'

'And why do the people follow them?' asked another voice. 'Surely they would be too big a drain on their resources?'

'I don't know,' said Caratacus. 'The workings of their minds are yet strange to me. What we need is someone who knows how they think.'

'What about Prydain of the Silures?' asked a chieftain. 'He was brought up in their ways and served in their Legions.'

'Perfect,' said Caratacus, 'summon him immediately – we need a Roman's perspective.'

Cassus's eyes widened slightly as he realised the implications. Several nights ago, he had been near the ex-Roman soldier but that had been in darkness. In a few moments' time he would be within a few paces of him inside a well-lit tent. The danger of discovery was huge as they had grown up together. He felt for his knife and vowed to himself that if there was a slightest inkling of recognition, he would cut Prydain's throat before any man could react.

Five minutes later, Prydain ducked into the tent and looked around at the gathered men.

Cassus stood at the back but maintained his gaze as Prydain looked in his direction. If Prydain recognised his old friend now, it was all over, for both of them.

Prydain glanced around the tent briefly. He had been here before but never in the presence of so many warlords. Some he knew but most were strangers, including the bearded one dressed in the ways of the Deceangli. There was something vaguely familiar about him, but he couldn't think what it was. He brushed the thought from his mind and turned to the king.

'My lord, you summoned me?'

'I did,' said Caratacus. 'Most here know your story but for the benefit of those who don't, explain your knowledge of the Roman ways.'

'My lord, I was brought up in Rome and fathered by a Roman but my mother was from Britannia. My heart and soul are Silures.'

'Yet you served in her Legions?'

'I did, but that was before I knew my heritage. My grandfather was Caedmon, chief of the Silures. Once this was revealed to me, my path was clear. I am Silures and challenge any man who says otherwise to trial of arms without quarter.'

At the back of the tent, Cassus seethed and it was all he could do not to step forward and accept Prydain's challenge yet he remained still, committed to the greater cause.

'Your loyalty is not in question, Prydain,' said Caratacus, 'we just need the benefit of your knowledge. There is a Legion marching on the Deceangli as we speak yet their actions are strange to us. This man is a scout and has watched them march. We seek your view of their intentions.'

Prydain nodded.

'I understand,' he said. 'Can I question the scout?'

'Proceed.'

Prydain asked the scout to repeat everything he had seen down to the tiniest detail. As he spoke, he placed pebbles on the map representing possible routes and other important features. Finally he finished and looked over at the king.

'So,' said Caratacus, 'do you have any idea what they are up to?'

'I think so,' said Prydain, 'but can't be sure.'

'Just spit it out,' said Caratacus, 'I will decide the worthiness of your views.'

'First of all, this isn't just a campaign march,' said Prydain. 'The many different uniforms suggest they march with all auxiliary units as well as Legionaries. Often a Legion splits into many parts and are spread out over a large area, but it seems they have called them all in for common purpose.'

'An assault,' suggested Caratacus.

'Possibly, but there is more; the fact that the camp followers have also lifted their roots suggests they are relocating and intend to form a new Legionary fortress elsewhere.'

'A fortress,' said Caratacus, 'but where?'

'I don't know,' said Prydain, 'but they are being shadowed by the fleet so I suggest it won't be far from the coast.'

'What possible military aid could a load of boats be?' asked Caratacus.

'Limited, agreed,' said Prydain, 'but I don't think these will be military support, I think they will contain supplies for the Legion.'

'What sort of supplies?'

'Food, water, weapons, clothing, you name it and it will be on board. But the first wave won't carry supplies; it will be full of timber for the initial palisades. This is not a normal military campaign, Caratacus, this is an invasion.'

-

'You think they intend to get a foothold in the Khymru?' asked Caratacus when the news had sunk in.

'I do,' said Prydain, 'and the route they take suggests they target the Cerrig of the Deceangli.'

'There's no way they can take the Cerrig,' said Caratacus, 'Idwal has it defended well.'

'There is nothing the Legions can't do when they set mind to it,' said Prydain. 'Their history shows they have levelled cities a thousand times the size of the Cerrig. All they need is time. First of all they will establish a fort and spread their control outward. After that they will move their attentions onto the centre of any local tribe and do whatever it takes to achieve their aims. For a fort the strength of the Cerrig they will bring in even bigger artillery, building Onagers from the great oaks of our forests, machines capable of throwing boulders half the size of a horse against its gates. They will surround it with thousands of men and starve them out, waiting for years if they have to. Make no mistake, once they are established, they will secure supply lines from the sea and will be reinforced by fresh men and constant supplies. Allow this to happen and the north of the Khymru will fall under their control by next spring and if that happens, the south will fall within a few years.'

'The Silures will never succumb,' growled one clan leader, 'our lands are protected by the great river to the east and the sea to the south and west.'

'Perhaps not immediately,' said Prydain, 'but these are mere inconveniences to a nation such as Rome. For hundreds of years they have conquered nations much bigger than ours. They are patient and their control spreads like a fungus, steady and all consuming. I am telling you, allow these people to establish a foothold in the Khymru and it is over, the whole of Britannia will fall.'

The gathered men fell silent. Finally Caratacus spoke up.

'Then we will not allow it to happen,' he said. 'The direction they take indicates the Deceangli are indeed the target. Idwal's forces are strong and his warriors brave but I have seen the Romans at close quarter and I fear he doesn't know what comes his way. But between Idwal's army and ours we have over forty-thousand men at arms, more than three times the numbers of their pathetic Legion. This is the opportunity we have been waiting for. If we join with the Deceangli, we can inflict a defeat of devastating proportions on the invaders, one which will send a signal to all other tribes. A signal that says they are not invincible and together we can triumph. What say you, do we sit back and watch the Romans swarm over our neighbours or do we stand alongside the Deceangli as brothers?'

The men in the tent roared their approval, showing support for the king.

'Then so be it,' said Caratacus, 'we move out at dawn. Send a message to Idwal to mobilise his army. Our time has come.'

—

The cheering continued and many men left the tent to pass the message to their respective clans. Cassus watched Prydain escape his reach for the second time in as many days. Inwardly he was seething, yet accepted his role had to be played out before he could pursue his oath to kill him.

'You have escaped me twice, slave boy,' he said under his breath, 'there won't be a third time.'

He turned and walked over to Caratacus who was leaning over the map with his warlords, planning the route they would take to the lands of the Deceangli.

'It has to be the coast,' said one of the Warlords, 'it is easier travelling and far enough away from Roman spies to ensure surprise when we get there.'

'What about straight over the mountains?' asked Caratacus.

'Much quicker,' agreed the warrior, 'but the paths are narrow in places, allowing only two abreast to pass. The army will be strung out over many miles and open to ambush.'

'The scout said they are only ten days march from the Cerrig,' said Caratacus, 'and it will take us that long whichever route we use, leaving little time for planning.'

'There is another option, my lord,' interrupted Cassus.

The men looked up at him with interest.

'Explain,' said Caratacus.

Cassus leaned over the map and pointed out a route on the eastern border of the Khymru, following the great river upstream to its source and beyond.

'If we follow the river,' said Cassus, 'it takes us through the lowlands of the Cornovii and up to the Deceangli coast. It cuts four days off the march and takes us directly into the path of the Victrix. All we have to do is inform Idwal of our intention and he can join us there for the battle. We will catch them unawares and our numbers will overwhelm them within hours.'

'I thought about that,' said Caratacus, 'it is indeed favourable but carries too much risk. By going east we encroach on the lands of the Dobunii and could draw the attention of the Legion Gemina. The last thing we want is to attract the attention of a second Legion.'

'That is a risk,' said Cassus, 'but what if they were too troubled dealing with other matters to look this way?'

'Explain,' said Caratacus.

'My lord, my men's swords still shine from cleaning and yearn to be dulled with blood. Our horses are fresh and we can be in the territory of the Dobunii in two days. Once there we can wreak havoc amongst the villages, striking quick and hard over a vast territory. The people will panic and word will spread to the fortress. The Gemina will think we are attacking them and do two things. First, they will stand to their garrison and focus on their defences, but secondly and more importantly, they will send out their cavalry to quell our aggression.'

'But you are no match for their cohorts,' said Caratacus.

'This is true,' said Cassus, 'but we don't intend to face them in conflict. We will be as shadows, striking hard and wreaking havoc before disappearing into the night.'

'But an army of this size cannot be hidden,' said Caratacus, 'and word of our movement would get back to the Gemina.'

'Perhaps so, but by then they will think they are the focus of the attack and won't risk sending out their forces until sure.'

'Your idea has merit,' said Caratacus, 'but you do realise what will happen when you are caught, for that is what you will be.'

'Perhaps so,' said Cassus, 'but if our blood adds time to you and Idwal's arm, then we will have died in a good cause.'

'Why would you do this?' asked Caratacus.

'To aid our people and free Britannia,' said Cassus.

Caratacus looked around and saw the approval in the eyes of his warlords.

'So be it,' said Caratacus. 'Brief your men and leave as soon as possible. You have four days until we reach the open plains and we need the Gemina Legion to be otherwise engaged. Can you do that?'

'Yes, my lord,' said Cassus, 'leave it to me.'

'I will spread word of your bravery to Idwal and your people,' said Caratacus, 'and the druids will carve your name in the stones of Mona.'

'I am honoured,' said Cassus. 'Now I will take my leave. We have a long ride before us.'

'Of course,' said Caratacus and watched Cassus duck through the flaps of the tent.

Cassus made his way back to the campfires of his men, his mind racing with the task before him. He did indeed intend riding toward the Gemina Legion but it wasn't to confront the Romans, it was to alert them about Caratacus's plan. This was exactly what they had hoped for and he knew one way or the other, Britannia's fate would be decided in the next few days.

Chapter 18

The Legionary Fort at Viriconium
50 AD

Ostorius Scapula stalked the ramparts of Viriconium, looking out into the forests surrounding the newly built fortress. His scarlet cloak was fastened down the front and he wore a fur-lined tunic against the chill of the Britannic night. Behind him, his auxiliary cavalrymen slept wrapped in their saddle blankets alongside the paddocks, enabling them to be riding from the fort within moments of receiving any command. Back in the barrack blocks, he knew thousands of Legionaries slept in their tunics, their armour within arm's reach and their packs ready with rations and water. Again, they were ready for instant mobilisation, though it would take far more time to organise them and by the time they left the fort, the cavalry could be miles away, racing toward wherever the conflict would take place. But of course, that depended on the actions of others.

He had been there for weeks waiting for news of Caratacus and the information feeding back from his scouts was limited. News had come that the Victrix was moving from the north and the second Augusta had Caratacus under pressure from the south so he knew

Caratacus had to act in the next few days. It was possible the king could turn and make his way back into the valleys of the Silures and Scapula knew that if he did, the campaign against Caratacus would stall for another year. There was no way the Legions could sustain a campaign through the winter in such hostile territory, so all he could hope for was that Caratacus's ego was as big as his stature. The noose was tightening and though they could afford to wait, Scapula was under pressure from Rome for results and craved the confrontation.

–

Twenty miles away, Cassus and his men waited on a hill above a village. He had briefed his men regarding the plan he had made with Caratacus and to their credit, they bought into it entirely, totally unaware Cassus was about to betray them.

Below them was a Dobunii village laying silent in the darkness. The plan was simple. They were to descend on the clan with burning torches and set fire to the thatched roofs, killing anyone appearing out of the huts. Cassus saw no problem with this as he had no respect for the Dobunii at all. The Roman in him saw them as heathen while the Deceangli influence saw them as traitors for bending their knee. They didn't deserve to live.

He knew he had to escape the fist of Deceangli warriors if he was to get to the fort but no opportunity had presented itself as yet. However, this was the chance he needed. He would lead the attack and, in the confusion, ride into the darkness unseen. His men would not notice him missing until first light and assume he had fallen in the fight. By then he would be at the fort and the Gemina would be mobilized.

He looked around at his men. Some held clay pots suspended from poles. Inside, the embers of a fire glowed red and they walked quickly amongst their comrades, pausing as each one held their rush torches against the flames. When they were all lit, Cassus nudged his horse forward and the rest of his men followed down the slope, gradually increasing the pace until they were galloping toward the village. It had started; the assault had begun.

--

In the camp of Caratacus, thousands of warriors also wrapped their cloaks around them as they struggled for sleep. Caratacus had temporarily prohibited the use of campfires at night, knowing too well that enemy forces often counted the glows to estimate their opponent's number. The march had been good so far and without incident but he knew the next few days would be crucial to their success. A day's march to the east lay Viriconium, the headquarters of the Gemina and though he was confident he had the strength to take on a Legion, he preferred it was on his terms and at a time of his choosing. Confronting them here would be of little value and end up in many lives lost for little gain, while combining with Idwal in the north to wipe out the Victrix could change history.

His tent was lit with oil lamps and hidden in a small valley to conceal the light from prying eyes. Around the table stood his warlords, going over the reports of the day. The command structure consisted of five men from his original Catuvellaunian army, all survivors from Medway – Gwydion of the Blaidd who had become a trusted lieutenant over the past few years and offered a Deceanglian viewpoint when making decisions, and four clan leaders from the Silures representing the combined clans from the south, each markedly different from the rest of the gathered men by their dress and face markings.

Catuvellauni and Deceangli wore mostly the same clothing, consisting of checked leggings and woollen jackets, possibly covered with chain mail armour. Each man wore a helmet bearing the emblem of their individual clans and wore swords strapped to their backs, a sign of the warrior and testament to their individual strength in battle.

The Silures on the other hand were more lightly attired. Their leggings were plain as were their tunics, both made of softened cow hide or deer skin. They wore no helmets on their heads, preferring to allow their black hair to fall freely about their shoulders interwoven with strips of blood red fabric, the colour of war. Every Silures warrior had facial tattoos on one side of their face, winding their way from brow to jaw and often down their necks. The intertwining, branchlike designs were representative of nature and the pagan gods they worshipped.

The Silures were formidable warriors and feared no one, yet they fought differently to all other tribes he knew. Rather than face an enemy across open ground and fight with honour head on, they preferred to hide in the forests and hills, making the most of the landscape and their affinity with nature. They would blend in amongst the foliage before descending on an enemy like an avalanche, striking swiftly to inflict as much devastation as they could before disappearing again as quickly as they had appeared. It was a strange way of war and one alien to the rest of the Britannic tribes, yet it had been successful for the Silures and they had grown to become the most feared tribes in the country. Even on this campaign they kept their distance from the main body, preferring to weave their ways through any available forests rather than use the well-worn footpaths of the Khymru.

Caratacus sighed inwardly. They were a strange people and not easily handled, yet without them he was hamstrung. He needed their strength if he was to become successful. Yet it was a temporary measure, for unbeknownst to anyone else, Caratacus's plan for the future didn't involve the Silures, at least not in their present form for they were far too troublesome. No, his ambition was to combine all the other tribes under his banner to drive out the Romans before claiming the title of King of a united Britannia. They would be one people in a united land with common cause and there would be no place for a tribe such as the Silures.

They could change or be changed, as simple as that, but that was for the future. At the moment he needed their swords and more importantly their reputation, but after the Romans were driven out and the island nation stood together as one, neither would count for anything and he would turn his attention to the fertile slopes of the Silures lands.

'So,' said Caratacus eventually, 'how goes the day?'

'The main force are spread throughout the valley, Lord,' said one of the Catuvellauni chiefs, 'and impatient to reach our goal.'

'And the food situation?'

'Is good at the moment. Our supply wagons are full and should last until we reach the Cerrig. Messages have been sent to the Cornovii asking for support and we have patrols raiding the villages of the Dobunii. The men eat cold Cawl and bread is being brought in from the local villages.'

'What about your men?' asked Caratacus to Wolfeye, one of the Silures' leaders.

'Worry not about our men, Caratacus,' he said, 'they are well looked after by our people and they too are impatient for battle.'

Caratacus nodded silently. It was well known that the Silures were constantly resupplied by their own people and to be fair, they never relied on the supply trains of Caratacus for anything.

'Good,' he said. 'What news of our allies?'

Gwydion stepped forward.

'Word was sent to Idwal,' he said, 'and the riders should be there by now. He has been told to assemble his army and travel east to face the Victrix here.' Gwydion leaned over and placed a row of pebbles across a drawn valley on the map. 'He is to take a holding position here until we arrive. Knowing the Romans as we do, they will pause and set up their own defensive lines to the front of Idwal while they assess the situation. That gives us time to join forces and launch an immediate attack before they can send for help. By the time the Gemina are notified, we will be caked in the blood of victory.'

'Excellent,' said Caratacus. 'So, tomorrow we leave the cloak of the forests behind us and travel the lowlands of the Cornovii. We will move fast but even if we face no challenge, we will not reach the safety of the Wrekin hills for two days and will still have to camp at least one night in the open. Even with the diversion being caused in the east by Cassus and his men, we can't afford to be complacent.' He leaned over the map once more. 'At this point,' he said, placing two stones on the map, 'my scouts tell me there is a ridge linking two hills. The ridge dominates the land and you can see in all directions from its peak. One of these has a hill fort used by a local Cornovii clan. It is of no great strength but will offer some protection for our men. Tomorrow night we will take over this hill fort and though it is not big enough for all, the rest of the army can camp on the other peak and the slopes to either side. All are linked by high ground and it affords a good defensive position should the need arise.'

'My men will not sleep like cattle within stone walls,' said Wolfeye.

'I understand that,' said Caratacus, 'but this is the area we are most at risk. There are no great forests nearby to hide an army but the adjacent peaks are open should you wish to use them.'

'Our foot soldiers will use the slopes,' said Wolfeye, 'and there is a forest an hour's ride away big enough for the horsemen. They will camp there and come to fight should the need arise.'

Caratacus grunted but knew better than to argue with these difficult men.

'So be it,' he said. 'Two more nights and we will be alongside Idwal. Get some sleep.'

The men left the tent while Caratacus stared down at the map, alone with his thoughts, unaware that to the east, a lone rider was about to change the course of history.

—

Outside the Legionary fort at Viriconium, a line of ten armed cavalry stood patiently either side of a solitary barbarian horseman. It was the middle of the night so a messenger had been sent to wake the Legatus.

Back in the officer's barracks, Scapula woke to the sound of someone knocking on the wooden door.

'My lord,' said a voice, 'your presence is needed.'

Scapula shot off his bunk and opened the door immediately.

'What news?' he asked.

'My lord, our scouts have captured an enemy rider and hold him outside the gates.'

'Why is this of interest to me?' asked Scapula.

'My lord, he demands audience with you and will speak to no other.'

'What is the nature of his demand?' asked Scapula.

'He refuses to say but said to give you this.' The soldier handed over a Pugio.

Scapula stared down at the dagger in confusion but suddenly his eyes opened wide in comprehension. A solitary Pugio was the sign of the Exploratores.

'This man,' he said, 'describe him.'

'No different to the rest of them,' said the soldier. 'We have disarmed him but he insists on speaking to you.'

'Tell me,' said Scapula, 'when he was caught, did he say anything else?'

'Only to hold and that he was friend not foe,' said the soldier.

'And in what language did he say this?'

The soldier paused as he realised he had missed the obvious difference between the warrior and those native to Britannia.

'Latin,' he said at last.

'Bring him to me,' shouted Scapula, 'and alert the garrison. Prepare to move out.'

'Yes, my lord,' said the soldier and turned away as the door slammed.

Inside the quarters, Scapula dressed quickly. If this man was who he thought he was then this was it – the message he had been waiting for.

–

Ten minutes later the door knocked again and this time was answered by one of Scapula's servants. Outside, an armed guard escorted a solitary man, taking no chances with the native warrior.

'Scapula expects us,' said the Decurion in charge.

'Bring them in,' called a voice, and the servant stepped aside to allow the guards to pass.

Scapula had dressed and now stood in full ceremonial armour. The guards halted and Scapula could see the warrior in their midst.

'Move,' said Scapula and the front rank opened to allow him full sight of the prisoner. Scapula stepped forward to stare at him.

'Who are you?' he asked.

'My name is Cassus Maecilius,' came the answer, 'son of Gaius Pelonius Maecilius of the province of Picenum.'

The guards turned to stare in confusion. Their prisoner was every inch a Britannic warrior yet he spoke Latin as well as any of them.

'How do I know you are who you say you are?' asked Scapula.

'You don't,' said Cassus. 'I seek Governor Ostorius Scapula and will share words with him only.'

'Then you have found him,' said Scapula. 'The rest of you men, return to your units.'

'My lord, are you sure?' asked the Decurion guard commander.

'I believe he is who he claims,' said Scapula. 'You men are dismissed.'

Cassus looked over his shoulder as the room cleared and finally he was alone with Scapula. The Legatus stepped forward and offered his forearm.

'Cassus Maecilius,' he said, 'I have been waiting for you. Welcome to the XIV *Gemina Martia Victrix*.'

Cassus returned the gesture.

'Are you hungry?' asked Scapula. 'Or perhaps you would like some wine?'

'Just some water,' said Cassus.

'So be it,' said Scapula, 'take a seat.'

They both sat at the table as a servant poured a mug of water from a pitcher.

'Leave us,' said Scapula and soon the two men were alone in the room.

'Well,' said Scapula, 'I have to admit your appearance is extraordinary. I suppose I should have expected this.'

Cassus looked down briefly. The way he was dressed seemed normal to him now and he often forgot the clean-shaven person with short hair he used to be.

'So,' said Scapula, 'do you have the news I crave?'

'I believe I do, my lord,' said Cassus, 'Caratacus has taken the bait and moves north as we speak.'

'Excellent,' said Scapula, 'do you know which route he intends to take?'

'I do,' said Cassus, 'and his army is less than two days march from here as we speak.'

Scapula stood up and looked at Cassus in disbelief.

'He takes the river route?' he said in astonishment. 'But surely he knows we are here; why risk our involvement?'

'Because he believes your cavalry will be too busy dealing with me and my men to take any rumours of his army seriously.'

'Your men?'

'There are a hundred horsemen laying waste to local Dobunii villages as we speak,' said Cassus. 'I was supposed to be amongst them but stole away to report here.'

'Won't you be missed?'

'They will think that I fell in battle but will continue with the assaults in the hope of attracting your attention. The plan is that while you are dealing with them, Caratacus will steal by under your very nose.'

'The plan has merit,' said Scapula, 'he knows we can't ignore the assaults on the Dobunii; we have pledged our protection and if we fall short, then future client kings will be more reluctant to bend their knee. We will have to deploy at least a cohort on their trail.'

'There is no need to split your forces, my lord,' said Cassus. 'Tomorrow night their target will be the village at the base of the black hill. Hide a century of archers within the village and the attackers will ride into the trap leaving you to concentrate on Caratacus.'

'I thought you rode with these men,' said Scapula, 'why do you offer them up for sacrifice?'

'They are Deceangli, my lord, and despite my similar attire, I am Roman. There is no conflict of allegiance.'

'Then it will be so,' said Scapula. 'Come, we will go to the map room and you can show me Caratacus's route. I want my cavalry to be gone within the hour and the Legion marching by dawn.'

For the next half hour Cassus showed Scapula the intended route and potential sites for confrontation. They soon worked out that even if they marched at double time, by the time they caught him up he would be well past the fort.

'Perhaps it's not a bad thing,' said Scapula. 'By approaching from the rear we can squeeze him between us and the Victrix. The only thing is by the time we reach him he will be clear of this open ground and amongst the mountains of the Wrekin on the northern edge of the Cornovii territory. Once there we may never get him out.'

'Perhaps I can help,' said Cassus. 'I may be able to get him to catch breath.'

'How?' asked Scapula.

'By telling him the truth,' said Cassus. 'Let him know he is walking into a trap and he will have no option but to form a defence. All we need to do is convince him the Victrix is closer than they actually are.'

'And you think he will believe you?'

'I have an idea that will make him believe me,' said Cassus, 'but I will need a hundred of your best cavalry on the fastest horses.'

'Consider it done,' said Scapula, 'I will place two centuries of scouts under your command. You do what you have to do and I will march the Legion north. If you can hold him up for one day, we have every chance of facing him in open ground here.' He pointed at a blank area of the map.

Cassus stood to leave.

'What about all this?' said Scapula, indicating Cassus's appearance. 'Don't you want to assume your true persona?'

'I don't have the time,' said Cassus, 'I'll just have to hope my fellow riders don't mistake me for the enemy and place an arrow in my back. In the meantime, the cover may well suit my needs one more time.'

'In what way?'

'To administer a long overdue retribution,' said Cassus, with a cold look in his eyes.

Scapula paused and considered asking him the nature but decided to let it go. As long as Cassus carried out his task, Scapula had no interest in petty squabbles of lesser men.

'Then leave as soon as you can,' said Scapula. 'You will have to ride like the wind to overtake Caratacus but the outcome of this campaign lies in your hands. Don't let me down.'

Cassus saluted, an act that felt strange in the guise of a Deceangli. He left the wooden building and an hour later he was riding north through the forests of the Dobunii along with a hundred and sixty scouts, hell bent on overtaking the army of Caratacus. Behind him he knew there were other patrols galloping in other directions to send word to Geta in the north and Vespasian in the south. They were to close in at double time with immediate effect and trap Caratacus between all three Legions. It was time to close the net.

Chapter 19

The Lands of the Cornovii
50 AD

Caratacus led his army across the plains of the Cornovii. Behind him, his warriors were spread out as far as the eye could see in case of attack. His mounted warriors covered his right flank to give warning of any unexpected assault from the Gemina but the longer the day went, the more confident Caratacus became.

Before him he could see the ridge that split the plains in two, the place where he and his men would stay overnight. His scouts had already secured the two peaks and the local clan had been pre-warned to make the king welcome.

As they approached the hills, a delegation from the local clan met them at a bridge across a fast-flowing river and gave him tribute of a pair of beautiful horses.

'My lord, we are honoured you have chosen our lands to rest,' said the old chief. 'Our homes are your homes.'

'We don't need your lodges, old man,' said Caratacus, 'though would make use of these two hills and the fort upon the summit.'

'Then they are yours, my lord,' said the man, 'and henceforth will be known as Caer Caradog in honour of your name.'

Caratacus nodded and accepted the horses.

'I am honoured,' he said, 'and your allegiance will be remembered.' Without further ado, he rode off and headed up the steep slopes to the fort on the summit. Over the next few hours the rest of the army crossed the bridge and spread out over the two hills. The only defences were those around the small fort, so patrols were deployed further afield to prevent any sneak attacks. By the time everyone was over the bridge, night was almost upon them and his men spread out to get some much-needed rest.

Up in the fort, Caratacus and his warlords made use of the few huts still standing and enjoyed the luxury of hot food from the fires of the locals. Overall it had been a successful campaign so far, with little attention from any enemy and they were on target to join with the Deceangli in days. Caratacus was exhausted and made his excuses before retiring to get some sleep in the corner of one of the huts. He knew that over the next few days there would be little chance to rest, let alone sleep.

–

Five miles to the North, Cassus and the two centuries of scouts sat waiting for night to fall. They had bypassed Caratacus's army the previous night and had been on the forward slopes of the Wrekin hills, frantically preparing the subterfuge they hoped would gain Scapula the much-needed time to catch them up. One of the centurions came up to Cassus and stood beside him, looking across the plains to the hills where they had watched Caratacus go to ground earlier in the day.

'He has got further than we thought,' said the centurion.

'He has,' said Cassus, 'but there is still hope. If we can fool him into staying there tomorrow, then at least two of the Legions can be here by daybreak the following day and if they can hold him until the Augusta arrive, we can close the trap.'

'But he will have the advantage of the high ground,' said the centurion.

'But we will have three Legions,' said Cassus. 'There is no way he can hold out against such a force.'

'So,' said the centurion, 'when do you want us to start?'

'Wait until midnight,' said Cassus, 'then tell the men to proceed as quickly as possible. We will have but one chance to get this right.'

-

Several hours later, a warrior on sentry duty stared in disbelief across the plain toward the Wrekin hills. At first, he couldn't believe what he was seeing, but soon realised the seriousness of what he was witnessing. He sent a runner to the fort to wake Caratacus and ten minutes later, the king came to the lookout post, accompanied by two of his men.

'What is so important that it drags me from my sleep?' he asked. 'Are we under attack?'

'No, my lord,' said the warrior, 'but I thought you should see this.' He pointed across the plain toward the Wrekin hills.

Caratacus stared and as the realisation sunk in, his heart fell. In the distance, he could see hundreds of pinpricks of light, littering the forward slopes of the distant mountains.

Though they were too far away to count, he knew that each was a campfire for resting men.

'Where did they come from?' he shouted. 'Where are my scouts? Why wasn't I warned about this?'

'My lord, they only appeared over the last hour, so whoever they are must have arrived after dark. Our scouts wouldn't have seen them.'

'Who do you think they are?' asked Gwydion.

'Who knows?' said Caratacus. 'It could be Cornovii, Deceangli or even the damned Victrix.'

'But they are in the north,' said Gwydion, 'over two days' march from here.'

'They could have turned south,' said Caratacus. 'Perhaps they got wind of our advance and decided to face us.'

'Possibly,' said Gwydion. 'The thing is, whoever they are, there seems to be more fires than stars on that hill. I don't know much about the structure of the Legions but I have spent much time with Prydain and know their units are built around groups of eight men called Contubernia. If each unit has a fire, there are close to ten thousand men waiting for us across that valley.'

'Of course,' said Caratacus, 'I forgot about him. Where is the Roman? I need his perspective.'

'He is out on patrol, my lord,' said Gwydion, 'and won't be back until daybreak.'

'*Shit*,' cursed Caratacus, staring at the far mountains once more. 'As soon as he is back, bring him to me, I need to make sense of this.'

'Yes, my lord,' said Gwydion and watched the king storm his way back up the hill.

Across the plain, Cassus and the scouts returned to the treeline and their horses. For the last few hours they had been out on the forward slopes of the hill, running from fire to fire making sure they kept burning through as much of the night as possible. The previous day had been spent collecting firewood and throughout the night, each man tended ten campfires, sending their light across the plains and reinforcing the false image of an entire army camped on the slopes. Now the sun was rising, they were happy for the fires to go out as their light would soon disappear with the dawn. But their work wasn't done yet. Quintus and Drusus, the centurions in charge of the two scout units, joined Cassus to discuss the events of the night.

'Do you think it has worked?' asked Quintus.

'Let's hope so,' said Cassus, 'it has been a long night, but the air was clear so hopefully we have given Caratacus pause for thought. Tell the men to grab some food for there is work yet to do. If they see no activity, they may suspect something so it is important to reinforce their doubts. Quintus, as soon as the sun is up, send patrols twenty men strong out onto the plains between us and the ridge. Make no attempt at concealment for we want them to think you are advance patrols of a Legion, scouting a route forward. Drusus, you take your century and head beyond the ridge to carry out the same task to their rear. They need to think that Vespasian is also to hand and think twice about retreat.'

'Tell me,' said Drusus, 'what rank were you in the Legion?'

'Decurion,' said Cassus.

'For such a lowly rank, it seems you enjoy commanding your betters,' said Drusus.

'I no longer have rank, nor indeed a Legion,' said Cassus, 'and work outside of their constraints. I understand your frustrations, but there is much at stake here and I speak with the authority of Scapula.'

'Fret not,' laughed the centurion, 'we will see this task completed, but when this is over, if you want to return to the comforting embrace of a Legion, seek me out. You would make a first class Optio.'

'Thanks,' said Cassus, 'we will see.'

Drusus mounted his horse to return to his men. Half an hour later he watched them gallop into the distance while the other century split into four patrols of twenty and spread out on the plain below him. Cassus chewed on some dry meat and stared over the rapidly lightening plains. He was looking for dust trails, a sign that Caratacus was on the move but as the sun appeared and the plains stayed empty, he knew the subterfuge had worked. Now all he could do was hope the messengers sent out by Scapula had made it through and the Legions were truly on their way.

–

Five miles away, Gwydion approached the hut occupied by Caratacus only to be stopped by his guards.

'Hold,' said one, 'the king still sleeps.'

'Still sleeping,' sneered Gwydion, 'the sun is almost over the horizon and his army chomps at the bit. Let me through.'

The guards looked at each other nervously, unsure of what action to take.

'Listen,' growled Gwydion, 'there are probably up to ten thousand men in those mountains before us, each sharpening their swords and relishing the opportunity to spill our blood. What king would sleep through such dire threat? Now let me in.'

'Let him through,' shouted a voice from within.

The guards stepped aside, relieved that the decision had been taken from their hands. Gwydion walked into the dimly lit hut expecting to see Caratacus sitting on a mattress, still struggling to wake. Instead, he found the king fully dressed and at a stone table, though obviously worse for wear. Several empty wine jugs stood testament to the long night's drinking behind him.

'Your men thought you were asleep, my lord,' said Gwydion.

'My eyes haven't closed throughout the night,' said Caratacus, 'though I now regret that decision.' His voice was slurred and his eyes were bloodshot. He lifted a goblet to his mouth before throwing it away in disgust when he found it empty.

'You haven't slept at all?'

'Nope, nor do I have strategy so I sought the answers in this excellent Roman wine. Did you know this wine comes from the Roman slopes overlooking the sea they call the Mare Nostrum? That's a full season's march away yet they deliver it to Britannia for their officers as fresh as the day they picked the grape. How do they do that, Gwydion? How does one nation grow so strong and become so advanced, that they can devote entire ships to delivering wine to mere men at the far side of the world? What gods enable such power?'

Gwydion was concerned. The king was obviously drunk, and in no state to lead the army.

'My lord,' he said, 'the men are impatient and seek direction. What are your orders?'

'Orders?' Caratacus sighed. 'My orders are to kill every Roman, drive them back to the sea and fire their cursed fleet with flaming arrows, as they flee with tails between their legs. How about that, Gwydion? Do you think the men will carry them out?'

Gwydion knew he had to do something. Men being drunk in battle was normal for the tribes but for a king to make decisions that could affect an entire army whilst in such a state was dangerous.

'My lord,' he said, 'you need to rest. I will speak to your warlords. When you are awake, we will make the decisions that need to be made. A few more hours will make no difference.'

'You are probably right,' said Caratacus. 'A few hours are all I need.' He staggered over to the cot in the corner and collapsed onto the dirty straw mattress. Within minutes he was snoring loudly and Gwydion left the hut to find the warlords.

Within the hour all the warlords with the exception of the absent Silures chiefs gathered on the ramparts of the hill fort. Voices were raised regarding what to do next, with some advocating an immediate assault while others suggested they withdraw until the situation became clear.

'We can't go forward,' said one of the warlords, 'we will be marching into the unknown. There have already been reports of Roman Scout patrols between us and the Wrekin; by now they surely know we are here and have constructed their defences.'

'And yet we have come so far for this opportunity,' said another, 'what honour would be in our retreat when finally faced by those whom we sought? No, we should wait until Caratacus regains his mind and heed his words. He is a great king and will know what to do.'

'So we should just stay here and wait?' the first man sneered. 'What sort of plan is that? The Romans make their strategy while our drunken king snores and our men sharpen already sharp blades in boredom.'

'No,' said Gwydion. 'While we wait, we get busy. This ridge is covered with loose rocks. Instruct our men to pile them into defensive walls in case of attack. Take the opportunity to form a defensive system. We may not need it but at least it keeps idle hands busy.'

'Build a temporary fort that we probably won't need,' sneered the warrior. 'Where is the sense in that?'

'There is every sense,' said Gwydion. 'The Romans build a new fortification every night, and they march and destroy it again the next morning before they leave. By using this tactic they are never taken by surprise and have become the greatest army in the world.'

'We are not Roman,' snarled one of the Warlords, 'we are Celts and fight in our own way.'

'I accept this,' said Gwydion, 'all I am saying is this; until Caratacus is able to take command again, at least do him the honour of protecting our men from unexpected attack. I'm sure that on the morrow we will confront the foe head on but until then, we need to cover all possibilities.'

Finally they all agreed and they set the men to building lines of loose stone walling around the base of the hills. With a workforce of thousands the results were soon visible and by the time midday passed, the walls were already waist high. Caratacus was still absent from the defences but by the time night fell, Gwydion at least felt they had done everything they could do to protect the army. Throughout the day, more and more reports came in about Roman patrols on all sides and by the time

Caratacus emerged from the hut, the news waiting for him was grim. Gwydion was summoned by the king and walked around the hill, examining the defences from the higher ground.

'You have done well, Gwydion,' he said, 'though it saddens me to have put you in this position.'

'To be honest, my lord, I think you would have done the same. The situation is still veiled and there are reports of Romans in all directions.'

'Who brings these reports?' asked Caratacus.

'Our own patrols,' said Gwydion. 'There have been skirmishes all day and we have managed to kill three of their number.'

'What about prisoners?' asked Caratacus.

'None, my lord.'

'How about the Legion on the Wrekin?'

'There has been no sign, my lord,' said Gwydion. 'They seem to have disappeared.'

'But why?' asked Caratacus. 'It makes no sense. Why would they withdraw unless they are up to something?'

'I have no idea, my lord.'

'Has Prydain returned from Patrol?'

'He has.'

'Then have him attend me immediately,' said Caratacus. 'We have wasted too much time.'

Gwydion sent a runner and five minutes later Prydain came into the hut.

'Prydain, yet again I seek your counsel,' said Caratacus. 'It seems there was a Legion encamped in the foothills of the Wrekin yet they have disappeared. I would know what tactics are these that play on my nerves.'

'I have just heard the rumours of a Legion on the Wrekin,' said Prydain, 'but paid it no heed. On what basis have these conclusions been drawn?'

'We saw them last night,' said Caratacus. 'The lights from their fires covered the hill like fireflies.'

Prydain shook his head.

'My lord, whatever force was on those hills, it wasn't Roman.'

'How can you be so sure?' asked Caratacus.

'My lord, the Romans camp on relatively flat ground and always build a marching camp for protection. Even if they were on the Wrekin, their campfires would have been hidden by the earthen banks they would have thrown up around them. To be honest, it seems there is something else afoot here. What army broadcasts its presence with hundreds of campfires unless they want to be seen?'

Caratacus stared at Prydain in horror as the realisation sunk in. He stood up and stamped around the room, muttering under his breath. Finally he returned to face the two men.

'You are right,' he said, 'I don't believe there ever was an enemy force on the Wrekin and I have been taken for a fool. We have wasted a whole day on this ridge and need to get off it as soon as possible. Pass word to the warlords, keep alert on the defences but prepare to move out at first light.'

'Which way, my lord?'

'Nothing has changed,' said Caratacus, 'our path lies northward to meet the Victrix head on. Their trickery has gained them a day but no more and I swear that before this day is out, our blades will still taste Roman blood.'

Both men left to spread the word while Caratacus called his warlords, knowing that one way or another, his destiny was now upon him.

–

A few miles away, Cassus met with one of the scout patrols in the shelter of a small ravine.

'Drusus,' he said, 'well met.'

'Cassus, it has been a long day.'

'You are wounded,' said Cassus.

'A mere scratch,' said Drusus, subconsciously touching the open wound on his face. 'Luckily their archers are not as good as ours.'

'And the rest of your men?'

'We lost three,' said Drusus, 'though they sold their lives dearly and I feel the task is well done. But my men need rest, Cassus. We have seen two nights and three days without sleep. Our senses are dulled and the horses are exhausted.'

'Your work here is done,' said Cassus, 'and I will see that Scapula hears about your part in this. Grasp this opportunity to rest; we are far enough from the ridge to be troubled by their patrols.'

'Where are you going?' asked Drusus.

'There is one more thing I have to do,' said Cassus, 'but I would ask that you pass on this message to Scapula. When battle is joined the tribes will wear their hair loose as I do now. If your eye is caught by one amongst their ranks whose hair is tied back, pause before you administer your death blow, for you may be slaying a fellow Roman.'

'You are returning to the enemy's ranks?' asked Drusus in disbelief.

'I am,' said Cassus, 'there is one more task that demands my attention. Fight well, Drusus,' he said, turning his horse, 'and perhaps one day, I may just take you up on the position of Optio.'

'May the gods be with you, Cassus,' said Drusus and watched in admiration as the Exploratore rode back toward the ridge and into the ranks of an entire army.

Chapter 20

The Forests of the Cornovii

50 AD

Geta wrapped his waterproof cloak tight around him as his horse plodded onward through the Khymric rain. In front of him was a cohort of cavalry while behind him marched an entire Legion. Over five thousand soldiers of various disciplines, each exhausted after a full day's march with little rest. They had received the message from Scapula the previous day and had immediately turned south into the path of Caratacus's army, marching all day at double time.

The pace was beginning to take its toll so centurion Rufius, the Primus Pilus of the Legion rode up to the Legatus and paced his horse alongside him.

'My lord, the men need to rest,' he said.

'I know,' said Geta, 'but there is no time. Scapula could be fighting with Caratacus as we speak and may need our swords.'

'My lord,' said the Primus Pilus, 'unless these men get some rest, those who reach the field will be in no fit state to fight and will be fodder for the enemy arrows. Surely Scapula will need fighting men, not exhausted boys too tired to wield a sword.'

Geta stopped his horse and looked across at the senior centurion in the Legion. His Primus Pilus had served with him for three years and Geta valued his opinion in all things military.

'Rufius,' he said, 'I know I push the men to the limit but this whole Britannic campaign may rely on our presence in the field. If we fail in this, our names will go down in history as the Legion who failed Claudius.'

'My lord,' said Rufius, 'I know the men. They are at the end of their strength. Allow them a few hours to catch some sleep and some hot food and I promise you we will make up the lost time. We will forego the marching camp and strive through the night if need be. Keep up this pace and tomorrow you won't have more than a cohort still able to fight.'

Geta considered carefully. He knew Rufius was right yet it was a wager he was reluctant to take. Finally he relented and turned to the Tribune on the other side.

'Rufius is right,' he said. 'Fall the infantry out but order the non-combatants to remain on duty. The engineers and the medics, the Immunes and the orderlies, all will remain on duty to cook hot food in the communal pots while the Legion sleeps. The cavalry will guard our flanks while all this happens.' He turned to the Primus Pilus. 'Rufius, the men have four hours before we march again. Let them sleep for the first three and wake them to eat. After that, the next time we stop will be on the plains before the Wrekin.'

'It will be enough, my lord,' said Rufius and turned to gallop back down the line. Five minutes later over five thousand men lay wrapped in their cloaks to either side of the path, most of them sleeping within minutes. All those tasked with cooking forced themselves forward to a clearing, where a group of slaves were already seeking the drier firewood from the forest to feed the cooking fires.

Geta dismounted and realised that despite riding most of the way, he was also exhausted and needed to sleep. His second in command walked over to speak to him.

'My lord, do you want your tent erected?'

'No,' said Geta, 'I will sleep with my Legion.' He walked back down alongside the never-ending rows of sleeping Legionaries until he found a space. Without a fuss, he pulled his cloak tighter and lay down between two sleeping soldiers, just one more Legionary in the armies of Rome.

–

After what seemed like only a few minutes, Geta was woken by an orderly with a bowl of soup.

'One between two, my lord,' said the orderly quietly.

Geta sat up and took the bowl of hot soup gratefully. More bowls were being handed out down the line as the Legion was woken by those still on duty and Geta realised he must have been asleep for at least three hours. It had seemed like three minutes.

The soldier next to him sat up and for a moment stared at the Legatus in confusion and disbelief. The commander of the entire Legion was sitting next to him in the drizzling rain, sharing a bowl of soup with a mere Legionary. Geta smiled at him.

'Dig in, Soldier,' he said, 'or I may just eat it all myself.'

Nervously, the Legionary retrieved his own spoon and shared the soup with his commanding officer, a story he would tell many times over the next few years.

Far to the south, Vespasian had also received the orders from Scapula and had turned his Legion northward to close Caratacus's escape route. Though he was several days away, he knew the Silures would already have riders galloping north to warn their people of the approaching threat from the Augusta and that was exactly what he wanted.

–

Scapula was the closest of all and his Legion lay concealed in the forests to the east of the ridge containing Caratacus's army. He hadn't received word from Geta and could only hope he was in striking distance. Caratacus was exactly where they wanted him, but if he left the ridge before the arrival of any of the other Legions, then Scapula would be forced to face Caratacus on less than favourable terms, a situation he wanted to avoid at all costs. He also knew that whatever happened, the confrontation would have to be the following day. The time for waiting was over.

Chapter 21

The Plains of the Cornovii
50 AD

Prydain walked from sentry to sentry along the eastern edge of the escarpment. He had been there for the last hour and had been tasked to ensure the sentries stayed alert to the possibility of a night attack. He approached two of the men sitting on a rock and talking quietly, as they blew on their hands to garner some warmth in the pre-dawn chill. Behind them, the horizon appeared slowly out of the darkness, heralding the imminent rising of the sun and the start of the army's continued march northward.

All around he could hear the sound of warriors stirring from their sleep and rummaging in their packs for food to break their fast. Horses snorted from the lower slopes as their riders approached to prepare them for the day's ride, and on the other hill he could see the movement of hundreds of men milling about, as the army stirred from its slumber. He turned around and looked to his front once more, knowing his stint would be over within the next half hour.

The plains below were still cloaked in darkness, and as the sun's rays crept through the fissures of the rocks they reached into the dense darkness below, long spears of light piercing the heart of the dark enemy.

Prydain turned to walk away but something caught his eye and he spun to stare into the valley. For a second there was nothing, but within moments it happened again; a flash of light where no flash of light should be. Subconsciously he grabbed the warrior's shoulder before him and stared into the darkness, hoping desperately he was wrong, but when it happened a third time he knew he was right – it was a reflection.

–

To the north, Cassus rode toward the hill in the darkness. He knew he was taking a risk but it was one he had to take. The slopes loomed high above and soon he heard the sound of a river ahead. Somewhere along the river, he knew there would be a bridge, but he could not afford to waste any time searching for it; he had to be back amongst the warriors before sunrise.

Realising there was little time, he jumped from his horse and slapped its haunches to send it back into the valley. He stripped naked and holding his clothes above his head, waded into the river, gasping as the icy water reached up to his midriff. He picked his way forward, feeling carefully with his feet for good purchase, expecting at any second to be washed away by the current.

Eventually he reached the far bank and wiped the worst of the water from his body with a handful of bracken. As he was dressing, he suddenly stopped and stood slowly upright as he felt a spear point rest lightly on the back of his neck.

'Declare yourself, stranger,' said a voice.

'I am Cassus,' he said, 'son of Bearskin, warrior of the Catuvellauni.'

'Why were you on the far side of the river?' asked the voice.

'I was sent on a special mission by Caratacus,' said Cassus, 'and need to reach him as soon as possible. I had no time to seek a bridge.'

'Turn around,' said the voice.

Cassus turned slowly and faced the warrior. He was a young man and even in the dark, Cassus could see the arrogance in his manner.

'I too am Catuvellauni,' said the warrior, 'and you have an accent that is strange to me.'

'I ride with the Deceangli,' said Cassus, 'or at least I did. My men are all dead, ambushed by the Romans. Only I survived and have important news for the king.'

'How do I know you are not a Roman spy?' asked the warrior.

'Take me to Caratacus,' said Cassus, 'he will vouch for me.'

'No, we will wait here until the next patrol passes and have you taken to be questioned by our leaders. If you are who you say you are, they will know the truth.'

Cassus thought quickly. Actually the last person he wanted to see was Caratacus as he had returned for one reason and one reason only – to kill Prydain. He turned his head quickly to look across the river.

'What was that noise?' he asked.

The warrior followed his gaze and Cassus took the opportunity to swipe aside the spear before plunging his knife up through the young warrior's throat and into his brain. For a second the man's eyes opened wide in terror before he fell silently to the floor, already dead.

Cassus withdrew his blade and wiped it on the man's tunic before replacing the knife in his belt. He dragged the body to the river and pushed it amongst the reeds, making sure it was hidden from prying eyes, before making his way up the hill toward the ridgeline.

–

Caratacus and his warlords ran from their huts and over to the ramparts of the small hill fort, to witness the events unfolding on the plains below. All around the hill, his warriors were running to collect their weapons and take station at the defences.

Before him in the growing morning light, thousands of Romans manoeuvred into position on the plain. Dust clouds raised by Centuries of galloping horses cast a haze over the infantry cohorts and Caratacus gazed in awe at the precision of the military discipline. From his position he could see the different arms of the Legion ranging from the slingers, archers and spear throwers to the magnificent auxiliary cavalry and the massed array of red caped Legionaries, each moving into position.

'How did they do this?' snapped Caratacus. 'How can one man move an army of thousands in the dark with no noise? It is impossible.'

Nobody answered; they were too busy staring at the army before them. Ordinarily they would not think twice about attacking an enemy head on, but the river formed an unmoveable barrier and they had been hemmed in by their own defences. Caratacus spun around.

'The bridge,' he called, 'have they reached it yet?'

'No my lord,' answered a voice.

'Then get down there,' he shouted, 'and get the cavalry across. *Hurry.*'

One of his warlords ran from the hill, shouting orders. Below him, men mounted their horses and galloped along the river toward the bridge, but as they drew close, they saw a horde of riders racing toward them on the other side.

'Too late,' shouted one of the warriors, 'their numbers are many.'

'Then deny them the crossing,' shouted the warlord, 'bring me fire.'

The riders dismounted and were joined by dozens of nearby infantry to pile bracken on the bridge.

'My lord, they draw close,' shouted a warrior.

'Then buy me some time,' shouted the warlord, 'we cannot give them this crossing.'

The man paused for a second before remounting his horse.

'*Follow me!*' he screamed, and led his unit of fifty cavalry galloping across the bridge toward the advancing cohort.

'*Keep working*,' shouted the warlord, and quickly the bridge was filled with bracken and brushwood. Within minutes the crossing was piled high and a line of slaves ran from the camp with burning torches.

'My lord,' said a warrior, 'the bridge is ready. What would you have us do?'

In the distance the warlord could see his men closing in on the much larger Roman force, and knew there would be no survivors.

'Burn it,' he said and turned his own horse to gallop back up the hill.

Behind him the flames caught the brushwood immediately and within moments the bridge was ablaze, denying the enemy a place to cross.

–

Back on the summit, Caratacus was busy issuing orders. He knew he couldn't retreat as the majority of his army were foot soldiers and the Roman army would cut them down within hours, so he had to make a stand here on the hill.

'*Get me some riders*,' he screamed and a few moments later, several men rode up in a cloud of dust.

'You men,' he said, 'there is a passable ford half a day to the south. Break through their lines and then split up. Half are to head west and find the Silures, while the rest will ride north and try to reach Idwal. He is two day's ride away but if we can hold this hill for a few days, Idwal's men will force them to turn and protect their rear. This day is not yet lost. With the Silures warriors and Idwal's army we can still emerge victorious. Now get moving and do not fail me.'

The riders turned their horses and galloped away.

'The rest of you,' he shouted, 'build up the walls and place our spear throwers along the riverbank. If they want this victory, they will pay in blood for every step they take.'

The warlords returned to their men, and as the Legion across the river continued their manoeuvres, Caratacus's army frantically searched for more boulders to strengthen their defences.

–

Two hours later, Geta sat astride his horse looking over his assembled Legion. He knew that from the hill it would look an awesome sight, yet close up he could see the exhaustion in every man's eyes. They had marched all night and were in no fit state to fight, but it was important they portrayed an image that would make Caratacus pause for thought.

Blood had already been drawn as a unit of riders had ridden from the hill and attacked a far stronger force of his own cavalry. The skirmish had lasted only minutes and every warrior had been slaughtered mercilessly.

Reports had come back regarding the burning of a bridge, a fact that amused Geta. The burning of a single bridge would have no effect on his Legion whatsoever. If they needed bridges, his engineers would build them, dozens of them if necessary and within a matter of days. It was as simple as that. These people had no idea who they were dealing with.

Rufius approached and reined in his horse alongside the Legate.

'My lord, the Legion is in position. What are your orders?'

Geta didn't answer but looked around at the massed ranks.

'They are exhausted,' said Geta. 'How can I ask them to fight?'

'They are Legionaries, my lord,' said Rufius. 'I promised you an army and an army is what we have. Yes they are tired but one word from you and we will assault this hill with every ounce of strength we have left.'

'To what effect?' asked Geta.

'Only the gods can foretell the outcome,' said Rufius, 'but once across the river, we will not retreat.'

'Any sign of Scapula or Vespasian?'

'No, my lord. We have sent out scouts but there is no sign as yet.'

'I don't know,' said Geta, 'perhaps we should wait.'

'My lord,' said the Primus Pilus, 'every minute we wait, those defences get higher and our men will grow more tired. We have waited years and marched hundreds of miles to get this opportunity, the longer we wait the higher the possibility he will escape.'

'I see the sense in your words, Rufius, but I cannot go against the orders of Scapula. He made it clear there were to be a minimum of two Legions for any assault.'

'Then at least unleash the Onagers,' said Rufius.

'To what end?' asked Geta. 'They will not reach the fortress from down here.'

'No, but it will at least keep their heads down and stop them building up the defences on the slopes. Scapula may be here at any moment and anything we can do to ease the assault will help.'

'You are right of course,' said Geta, 'and my hesitation shames me. Give the order for the engineers to prepare the machines. Support them with archers and make sure every man in earshot knows about our intentions. Prepare to advance the Legion and let's send this heathen king a message he will never forget.'

The orders were quickly passed down the line and within moments, ranks of Cornicines blasted out the signal. Every soldier in the Legion stood to attention and from the depths of their ranks, a squad of riders galloped out to join Geta. The front rank opened and a fully armoured Legionary rode forward draped in a lion's skin cloak, holding up the sacred emblem of the Legion, the Aquila.

Every pair of eyes stared at the sculptured eagle perched on its golden laurel wreath, wings outstretched and grasping a thunderbolt in its talons. Geta rode up alongside the Aquilifer and together they turned to face the hill.

Geta drew his Gladius and held it high.

'Twentieth Valeria Victrix,' he called, 'before us lays the king of this cursed country. Take this day and we take

Britannia.' He dropped his sword to point toward the hill. 'For the Emperor and for Rome, *advance!*'

Immediately, five hundred drums beat out a march and as one, thousands of soldiers stepped forward in time to the beat, the whole plain a chequerboard of trained soldiers marching toward the ultimate battle, each one exhausted yet determined to win the day.

–

Yet again, Caratacus looked down in awe. The entire plain was full of manoeuvring cohorts and as one they approached the base of the hills.

'*Get more men to the river,*' he screamed, and watched as hundreds of men reinforced those already in the front line. 'Get me archers and prepare to darken the skies.'

The hill was alive with running men, and within minutes they had each taken up their defensive positions. Along the nearest bank, a thousand warriors held spears before them, ready to repel anyone wading across the river. Behind them rows of archers waited patiently for their opportunity to release their arrows and further back stood the main bulk of the army, the experienced warriors armed with sword or axe.

Caratacus descended the hill and faced the oncoming enemy. Over the water he could see his counterpart leading the Legion toward him. Suddenly, the drums stopped and the army ground to a halt in a cloud of dust. Caratacus stared at the Romans, impatient for the battle to begin.

–

Across the river, Geta turned to his second in command.

'Hold the Legion here,' he said, 'I will give this so-called king one more chance to save his people's lives. Rufius, attend me. And bring an interpreter.'

With a gentle kick, he urged his horse forward in the company of his Aquilifer. Though the sun was still low in the sky, a bead of sweat ran down his cheek and dripped from his chin onto the breast plate of his gleaming bronze Lorica Segmentata. It was ceremonial armour and unwieldy in battle, but every Roman knew that image was important when dealing with barbarians. His scarlet cloak blew gently in the wind and he glanced nervously at the standard bearer at his side, slightly satisfied that he was also awash with sweat.

Centurion Rufius rode up beside them, his own scarlet cloak blowing in the wind, though his armour consisted of a leather tunic covered with a chain link over-vest. It wasn't as ornate as the one worn by the Legate but was far more suitable for close quarter battle. When they were within shouting distance, Geta turned to his interpreter.

'Repeat my words exactly,' he said before facing the warriors on the far side of the river.

'Warriors of Britannia,' he called, 'I am Geta, Legatus of the Twentieth Valeria Victrix. Behold our strength and witness our resolve. You have been a valiant foe and your blades are dull with blood from your campaign but your time is over. End this now and no more blood need be shed.'

Across the river Caratacus walked forward until he stood alone in front of his own army.

'I am Caratacus,' he called, 'King of Britannia and leader of these men. Who are you to come into our lands and demand our servitude? By what right do you declare yourselves master and we slaves?'

'By the right of arms,' shouted Geta. 'As you once conquered enemy tribes, so we now conquer your lands. It is the way of warfare and has been so since time began. It is the way it will always be. You have run your race, Caratacus and have come up second. Show us your mettle and give your people a chance to live their lives. Cede to me and my Legion will leave this field before darkness falls, their blades un-blooded.'

'And what of me?' shouted Caratacus. 'What fate awaits a king?'

'You will be taken to Rome and answer to the Senate,' said Geta, 'King and Emperor face to face, talking as equals as things should be.'

'Yet I will be vanquished and my fate will be in his hands,' said Caratacus.

'It is the way of the world, Caratacus. In war, there is always a victor.'

'You are right,' said Caratacus, 'there is always a victor and perhaps this day he stands on this side of the river.'

Geta shook his head slowly.

'Do not fool yourself, Caratacus. My men already have the betterment of yours. We outnumber you, are better trained and hunger for battle. We will call upon weapons you cannot even imagine, machines that will shatter your puny walls and pour fire from the heavens. We have cross-bows that can carry death even unto your fort on the hill. Our numbers are endless and our resolve limitless. This alone will see us victorious but if you still doubt our ability, consider this. As we speak, there are two more Legions within an hour of this place. Each is larger than that before you, each as eager to end this today. Our numbers alone will overwhelm you.'

'You boast of numbers,' shouted Caratacus, 'yet we too have armies yet uncounted who ride to aid our cause. Look to your rear for they may appear at any moment.'

Geta turned and gave a hand signal. Behind him a rider galloped forward carrying a sack and pulled up beside the Legatus.

'If you refer to the armies you sent for, Caratacus,' he shouted, 'then they are not even aware we are here. Behold your messengers.'

The rider emptied the sack on the ground and ten severed heads rolled in the dust.

'You cannot win this, Caratacus,' called Geta. 'Show true kingship and enable your men to grow old in their lodges, telling tales of how they once faced a Legion. The decision is yours, Caratacus and the answer is simple, life or death.'

Caratacus stared at the severed heads on the far bank. His mind raced at the implications, for if Geta was right, they were alone with no chance of reinforcements. If they had to face three Legions then there was indeed no hope, but Geta had made an error; he had let slip that the Legion opposite was still alone and their own reinforcements may still be far off. Caratacus was confident that should battle be joined between just the two forces then the outcome was not guaranteed and he may still win the day, but he could not afford to wait; time was not on his side.

Quickly he gave an order over his shoulder, before turning once more to face Geta.

'We do not fear your shiny army, Roman,' he called, 'and we welcome the chance to greet our ancestors. I have listened to your words and now deliver an answer to mirror my contempt.' His hand moved slightly, giving a signal to a nearby archer and an arrow flew above the king's head, piercing the air and heading straight for Geta's heart.

Across the river, Rufius reacted first and instinctively swung his shield forward to cover the Legate. The arrow thudded into the laminated wood, piercing through and sending a shower of splinters against Geta's armour.

'*Treachery*,' shouted Rufius as he grabbed the Legate, and immediately hundreds of Roman archers replied with a barrage of their own, covering the four men as they galloped back to the lines. Across the river, the defending army crouched low and hid behind their shields, waiting patiently until the hail of death stopped. Finally they stood up and Caratacus stared after the retreating Legatus. The first success, albeit minor, belonged to Britannia but he knew the real fight was about to begin.

Chapter 22

Caer Caradog
50 AD

'Rufius, deploy all artillery immediately,' shouted Geta. 'Spread them across as wide a front as possible, yet out of reach of their archers. Empty every cart of missiles and pour fire upon them until we have nothing else to use. I want every Onager, Ballistae and Scorpio in the front line throwing a hail of death at these barbaric people and their king. I want every wall they have built demolished by midday, and I want to see rivers of blood running down the slopes of that hill before we assault.'

'What about the engineers, my lord?' asked Rufius. 'We will need trees to form bridges.'

'We have no time,' said Geta, 'the nearest trees large enough to span the river lay an hour away and we need to take this hill before nightfall.'

'Why before nightfall?' asked Rufius. 'The enemy is trapped on the hill and are not going anywhere. We can wear them down throughout the day and launch an attack after dark.'

'We can't,' said Geta, 'the Silures hordes could be here at any time and without the swords of Scapula, we would be at their mercy.'

'But I thought you intercepted his messengers,' said Rufius.

'We captured some,' said Geta, 'but five more escaped and will be well on their way to their allies.'

'But I counted ten heads,' said Rufius.

'Five of their warriors,' said Geta, 'and five of our own slaves. It was necessary to cast doubt in the heart of Caratacus.'

Rufius nodded in agreement, the death of five slaves to meet the needs of the Legion not even registering as an event on his military mind.

'Consider it done,' he said and turned to ride back to the first cohort.

–

Five miles away Legate Ostorius Scapula led his Legion out of the wood line and onto the plain. His Legion had been held up by marauding bands of cavalry and though they offered no serious threat to the Legion, they were a problem that had to be dealt with. Finally his scouts had run the last of them down and reported back to him.

'My lord,' said the Decurion, 'the enemy are routed and the Gemina is free to advance.'

'About time,' growled Scapula, and mounted his horse.

'My lord, there is something you should know,' said the Decurion.

'Spit it out,' said Scapula.

'There is black smoke above the hills, my lord. It would seem that Caratacus has been engaged.'

'*On whose command?*' screamed Scapula. 'I gave explicit orders that he was not to be faced until we had all three Legions to hand.'

'My men tell me it's the Victrix, my lord,' said the Decurion. 'I am also informed that the Augusta is still two days march from here.'

'That cursed Geta will pay for this,' growled Scapula. 'He puts an entire Legion at risk and if Claudius loses a Legion, I will be recalled to Rome before the first snow falls. Decurion, we have wasted too much time. Tell your men they will lead the vanguard across this plain and are responsible for ensuring there are no more hold ups. Use every weapon and man at your disposal to clear the way for your comrades. This Legion will march as they have never marched before. Bring me the Primus Pilus and then set out to clear a path and protect our flanks. Let's hope we are not too late.'

The Decurion turned and galloped away while a tribune gave the signal for an entire Legion to get to their feet.

'March us out, Tribune,' called Scapula, 'the Victrix may need our help and are still three hours march away. Get us there in two.'

'Yes, my lord,' answered the Tribune and the trumpeters rang out the advance. The Fourteenth Gemina were on their way.

–

The two hills were ablaze from the fire pots launched from the Ballistae and clouds of black smoke swirled amongst the warriors, causing them to cough as the acrid fumes reached into their lungs and burnt their eyes. Huge swathes of bracken caught light and walls of fire leapt hungrily up the hill, causing warriors to flee their defensive positions like frightened hares, eagerly targeted by the Scorpio operators on the far bank.

Boulders hurled from the Onagers smashed into defending walls built only hours earlier, and men screamed from crush injuries and lacerations caused by the thousands of mini shards from the shattering missiles. Defenders crouched low to avoid the maelstrom and though there were indeed many casualties, their number were few compared to the army's overall strength.

Geta watched the bombardment with satisfaction, assuming the enemy's strength would be devastated by the assault and he ordered his auxiliary infantry cohorts to advance to the river's edge.

The wind was blowing from the Victrix toward the hill and Geta ordered dozens of fires to be built on his side of the river. When raging, green foliage was added and even more clouds of smoke encompassed the enemy positions, enabling his forces to approach the river unchallenged.

'*On my order*,' he screamed, '*advance!*'

Over a two-mile stretch, a thousand men climbed down the bank and waded toward the centre of the river, each determined to gain the far shore as quickly as possible. For a few moments their approach went unnoticed but suddenly disaster loomed and Geta watched in horror as the assault started to unravel.

Many of the front rank faltered as the fast-flowing current beat against their bodies and tried to push them over. Unstable soldiers grabbed their comrades instinctively as they tried to stay upright and the ordered advancing line began to break up. The ranks behind added to the confusion as they pushed through the smoke, unaware of the problems to their front and the pressure from behind meant many of the front line stumbled and were washed downstream, crashing into their comrades and adding to the confusion in the river.

The cries of panic alerted the defenders and hundreds of warriors ran forward, taking advantage of the gaps in the smoke to launch their spears at the struggling men. Combined with the strong current, the slaughter of the front rank meant the situation descended into chaos and soldiers were stranded in the full view of the enemy, unable to advance or retreat.

Up above Caratacus saw the confusion and, grasping the opportunity presented to him, sent more spear throwers to the water's edge. Geta's cohorts were in disarray and were cut down mercilessly. Some managed to reach the far shore but Caratacus's men were waiting, cutting them down as they climbed the banks. As the smoke cleared the Roman officers spotted the threat and realising the assault had failed, ordered the retreat; surprise had been lost.

Archers hurried forward to give covering fire and the opposing warriors retreated to their defences under a hail of arrows.

'*Help them out,*' screamed Rufius, and the reserve Legionaries still in their cohorts broke ranks to run forward and haul the survivors from the river. Hundreds of dead bodies floated downstream, many amidst slicks of their own blood and mingling with the struggling wounded without the strength to swim back. Some of those still able managed to crawl to the far bank only to be picked off by the enemy, but many more managed to hide amongst the reeds at the water's edge, unable to make it back but stranded on the enemy side of the river.

For the next hour they expended time and effort saving those they could but by the time they had rescued everyone possible, they could see that hundreds more were stranded on the far side, many of them wounded.

Geta was shocked. Not only had his very first assault been totally devastated but it had left him with an impossible problem. Hundreds of his men were stranded on the far side and though the enemy were being kept back by the Legion's archers, when night fell, he knew Caratacus's men would trawl along the riverbank picking them off with ease.

He paced back and forth, turning the problem over and over in his mind. If he sent over any more of the Legion to help them, the same thing could happen, yet if he left them there, it would have a terrible demoralising effect on his Legion and besides, every man under his command had trained together and had vowed never to abandon a comrade in need. This was bordering on a disaster yet had been entirely unforeseen. Nobody had judged the river's current correctly and it had been a terrible lesson costing the lives of hundreds.

In the distance he heard the sound of a Cornicine and a rider galloped up, coming to a halt before him.

'My lord, a Legion approaches,' he called, 'it looks like it's the Gemina.'

'Shit,' cursed Geta under his breath. Despite his need for more men, the last thing he needed was another Legatus witnessing his failure.

'Maintain the archers on station,' he ordered, 'and form up the ranks. This is but a setback and we are still Romans. Ensure we greet Scapula as befits a governor.'

Geta sent a slave for his horse and tidied up his uniform before riding out to meet Scapula. Ten minutes later, the two men rode side by side toward the mountain. As they approached, Geta filled him in on the disastrous events of the day and Scapula looked on with concern as they passed the hundreds of wounded auxiliaries now being tended by their bedraggled comrades and medical orderlies.

Scapula ordered his army to halt while he rode forward with Geta to survey the battlefield. They rode close to the river yet remained out of range of the enemy bows.

'Why wasn't this river taken into consideration?' asked Scapula, looking at the fast-flowing water before him.

'It was,' said Geta, 'and was deemed crossable but the heavy rain in the far mountains increased the flow. There are fordable points but they are few and narrow.'

'Why weren't these used?'

'They provide bottlenecks that are easily defended and I judged the cost would be too high. We had no idea where you were and there is a risk that the king may receive reinforcements at any moment. We have to take these hills as soon as possible or this whole thing may explode into something we can't handle.'

Scapula nodded but did not comment. They rode together for a mile or so up the riverbank, all the while being jeered by the enemy on the far bank and subject to hails of arrows that fell far short of their targets. Finally, Scapula had seen enough and they turned to return downstream.

'Geta, the outcome of this assault is indeed unfortunate and a conversation needs to be had but now is not the time. What is the mettle of your men?'

'They froth at the mouth for retribution, my lord,' said Geta.

'Then retribution is what they shall have,' said Scapula and kicked his horse to gallop back to the command post, closely followed by Geta. They summoned the Tribunes of the Victrix as well as the senior centurions for a briefing and when everyone was present, they stood in a wide circle as Scapula outlined his plan.

'Men of the Victrix,' he said, 'today you have suffered a setback but it is no defeat. In battle, both sides suffer losses; it is the nature of the beast. This Caratacus has selected his positions well and our machines are all but useless against mountainous slopes. Legatus Geta read the situation well and I concur with his actions. The fact that the river had risen was unforeseen and it is a formidable barrier to equal the strongest palisade. With time, we would cross it on a hundred bridges but time is something we do not have. What we do have is men, horses and a discipline these barbarians have never seen. I promise you that before this day is out, there will be ten thousand Legionaries on that far bank, and many more to either side. By nightfall this hill will be red with barbarian blood and our fallen will be avenged.'

The assembled officers shouted their approval and Scapula allowed them to continue. For this to succeed, he needed every man's complete approval including the officers and ordinary men. Finally the noise subsided and he spoke again.

'The plan is this,' he said, and stepped out into the centre of the circle of men. He drew his Gladius and scratched a snakelike line in the dust.

'This is the river,' he said, 'and these are the two hills. A mile upstream, there is a narrow ford, able to take two riders abreast, however it is heavily defended. The Gemina will concentrate all their artillery on these defences and at a signal, a cohort of cavalry will gallop at full speed across the ford and smash into whatever remains of their strength.'

'My lord, cavalry are no use on the steep slopes,' said a voice.

'I know,' said Scapula, 'but their purpose is to gain time for the auxiliary cohorts of the Gemina to cross in strength behind them. At the same time, every archer from both Legions will assemble here and here.' He indicated two points further downstream on the map. 'These two points are two hundred paces apart and will be the main thrust of the assault. It is here that the Victrix will lead the assault across the river and into the heart of the enemy.'

'That is where we lost a lot of men this morning,' said one of the Tribunes.

'I am aware of that,' said Scapula, 'but the slopes beyond still present the best route for an assault on the hill. The main problem is the force of the current so we will take that problem away.'

'How?' asked Geta.

'With our cavalry,' said Scapula. 'We will place a hundred horses across the river both upstream and downstream of the crossing point, covered by archers. The size and strength of the horses will withstand the flow and disrupt the current enough for our men to get across without being washed away. However, it is important that the men at the front know this. If they lose their footing, they are not to try and fight it but allow the current to take them. If they struggle, they will affect those behind and the advance will falter. For those that do lose their footing, the cavalry downstream will pluck them from the water as they pass.'

The officers nodded in appreciation. It was an effective use of resources and a way of getting the main force across as quickly as possible.

'I won't insult you by explaining what protective measures you need to take once across,' said Scapula, 'that is your job. The initial landing on the far side will be the most dangerous but once there, I see no reason why we can't mop this up by night fall. Now, are there any questions? No? Good, make your preparations, we move immediately.'

The officers and centurions dispersed to their units and Scapula rode to brief his Legion. Rufius walked over to Geta.

'My lord, I would have word.'

'Speak,' said Geta.

'My lord, despite his fine words, I detect a cynicism in his voice about the ability of our men and it leaves a sour taste in my mouth.'

'You noticed too?' said Geta.

'I did and I would request the opportunity to prove the governor wrong.'

'How?'

'By allowing me to lead the assault with the first cohort,' said Rufius.

'Rufius,' said Geta, 'this is no ordinary battle. Out on the field the first cohort will always lead us into the fray, but they are my most valuable men and despite the plan of Scapula, I fear they could suffer the same fate as the men this morning.'

'My men are veterans, my lord, and have a discipline of iron. Give me this opportunity and not only will we secure the far bank, but will wipe out any threat to those following behind.'

Geta thought for a moment before nodding.

'So be it,' he said. 'Pass the word.'

The next hour flew by as everyone found their places, and gradually the commotion died down as the Legions faced the two hills Caratacus had chosen to defend. Siege engines were primed, ready for covering fire, quivers were packed with arrows ready to pick off defenders and slingers were deployed within the foliage of the riverbank. Riders talked quietly to their horses, anticipating the frenzy of battle they knew was imminent. To the front of them all, Rufius stood alone before his cohort of veterans, waiting for the command to come.

—

Across the river, Caratacus and his warlords had seen the deployment and knew a big push was coming. Frantically they strode between their men, encouraging each group to fight to the last and reminding them for every man who fell, ten thousand would live in freedom. Skins of ale and wine were handed from man to man adding fuel to the growing confidence. In contrast to the silence of the Romans, the hill was a wall of sound with every man screaming their defiance at the enemy across the river.

On one flank, Cassus had been noticed by a warlord and ordered into line to face the forthcoming assault. Though he had other things on his mind, he complied, knowing that when battle was joined, he could slip away in the confusion. He knew that wherever Caratacus was, Prydain wouldn't be far away and he would seize his chance at the first opportunity.

—

Geta waited for the signal. His Legionaries were ready. This time they were disciplined, battle hardened men, all veterans of many battles and he knew that whatever happened, they would not retreat. He looked up as a burning arrow sailed through the air, trailing a line of black smoke; the first signal.

'*Ballistae ready*,' he screamed. 'Onagers ready, on my mark, *fire!*'

Once again, the thump of catapults filled the air and fire pots rained down on the enemy positions. Loose bundles of ten arrows at a time were shot from the Ballistae, providing a wall of death aimed randomly across the river. Slingers picked out individuals across the water, aiming their lead shot at the heads of the barbarians with surprising accuracy, while ranks of archers stood ready to add their own skills to the wall of covering fire. A Cornicine sounded across the battle front and Geta saw the cavalry ride into the river to disrupt the flow, covered from assault by the intensive bombardment from their allies.

Geta held his breath, hoping the strategy would work. He knew that one way or the other he would have to commit his men within the next minute or so.

'Rufius,' he shouted and the Primus Pilus turned to face him. In his left hand he held the large, oblong shaped shield with the Legion's wild boar crest emblazoned across the front, while in his right his Gladius was already drawn. He had discarded his cloak and the faceguards of his scarlet plumed helmet were secured under his chin. On his face he wore a look of pure determination.

'Yes, my lord,' answered Rufius.

'Rufius, the barbarians voice their eagerness for the fray. What say you we show them the same.'

'Aye, my lord,' shouted Rufius and turned to his cohort.

'First cohort,' he shouted, 'we have been selected this day for glory and once more lead our Legion, nay, our Empire on the assault of a heathen king. Let these barbarians hear the sound of oncoming death.'

Six hundred voices of the first cohort filled the air, screaming their support and readiness.

'*Twentieth Valeria Victrix*,' shouted Rufius when the sound had died down, 'your forebears led the way in Illyricum, Hispana and Germania. Pay tribute this day to their sacrifice and send a message they will hear at the tables of the gods. Join the first cohort in their defiance and make Caratacus tremble in his boots.'

Across the entire front and throughout the deep reserves, every man screamed their readiness in defiance of the enemy facing them. Geta felt his heart race with pride and as the shouting eased, their noise was replaced with a cacophony of sound from every drum and Cornicine from both Legions. He glanced down at the water and could see that though still deep, the flow had eased, broken by hundreds of horses up stream.

'*Valeria Victrix*,' roared Geta, '*advance!*'

Rufius ran to the water's edge closely followed by over six hundred veterans. This was no time for orderly lines; they would come later. The most important thing was to get across as quickly as possible.

'*Archers*,' screamed Geta over the sound of the drums, 'their lives lie in your hands and I will personally crucify any man who misses an easy target. Load your bows and aim true.'

Rufius waded waist deep across the river. Out of the corner of his eye he saw a man fall but as ordered, the disciplined Legionary released his shield and struck out to avoid becoming an obstacle to his comrades. If he failed to reach the far bank, the cavalry downstream were waiting to fish him out.

Along the edge of the far bank, Rufius could see dozens of frightened faces peering from their hiding places amongst the reeds, each grateful that they could soon be released from the freezing mud and threat of impeding death.

–

Up on the slopes, Caratacus was alert to the threat and stormed amongst his own warriors, screaming his commands and urging them to greater feats of bravery.

'*Get off your bellies,*' he screamed, 'and let them feel the anger in our souls. Their arrows are but feathers; take the battle to the invaders.'

A thousand men raced forward to confront the Romans climbing the banks.

'*Archers, volley fire,*' and a wall of iron tipped ash flew across the river into the onrushing enemy.

Men fell in their hundreds, but their places were quickly taken by their fellow warriors as they raced to the battle. Over and over again the archers cut them down but their numbers were too many. As soon as they were in range, the warriors threw their spears and Romans fell like scythed corn on the banks of the river. Rufius crouched below his shield, frustrated that although they had bettered the current, the ferocious onslaught of arrows, spears and rocks from above meant they were finding it hard to secure a bridge head. Finally a few more men managed to crawl onto the bank and Rufius called out.

'*You men, on me,*' he screamed, 'shield wall now.'

All five men knelt down and planted their Scuta in the damp soil. Another four joined them and stood between the first five, placing their own shields above the lower ones to provide a protective wall higher than a man. It wasn't much but it gave a narrow channel of safety behind which men could climb from the killing zone of the river without being in line of sight of the enemy archers.

Very quickly the numbers grew, and the shield wall expanded both ways, an ever-growing barricade that fed itself, growing larger by the second as more men reached the bank. The enemy warriors were kept back by the Legion's archers though some managed to get through the deadly storm and fall upon the shield wall with a ferocity born of frustration.

Rufius looked around in triumph. Men were pouring ashore in their hundreds and he knew he could now do what he did best.

'*You men,*' he screamed, 'on my command, twenty paces forward and form into century level Testudo. Those to each side, close the gap and prepare to do the same. Ready; *move!*'

Approximately eight men ran forward as ordered and the first ten planted their shields once more in the soil before crouching low behind them. The second ten crouched behind the first and raised their shields above their heads, protecting the first ten and themselves from the constant rain of rocks and arrows. As each man arrived, they placed their shields either to a flank or above their heads depending on their location in the square and finally they had a group of eighty men, entirely encased in a protective wall of shields, the infamous tortoise defence, the Testudo.

A mile away, the barrage from the Gemina's artillery continued, raining hell on the strong defences protecting the ford across the river. The bombardment from the fire pots of the Onagers had been so severe even the rocks seemed to be ablaze, and men were screaming in pain from the unrelenting flames as they burned to death.

In the forest behind the siege machines an entire Alae of cavalry waited patiently. The unit consisted of sixteen Turmae, each of thirty riders commanded by a Decurion, a mounted unit of four hundred and eighty men. Behind them, another four cohorts of auxiliary infantry totalling almost two thousand men waited their turn to cross the ford and assault the flank of Caratacus's army.

'*Stand by*,' shouted Scapula, 'Praefectus Ruga, on my command, secure me this crossing.'

'We are ready, my lord.'

'Cease the barrage, Ruga, make it happen, *advance!*'

'Alae Fourth Claudia,' bellowed Ruga drawing his sword, 'no retreat, no surrender, *charge!*'

The entire wing of cavalry leapt forward at full gallop, almost five hundred armed men taking advantage of the confusion caused by the barrage.

Within moments they were through the river and piercing the enemy lines. Those warriors who had survived the fire-rain stumbled from their hiding places to meet the enemy, only to be cut down by lances or the curved blades of the riders. Within minutes the entire Alae was across, causing mayhem in the ranks of the enemy.

'*Fourteenth Gemina*,' screamed Scapula, 'for the glory of Rome, *advance!*'

Two thousand infantry followed Scapula across the ford, each adding their swords to the havoc being caused by the cavalry and swarming over the slope like an army of ants. Despite their numbers, Scapula didn't have it all his own way and a fresh impetus of Caratacus's warriors stormed down the hill to plug the gap.

All around, man faced man in one on one combat, each fighting furiously in the knowledge that no quarter would be asked or given. For several minutes the outcome was uncertain but as more reinforcements crossed the narrow ford, the Roman numbers gradually overwhelmed the defenders and hundreds of men fell before the onslaught. Finally the remaining warriors turned and retreated up the steep slopes, climbing frantically to escape the attentions of the Batavians. Many of the Auxiliaries started to follow but were ordered back by their commanders.

Scapula rode forward and took command of the situation.

'Ruga, gather your cavalry and protect this crossing at all costs. The infantry will form up in Cuneus formation and follow the river downstream to squeeze the enemy between us and Geta's forces. I just hope they managed to get across.'

Chapter 23

Caer Caradog
50 AD

Caratacus was frantic. He had thrown everything he had at the defences and though their spears and arrows had accounted for hundreds of the enemy, their own casualties were horrendous and he knew that all he had left were the elite warriors kept behind above the higher lines of walls where the enemy catapults couldn't reach. He stormed from position to position, encouraging the defenders and promising the freedom of their lands from Roman tyranny. He glared at the enemy on the lower slopes of the hills. The entire bottom half was now in the hands of the Romans and he could see them forming up into their centuries, preparing for the assault up the slopes. He climbed up onto a prominent rock and addressed the men before him.

'Men of Britannia,' he called, 'do not let their numbers or meaningless drills affect the truth of your hearts. They are just men as you or I and their blood runs as red as ours. They are not invincible and they have faced defeat at our hands before. Do not forget, in the times of our grandfathers these Romans set covetous eyes on our homeland and twice came ashore with swords drawn and murder in their eyes. On both occasions our forefathers drove them away, shedding their own blood so we can sleep in our own lodges in our own lands. Do not let their sacrifice be in vain this day for make no mistake, if we fail in this task then servitude and bondage beckons. Emerge victorious and our lands will be free for another generation.'

Below him the men roared their approval and beat their weapons against their shields. Caratacus grabbed the moment, urging them to greater things and before he had finished, the slopes were alive again with the cheers and support of his army. Slowly the sounds of cheering died and they looked around, realising there was another sound vibrating through the evening air; the sound of Roman drums.

Caratacus stared down and could see the Legion was moving. Dozens of military squares, each containing eighty men marched in step across the lower slopes and up toward the higher defences, each step in time with the beat of the drums.

'*Men of Britannia*,' screamed Caratacus, 'look to your weapons and listen to your hearts. Over the next few hours, the freedom of these lands lies in your hands.'

–

Cassus crouched behind one of the hastily erected walls. He had been stuck there for hours, unable to move further up the hill due to the accuracy of the Roman archers. On several occasions, one or more of the defenders had taken the chance to run between positions but every time they were struck down by arrows before they had gone more than a few paces. He knew his options were limited and the only way the archers would cease their deadly fire was when the infantry closed in on the defences.

Occasionally he saw Caratacus high above his position, out of reach of the arrows and once he was almost certain he saw Prydain at his side. That gave Cassus strength to continue. He had waited six years; he could handle a few more hours.

–

Gwydion and Prydain stood alongside each other on the ramparts of the fort. Gwydion looked down at the manoeuvring Centuries and turned to Prydain.

'What do you think?' he asked.

'It's not good,' said Prydain. 'Now they have bettered the river, they'll revert to type and use their might to work their way upward.'

'We still have a lot of warriors down there,' said Gwydion, 'they will sell themselves dearly.'

'In the end it will make no difference,' said Prydain, 'they are a tide that cannot be stopped. Dam them in one place and they pour around the end. Defend that point and they will come over the top. There is no defence against them, Gwydion – this day is doomed.'

'Caratacus thinks otherwise,' said Gwydion, 'his words extol victory.'

'His words might,' said Prydain, 'but his actions suggest otherwise.'

'What do you mean?'

'He keeps horses ready for a quick exit,' said Prydain, 'and has instructed ten of his closest advisers to stay close in case the day does not go well.'

'He means to run?'

'He has seen the futility of the task,' said Prydain, 'and only lingers in the hope that my people's cavalry fall upon the rear of the attackers to dull their strike.'

'Is this likely?'

Prydain shook his head.

'I fear not,' he said, 'they would have been here by now and even if they were to arrive, that river is as much a barrier to them as it was to the Romans. This day is done, Gwydion. Make your plans to escape this place.'

'You know I cannot run, Prydain. I am Britannic and our fate lies here. If I run then others will run with good reason. I am no coward, Prydain, and if I fall this day, then at least I will die defending my homeland.'

'Gwydion, unveil your eyes,' said Prydain. 'Your own king has already decided the fight is over and makes plans to leave.'

'What about the women?' asked Gwydion. 'There are over a hundred within the camp. Surely he doesn't mean to leave them behind?'

'They are already hidden in the cave on the other summit,' said Prydain. 'They have supplies and the entrance has been hidden with bracken. The hope is the Romans will sweep by and the women will emerge in a few days when they have gone.'

'This is unbelievable,' said Gwydion. 'Facing defeat is one thing, but to extol victory to his men while preparing to flee is another.'

'Don't be too hard on him, Gwydion,' said Prydain, 'for such is the way of kings. They see themselves as above battles but winners of wars. Perhaps he is right and we need him to continue the fight on another field at a different time.'

'Your words are wise,' said Gwydion, 'but yet I cannot flee and leave those I call brother to die so I may live.'

'I understand,' said Prydain, 'and your honour is evident. All I am saying is if the day is lost and the lines are routed, then there is no shame in fleeing a lost cause. Do not delay just to add your name to the fallen. Live to fight another day.'

'What about you, Prydain?' asked Gwydion.

'I too will stay until the last moment,' said Prydain, 'but will make my way back to my people if we lose the day.'

Both men jumped as a blast from the Roman trumpeters echoed across the hill and they looked down to see the Roman formations approaching the lines of loosely packed stone walls.

'Until next we meet,' said Prydain and grabbed Gwydion's forearm.

'In this life or the next,' said Gwydion.

Prydain strode away to join Caratacus while Gwydion unwrapped Angau for what was possibly the last time. The Parthenian recurved bow had been in his family for generations and there was no better archer than Gwydion. He placed his two quivers of arrows on the wall to his front and loosened the straps that kept them tightly together, knowing that even if he made every one fly true, the deaths of forty Romans would have little bearing on the outcome of the day.

–

Rufius stood to the front of the first century leading the way up the hill, his eyes constantly scanning the slopes for the first sign of the counter assault he knew would come. Sure enough, movement caught his eye and he saw a volley of arrows fly from the higher rocks above.

'*Testudo*,' he screamed and immediately the Legion stopped to present their shields into the formation of the tortoise.

Rufius crouched down behind his own Scutum and the whole advance halted momentarily while the first volley slammed into their shields. Immediately Rufius peered over the top of his shield and took advantage of the lull between volleys.

'*Ten paces, advance,*' and each Testudo lifted their shields to run ten paces before presenting their shields once more.

Again and again the arrows fell but each time the Roman formations gained ground a few steps at a time. Their shields were bristling with arrow shafts but the advance had cost less than a dozen men from their strength, each the result of a lucky arrow finding its way through a hole or a gap between the defensive shields.

Within minutes, the first century reached the wall and while frantic defenders hammered the Testudo from above with sword and axe, the men at the front reached between their shields and pulled at the loose stones to form a breach. All across the defensive walls, other Centuries reached their objectives and the loose rocks were torn from the barricades.

Rufius was frantic, screaming at the men at the walls to pull them down. The front rank levered at the stones with stout poles cut especially for the task, forcing them outward while their comrades tried their best to deflect the blows from above with their Pilae.

–

A mile away Scapula's auxiliary infantry were also in formation though this time in line abreast ten men deep and a hundred men across. The rocks above had been cleared of any remaining enemy and the front of the line faced downstream, at right angles to the river. They too heard the drums of Geta's Legion and strained at the leash to be released against the enemy. The Auxiliary infantry had smaller shields and wore armour of leather as opposed to the Lorica Segmentata worn by the Roman regulars. This meant that though they were not so good in military formation, they would be much more effective in the broken ground and rocky slopes before them.

'Gallic cohorts,' shouted Scapula, 'the Victrix face the enemy in a bloody confrontation with Caratacus. Before us lie the cream of the enemy and it is a task worthy of the best. I know you will not let me, your fellows or your country down. Use this day to carve your names into history.'

He drew his Gladius and held it high.

'Gallic cohorts of the Fourteenth Gemina,' he shouted, 'onward into glory. *Advance!*'

A thousand men stepped forward in rough formation. Not the disciplined lines of their Roman comrades but two cohorts of ferocious individuals with fire in their heart and murder in their soul. For the first hundred yards they maintained their pace before gathering speed toward the rocky slopes that led to the ground between the peaks. Within moments they were running at half speed and when a few defenders appeared from their hiding places before them, a great cry arose from the Gauls and they broke into full speed to drive home their assault. Warriors appeared in their hundreds from between the rocks, hurling their missiles at the oncoming horde and the front line of the auxiliaries took the full force of the barrage, decimated by the spears and throwing axes. Row after row met similar fates but their numbers and impetus were too great and those behind the fallen descended on the warrior defenders like packs of rabid wolves.

Hand to hand fighting broke out across the slopes, spreading like a bush fire as those behind ran past those already engaged to roll the attack forward. Steel clashed on steel, but though the defenders had neither armour nor helmets they fought with animalistic ferocity. Within minutes the whole slope was a battlefield of screaming men, each in mortal combat with life the desperate prize.

Back on the slopes below the fort, Rufius heard a shout from beneath the shields of the first century as the first wall was breached and boulders rolled at the attacker's feet. Pilae were thrust forward through the gap and the Legionaries widened the gap until three could squash through together. Their comrades piled through behind them and the Legion burst through the walls like blood from a severed limb. Around them the defenders ran forward, smashing into them in a frenzy, desperate to block the breach. Up above, Gwydion picked his targets carefully, killing the Romans one by one as they cleared the growing gaps. Men fell on men but still they came and soon breaches appeared all along the wall. Gwydion did his best to stem the tide and though every arrow found a mark, soon he was down to the last six arrows.

Wolfeye gave the order to retreat to the second hill and hundreds of warriors turned to gather on the steeper slopes.

'*After them,*' screamed Rufius, 'don't let them reform.'

Before them the warriors scrambled toward the safety of the second hill but before they got within a few hundred paces, lines of Gallic infantry appeared from beyond the slopes.

'Who are they?' shouted a Legionary.

'By the gods,' shouted Rufius, 'it's the Gemina. Onward, Victrix and squeeze them between the Legions.'

—

With enemy before and behind them, the warrior defenders sought a way out but with an escarpment to their right and the river down below they were hemmed in with no chance of escape.

Wolfeye climbed up onto a rock and addressed the few hundred warrior survivors.

'*Now is not the time to falter*,' he screamed, 'for every one of us who fall, three of this filth will join us on the journey to the gods and our forefathers will see we have honoured their names. Even as we die, our blood will enrich Britannic soil. The day is done, countrymen, but meet the night with sword in hand. Turn from flight and face the foe and meet our gods with honour.'

He jumped down from the rock and with hundreds of screaming men behind him, raced into the face of the oncoming Romans.

—

Gwydion cursed out loud. To one side he could see a huge battle breaking out between the remainder of the defenders and two different fronts of attackers. Below him the Testudos were reforming this side of what remained of the defensive walls and behind them he could see groups of men crossing the river with dozens of ladders, ready to scale the palisades. The day was lost and he knew Prydain had been right. No matter what he did now, it would have no bearing on the outcome. It was time to go but before he did, he drew the last arrow from his quiver and aimed carefully at the mass of men approaching the palisades.

–

The morale of Legionaries beneath the shields of the Testudo was high and they were shouting in time with their own advance. The Decurions of each unit roared their encouragement from amongst their sweating ranks and behind each unit, the centurions and Optios screamed their orders, ensuring the momentum of the assault was maintained. Still the missiles rained down from above, yet the effect was minimal against the solid walls of shields.

Rufius stayed close to the lead Centuries, ducking low behind his own Scutum and controlling the advancing lines. He needed them all to reach the walls of the palisade more or less at the same time to dilute the defender's fire across many targets, rather than suffer intense bombardment on one or two. His shield bristled with arrow shafts, each blocked with skilful manipulation born through years of experience on battlefields throughout half the known world. He knew his solitary figure attracted the attention of the enemy but even when closing in on the fort, his defensive skills and battle awareness meant he presented a minimal target to the archers above.

Despite this, Gwydion had watched him since the Legion crossed the river, singling him out as a prominent leader and the fulcrum around which the advance revolved. The magnificent red crest sweeping across his helmet made him easy to spot amongst the chaos of the battlefield and Gwydion willed him onward, hoping he would come within range before the ladders fell against the palisade.

'Come on,' murmured Gwydion to himself as the attackers drew close, a few more steps. Slowly he picked up the last arrow and placed it in the bow, taking his time to ensure the bowstring fitted snuggly in the notch of the shaft.

Below the palisade, the first of the attackers reached the timber façade and lifted their shields above their heads, slamming the forward edges into the timbers. The rows behind placed their shields overlapping those in front until they had a platform stretching back ten men. The last two lines knelt down and leaned their shields forward, forming a steep ramp onto the makeshift platform. No sooner had the last shield locked into place when another line of men ran forward and leapt onto the shields of their comrades and formed a further, smaller platform reaching halfway up the palisade. Finally, under the protective barrage from the Sagittaria, hundreds of lightly armoured auxiliaries stormed forward to climb onto the ledge of shields, before leaping over the palisade and into the faces of the enemy. All across the defences the same tactic was used to propel attackers over the walls and in between, hundreds of ladders filled the gaps to be scaled by those specially trained in siege warfare.

Gwydion knew he had to move, but the situation had taken a dramatic turn. From behind the advancing army he could see the Legion's Eagle standard appear over the attackers, closely followed by the easily recognised Roman commander. He gasped at the audacity of the man and held his breath as Legatus Geta came into range of his one remaining arrow.

A few steps away defenders and attackers fought ferociously on the ramparts and he knew he could wait no longer. He lifted his bow slowly and aimed at the Legatus, knowing that a successful shot may not halt the attack but would strike a devastating blow against Rome. Just as his shot became clear his eyes widened as he recognised a figure running amongst the retreating warriors.

Gwydion lowered his bow momentarily as he stared at the man running to safety. He couldn't believe it. The warrior before him had lost his helmet and as his hair fell about his terrified face, Gwydion could see the blackness was interrupted by a long streak of white.

'*Gwydion*,' screamed a voice from below, 'the day is lost; we have to leave.'

Gwydion looked down at Prydain in the courtyard of the fort. Without answering he picked up his bow and ran along the ramparts to get a better view of the man on the hill and as he reached the corner, the running warrior looked up into his eyes.

There was no doubt in Gwydion's mind; it was the man who had haunted his nightmares for the past five years. Below him ran the man called Badger, the brigand who had killed his woman and forced him to give up his son.

Gwydion's heart raced. He had two targets and one arrow. The warrior in him demanded he kill the Legatus of a Legion, but he had sworn on the memory of his wife that one day he would repay her death with that of her killer.

Behind him the Roman force had taken the ramparts and were pouring over the palisade. He knew he had seconds to decide, so without any more thought he finally lifted his bow and aimed at the man he had chosen to die.

Chapter 24

Caer Caradog

50 AD

Rufius climbed over the palisades and onto the ramparts, following the men who had slaughtered the remaining defenders. All along the walls his fellow Romans were pouring over the defences and dropping to the inner courtyard to continue the battle with the last stubborn defenders.

Gone were the lines of disciplined soldiers who had marched their way up the slopes and auxiliary infantry men fought alongside the heavier armoured Legionaries as they made their way toward the centre of the fort. The scene was chaos as men and boys fought frantically to save their own lives, but were no match for overwhelming power of the attackers.

Rufius watched his men advance, knowing that the next few hours would be filled with uncompromising slaughter as they took out their frustration on the enemy forces. He looked around the ramparts, littered with dozens of bodies both Britannic and Roman, and walked slowly among them, checking for friendly wounded. A man groaned and he looked to one side where a defender was trying to crawl away. Rufius bent over and grasping his hair, slit the man's throat with his Pugio. He stood to continue his task but suddenly a movement caught his eye and he saw a warrior leaning outward over the palisade, aiming a bow toward the on-going battle on the slopes of the hill. He followed the archer's gaze and his heart missed a beat as he saw Scapula riding his horse up the hill.

Rufius roared in anger and ran forward, drawing his Gladius as he went, hoping he had distracted the man for just enough to affect his aim. If he hadn't, this field could see the death of a Legate and victory or not, that would be a disaster.

—

Gwydion heard the roar and glance sideways at the oncoming Roman, realising instantly he had but seconds to decide and if he hesitated to defend himself, the opportunity would be lost. He drew back his arm and focussing on his chosen target, let the arrow fly.

He did not know if the arrow flew true, as by the time it was halfway through the flight, the Roman fell upon him and swung his Gladius toward his face. Gwydion ducked instinctively but the blade smashed against his helmet and caused him to fall sideways off the rampart and into the fortress below.

Rufius leapt off the rampart onto the roof of a hut and then down onto the dirt of the fort, determined to finish him off. Gwydion struggled to his feet, dazed, and with his sword arm hanging uselessly at his side. He tried to stagger away but Rufius appeared before him and smashed him in the face with the hilt of his Gladius, sending him sprawling in the dust once more.

Rufius walked over and stood over the semi-conscious body of Gwydion, staring down at him with hatred.

'Nice try, heathen,' he said, 'but you wasted your time. The arrow missed and Scapula still lives; you wasted your life in vain.'

Gwydion didn't understand the Latin but gave a response of his own.

'Do your worst, Roman,' he said, 'for your time in these lands is fleeting.' He drew a breath and spat a mouthful of blood over him.

Rufius wiped a speck of bloody saliva from his face and changed the grip on his Gladius.

'A pathetic gesture from a pathetic man,' he said. 'Time to die, heathen and share the fate of this godforsaken country.' He stepped forward and, crouching low, plunged his Gladius into Gwydion's stomach.

Gwydion gasped and his head flew backward in agony as the centurion twisted the blade in the wound.

'If you know anything about warfare, heathen, then you will know a gut wound kills slowly and you will soon die, screaming, as will Britannia.'

Gwydion's eyes rolled backward as the pain increased and the stench of his pierced entrails escaped the wound.

Rufius cleaned his Gladius on the dying man's tunic before turning away to join the assault further within the fort.

—

Prydain appeared from around a corner, searching frantically for his friend. He had seen him fall from the ramparts but had been held up fighting a Gallic swordsman. Finally he recognised Gwydion and ran over to crouch low beside him, knowing instantly the wound was lethal. He lifted his friend's head gently and Gwydion opened his eyes to look up at him.

'Prydain,' gasped Gwydion, 'you are here, thank the gods.'

'I am here, friend,' said Prydain, 'and will stay until you start the journey.'

'No,' gasped Gwydion, 'you can't. You must do something for me.'

'Anything,' said Prydain.

'Then save yourself and travel north. Go to the village of Lanbard and seek the woodsman called Derwen.'

'Why?' asked Prydain.

'He has a boy in his care called Taliesin,' said Gwydion, 'the true blood leader of his mother's clan. He is my son, Prydain, and I entrust him into your care. Check he is well and one day take him to claim his rightful place as leader of the Blaidd.'

'I will,' said Prydain, 'I swear.'

Gwydion started coughing and he gasped in pain.

'Then go now,' he said, 'and save your life, if not for yourself, then for Taliesin. I am done here, Prydain, leave while you have the chance.'

Prydain knew he was right and if he was to escape the battle, he had to leave right away. He stood up before turning to his friend once more.

'Travel well, friend,' said Prydain, 'and one day we will ride together in the lands of the gods.'

'Prydain, one more thing,' gasped Gwydion, 'when the boy becomes a man, tell him… tell him…'

'Tell him what?' asked Prydain.

Gwydion's head fell sideways and Prydain turned away, knowing that his friend would talk no more.

On the other side of the fort wall, the hill was covered with thousands of dead. Most were native to Britannia and most had the jet-black hair that was common to their tribes, but amongst their number, one body stood out. His black hair was streaked with white and deep in his heart was Gwydion's arrow.

Chapter 25

The Lands of the Deceangli
50 AD

Prydain ran amongst the huts of the hill fort, avoiding the hordes of attackers now laying waste to the village. He scrambled over the rear wall and joined the hundreds of men fleeing for their lives down the reverse of the hill. Below he could see a disorganised battle covering the slopes, thousands of men in lethal hand to hand combat fighting for their lives. In the distance he could see the silver gleam of another river though he knew there were no fords in this one, and it provided a massive obstacle for any men lucky enough to reach it. Down on the flood plain an Alae of cavalry was forming up to sweep along the valley and mop up the last of the escapees.

Prydain realised there was no way he could reach the river and looked around frantically for somewhere to hide, but a movement caught his eye and he noticed a lone horse standing over a dead rider. Prydain ran forward and grabbed the reins, talking quietly to calm the beast. Despite having a mount, he knew he would not get far in the face of the rapidly approaching cavalry. Finally he made his decision. He knew it was risky but there was only one option. He climbed up into the saddle and kicked his heels hard into the horse's flanks. The beast leaped forward and responding to Prydain's control, galloped down the slope at breakneck speed.

The smaller rocks flew about the feet of his mount and Prydain expected it to fall at any second, but they eventually reached the floodplain and turned to face the river.

Hundreds of men raced toward the water, terrified of the wall of death they knew was about to fall upon them but still they ran, desperate to reach the perceived safety of the forests on the far bank.

Prydain kicked the horse again and galloped hard toward the river, passing running boys and men, each just as desperate to reach the water. To the north he could see the dust cloud of the Alae approaching fast, almost five hundred cavalry descending on the last of Caratacus's army to administer the final defeat.

Prydain's mind was set hard and he deafened his ears to the countless cries of help from thousands of doomed men. Despite their pleas he rode hard, knowing that most of those he passed were about to die a horrible death, but there was no way he could help them all and he had promised to live, for Gwydion's sake.

Within moments he reached the river and pulled up amongst hundreds of refugees, each mingling at the bank, terrified and unwilling to take the leap into the fast-flowing water.

'*What are you waiting for*? Swim for your lives, their cavalry rides down on us as we wait.'

'The water is too fast,' shouted a man, 'we will be drowned.'

'Stay here and you will be cut down like corn,' replied Prydain, 'at least this way you have a chance.'

'It is too wide,' another said, 'we will never make it.'

Prydain stood up in the stirrups.

'*Listen to me,*' he screamed, 'you have to do this. The Roman cavalry will be here in minutes. Remove what armour you have and throw away your weapons. Discard your cloaks and tunics for the wool will drag you down. Walk out as far as you can but when the water takes you, don't fight it. Let it carry you downstream. Swim with the current and as the river turns the bend, strike out where the water washes against the far bank.'

Still the crowd hesitated.

'*What are you waiting for?*' repeated Prydain. 'You are going to die.' Realising he was wasting his time, he jumped off the horse and started to strip his clothes.

'Fine,' he shouted, 'stay and feed their lances. I am going.'

Within moments he had stripped to the waist and threw everything he had to one side.

'You have no more time,' he shouted, 'take your chances in the river or die where you stand. The choice is yours.' Without any more hesitation, he turned and plunged into the brown, freezing water.

Seconds later, others followed suit and within a minute hundreds of terrified refugees followed Prydain's example, striking out into the fast-moving current. Prydain had learned to swim in the Legions, as did all Legionaries, so he found it relatively easy but behind him the natives of Britannia struggled in the current. Many had ignored Prydain's instructions and had kept their clothing, not realizing that by doing so they had guaranteed their own deaths.

Screaming men sank beneath the water, dragged down by the weight of the sodden wool and as they panicked, they reached out to grab whatever they could, pulling others down with them. Despite the panic, many managed to pull clear and as Prydain reached the opposite bank, he could see other survivors hauling themselves up the muddy bank, gasping for breath and exhausted from the punishing, freezing water.

'Keep going,' shouted Prydain, 'we are still within range of their archers.' All along the bank, those lucky enough to survive staggered to the relative safety of the treeline and disappeared within their welcoming shelter. Prydain glanced back and saw the Roman cavalry descend upon those who had decided to stay, and despite the plaintive cries for mercy, they fell in their hundreds, slaughtered by the blades of the blood hungry riders.

The last of the survivors struggled up the bank and Prydain saw someone crawling in the mud, too exhausted to stand. He ran forward and helped them up, surprised to see that the silt covered figure was actually a young woman.

'Come,' he said, lifting her up from the floor, 'quickly before the archers arrive.'

They both staggered into the treeline as the screams of those left behind echoed across the river. On and on they ran until they were deep into the forest and finally, they both fell to the forest floor, exhausted.

'Thank you,' said the young woman eventually.

'No problem,' said Prydain, sitting up, 'but we can't wait here; the Legions will be deploying the Batavians as we speak.'

'Batavians?'

'People to track us down,' said Prydain, 'and they're also very good at crossing rivers. Now, come on, we have to go.'

'Where to?' asked the woman.

Prydain paused, realising this was a very pertinent question. He couldn't go south as the Augusta Legion were marauding through the Silures countryside. West was back into the arms of the attacking Romans and east was into Dobunii territory, the client kingdom working with the Gemina fortress. That meant there was only one option left.

'We have to go north,' he said eventually, 'into the lands of the Deceangli.'

'My people also lie north,' said the girl, 'they will give us protection.'

'Good,' said Prydain, 'then we should move. We need to find shelter and some extra clothing by nightfall.'

'Where will we find clothes?' asked the woman.

'From the dead,' said Prydain, 'now let's go.' He helped her up and like hundreds of similarly bedraggled people around them, headed north into the denser parts of the forest.

–

Hours later, Ostorius Scapula was walking around the battlefield, surveying the carnage inflicted on both sides. It had been a mighty battle and men lay dead in their thousands. Eventually even the bloodthirsty Batavians had lost the lust for blood and prisoners were being rounded up in their hundreds.

Praefectus Ruga approached and walked alongside the Legatus.

'A great day, my lord, and one that will see your name inscribed in the annals of history.'

'Do you think so, Ruga?' asked Scapula. 'All these men have been sent to greet their gods yet Caratacus has escaped my reach. What sort of victory is this?'

'You have sent a message out, my lord. A message that states that no matter how big the army or great the king, nobody stands against Rome. Caratacus may flee, but he cannot hide. Most of the country lies in our hands and after today, I cannot see the Silures offering him further sanctuary. A lot of their people died under his banner.'

'We will see,' said Scapula. 'What news of our wounded?'

'Still being counted, my lord. The men are quiet despite the victory for a lot of their comrades died this day.'

'And prisoners?'

'About a thousand. Amongst their number are the brothers of Caratacus and a group found hiding in a cave. We believe they are the wife and family of Caratacus.'

'So the mighty king fled and left his loved ones behind?'

'It would seem so,' said Ruga.

'Have them taken to Londinium,' said Scapula. 'The rest of the prisoners can gather the dead and build the funeral pyres.'

'What about the enemy dead, my lord?'

'Burn them too, they fought well.'

'One more thing, my lord, there is a warrior within their midst who speaks Latin and claims asylum. He said to mention his name to you.'

'Is the name Cassus?' asked Scapula.

'It is,' said Ruga.

'Have him released and looked after,' said Scapula, 'he is one of ours.'

'Yes, my lord,' said Ruga and marched away.

Scapula picked his way amongst the bloody pools and made his way up to the fort. Legatus Geta watched him approach.

'Hail Scapula,' he said.

'Geta,' said Scapula, 'your Legions fought well today. We will seek approval from Emperor Claudius to add the battle honour to your Legion's name.'

'My men will be honoured, my lord,' answered Geta.

'So do you think this day will be worth it?' asked Scapula.

'I do,' said Geta. 'I believe it is the fulcrum around which the defeat of Britannia will hinge. To date there have been two schools of thought, victory and defeat. I now believe the inhabitants will see that resistance is pointless and they will all bend their knee to Rome.'

'Most perhaps,' Scapula sighed, 'but not all. I hear fearsome stories about the Silures and suspect there will have to be more days such as this before they acknowledge our banners.'

'Then so be it,' said Geta. 'Let them resist. Rome is greater than one battle. This day or next year, their tribes will fall. Whether it be our blades or those of our grandchildren, the end result is inevitable. Rome is eternal and there is always plenty of time.'

'Perhaps Rome has time,' sighed Scapula, 'but I fear I do not share that luxury.'

'My lord?'

'It's nothing,' said Scapula. 'Right, let's get this day over. Our dead need honouring and there are wounded to attend to.'

'Who's this?' asked Geta, looking over to a Praefectus approaching with a Britannic warrior.

'This is Praefectus Ruga,' said Scapula, 'and that is Decurion Cassus Maecilius.'

'The Exploratore?' asked Geta with interest.

'Yes,' said Scapula, 'and probably the main reason we were victorious today.'

Cassus approached and saluted the Legates.

'Cassus, I am glad you survived,' said Scapula.

'It was difficult,' said Cassus, 'the battle was unstructured and I found myself fighting both Briton and Roman at times just to stay alive.'

Geta's eyes narrowed.

'I hope you didn't kill any of your true comrades,' he scowled.

Cassus turned and stared at the Legate.

'I did what I had to do,' he said.

'Enough!' Scapula intervened. 'What is done is done. You have Rome's gratitude. So, are you ready to embrace her Legions once more?'

'Not yet, my lord. I believe the man responsible for my disgrace six years ago still lives and I beg your approval to seek him out and end my oath once and for all.'

'How do you know he is alive?' asked Scapula. 'He could be amongst all these.' He waved his arm around the battlefield.

'I have been held amongst the prisoners these past few hours,' said Cassus, 'and my quarry is well known to them. They talked of the outcome, not suspecting my true alliance and I heard tell of Prydain crossing the river. I would seek permission to pursue him and end this once and for all.'

'And when this is done?'

'I will return to Londinium to serve as you see fit,' said Cassus.

'You have earned this boon,' said Scapula, 'and permission is granted.'

'Thank you, my lord,' said Cassus and turned to walk away but within a few steps he stopped and turned around.

'My lord, during my time with the prisoners, I heard rumour of one other thing.'

'Which is?'

'The destination of Caratacus.'

Both Legates stared at the Exploratore in astonishment.

'Where is he going?' asked Scapula eventually.

'He is to seek refuge with Cartimunda,' said Cassus. 'She is queen of the Brigantes and they lie in the north of Britannia.'

Scapula glanced at Geta, realising the implications of the unexpected news.

'Thank you, Cassus,' said Scapula, 'this is truly powerful knowledge. Pursue this man who haunts your dreams and may the gods grant you the outcome you require.'

'Thank you, my lord,' said Cassus, 'but this has nothing to do with the gods; it is between me and Prydain and long overdue.'

Without further ado he left the fort with the Praefectus and obtained a horse from the many abandoned by the defenders. Within the hour, he had crossed the river and was riding northward, once more on the trail of Prydain.

Chapter 26

The Lands of the Ordovices
50 AD

Prydain rode from Lanbard having received directions to the home of Derwen the woodsman. The battle of Caer Caradog had ended weeks earlier and though they had been pursued through the forests for days, many of the remnants of Caratacus' army had survived and sought refuge throughout the tribes of the south.

The young woman whom he had rescued from the river on the day of the battle had disappeared into the night soon after, and as soon as Prydain knew he was safe from pursuit, he made his way to Lanbard to seek out the son of Gwydion.

He rode into the clearing and waited on the outskirts, waiting for an invite as was their way.

'Hail, Derwen,' he called, 'I am Prydain, friend of Gwydion of the Blaidd and would seek respite.'

A man ducked out of a hut and walked toward him.

'A friend of Gwydion,' he said, 'then I bid you welcome. Come, stable your horse. We offer simple fare and a straw bed but it is warm and dry.'

'And no man could ask for more,' said Prydain and urged his horse forward.

As soon as the horse was secure for the night, Prydain followed Derwen into the hut and met Lynwen, the woodsman's wife. In the corner, two girls played with a young boy of about five years and Prydain guessed he was Taliesin. Derwen saw his look and glanced at his wife.

Nobody talked about Gwydion as protocol demanded that any guest was looked after before a host could ask for news.

Lynwen brought a platter of cheese with a thick slab of pork accompanied by ale and bread. Everyone ate quietly and after the children had been fed, Derwen filled up Prydain's tankard with fresh ale.

'So, Prydain,' he said, 'you say you are a friend of Gwydion. Have you seen him these past few months?'

'I have,' said Prydain.

'Where?' asked Lynwen.

'I fought alongside him at a place they now call Caer Caradog,' said Prydain.

Lynwen's hand flew to her mouth to stifle the gasp.

'You were there?' she asked.

'I was,' said Prydain, 'and the stories you hear in the markets of Lanbard do not do the day justice. It was everything they say and more. Never have I seen a battle more brutal or futile. We never stood a chance.'

'And what about Gwydion?' asked Lynwen, asking the question everyone knew had to be answered. 'Did he survive?'

Prydain glanced at Derwen before shaking his head.

'I'm sorry, Lynwen,' he said, 'Gwydion died in the fort on Caer Caradog.'

Lynwen gasped once more and this time tears welled up in her eyes.

'Oh that poor man,' she said, her voice breaking with emotion.

'He fought well,' said Prydain, 'and sold his life dearly.'

Over the next half hour, Prydain recounted the battle of Caer Caradog while Derwen listened silently, engrossed in the stories of valour and tragedy. Finally Prydain told of how Gwydion had met his death and the pledge he had made to his dying friend.

'So you have come to take Taliesin from us?' gasped Lynwen.

'I don't know,' said Prydain. 'My own people are now under threat from these Legions and I have to join them to protect our lands. But I made a pledge and it is only fair that you know the truth. Taliesin is no ordinary child, Lynwen. He is Gwenno's son and as such, the true blood leader of the Blaidd. The usurper Robbus carries the title chieftain but only by treachery and murder. One day, Taliesin must challenge Robbus or indeed his successor, but that time is many years away.'

'Why can't he just stay here?' asked Derwen.

'Because the country is at war,' said Prydain, 'and the Romans spread like fungus.'

'But why would they bother with a simple woodsman?'

'It's not the Legions I worry about,' said Prydain, 'but at times such as these many of those displaced by warfare get desperate. Brigands abound and your family is an easy target.'

'So what would you have us do?' asked Lynwen.

'He wants us to move to the village,' said Derwen, guessing the obvious answer.

'It makes sense,' said Prydain. 'You would be safe from brigands and should the Romans come, they will always try and negotiate with villages the size of Lanbard. Either way, the chance of you all surviving is much higher.'

Derwen looked at Lynwen.

'What do you think?' he asked.

'We have lived most of our lives in the forest,' she said, 'but the times are changing. Our life is hard but good and if it was only our own lives we risked, then I would stay in a heartbeat. But I see the sense in Prydain's words and fear for the safety of the children, not just for Taliesin but for the girls. I think we should consider this carefully.'

Derwen nodded and stood up.

'There is much to think about,' he said, 'and I would sleep on such a decision.'

Prydain nodded and got to his feet.

'Think well, Derwen,' he said, 'for you have the fate of a king in your care.'

'There is a straw bed in the stable,' said Derwen, 'and you will find it warm. One way or another, you will have my decision at dawn.'

'So be it,' said Prydain, 'I will see you in the morning.' He left the hut and made his way over to the stable, mentally exhausted from the strain of the last few weeks.

–

The following morning, Prydain woke to the smell of burning and for a few seconds, struggled to realise where he was. Finally he jumped up and ran out into the clearing between the huts, not believing what he was seeing.

The main hut was ablaze, and to the far side of the clearing he could see Derwen lying in the dust with his throat opened from an assassin's blade. Prydain ran over to the hut and tried to get inside but was beaten back by the smoke. He looked around frantically but could not see any sign of Lynwen or the children. Realising the brigand responsible was probably still around, he ran back to the stable to get his sword but as he entered, he could see his weapon was gone and his horse laying on the floor snorting its dying breaths as the blood poured from its own slashed throat.

Prydain spun around, expecting an attack at any second but there was no one to be seen. He ran outside once more, not understanding what was happening, but had only gone a few paces when he stopped dead in his tracks, staring across the clearing in disbelief.

A few paces to his front, his sword was stuck in the ground, while across the clearing a second sword mirrored his own but behind this one, a fellow warrior stood calmly, his head slightly bowed but eyes watching his every move.

–

It was obviously a challenge and though the man looked familiar, Prydain couldn't place him.

'Who are you?' he asked, 'and what do you want?'

The warrior sneered before answering.

'You know who I am,' he said, 'and what I want is for you to die.'

Prydain still couldn't place him but as the man lifted his head, to face him head on, he recognised the person he had grown up with. Cassus Maecilius.

'*Cassus*,' he said eventually, 'I thought you were dead.'

'You thought wrong,' answered Cassus.

'What have you done with these people?' asked Prydain.

'They are all dead,' answered Cassus, 'you Britons sleep far too soundly.'

326

'And the children?' asked Prydain.

'The girls died quickly,' said Cassus, 'as did the mother. The boy, however, is still alive.' He nodded to one side.

Prydain looked over and could see Taliesin sat against a tree, his tear stained face evidence of the fear that coursed through him. Prydain couldn't believe his luck that the boy was still alive.

'Why keep him alive?' asked Prydain.

'Because I wanted you to have a reason to stay and fight,' said Cassus. 'I tire from chasing you and this will end right now.'

'What is it you want, Cassus?' asked Prydain.

'I want to kill you, Prydain,' said Cassus menacingly, 'it's as simple as that. I want to pierce your heart with my sword and stare into your eyes as your life drains from your body.'

'I once gave you your life,' said Prydain.

'Yet allowed all my men to die,' said Cassus. 'There is a debt to be paid.'

'Perhaps you are right,' said Prydain, 'and it is my time. I could never better you with sword, Cassus, and probably can't still. Why should I give you the pleasure of combat when the outcome is almost certain?'

'Because of him,' said Cassus, nodding toward the child. 'Fight well and when you die, which you will, I will leave the boy at the gates of the village. Fight poorly and after I kill you, I will throw him to the flames. Is that reason enough?'

'How do I know you will keep your word?' asked Prydain.

'You don't,' said Cassus, 'now take your sword, slave-boy. I have waited for this moment for six years.'

Prydain walked forward and slowly pulled his sword from the soil. As boys, he and Cassus had played at being Legionaries within the vineyards of Cassus' family farm, Cassus the son of a landowner and Prydain the adopted son of a freed Gladiator. Despite this, they had grown up as friends and even joined the Legions together as young men. Throughout that time, Cassus had always been the better swordsman but that was with a Gladius, the short stabbing sword of the Legions. These swords were different and Prydain had used one for six years. They were much heavier and needed two hands to wield them properly. He looked up at Cassus.

'You choose a Barbarian weapon over a Roman one,' he said. 'That's not like you, Cassus.'

'Let's just say I have had a bit of training, since last we met,' said Cassus, swinging his sword back and fore in one hand. 'Now enough talking, slave boy, it's time to meet your fate.' He stepped forward to meet Prydain's advance and the clash of steel rang out across the forest.

–

Prydain's own sword skills were excellent and he was considered an expert in his tribe, but the ability of Cassus took him by surprise. There were no brutal swings of strength, aimed aimlessly at his body but skilfully crafted swipes followed up by clever defensive strokes and sleights of hand to fend off the blows.

Over and over again, Prydain took the initiative and forced Cassus back but at all times, he sensed Cassus was playing with him, allowing him the luxury of believing he had the upper hand.

Prydain knew he was in trouble. Repeatedly he swung blow after blow at his opponent, but every time it was deflected with the skilful defence of Cassus. Finally he started to miss altogether and Cassus looked at him in derision as he stumbled and fell into the dust.

'This is pathetic,' snarled Cassus. 'Call yourself a warrior? I feel I will have better contest from that boy before I burn him.'

Prydain staggered to his feet but knew he was finished. His body ached and the strength had gone from his legs. He picked up his sword and raised it high above his shoulder before charging toward Cassus, screaming in rage.

Cassus stepped to one side and spinning round swung his sword to cut through Prydain's armour. Prydain cried out in pain and dropped to his knees, knowing his time had come. His sword fell from his hand as he awaited the final blow.

Cassus threw away his own sword and pulled a knife from his boot. He kicked Prydain in the back sending him sprawling in the dust before rolling him over onto his back. He dropped down onto Prydain's chest and stared into the injured man's eyes.

'You disappoint me, Prydain,' he said. 'I have waited six years for this moment and have barely broken sweat. What does it feel like, slave boy? What thoughts go through the mind of a man about to die? The pain, the afterlife; tell me, what is in your mind's eye?'

'Just do it, Cassus,' said Prydain, 'you'll get no more sport from me.'

'You're right,' said Cassus, 'I waste too much time. Goodbye, slave boy, I'll see you in hell.' He placed the point of his blade against Prydain's chest and as he changed his grip, Prydain closed his eyes and braced himself for the pain that would precede his death.

–

'Stay your hand,' said a quiet voice and Cassus spun his head around, thinking he was in danger. A few steps away, a pretty young woman wearing a hooded cloak stood motionless in the dust.

'Who are you?' he asked.

'Don't you remember me?' asked the girl. 'We once spent several days together as I nursed you back to health.' She lifted her hands and slipped the hood from her head.

'Heulwen,' he said, 'the Shaman from the Asbri.'

'That's right,' she said, 'and if you recall, I told you we would one day reclaim the debt.'

'Not now, Witch,' he snarled, 'I have death to administer.'

'It has to be now,' said Heulwen, 'for the price demanded is the life of this man.'

'That is not going to happen,' said Cassus. 'I have waited too long. This man dies here, even if it costs me my own life.'

'Kill him if you must,' said Heulwen, 'but we demand a life in return.'

'I care not if I live or die,' said Cassus, 'do what you must.'

'Oh it's not your life we will take, but that of another,' said Heulwen.

'Who?' asked Cassus, his eyes narrowing in suspicion.

'That of Sioned,' said Heulwen.

Cassus paused. During his time with the Deceangli he had grown very close to Sioned and intended to seek her out when this was all over.

'You lie,' said Cassus, 'I have made arrangements for her safety.'

'The man you knew as Dento is dead,' said Heulwen, 'and Sioned has sought safety with the Asbri. As we speak, she sleeps within the caves of my people. Take this man's life and she will share his fate.'

Cassus was in turmoil. At last he had the opportunity to kill the man he had hated for six years, yet the thought of Sioned being killed for his actions stayed his hand. Prydain stared up at him, holding his breath, not knowing what decision his attacker would take.

Finally, Cassus roared his frustration and threw his knife from him before putting his face close to Prydain's.

'This isn't over, slave boy,' he spat. 'You gave me my life once, now we are even. The next time we meet, one of us dies.'

Without another word he stood up and, retrieving his sword, vaulted onto his horse before turning to face them once more.

'I *will* kill you, Prydain,' he shouted. 'As the gods are my witness, one day my blade will send you to hell.'

Turning his horse, he galloped out of the clearing, leaving the girl and Prydain alone. Heulwen walked over and crouched down beside him to look at his wound.

'Hello again,' she said.

Prydain's eyes opened in astonishment as he recognised the face before him.

'River girl,' he said.

'The very same,' she said.

'I don't understand,' he said. 'Why were you at Caer Caradog and why did you disappear when you did?'

'My people are tasked as healers across all tribes,' said Heulwen, 'and there were four sent to aid Caratacus in his campaign. Only I survived and that is down to you.'

'But why did you leave when you did?'

'Do you remember that second night after the battle?'

'Vaguely. We were sheltered in a hut, if I recall.'

'We were and you told me the tale of Gwydion and his son.'

'I did.'

'Well, I knew then that I had to tell the Asbri elders of his existence. The forest is my home and I travel faster alone. I knew if I explained, you would stop me going so I just left.'

'But what are you doing here?'

'I came to find Taliesin,' she said. 'When I told my people the story, they sent me after him, for the forest is no place for an orphaned king. We will take him, Prydain and make sure he becomes a good man.'

Prydain winced as his body was wracked with pain.

'Where is he?' asked Prydain.

'He has already left,' said Heulwen, 'and is in the safe hands of my people.'

'I never saw anyone else,' said Prydain.

'No, you wouldn't,' she smiled. 'Now, let me see this wound.'

'Am I about to die?' he asked as Heulwen cut away his tunic.

'I don't think so,' she answered, 'I guess the gods have plans for you yet. Now, enough talking, I need to see to this wound.'

Prydain laid back, wincing as Heulwen administered her herbs.

Around him the farm burned, and he knew he had flirted with death once again. He had survived the slaughter of Caer Caradog, been saved from death at the hands of Cassus and delivered a future king into safety. Perhaps Heulwen was right. Perhaps the gods did have bigger plans for him.

...Only time would tell...

Epilogue

The Lands of the Brigantes
51 AD

Caratacus and his fellows were exhausted. They had hidden from the Romans for many months, hiding amongst the villages of those tribes that still resented the occupation. Most of the tribes were weak and Caratacus knew he couldn't stay with them for they had no spirit, no fire to fight against the invaders. He had enjoyed many small victories against the enemy over the last seven years, sandwiched between two great defeats, Medway and Caer Caradog.

Again fate had snatched defeat from the jaws of victory and he knew that with a bit more cohesion and a bigger force then the Romans would be beatable. With this in mind, he made his way through the country, hiding in the forests like a brigand but always with a greater purpose in mind – to join with the one great tribe left in Britannia, the Brigantes. The Brigantes were a powerful tribe and led by a warlike queen called Cartimunda. If he could persuade her to march to war then there was still hope and the Romans could still be defeated.

Slowly they had travelled north, avoiding the Roman patrols and eventually rode up the gate of Cartimunda's hill fort. Caratacus had sent one of his riders ahead a day earlier to announce his arrival and had been assured of a welcome fit for a king.

The great gates lay open and Caratacus rode in, followed by the few dozen men who had stayed loyal to him over the past few months.

Cartimunda's people stood either side of the track, watching him silently as he rode toward the village centre.

'They are strangely quiet, Lord,' said a rider alongside him.

Caratacus agreed but they kept going. Finally he reached the centre and as they dismounted, a group of men ran forward to take their horses.

'Where is Cartimunda?' asked Caratacus, 'I was told I was to be met.'

'She will be here,' said one of the grooms and they led the horses away, leaving Caratacus and his men waiting.

Finally a commotion caused them to turn and they saw part of the surrounding crowd open to allow someone through. A woman walked toward Caratacus, flanked by two lines of heavily armed warriors.

'Cartimunda,' said Caratacus, 'it is good to see you again.'

'I wish I could say the same,' she said.

'What do you mean?' asked Caratacus. 'I sent word of my arrival and received a positive message.'

'These are troubling times, Caratacus,' she said, 'and we need to bend in the wind if we are not to snap.'

'I don't understand,' he answered, 'what wind do you talk of?'

'The storm that Rome has sent against us,' said Cartimunda. 'We cannot resist them, Caratacus.'

'But we can,' he said, 'with your warriors and my knowledge we can take the battle to them. These last seven years I have learned so much about them and know their weaknesses. Nobody knows them as I do.'

'Yet still you fell short at Caer Caradog.'

'A twist of fate,' he said. 'If Idwal had sent his men or the Silures had sent their cavalry, then the outcome would have been so different.'

'But they didn't and it wasn't,' said Cartimunda. 'It's over, Caratacus. The Romans are here to stay and the best thing we can do is work with them rather than under them.'

'No, you are wrong,' he answered. 'They can be bettered and with your help, I will be the one to defeat them.'

'Not with my warriors,' she said. 'My people need corn and cattle, not blood and tears.'

'You are refusing to help me?'

'I'm sorry Caratacus, but I have reached an agreement with the Romans. They will let us continue to rule our own lands in return for tribute.'

'You have bent your knee,' he gasped. 'The great Cartimunda of the Brigantes has given up without a fight.'

'It was in the interests of my people, Caratacus, a trait that perhaps you could learn.'

'Never,' snarled Caratacus, 'I will fight until there is no breath left in my body.'

'Then you will fight alone,' she said.

'Where are my horses?' shouted Caratacus. 'The air stinks of cowardice; I need to get out of here.'

'I'm afraid I can't allow that,' said Cartimunda.

'*On whose authority?*' shouted Caratacus.

'On mine,' said a voice, and a man wearing the full polished bronze armour and scarlet cloak of a Legionary Legatus, stepped from behind a building.

'*Treachery,*' gasped Caratacus.

'It is for the best,' said Cartimunda, 'too many people have died already. This is Legatus Scapula and he is here to accept your surrender.'

Caratacus drew his sword and spun around frantically, looking for a way out but the crowd had opened up and hundreds of Legionaries marched forward with levelled Pilae. Within moments Caratacus and his men were hemmed in on all sides by the points of the spears and the king knew his time was up.

Scapula stepped forward and spoke to him.

'It is over, Caratacus. You fought and lost. Accept your defeat graciously.'

'Never,' scowled Caratacus, 'I am a king and demand I be treated as an equal.'

'*You are nothing,*' shouted Scapula, 'and I tire of your arrogance. I have won, Caratacus, Rome has won. Don't you understand? You and your country have failed, it is over.'

'*It is never over,*' shouted Caratacus, 'and as we speak, children nurture dreams of driving you out when they are men. Do your worst, Roman. Enjoy it while you can.'

Scapula shook his head in derision.

'Tribune,' he called over his shoulder, 'take these men into custody and chain them like criminals.'

'And the king, my lord?' asked a voice.

'King?' asked Scapula. 'I see no king. I see a bitter, defeated man who puts his own glory above the lives of his people. Chain him alongside the others.'

The Legionaries fell on the prisoners and chained them together as Cartimunda and Scapula looked on.

'What will become of him?' asked Cartimunda.

'That is not my decision,' said Scapula. 'He will be sent to Rome to face the Senate.'

'Really?' said Cartimunda. 'And who will have the final say?'

'His fate will be decided by Emperor Claudius,' said Scapula, 'and history will show that he and he alone decided the fate of Caratacus, would-be King of Britannia.'

Author's Notes

Caratacus

After the battle of the Medway and the battle of the Thames, Caratacus fled with the remnants of his army to the lands of the Silures in modern day South Wales. There he eventually led the Silures and campaigned against the Romans along the Welsh/English Border and into the Midlands of England.

Eventually, Legatus Ostorius Scapula led a campaign against Caratacus and though versions vary, it is believed that he defeated him at the Battle of Caer Caradog in Shropshire using the XIV *Gemina Martia Victrix* and the Legio Vigesima Valeria Victrix.

Caratacus' family were captured at the battle, and though he escaped to the Brigantes tribe in the north of modern-day England, he was handed over to the Romans by Queen Cartimunda.

Exploratores

The Exploratores were Rome's equivalent of today's Special Forces. They were known to sometimes join the enemy in order to gain inside information and often spent many years undercover.

The Silures

The Silures were a fearsome tribe based in South Wales and conducted an on-going guerrilla campaign against the Romans. They were never finally defeated but accepted Roman integration over a period of time. Their Capital was at a place called Llanmelin hill in Wales and the remains of their hill fort can still be seen today.

Vespasian

Legatus Vespasian did indeed campaign through southern England and subdued all the tribes in the south including the Durotriges. The Augusta Legion were eventually tasked against the Silures in Wales and many years later, Vespasian went on to become Emperor of Rome.

Ostorius Scapula

Scapula took over from Plautius as Governor of Britain and successfully campaigned against Caratacus. Reports show that shortly after, he died through exhaustion.

Afterword

Accurate information from the time is limited and different sources quote different things. For instance, some sources state that the Gemina and Victrix took part in the final battle with Caratacus while others include the Augusta in the conflict. The information within this book has been used to support the main story line of the characters and as such may not accurately reflect the history. However, the Roman historian Tacitus has documented one of the few records from the time. Please see below.

The Report of the Battle with Caratacus as recorded by Tacitus, the Roman Historian.

'The army then marched against the Silures, a naturally fierce people and now full of confidence in the might of Caratacus, who by many an indecisive and many a successful battle had raised himself far above all the other generals of the Britons. Inferior in military strength but deriving an advantage from the deceptiveness of the country, he at once shifted the war by a stratagem into the territory of the Ordovices, where, joined by all who dreaded peace with us, he resolved on a final struggle. He selected a position for the engagement in which advance and retreat alike would be difficult for our men and comparatively easy for his own, and then on some lofty hills, wherever their sides could be approached by a gentle slope, he piled up stones to serve as a rampart. A river too of varying depth was in his front, and his armed bands were drawn up before his defences.'

'Then too the chieftains of the several tribes went from rank to rank, encouraging and confirming the spirit of their men by making light of their fears, kindling their hopes, and by every other warlike incitement. As for Caratacus, he flew hither and thither, protesting that that day and that battle would be the beginning of the recovery of their freedom, or of everlasting bondage. He appealed, by name, to their forefathers who had driven back the dictator Caesar, by whose valour they were free from the Roman axe and tribute, and still preserved inviolate the persons of their wives and of their children. While he was thus speaking, the host shouted applause; every warrior bound himself by his national oath not to shrink from weapons or wounds.'

'Such enthusiasm confounded the Roman general. The river too in his face, the rampart they had added to it, the frowning hilltops, the stern resistance and masses of fighting men everywhere apparent, daunted him. But his soldiers insisted on battle, exclaiming that valour could overcome all things; and the prefects and tribunes, with similar language, stimulated the ardour of the troops. Ostorius having ascertained by a survey the inaccessible and the assailable points of the position, led on his furious men, and crossed the river without difficulty. When he reached the barrier, as long as it was a fight with missiles, the wounds and the slaughter fell chiefly on our soldiers; but when he had formed the military Testudo, and the rude, ill-compacted fence of stones was torn down, and

344

it was an equal hand-to-hand engagement, the barbarians retired to the heights. Yet even there, both light and heavy-armed soldiers rushed to the attack; the first harassed the foe with missiles, while the latter closed with them, and the opposing ranks of the Britons were broken, destitute as they were of the defence of breastplates or helmets. When they faced the auxiliaries, they were felled by the swords and javelins of our Legionaries; if they wheeled round, they were again met by the sabres and spears of the auxiliaries. It was a glorious victory; the wife and daughter of Caratacus were captured, and his brothers too were admitted to surrender.'